9.95
2

D1247650

EDWARD BELLAMY

The Blindman's World and Other Stories

The American Short Story Series

VOLUME 4.

GARRETT PRESS

Library of Congress Catalog Card No. 68-55664

*This volume was reprinted from the 1898 edition
published by Houghton, Mifflin and Company
First Garrett Press Edition published 1968*

The American Short Story Series
Volume 4
©1968

Manufactured in the United States of America

GARRETT PRESS, INC.
Publishers
250 West 54th Street, New York, N.Y. 10019

CONTENTS

	PAGE
THE BLINDMAN'S WORLD	1
AN ECHO OF ANTIETAM	30
THE OLD FOLKS' PARTY	59
THE COLD SNAP	89
TWO DAYS' SOLITARY IMPRISONMENT	104
A SUMMER EVENING'S DREAM	129
POTTS'S PAINLESS CURE	157
A LOVE STORY REVERSED	192
DESERTED	237
HOOKING WATERMELONS	264
A POSITIVE ROMANCE	295
LOST	315
WITH THE EYES SHUT	335
AT PINNEY'S RANCH	366
TO WHOM THIS MAY COME	389

EDWARD BELLAMY

26 MARCH, 1850 — 22 MAY, 1898

THE first book of Edward Bellamy's which I read was "Dr. Heidenhoff's Process," and I thought it one of the finest feats in the region of romance which I had known. It seemed to me all the greater because the author's imagination wrought in it on the level of average life, and built the fabric of its dream out of common clay. The simple people and their circumstance were treated as if they were persons whose pathetic story he had witnessed himself, and he was merely telling it. He wove into the texture of their sufferings and their sorrows the magic thread of invention so aptly and skillfully that the reader felt nothing improbable in it. One even felt a sort of moral necessity for it, as if such a clue not only could be, but must be given for their escape. It became not merely probable, but imperative, that there should be some means of extirpating the memory which fixed a sin in lasting remorse, and of thus saving the soul from the depravity of despair. When it finally appeared that there was no such means, one reader, at least, was inconsolable. Nothing from romance remains to me more poignant than the pang that this plain, sad tale imparted.

The art employed to accomplish its effect was the art which Bellamy had in degree so singular that one might call it supremely his. He does not so much transmute our every-day reality to the substance of romance as make the airy stuff of dreams one in quality with veritable experience. Every one remembers from " Looking Backward " the allegory which figures the pitiless prosperity of the present conditions as a coach drawn by slaves under the lash of those on its top, who have themselves no firm hold upon their places, and sometimes fall, and then, to save themselves from being ground under the wheels, spring to join the slaves at the traces. But it is not this, vivid and terrible as it is, which most wrings the heart; it is that moment of anguish at the close, when Julian West trembles with the nightmare fear that he has been only dreaming of the just and equal future, before he truly wakes and finds that it is real. That is quite as it would happen in life, and the power to make the reader feel this, like something he has known himself, is the distinctive virtue of that imagination which revived throughout Christendom the faith in a millennium.

A good deal has been said against the material character of the happiness which West's story promises men when they shall begin to do justice, and to share equally in the fruits of the toil which operates life; and I confess that this did not attract me. I should have preferred, if I had been chooser, to have the millennium much simpler, much more independent of modern inventions, modern conveniences, modern facilities. It seemed to me that in an ideal condition (the only condition finally worth having) we should get on without most of these things, which are but sorry patches on the rags of our outworn civilization, or only toys to amuse our greed and vacancy. Æsthetically, I sympathized with those select spirits who were shocked that nothing better than the futile luxury of their own selfish lives could be imagined for the lives which overwork and underpay had forbidden all pleasures; I acquired considerable merit with myself by asking whether the hope of these formed the highest appeal to human nature. But I overlooked an important condition which the other critics overlooked; I did not reflect that such things were shown as merely added unto those who had first sought the kingdom of God and his righteousness, and that they were no longer vicious or even so foolish when they were harmlessly come by. I have since had to own that the joys I thought trivial and sordid did rightly, as they did most strenuously, appeal to the lives hitherto starved of them. In depicting them as the common reward of the common endeavor, Edward Bellamy builded better than we knew, whether he knew better or not; and he builded from a thorough sense of that level of humanity which he was destined so potently to influence, — that American level which his book found in every Christian land.

I am not sure whether this sense was ever a full consciousness with him ; very possibly it was not ; but in any case it was the spring of all his work, from the earliest to the latest. Somehow, whether he *knew* or not, he unerringly *felt* how the average man would feel ; and all the webs of fancy that he wove were essentially of one texture through this sympathy. His imagination was intensely democratic, it was inalienably plebeian, even, — that is to say, humane. It did not seek distinction of expression ; it never put the simplest and plainest reader to shame by the assumption of those fine-gentleman airs which abash and dishearten more than the mere literary swell can think. He would use a phrase or a word that was common to vulgarity, if it said what he meant ; sometimes he sets one's teeth on edge, in his earlier stories, by his public school diction. But the nobility of the heart is never absent from his work ; and he has always the distinction of self-forgetfulness in his art.

I have been interested, in recurring to his earlier work, to note how almost entirely the action passes in the American village atmosphere. It is like the greater part of his own life in this. He was not a man ignorant of other keeping. He was partly educated abroad, and he knew cities both in Europe and in America. He was a lawyer by profession, and he was sometime editor of a daily newspaper in a large town. But I remember how, in one of our meetings, he spoke with distrust and dislike of the environment of cities as unwholesome and distracting, if not demoralizing (very much to the effect of Tolstoi's philosophy in the matter), and in his short stories his types are village types. They are often such when he finds them in the city, but for much the greater part he finds them in the village; and they are always, therefore, distinctively American; for we are village people far more than we are country people or city people. In this as in everything else we are a medium race, and it was in his sense, if not in his knowledge of this fact, that Bellamy wrote so that there is never a word or a look to the reader implying that he and the writer are of a different sort of folk from the people in the story.

" Looking Backward," with its material delights, its communized facilities and luxuries, could not appeal to people on lonely farms who scarcely knew of them, or to people in cities who were tired of them, so much as to that immense average of villagers, of small-town-dwellers, who had read much and seen something of them, and desired to have them. This average, whose intelligence forms the prosperity of our literature, and whose virtue

forms the strength of our nation, is the environment which Bellamy rarely travels out of in his
airiest romance. He has its curiosity, its princi-
ples, its aspirations. He can tell what it wishes
to know, what problem will hold it, what situation
it can enter into, what mystery will fascinate it,
and what noble pain it will bear. It is by far the
widest field of American fiction; most of our finest
artists work preferably in it, but he works in it
to different effect from any other. He takes that
life on its mystical side, and deals with types
rather than with characters; for it is one of the
prime conditions of the romancer that he shall do
this. His people are less objectively than subjec-
tively present; their import is greater in what
happens to them than in what they are. But he
never falsifies them or their circumstance. He
ascertains them with a fidelity that seems almost
helpless, almost ignorant of different people, different circumstance; you would think at times that
he had never known, never seen, any others; but
of course this is only the effect of his art.

When it comes to something else, however, it is
still with the same fidelity that he keeps to the
small-town average, the American average. He
does not address himself more intelligently to the
mystical side of this average in " Dr. Heidenhoff's
Process," or " Miss Ludington's Sister," or any of
his briefer romances, than to its ethical side in
" Equality." That book disappointed me, to be

frank. I thought it artistically inferior to anything else he had done. I thought it was a mistake
to have any story at all in it, or not to have vastly
more. I felt that it was not enough to clothe the
dry bones of its sociology with paper garments
out of " Looking Backward." Except for that
one sublime moment when the workers of all sorts
cry to the Lords of the Bread to take them and
use them at their own price, there was no thrill
or throb in the book. But I think now that any
believer in its economics may be well content to let
them take their chance with the American average,
here and elsewhere, in the form that the author
has given them. He felt that average so wittingly
that he could not have been wrong in approaching it with all that public school exegesis which
wearies such dilettanti as myself.

Our average is practical as well as mystical; it
is first the dust of the earth, and then it is a living
soul; it likes great questions simply and familiarly
presented, before it puts its faith in them and
makes its faith a life. It likes to start to heaven
from home, and in all this Bellamy was of it, voluntarily and involuntarily. I recall how, when we
first met, he told me that he had come to think of
our hopeless conditions suddenly, one day, in looking at his own children, and reflecting that he
could not place them beyond the chance of want
by any industry or forecast or providence; and
that the status meant the same impossibility for

others which it meant for him. I understood then that I was in the presence of a man too single, too sincere, to pretend that he had begun by thinking of others, and I trusted him the more for his confession of a selfish premise. He never went back to himself in his endeavor, but when he had once felt his power in the world, he dedicated his life to his work. He wore himself out in thinking and feeling about it, with a belief in the good time to come that penetrated his whole being and animated his whole purpose, but apparently with no manner of fanaticism. In fact, no one could see him, or look into his quiet, gentle face, so full of goodness, so full of common sense, without perceiving that he had reasoned to his hope for justice in the frame of things. He was indeed a most practical, a most American man, without a touch of sentimentalism in his humanity. He believed that some now living should see his dream — the dream of Plato, the dream of the first Christians, the dream of Bacon, the dream of More — come true in a really civilized society; but he had the patience and courage which could support any delay.

These qualities were equal to the suffering and the death which came to him in the midst of his work, and cut him off from writing that *one more book* with which every author hopes to round his career. He suffered greatly, but he bore his suffering greatly; and as for his death, it is told that when, toward the last, those who loved him were loath to leave him at night alone, as he preferred to be left, he asked, " What can happen to me ? I can only die."

I am glad that he lived to die at home in Chicopee, — in the village environment by which he interpreted the heart of the American nation, and knew how to move it more than any other American author who has lived. The theory of those who think differently is that he simply moved the popular fancy ; and this may suffice to explain the state of some people, but it will not account for the love and honor in which his name is passionately held by the vast average, East and West. His fame is safe with them, and his faith is an animating force concerning whose effect at this time or some other time it would not be wise to prophesy. Whether his ethics will keep his æsthetics in remembrance I do not know ; but I am sure that one cannot acquaint one's self with his merely artistic work, and not be sensible that in Edward Bellamy we were rich in a romantic imagination surpassed only by that of Hawthorne.

W. D. HOWELLS.

THE BLINDMAN'S WORLD

THE narrative to which this note is introductory was found among the papers of the late Professor S. Erastus Larrabee, and, as an acquaintance of the gentleman to whom they were bequeathed, I was requested to prepare it for publication. This turned out a very easy task, for the document proved of so extraordinary a character that, if published at all, it should obviously be without change. It appears that the professor did really, at one time in his life, have an attack of vertigo, or something of the sort, under circumstances similar to those described by him, and to that extent his narrative may be founded on fact. How soon it shifts from that foundation, or whether it does at all, the reader must conclude for himself. It appears certain that the professor never related to any one, while living, the stranger features of the experience here narrated, but this might have been merely from fear that his standing as a man of science would be thereby injured.

THE PROFESSOR'S NARRATIVE

At the time of the experience of which I am about to write, I was professor of astronomy and

higher mathematics at Abercrombie College. Most
astronomers have a specialty, and mine was the
study of the planet Mars, our nearest neighbor
but one in the Sun's little family. When no important celestial phenomena in other quarters demanded attention, it was on the ruddy disc of Mars
that my telescope was oftenest focused. I was
never weary of tracing the outlines of its continents
and seas, its capes and islands, its bays and straits,
its lakes and mountains. With intense interest I
watched from week to week of the Martial winter
the advance of the polar ice-cap toward the equator,
and its corresponding retreat in the summer; testi-
fying across the gulf of space as plainly as written
words to the existence on that orb of a climate like
our own. A specialty is always in danger of becoming an infatuation, and my interest in Mars, at
the time of which I write, had grown to be more
than strictly scientific. The impression of the near-
ness of this planet, heightened by the wonderful
distinctness of its geography as seen through a
powerful telescope, appeals strongly to the imagination of the astronomer. On fine evenings I used
to spend hours, not so much critically observing as
brooding over its radiant surface, till I could almost
persuade myself that I saw the breakers dashing
on the bold shore of Kepler Land, and heard the
muffled thunder of avalanches descending the snow-
clad mountains of Mitchell. No earthly landscape had the charm to hold my gaze of that far-

off planet, whose oceans, to the unpracticed eye, seem but darker, and its continents lighter, spots and bands.

Astronomers have agreed in declaring that Mars is undoubtedly habitable by beings like ourselves, but, as may be supposed, I was not in a mood to be satisfied with considering it merely habitable. I allowed no sort of question that it was inhabited. What manner of beings these inhabitants might be I found a fascinating speculation. The variety of types appearing in mankind even on this small Earth makes it most presumptuous to assume that the denizens of different planets may not be characterized by diversities far profounder. Wherein such diversities, coupled with a general resemblance to man, might consist, whether in mere physical differences or in different mental laws, in the lack of certain of the great passional motors of men or the possession of quite others, were weird themes of never-failing attractions for my mind. The El Dorado visions with which the virgin mystery of the New World inspired the early Spanish explorers were tame and prosaic compared with the speculations which it was perfectly legitimate to indulge, when the problem was the conditions of life on another planet.

It was the time of the year when Mars is most favorably situated for observation, and, anxious not to lose an hour of the precious season, I had spent the greater part of several successive nights

in the observatory. I believed that I had made
some original observations as to the trend of the
coast of Kepler Land between Lagrange Peninsula
and Christie Bay, and it was to this spot that my
observations were particularly directed.

On the fourth night other work detained me
from the observing-chair till after midnight.
When I had adjusted the instrument and took
my first look at Mars, I remember being unable
to restrain a cry of admiration. The planet was
fairly dazzling. It seemed nearer and larger than
I had ever seen it before, and its peculiar rud-
diness more striking. In thirty years of observations, I recall, in fact, no occasion when the
absence of exhalations in our atmosphere has coin-
cided with such cloudlessness in that of Mars as
on that night. I could plainly make out the white
masses of vapor at the opposite edges of the lighted
disc, which are the mists of its dawn and evening.
The snowy mass of Mount Hall over against Kepler Land stood out with wonderful clearness, and
I could unmistakably detect the blue tint of the
ocean of De La Rue, which washes its base, — a
feat of vision often, indeed, accomplished by star-
gazers, though I had never done it to my complete
satisfaction before.

I was impressed with the idea that if I ever
made an original discovery in regard to Mars, it
would be on that evening, and I believed that I
should do it. I trembled with mingled exultation

and anxiety, and was obliged to pause to recover my self-control. Finally, I placed my eye to the eye-piece, and directed my gaze upon the portion of the planet in which I was especially interested. My attention soon became fixed and absorbed much beyond my wont, when observing, and that itself implied no ordinary degree of abstraction. To all mental intents and purposes I was on Mars. Every faculty, every susceptibility of sense and intellect, seemed gradually to pass into the eye, and become concentrated in the act of gazing. Every atom of nerve and will power combined in the strain to see a little, and yet a little, and yet a little, clearer, farther, deeper.

The next thing I knew I was on the bed that stood in a corner of the observing-room, half raised on an elbow, and gazing intently at the door. It was broad daylight. Half a dozen men, including several of the professors and a doctor from the village, were around me. Some were trying to make me lie down, others were asking me what I wanted, while the doctor was urging me to drink some whiskey. Mechanically repelling their offices, I pointed to the door and ejaculated, " President Byxbee — coming," giving expression to the one idea which my dazed mind at that moment contained. And sure enough, even as I spoke the door opened, and the venerable head of the college, somewhat blown with climbing the steep stairway,

stood on the threshold.   With a sensation of prodigious relief, I fell back on my pillow.

It appeared that I had swooned while in the
observing-chair, the night before, and had been
found by the janitor in the morning, my head
fallen forward on the telescope, as if still observing, but my body cold, rigid, pulseless, and apparently dead.

In a couple of days I was all right again, and
should soon have forgotten the episode but for a
very interesting conjecture which had suggested
itself in connection with it.   This was nothing less
than that, while I lay in that swoon, I was in
a conscious state outside and independent of the
body, and in that state received impressions and
exercised perceptive powers.   For this extraordinary theory I had no other evidence than the fact
of my knowledge in the moment of awaking that
President Byxbee was coming up the stairs.   But
slight as this clue was, it seemed to me unmistakable in its significance.   That knowledge was certainly in my mind on the instant of arousing from
the swoon.   It certainly could not have been there
before I fell into the swoon.   I must therefore
have gained it in the mean time ; that is to say, I
must have been in a conscious, percipient state
while my body was insensible.

If such had been the case, I reasoned that it was
altogether unlikely that the trivial impression as
to President Byxbee had been the only one which

I had received in that state. It was far more probable that it had remained over in my mind, on
waking from the swoon, merely because it was the
latest of a series of impressions received while outside the body. That these impressions were of a
kind most strange and startling, seeing that they
were those of a disembodied soul exercising faculties more spiritual than those of the body, I could
not doubt. The desire to know what they had
been grew upon me, till it became a longing which
left me no repose. It seemed intolerable that I
should have secrets from myself, that my soul
should withhold its experiences from my intellect.
I would gladly have consented that the acquisi-
tions of half my waking lifetime should be blotted
out, if so be in exchange I might be shown the
record of what I had seen and known during those
hours of which my waking memory showed no
trace. None the less for the conviction of its hope-
lessness, but rather all the more, as the perversity
of our human nature will have it, the longing for
this forbidden lore grew on me, till the hunger of
Eve in the Garden was mine.

Constantly brooding over a desire that I felt to
be vain, tantalized by the possession of a clue
which only mocked me, my physical condition became at length affected. My health was disturbed
and my rest at night was broken. A habit of
walking in my sleep, from which I had not suffered since childhood, recurred, and caused me fre-

quent inconvenience. Such had been, in general, my condition for some time, when I awoke one morning with the strangely weary sensation by which my body usually betrayed the secret of the impositions put upon it in sleep, of which otherwise I should often have suspected nothing. In going into the study connected with my chamber, I found a number of freshly written sheets on the desk. Astonished that any one should have been in my rooms while I slept, I was astounded, on looking more closely, to observe that the handwriting was my own. How much more than astounded I was on reading the matter that had been set down, the reader may judge if he shall peruse it. For these written sheets apparently contained the longed-for but despaired-of record of those hours when I was absent from the body. They were the lost chapter of my life; or rather, not lost at all, for it had been no part of my waking life, but a stolen chapter, — stolen from that sleep-memory on whose mysterious tablets may well be inscribed tales as much more marvelous than this as this is stranger than most stories.

It will be remembered that my last recollection before awaking in my bed, on the morning after the swoon, was of contemplating the coast of Kepler Land with an unusual concentration of attention. As well as I can judge, — and that is no better than any one else, — it is with the moment that my bodily powers succumbed and I became unconscious that the narrative which I found on my desk begins.

THE DOCUMENT FOUND ON MY DESK

Even had I not come as straight and swift as the beam of light that made my path, a glance about would have told me to what part of the universe I had fared. No earthly landscape could have been more familiar. I stood on the high coast of Kepler Land where it trends southward. A brisk westerly wind was blowing and the waves of the ocean of De La Rue were thundering at my feet, while the broad blue waters of Christie Bay stretched away to the southwest. Against the northern horizon, rising out of the ocean like a summer thunder-head, for which at first I mistook it, towered the far-distant, snowy summit of Mount Hall.

Even had the configuration of land and sea been less familiar, I should none the less have known that I stood on the planet whose ruddy hue is at once the admiration and puzzle of astronomers. Its explanation I now recognized in the tint of the atmosphere, a coloring comparable to the haze of Indian summer, except that its hue was a faint rose instead of purple. Like the Indian summer haze, it was impalpable, and without impeding the view bathed all objects near and far in a glamour not to be described. As the gaze turned upward, however, the deep blue of space so far overcame the

roseate tint that one might fancy he were still on
Earth.

As I looked about me I saw many men, women,
and children. They were in no respect dissimi-
lar, so far as I could see, to the men, women, and
children of the Earth, save for something almost
childlike in the untroubled serenity of their faces,
unfurrowed as they were by any trace of care, of
fear, or of anxiety. This extraordinary youthful-
ness of aspect made it difficult, indeed, save by
careful scrutiny, to distinguish the young from the
middle-aged, maturity from advanced years. Time
seemed to have no tooth on Mars.

I was gazing about me, admiring this crimson-
lighted world, and these people who appeared to
hold happiness by a tenure so much firmer than
men's, when I heard the words, "You are welcome," and, turning, saw that I had been accosted
by a man with the stature and bearing of middle
age, though his countenance, like the other faces
which I had noted, wonderfully combined the
strength of a man's with the serenity of a child's.
I thanked him, and said, —

"You do not seem surprised to see me, though I
certainly am to find myself here."

"Assuredly not," he answered. "I knew, of
course, that I was to meet you to-day. And not
only that, but I may say I am already in a sense
acquainted with you, through a mutual friend, Professor Edgerly. He was here last month, and I

met him at that time.   We talked of you and your
interest in our planet.   I told him I expected you."

"Edgerly!" I exclaimed.   "It is strange that
he has said nothing of this to me.   I meet him
every day."

But I was reminded that it was in a dream that
Edgerly, like myself, had visited Mars, and on
awaking had recalled nothing of his experience,
just as I should recall nothing of mine.   When will
man learn to interrogate the dream soul of the
marvels it sees in its wanderings?   Then he will
no longer need to improve his telescopes to find out
the secrets of the universe.

"Do your people visit the Earth in the same
manner?" I asked my companion.

"Certainly," he replied; "but there we find no
one able to recognize us and converse with us as I
am conversing with you, although myself in the
waking state.   You, as yet, lack the knowledge we
possess of the spiritual side of the human nature
which we share with you."

"That knowledge must have enabled you to learn
much more of the Earth than we know of you," I
said.

"Indeed it has," he replied.   "From visitors
such as you, of whom we entertain a concourse constantly, we have acquired familiarity with your
civilization, your history, your manners, and even
your literature and languages.   Have you not
noticed that I am talking with you in English,

which is certainly not a tongue indigenous to this planet?"

"Among so many wonders I scarcely observed that," I answered.

"For ages," pursued my companion, "we have been waiting for you to improve your telescopes so as to approximate the power of ours, after which communication between the planets would be easily established. The progress which you make is, however, so slow that we expect to wait ages yet."

"Indeed, I fear you will have to," I replied. "Our opticians already talk of having reached the limits of their art."

"Do not imagine that I spoke in any spirit of petulance," my companion resumed. "The slowness of your progress is not so remarkable to us as that you make any at all, burdened as you are by a disability so crushing that if we were in your place ·I fear we should sit down in utter despair."

"To what disability do you refer?" I asked. "You seem to be men like us."

"And so we are," was the reply, "save in one particular, but there the difference is tremendous. Endowed otherwise like us, you are destitute of the faculty of foresight, without which we should think our other faculties well-nigh valueless."

"Foresight!" I repeated. "Certainly you cannot mean that it is given you to know the future?"

"It is given not only to us," was the answer, "but, so far as we know, to all other intelligent beings of the universe except yourselves. Our positive knowledge extends only to our system of moons and planets and some of the nearer foreign systems, and it is conceivable that the remoter parts of the universe may harbor other blind races like your own; but it certainly seems unlikely that so strange and lamentable a spectacle should be duplicated. One such illustration of the extraordinary deprivations under which a rational existence may still be possible ought to suffice for the universe."

"But no one can know the future except by inspiration of God," I said.

"All our faculties are by inspiration of God," was the reply, "but there is surely nothing in foresight to cause it to be so regarded more than any other. Think a moment of the physical analogy of the case. Your eyes are placed in the front of your heads. You would deem it an odd mistake if they were placed behind. That would appear to you an arrangement calculated to defeat their purpose. Does it not seem equally rational that the mental vision should range forward, as it does with us, illuminating the path one is to take, rather than backward, as with you, revealing only the course you have already trodden, and therefore have no more concern with? But it is no doubt a merciful provision of Providence that renders you unable to realize the grotesqueness of your predicament, as it appears to us."

"But the future is eternal!" I exclaimed. "How can a finite mind grasp it?"

" Our foreknowledge implies only human faculties," was the reply. " It is limited to our individual careers on this planet. Each of us foresees
the course of his own life, but not that of other
lives, except so far as they are involved with his."

" That such a power as you describe could be
combined with merely human faculties is more than
our philosophers have ever dared to dream," I said.
" And yet who shall say, after all, that it is not
in mercy that God has denied it to us? If it is
a happiness, as it must be, to foresee one's happiness, it must be most depressing to foresee one's
sorrows, failures, yes, and even one's death. For
if you foresee your lives to the end, you must anticipate the hour and manner of your death, — is it
not so?"

" Most assuredly," was the reply. " Living
would be a very precarious business, were we unin-
formed of its limit. Your ignorance of the time
of your death impresses us as one of the saddest
features of your condition."

" And by us," I answered, " it is held to be one
of the most merciful."

" Foreknowledge of your death would not, indeed, prevent your dying once," continued my companion, " but it would deliver you from the thousand deaths you suffer through uncertainty whether
you can safely count on the passing day. It is not
the death you die, but these many deaths you do not
die, which shadow your existence. Poor blindfolded

creatures that you are, cringing at every step in apprehension of the stroke that perhaps is not to fall till old age, never raising a cup to your lips with the knowledge that you will live to quaff it, never sure that you will meet again the friend you part with for an hour, from whose hearts no happiness suffices to banish the chill of an ever-present dread, what idea can you form of the Godlike security with which we enjoy our lives and the lives of those we love! You have a saying on earth, 'To-morrow belongs to God;' but here to-morrow belongs to us, even as to-day. To you, for some inscrutable purpose, He sees fit to dole out life moment by moment, with no assurance that each is not to be the last. To us He gives a lifetime at once, fifty, sixty, seventy years, — a divine gift indeed. A life such as yours would, I fear, seem of little value to us; for such a life, however long, is but a moment long, since that is all you can count on."

"And yet," I answered, "though knowledge of the duration of your lives may give you an enviable feeling of confidence while the end is far off, is that not more than offset by the daily growing weight with which the expectation of the end, as it draws near, must press upon your minds?"

"On the contrary," was the response, "death, never an object of fear, as it draws nearer becomes more and more a matter of indifference to the moribund. It is because you live in the past that death

is grievous to you. All your knowledge, all your
affections, all your interests, are rooted in the past,
and on that account, as life lengthens, it strength-
ens its hold on you, and memory becomes a more
precious possession. We, on the contrary, despise
the past, and never dwell upon it. Memory with
us, far from being the morbid and monstrous
growth it is with you, is scarcely more than a rudi-
mentary faculty. We live wholly in the future
and the present. What with foretaste and actual
taste, our experiences, whether pleasant or painful,
are exhausted of interest by the time they are past.
The accumulated treasures of memory, which you
relinquish so painfully in death, we count no loss
at all. Our minds being fed wholly from the
future, we think and feel only as we anticipate ;
and so, as the dying man's future contracts, there
is less and less about which he can occupy his
thoughts. His interest in life diminishes as the
ideas which it suggests grow fewer, till at the last
death finds him with his mind a *tabula rasa*, as
with you at birth. In a word, his concern with life
is reduced to a vanishing point before he is called
on to give it up. In dying he leaves nothing behind."

" And the after-death," I asked, — " is there no
fear of that ? "

" Surely," was the reply, " it is not necessary
for me to say that a fear which affects only the
more ignorant on Earth is not known at all to us,

and would be counted blasphemous. Moreover, as
I have said, our foresight is limited to our lives
on this planet. Any speculation beyond them
would be purely conjectural, and our minds are
repelled by the slightest taint of uncertainty. To
us the conjectural and the unthinkable may be
called almost the same."

"But even if you do not fear death for itself,"
I said, "you have hearts to break. Is there no
pain when the ties of love are sundered?"

"Love and death are not foes on our planet,"
was the reply. "There are no tears by the bed-
sides of our dying. The same beneficent law which
makes it so easy for us to give up life forbids us to
mourn the friends we leave, or them to mourn us.
With you, it is the intercourse you have had with
friends that is the source of your tenderness for
them. With us, it is the anticipation of the intercourse we shall enjoy which is the foundation of
fondness. As our friends vanish from our future
with the approach of their death, the effect on our
thoughts and affections is as it would be with you
if you forgot them by lapse of time. As our dying
friends grow more and more indifferent to us, we,
by operation of the same law of our nature, become
indifferent to them, till at the last we are scarcely
more than kindly and sympathetic watchers about
the beds of those who regard us equally without
keen emotions. So at last God gently unwinds instead of breaking the bands that bind our hearts

together, and makes death as painless to the surviving as to the dying. Relations meant to produce our happiness are not the means also of torturing us, as with you. Love means joy, and that alone, to us, instead of blessing our lives for a while only to desolate them later on, compelling us to pay with a distinct and separate pang for every thrill of tenderness, exacting a tear for every smile."

"There are other partings than those of death. Are these, too, without sorrow for you?" I asked.

"Assuredly," was the reply. "Can you not see that so it must needs be with beings freed by foresight from the disease of memory? All the sorrow of parting, as of dying, comes with you from the backward vision which precludes you from beholding your happiness till it is past. Suppose your life destined to be blessed by a happy friendship. If you could know it beforehand, it would be a joyous expectation, brightening the intervening years and cheering you as you traversed desolate periods. But no; not till you meet the one who is to be your friend do you know of him. Nor do you guess even then what he is to be to you, that you may embrace him at first sight. Your meeting is cold and indifferent. It is long before the fire is fairly kindled between you, and then it is already time for parting. Now, indeed, the fire burns well, but henceforth it must consume your heart. Not till they are dead or gone do you fully realize how dear your friends were and how sweet was their companionship. But we — we see our friends afar off coming to meet us, smiling already in our eyes, years before our ways meet. We greet them at first meeting, not coldly, not uncertainly, but with exultant kisses, in an ecstasy of joy. They enter at once into the full possession of hearts long warmed and lighted for them. We meet with that delirium of tenderness with which you part. And when to us at last the time of parting comes, it only means that we are to contribute to each other's happiness no longer. We are not doomed, like you, in parting, to take away with us the delight we brought our friends, leaving the ache of bereavement in its place, so that their last state is worse than their first. Parting here is like meeting with you, calm and unimpassioned. The joys of anticipation and possession are the only food of love with us, and therefore Love always wears a smiling face. With you he feeds on dead joys, past happiness, which are likewise the sustenance of sorrow. No wonder love and sorrow are so much alike on Earth. It is a common saying among us that, were it not for the spectacle of the Earth, the rest of the worlds would be unable to appreciate the goodness of God to them; and who can say that this is not the reason the piteous sight is set before us?"

"You have told me marvelous things," I said, after I had reflected. "It is, indeed, but reason-

able that such a race as yours should look down
with wondering pity on the Earth. And yet, before I grant so much, I want to ask you one question. There is known in our world a certain sweet
madness, under the influence of which we forget
all that is untoward in our lot, and would not
change it for a god's. So far is this sweet madness regarded by men as a compensation, and more
than a compensation, for all their miseries that if
you know not love as we know it, if this loss be
the price you have paid for your divine foresight,
we think ourselves more favored of God than you.
Confess that love, with its reserves, its surprises,
its mysteries, its revelations, is necessarily incom-
patible with a foresight which weighs and measures
every experience in advance."

"Of love's surprises we certainly know nothing,"
was the reply. "It is believed by our philosophers
that the slightest surprise would kill beings of our
constitution like lightning; though of course this
is merely theory, for it is only by the study of
Earthly conditions that we are able to form an idea
of what surprise is like. Your power to endure
the constant buffetings of the unexpected is a matter of supreme amazement to us; nor, according to
our ideas, is there any difference between what you
call pleasant and painful surprises. You see, then,
that we cannot envy you these surprises of love
which you find so sweet, for to us they would be
fatal. For the rest, there is no form of happiness

which foresight is so well calculated to enhance as
that of love. Let me explain to you how this be-
falls. As the growing boy begins to be sensible of
the charms of woman, he finds himself, as I dare
say it is with you, preferring some type of face and
form to others. He dreams oftenest of fair hair,
or may be of dark, of blue eyes or brown. As the
years go on, his fancy, brooding over what seems to
it the best and loveliest of every type, is constantly
adding to this dream-face, this shadowy form, traits
and lineaments, hues and contours, till at last the
picture is complete, and he becomes aware that
on his heart thus subtly has been depicted the
likeness of the maiden destined for his arms.

" It may be years before he is to see her, but
now begins with him one of the sweetest offices
of love, one to you unknown. Youth on Earth is
a stormy period of passion, chafing in restraint or
rioting in excess. But the very passion whose
awaking makes this time so critical with you is
here a reforming and educating influence, to whose
gentle and potent sway we gladly confide our children. The temptations which lead your young
men astray have no hold on a youth of our happy
planet. He hoards the treasures of his heart for
its coming mistress. Of her alone he thinks, and to
her all his vows are made. The thought of license
would be treason to his sovereign lady, whose
right to all the revenues of his being he joyfully
owns. To rob her, to abate her high prerogatives,

would be to impoverish, to insult, himself; for she is to be his, and her honor, her glory, are his own. Through all this time that he dreams of her by night and day, the exquisite reward of his devotion is the knowledge that she is aware of him as he of her, and that in the inmost shrine of a maiden heart his image is set up to receive the incense of a tenderness that needs not to restrain itself through fear of possible cross or separation.

"In due time their converging lives come together. The lovers meet, gaze a moment into each other's eyes, then throw themselves each on the other's breast. The maiden has all the charms that ever stirred the blood of an Earthly lover, but there is another glamour over her which the eyes of Earthly lovers are shut to, — the glamour of the future. In the blushing girl her lover sees the fond and faithful wife, in the blithe maiden the patient, pain-consecrated mother. On the virgin's breast he beholds his children. He is prescient, even as his lips take the first-fruits of hers, of the future years during which she is to be his companion, his ever-present solace, his chief portion of God's goodness. We have read some of your romances describing love as you know it on Earth, and I must confess, my friend, we find them very dull.

"I hope," he added, as I did not at once speak, "that I shall not offend you by saying we find them also objectionable. Your literature possesses in general an interest for us in the picture it presents of the curiously inverted life which the lack of foresight compels you to lead. It is a study especially prized for the development of the imagination, on account of the difficulty of conceiving conditions so opposed to those of intelligent beings in general. But our women do not read your romances. The notion that a man or woman should ever conceive the idea of marrying a person other than the one whose husband or wife he or she is destined to be is profoundly shocking to our habits of thought. No doubt you will say that such instances are rare among you, but if your novels are faithful pictures of your life, they are at least not unknown. That these situations are inevitable under the conditions of earthly life we are well aware, and judge you accordingly ; but it is needless that the minds of our maidens should be pained by the knowledge that there anywhere exists a world where such travesties upon the sacredness of marriage are possible.

" There is, however, another reason why we discourage the use of your books by our young people, and that is the profound effect of sadness, to a race accustomed to view all things in the morning glow of the future, of a literature written in the past tense and relating exclusively to things that are ended."

" And how do you write of things that are past except in the past tense ? " I asked.

" We write of the past when it is still the future, and of course in the future tense," was the reply. " If our historians were to wait till after the events to describe them, not alone would nobody care to read about things already done, but the histories themselves would probably be inaccurate ; for memory, as I have said, is a very slightly developed faculty with us, and quite too indistinct to be trustworthy. Should the Earth ever establish communication with us, you will find our histories of interest ; for our planet, being smaller, cooled and was peopled ages before yours, and our astronomical records contain minute accounts of the Earth from the time it was a fluid mass. Your geologists and biologists may yet find a mine of information here."

In the course of our further conversation it came out that, as a consequence of foresight, some of the commonest emotions of human nature are unknown on Mars. They for whom the future has no mystery can, of course, know neither hope nor fear. Moreover, every one being assured what he shall attain to and what not, there can be no such thing as rivalship, or emulation, or any sort of competition in any respect ; and therefore all the brood of heart-burnings and hatreds, engendered on Earth by the strife of man with man, is unknown to the people of Mars, save from the study of our planet. When I asked if there were not, after all, a lack of spontaneity, of sense of

freedom, in leading lives fixed in all details beforehand, I was reminded that there was no difference
in that respect between the lives of the people of
Earth and of Mars, both alike being according to
God's will in every particular. We knew that will
only after the event, they before, — that was all.
For the rest, God moved them through their wills
as He did us, so that they had no more sense of
compulsion in what they did than we on Earth
have in carrying out an anticipated line of action,
in cases where our anticipations chance to be correct. Of the absorbing interest which the study
of the plan of their future lives possessed for the
people of Mars, my companion spoke eloquently.
It was, he said, like the fascination to a mathe-
matician of a most elaborate and exquisite demonstration, a perfect algebraical equation, with the
glowing realities of life in place of figures and
symbols.

When I asked if it never occurred to them to
wish their futures different, he replied that such a
question could only have been asked by one from
the Earth. No one could have foresight, or clearly
believe that God had it, without realizing that the
future is as incapable of being changed as the
past. And not only this, but to foresee events
was to foresee their logical necessity so clearly
that to desire them different was as impossible as
seriously to wish that two and two made five instead of four. No person could ever thoughtfully

wish anything different, for so closely are all things, the small with the great, woven together by God that to draw out the smallest thread would unravel creation through all eternity.

While we had talked the afternoon had waned, and the sun had sunk below the horizon, the roseate atmosphere of the planet imparting a splendor to the cloud coloring, and a glory to the land and sea scape, never paralleled by an earthly sunset. Already the familiar constellations appearing in the sky reminded me how near, after all, I was to the Earth, for with the unassisted eye I could not detect the slightest variation in their position. Nevertheless, there was one wholly novel feature in the heavens, for many of the host of asteroids which circle in the zone between Mars and Jupiter were vividly visible to the naked eye. But the spectacle that chiefly held my gaze was the Earth, swimming low on the verge of the horizon. Its disc, twice as large as that of any star or planet as seen from the Earth, flashed with a brilliancy like that of Venus.

" It is, indeed, a lovely sight," said my companion, "although to me always a melancholy one, from the contrast suggested between the radiance of the orb and the benighted condition of its inhabitants. We call it 'The Blindman's World.'" As he spoke he turned toward a curious structure which stood near us, though I had not before particularly observed it.

"What is that?" I asked.

"It is one of our telescopes," he replied. "I am going to let you take a look, if you choose, at your home, and test for yourself the powers of which I have boasted;" and having adjusted the instrument to his satisfaction, he showed me where to apply my eye to what answered to the eye-piece.

I could not repress an exclamation of amazement, for truly he had exaggerated nothing. The little college town which was my home lay spread out before me, seemingly almost as near as when I looked down upon it from my observatory windows. It was early morning, and the village was waking up. The milkmen were going their rounds, and workmen, with their dinner-pails, where hurrying along the streets. The early train was just leaving the railroad station. I could see the puffs from the smoke-stack, and the jets from the cylinders. It was strange not to hear the hissing of the steam, so near I seemed. There were the college buildings on the hill, the long rows of windows flashing back the level sunbeams. I could tell the time by the college clock. It struck me that there was an unusual bustle around the buildings, considering the earliness of the hour. A crowd of men stood about the door of the observatory, and many others were hurrying across the campus in that direction. Among them I recognized President Byxbee, accompanied by the college janitor. As I gazed they reached the observatory, and,

passing through the group about the door, entered
the building. The president was evidently going
up to my quarters. At this it flashed over me
quite suddenly that all this bustle was on my
account. I recalled how it was that I came to be
on Mars, and in what condition I had left affairs
in the observatory. It was high time I were back
there to look after myself.

Here abruptly ended the extraordinary document which I found that morning on my desk.
That it is the authentic record of the conditions of
life in another world which it purports to be I do
not expect the reader to believe. He will no doubt
explain it as another of the curious freaks of som-
nambulism set down in the books. Probably it
was merely that, possibly it was something more.
I do not pretend to decide the question. I have
told all the facts of the case, and have no better
means for forming an opinion than the reader.
Nor do I know, even if I fully believed it the true
account it seems to be, that it would have affected
my imagination much more strongly than it has.
That story of another world has, in a word, put me
out of joint with ours. The readiness with which
my mind has adapted itself to the Martial point of
view concerning the Earth has been a singular experience. The lack of foresight among the human
faculties, a lack I had scarcely thought of before,
now impresses me, ever more deeply, as a fact out

of harmony with the rest of our nature, belying its promise, — a moral mutilation, a deprivation arbitrary and unaccountable. The spectacle of a race doomed to walk backward, beholding only what has gone by, assured only of what is past and dead, comes over me from time to time with a sadly fantastical effect which I cannot describe. I dream of a world where love always wears a smile, where the partings are as tearless as our meetings, and death is king no more. I have a fancy, which I like to cherish, that the people of that happy sphere, fancied though it may be, represent the ideal and normal type of our race, as perhaps it once was, as perhaps it may yet be again.

AN ECHO OF ANTIETAM

THE air was tremulous with farewells. The regiment, recruited within sight of the steeples of Waterville, and for three months in camp just outside the city, was to march the next morning. A series of great battles had weakened the Federal armies, and the authorities at Washington had ordered all available men to the front.

The camp was to be broken up at an early hour, after which the regiment would march through the city to the depot to take the cars. The streets along the route of the march were already being decorated with flags and garlands. The city that afternoon was full of soldiers enjoying their last leave of absence. The liquor shops were crowded with parties of them drinking with their friends, while others in threes and fours, with locked arms, paraded the streets singing patriotic songs, sometimes in rather maudlin voices, for to-day in every saloon a soldier might enter, citizens vied for the privilege of treating him to the best in the house. No man in a blue coat was suffered to pay for anything.

For the most part, however, the men were sober

enough over their leave-taking. One saw every-
where soldiers and civilians, strolling in pairs,
absorbed in earnest talk. They are brothers,
maybe, who have come away from the house to be
alone with each other, while they talk of family
affairs and exchange last charges and promises as
to what is to be done if anything happens. Or
perhaps they are business partners, and the one
who has put the country's business before his own
is giving his last counsels as to how the store or
the shop shall be managed in his absence. Many
of the blue-clad men have women with them, and
these are the couples that the people oftenest turn
to look at. The girl who has a soldier lover is the
envy of her companions to-day as she walks by
his side. Her proud eyes challenge all who come,
saying, " See, this is my hero. I am the one he
loves."

You could easily tell when it was a wife and
not a sweetheart whom the soldier had with him.
There was no challenge in the eyes of the wife.
Young romance shed none of its glamour on the
sacrifice she was making for her native land. It
was only because they could not bear to sit any
longer looking at each other in the house that she
and her husband had come out to walk.

In the residence parts of the town family groups
were gathered on shady piazzas, a blue-coated figure the centre of each. They were trying to talk
cheerfully, making an effort even to laugh a little.

Now and then one of the women stole unobserved
from the circle, but her bravely smiling face as she
presently returned gave no inkling of the flood of
tears that had eased her heart in some place apart.
The young soldier himself was looking a little pale
and nervous with all his affected good spirits, and
it was safe to guess that he was even then thinking how often this scene would come before him
afterwards, by the camp-fire and on the eve of
battle.

In the village of Upton, some four or five miles
out of Waterville, on a broad piazza at the side
of a house on the main street, a group of four
persons were seated around a tea-table.

The centre of interest of this group, as of so
many others that day, was a soldier. He looked
not over twenty-five, with dark blue eyes, dark
hair cut close to his head, and a mustache trimmed
crisply in military fashion. His uniform set off
to advantage an athletic figure of youthful slender-
ness, and his bronzed complexion told of long days
of practice on the drill-ground in the school of the
company and the battalion. He wore the shoulder-
straps of a second lieutenant.

On one side of the soldier sat the Rev. Mr.
Morton, his cousin, and on the other Miss Bertha
Morton, a kindly faced, middle-aged lady, who was
her brother's housekeeper and the hostess of this
occasion.

The fourth member of the party was a girl of nineteen or twenty. She was a very pretty girl, and although to-day her pallid cheeks and red and swollen eyelids would to other eyes have detracted somewhat from her charms, it was certain that they did not make her seem less adorable to the young officer, for he was her lover, and was to march with the regiment in the morning.

Lieutenant Philip King was a lawyer, and by perseverance and native ability had worked up a fair practice for so young a man in and around Upton. When he volunteered, he had to make up his mind to leave this carefully gathered clientage to scatter, or to be filched from him by less patriotic rivals; but it may be well believed that this seemed to him a little thing compared with leaving Grace Roberts, with the chance of never returning to make her his wife. If, indeed, it had been for him to say, he would have placed his happiness beyond hazard by marrying her before the regiment marched; nor would she have been averse, but her mother, an invalid widow, took a sensible rather than a sentimental view of the case. If he were killed, she said, a wife would do him no good; and if he came home again, Grace would be waiting for him, and that ought to satisfy a reasonable man. It had to satisfy an unreasonable one. The Robertses had always lived just beyond the garden from the parsonage, and Grace, who from a little girl had been a great pet of the childless minister

and his sister, was almost as much at home there
as in her mother's house. When Philip fell in
love with her, the Mortons were delighted. They
could have wished nothing better for either. From
the first Miss Morton had done all she could to
make matters smooth for the lovers, and the present little farewell banquet was but the last of
many meetings she had prepared for them at the
parsonage.

Philip had come out from camp on a three-hours'
leave that afternoon, and would have to report
again at half-past seven. It was nearly that hour
now, though still light, the season being midsummer. There had been an effort on the part of all
to keep up a cheerful tone ; but as the time of the
inevitable separation drew near, the conversation
had been more and more left to the minister and
his sister, who, with observations sometimes a little
forced, continued to fend off silence and the demoralization it would be likely to bring to their young
friends. Grace had been the first to drop out
of the talking, and Philip's answers, when he was
addressed, grew more and more at random, as the
meetings of his eyes with his sweetheart's became
more frequent and lasted longer.

" He will be the handsomest officer in the regiment, that's one comfort. Won't he, Grace ? "
said Miss Morton cheerily.

The girl nodded and smiled faintly. Her eyes
were brimming, and the twitching of her lips from

time to time betrayed how great was the effort with
which she kept her self-command.

"Yes," said Mr. Morton; "but though he looks
very well now, it is nothing to the imposing appearance he will present when he comes back with a
colonel's shoulder-straps. You should be thinking
of that, Grace."

"I expect we shall hear from him every day,"
said Miss Morton. "He will have no excuse for
not writing with all those envelopes stamped and
addressed, with blank paper in them, which Grace
has given him. You should always have three or
four in your coat pocket, Phil."

The young man nodded.

"I suppose for the most part we shall learn of
you through Grace; but you must n't forget us
entirely, my boy," said Mr. Morton. "We shall
want to hear from you directly now and then."

"Yes; I'll be sure to write," Philip replied.

"I suppose it will be time enough to see the regiment pass if we are in our places by nine o'clock,"
suggested Miss Morton, after a silence.

"I think so," said her brother. "It is a great
affair to break camp, and I don't believe the march
will begin till after that time."

"James has got us one of the windows of Ray
& Seymour's offices, you know, Philip," resumed
Miss Morton; "which one did you say, James?"

"The north one."

"Yes, the north one," she resumed. "They say

every window on Main Street along the route of
the regiment is rented. Grace will be with us, you
know. You must n't forget to look up at us as you
go by " — as if the young man were likely to!

He was evidently not now listening to her at all.
His eyes were fastened upon the girl's opposite
him, and they seemed to have quite forgotten the
others. Miss Morton and her brother exchanged
compassionate glances. Tears were in the lady's
eyes. A clock in the sitting-room began to strike:

" One, two, three, four, five, six, seven."

Philip started.

" What time is that ? " he asked, a little huskily.
No one replied at once. Then Mr. Morton said :

" I am afraid it struck seven, my boy."

" I must leave in ten minutes then," said the
young man, rising from the table. The rest followed his example.

" I wonder if the buggy will be in time ? " said
he.

" It is at the gate," replied Miss Morton. " I
heard it drive up some time ago."

Unmindful of the others now, Philip put his arm
about Grace's waist and drew her away to the end
of the piazza and thence out into the garden.

" Poor young things," murmured Miss Morton,
the tears running down her cheeks as she looked
after them. " It is pitiful, James, to see how they
suffer."

" Yes," said the minister ; " and there are a

great many just such scenes to-day. Ah, well,
as St. Paul says, we see as yet but in part."

Passing in and out among the shrubbery, and
presently disappearing from the sympathetic eyes
upon the piazza, the lovers came to a little summer-
house, and there they entered. Taking her wrists
in his hands, he held her away from him, and his
eyes went slowly over her from head to foot, as if
he would impress upon his mind an image that
absence should not have power to dim.

" You are so beautiful," he said, " that in this
moment, when I ought to have all my courage, you
make me feel that I am a madman to leave you
for the sake of any cause on earth. The future to
most men is but a chance of happiness, and when
they risk it they only risk a chance. In staking
their lives, they only stake a lottery ticket, which
would probably draw a blank. But my ticket has
drawn a capital prize. I risk not the chance, but
the certainty, of happiness. I believe I am a fool,
and if I am killed, that will be the first thing they
will say to me on the other side."

" Don't talk of that, Phil. Oh, don't talk of
being killed ! "

" No, no ; of course not ! " he exclaimed. " Don't
fret about that ; I shall not be killed. I 've no
notion of being killed. But what a fool I am to
waste these last moments staring at you when I
might be kissing you, my love, my love ! " And
clasping her in his arms, he covered her face with
kisses.

She began to sob convulsively.

"Don't, darling; don't! Don't make it so hard for me," he whispered hoarsely.

"Oh, do let me cry," she wailed. "It was so hard for me to hold back all the time we were at table. I must cry, or my heart will break. Oh, my own dear Phil, what if I should never see you again! Oh! Oh!"

"Nonsense, darling," he said, crowding down the lump that seemed like iron in his throat, and making a desperate effort to keep his voice steady. "You will see me again, never doubt it. Don't I tell you I am coming back? The South cannot hold out much longer. Everybody says so. I shall be home in a year, and then you will be my wife, to be God's Grace to me all the rest of my life. Our happiness will be on interest till then; ten per cent. a month at least, compound interest, piling up every day. Just think of that, dear; don't let yourself think of anything else."

"Oh, Phil, how I love you!" she cried, throwing her arms around his neck in a passion of tenderness. "Nobody is like you. Nobody ever was. Surely God will not part us. Surely He will not. He is too good."

"No, dear, He will not. Some day I shall come back. It will not be long. Perhaps I shall find you waiting for me in this same little summerhouse. Let us think of that. It was here, you know, we found out each other's secret that day."

" I had found out yours long before," she said, faintly smiling.

" Time 's up, Phil." It was Mr. Morton's voice calling to them from the piazza.

" I must go, darling. Good-by."

" Oh, no, not yet ; not quite yet," she wailed, clinging to him. " Why, we have been here but a few moments. It can't be ten minutes yet."

Under the influence of that close, passionate embrace, those clinging kisses and mingling tears, there began to come over Philip a feeling of weakness, of fainting courage, a disposition to cry out, "Nothing can be so terrible as this. I will not bear it ; I will not go." By a tyrannical effort of will, against which his whole nature cried out, he unwound her arms from his neck and said in a choked voice : —

" Darling, this is harder than any battle I shall have to fight, but this is what I enlisted for. I must go."

He had reached the door of the summer-house, not daring for honor's sake to look back, when a heartbroken cry smote his ear.

" You have n't kissed me good-by ! "

He had kissed her a hundred times, but these kisses she apparently distinguished from the good-by kiss. He came back, and taking her again in his embrace, kissed her lips, her throat, her bosom, and then once more their lips met, and in that kiss of parting which plucks the heart up by the roots.

How strong must be the barrier between one soul and another that they do not utterly merge in moments like that, turning the agony of parting to the bliss of blended being!

Pursued by the sound of her desolate sobbing, he fled away.

The stable-boy held the dancing horse at the gate, and Mr. Morton and his sister stood waiting there.

" Good-by, Phil, till we see you again," said Miss Morton, kissing him tenderly. " We 'll take good care of her for you."

" Will you please go to her now?" he said huskily. " She is in the summer-house. For God's sake try to comfort her."

"Yes, poor boy, I will," she answered. He shook hands with Mr. Morton and jumped into the buggy.

" I 'll get a furlough and be back in a few months, maybe. Be sure to tell her that," he said.

The stable-boy stood aside; the mettlesome horse gave a plunge and started off at a three-minute gait. The boy drew out his watch and observed: " He hain't got but fifteen minutes to git to camp in, but he 'll do it. The mare's a stepper, and Phil King knows how to handle the ribbons."

The buggy vanished in a cloud of dust around the next turn in the road. The stable-boy strode whistling down the street, the minister went to his

study, and Miss Morton disappeared in the shrubbery in the direction of the summer-house.

II

Early next morning the country roads leading
into Waterville were covered with carts and wag-
ons and carriages loaded with people coming into
town to see the regiment off. The streets were
hung with flags and spanned with decorated arches
bearing patriotic inscriptions. Red, white, and
blue streamers hung in festoons from building to
building and floated from cornices. The stores
and places of business were all closed, the side-
walks were packed with people in their Sunday
clothes, and the windows and balconies were lined
with gazers long before it was time for the regiment to appear. Everybody — men, women, and
children — wore the national colors in cockades or
rosettes, while many young girls were dressed
throughout in red, white, and blue. The city
seemed tricked out for some rare gala-day, but the
grave faces of the expectant throng, and the subdued and earnest manner which extended even to
the older children, stamped this as no ordinary
holiday.

After hours of patient waiting, at last the word
passes from mouth to mouth, "They are coming!"
Vehicles are quickly driven out of the way, and in
a general hush all eyes are turned towards the

head of the street. Presently there is a burst of martial music, and the regiment comes wheeling round the corner into view and fills the wide street from curb to curb with its broad front. As the blue river sweeps along, the rows of polished bayonets, rising and falling with the swinging tread of the men, are like interminable ranks of foam-crested waves rolling in upon the shore. The imposing mass, with its rhythmic movement, gives the impression of a single organism. One forgets to look for the individuals in it, forgets that there are individuals. Even those who have brothers, sons, lovers there, for a moment almost forget them in the impression of a mighty whole. The mind is slow to realize that this great dragon, so terrible in its beauty, emitting light as it moves from a thousand burnished scales, with flaming crest proudly waving in the van, is but an aggregation of men singly so feeble.

The hearts of the lookers-on as they gaze are swelling fast. An afflatus of heroism given forth by this host of self-devoted men communicates itself to the most stolid spectators. The booming of the drum fills the brain, and the blood in the veins leaps to its rhythm. The unearthly gayety of the fife, like the sweet, shrill song of a bird soaring above the battle, infects the nerves till the idea of death brings a scornful smile to the lips. Eyes glaze with rapturous tears as they rest upon the flag. There is a thrill of voluptuous sweetness

in the thought of dying for it. Life seems of
value only as it gives the poorest something to
sacrifice. It is dying that makes the glory of the
world, and all other employments seem but idle
while the regiment passes.

The time for farewells is gone by. The lucky
men at the ends of the ranks have indeed an
opportunity without breaking step to exchange
an occasional hand-shake with a friend on the side-
walk, or to snatch a kiss from wife or sweetheart,
but those in the middle of the line can only look
their farewells. Now and then a mother intrusts
her baby to a file-leader to be passed along from
hand to hand till it reaches the father, to be sent
back with a kiss, or, maybe, perched aloft on his
shoulder, to ride to the depot, crowing at the music
and clutching at the gleaming bayonets. At every
such touch of nature the people cheer wildly.
From every window and balcony the ladies shower
garlands upon the troops.

Where is Grace? for this is the Upton company
which is passing now. Yonder she stands on a
balcony, between Mr. Morton and his sister. She
is very pale and the tears are streaming down her
cheeks, but her face is radiant. She is smiling
through her tears, as if there was no such thing on
earth as fear or sorrow. She has looked forward
to this ordeal with harrowing expectations, only to
find herself at the trying moment seized upon and
lifted above all sense of personal affliction by the

passion of self-devotion with which the air is electric. Her face as she looks down upon her lover
is that of a priestess in the ecstasy of sacrifice.
He is saluting with his sword. Now he has passed.
With a great sob she turns away. She does not
care for the rest of the pageant. Her patriotism
has suddenly gone. The ecstasy of sacrifice is
over. She is no longer a priestess, but a broken-
hearted girl, who only asks to be led away to some
place where she can weep till her lover returns.

III

There was to be a great battle the next day.
The two armies had been long manœuvring for
position, and now they stood like wrestlers who
have selected their holds and, with body braced
against body, knee against knee, wait for the sig-
nal to begin the struggle. There had been during
the afternoon some brisk fighting, but a common
desire to postpone the decisive contest till the morrow had prevented the main forces from becoming
involved. Philip's regiment had thus far only
been engaged in a few trifling skirmishes, barely
enough to stir the blood. This was to be its
first battle, and the position to which it had been
allotted promised a bloody baptism in the morning.
The men were in excellent heart, but as night settled down, there was little or no merriment to be
heard about the camp-fires. Most were gathered

in groups, discussing in low tones the chances of the morrow. Some, knowing that every fibre of muscle would be needed for the work before them, had wisely gone to sleep, while here and there a man, heedless of the talk going on about him, was lying on his back staring up at the darkening sky, thinking.

As the twilight deepened, Philip strolled to the top of a little knoll just out of the camp and sat down, with a vague notion of casting up accounts a little in view of the final settlement which very possibly might come for him next day. But the inspiration of the scene around him soon diverted his mind from personal engrossments. Some distance down the lines he could see the occasional flash of a gun, where a battery was lazily shelling a piece of woods which it was desirable to keep the enemy from occupying during the night. A burning barn in that direction made a flare on the sky. Over behind the wooded hills where the Confederates lay, rockets were going up, indicating the exchange of signals and the perfecting of plans which might mean defeat and ruin to him and his the next day. Behind him, within the Federal lines, clouds of dust, dimly outlined against the glimmering landscape, betrayed the location of the roads along which artillery, cavalry, infantry were hurrying eagerly forward to take their assigned places for the morrow's work.

Who said that men fear death? Who concocted

that fable for old wives? He should have stood that night with Philip in the midst of a host of one hundred and twenty-five thousand men in the full flush and vigor of life, calmly and deliberately making ready at dawn to receive death in its most horrid forms at one another's hands. It is in vain that Religion invests the tomb with terror, and Philosophy, shuddering, averts her face; the nations turn from these gloomy teachers to storm its portals in exultant hosts, battering them wide enough for thousands to charge through abreast. The heroic instinct of humanity with its high contempt of death is wiser and truer, never let us doubt, than superstitious terrors or philosophic doubts. It testifies to a conviction, deeper than reason, that man is greater than his seeming self; to an underlying consciousness that his mortal life is but an accident of his real existence, the fashion of a day, to be lightly worn and gayly doffed at duty's call.

What a pity it truly is that the tonic air of battlefields — the air that Philip breathed that night before Antietam — cannot be gathered up and preserved as a precious elixir to reinvigorate the atmosphere in times of peace, when men grow faint of heart and cowardly, and quake at thought of death.

The soldiers huddled in their blankets on the ground slept far more soundly that night before the battle than their men-folk and women-folk in

their warm beds at home. For them it was a
night of watching, a vigil of prayers and tears.
The telegraph in those days made of the nation an
intensely sensitive organism, with nerves a thousand miles long. Ere its echoes had died away,
every shot fired at the front had sent a tremor to
the anxious hearts at home. The newspapers and
bulletin boards in all the towns and cities of the
North had announced that a great battle would
surely take place the next day, and, as the night
closed in, a mighty cloud of prayer rose from
innumerable firesides, the self-same prayer from
each, that he who had gone from that home might
survive the battle, whoever else must fall.

The wife, lest her own appeal might fail, taught
her cooing baby to lisp the father's name, thinking that surely the Great Father's heart would not
be able to resist a baby's prayer. The widowed
mother prayed that if it were consistent with God's
will he would spare her son. She laid her heart,
pierced through with many sorrows, before Him.
She had borne so much, life had been so hard, her
boy was all she had to show for so much endured,
— might not this cup pass? Pale, impassioned
maids, kneeling by their virgin beds, wore out the
night with an importunity that would not be put
off. Sure in their great love and their little knowledge that no case could be like theirs, they be-
seeched God with bitter weeping for their lovers'
lives, because, forsooth, they could not bear it if

hurt came to them. The answers to many thousands of these agonizing appeals of maid and wife and mother were already in the enemy's cartridge-boxes.

IV

The day came. The dispatches in the morning papers stated that the armies would probably be engaged from an early hour.

Who that does not remember those battle-summers can realize from any telling how the fathers and mothers, the wives and sisters and sweethearts at home, lived through the days when it was known that a great battle was going on at the front in which their loved ones were engaged? It was very quiet in the house on those days of battle. All spoke in hushed voices and stepped lightly. The children, too small to understand the meaning of the shadow on the home, felt it and took their noisy sports elsewhere. There was little conversation, except as to wher definite news might be expected. The household work dragged sadly, for though the women sought refuge from thought in occupation, they were constantly dropping whatever they had in hand to rush away to their chambers to face the presentiment, perhaps suddenly borne in upon them with the force of a conviction, that they might be called on to bear the worst. The table was set for the regular meals, but there was little pretense of eating. The eyes of all had a

far-off expression, and they seemed barely to see
one another. There was an intent, listening look
upon their faces, as if they were hearkening to the
roar of the battle a thousand miles away.

Many pictures of battles have been painted, but
no true one yet, for the pictures contain only men.
The women are unaccountably left out. We ought
to see not alone the opposing lines of battle writhing and twisting in a death embrace, the batteries
smoking and flaming, the hurricanes of cavalry,
but innumerable women also, spectral forms of mothers, wives, sweethearts, clinging about the necks
of the advancing soldiers, vainly trying to shield
them with their bosoms, extending supplicating
hands to the foe, raising eyes of anguish to Heaven.
The soldiers, grim-faced, with battle-lighted eyes,
do not see the ghostly forms that throng them, but
shoot and cut and stab across and through them
as if they were not there, — yes, through them, for
few are the balls and bayonets that reach their
marks without traversing some of these devoted
breasts. Spectral, alas, is their guardianship, but
real are their wounds and deadly as any the com-
batants receive.

Soon after breakfast on the day of the battle
Grace came across to the parsonage, her swollen
eyes and pallid face telling of a sleepless night.
She could not bear her mother's company that day,
for she knew that she had never greatly liked
Philip. Miss Morton was very tender and sym-

pathetic. Grace was a little comforted by Mr.
Morton's saying that commonly great battles did
not open much before noon. It was a respite to
be able to think that probably up to that moment
at least no harm had come to Philip. In the early
afternoon the minister drove into Waterville to
get the earliest bulletins at the " Banner " office,
leaving the two women alone.

The latter part of the afternoon a neighbor who
had been in Waterville drove by the house, and
Miss Morton called to him to know if there were
any news yet. He drew a piece of paper from his
pocket, on which he had scribbled the latest bulletin before the " Banner " office, and read as follows : " The battle opened with a vigorous attack
by our right. The enemy was forced back, stub-
bornly contesting every inch of ground. General
——'s division is now bearing the brunt of the
fight and is suffering heavily. The result is yet
uncertain."

The division mentioned was the one in which
Philip's regiment was included. " Is suffering
heavily," — those were the words. There was
something fearful in the way the present tense
brought home to Grace a sense of the battle as
then actually in progress. It meant that while she
sat there on the shady piazza with the drowsy hum
of the bees in her ears, looking out on the quiet
lawn where the house cat, stretched on the grass,
kept a sleepy eye on the birds as they flitted in the

branches of the apple-trees, Philip might be facing
a storm of lead and iron, or, maybe, blent in some
desperate hand-to-hand struggle, was defending his
life — her life — against murderous cut and thrust.

To begin to pray for his safety was not to dare
to cease, for to cease would be to withdraw a sort
of protection — all, alas ! she could give — and
abandon him to his enemies. If she had been
watching over him from above the battle, an actual
witness of the carnage going on that afternoon on
the far-off field, she could scarcely have endured a
more harrowing suspense from moment to moment.
Overcome with the agony, she threw herself on the
sofa in the sitting-room and lay quivering, with her
face buried in the pillow, while Miss Morton sat
beside her, stroking her hair and saying such
feeble, soothing words as she might.

It is always hard, and for ardent temperaments
almost impossible, to hold the mind balanced in
a state of suspense, yielding overmuch neither to
hope nor to fear, under circumstances like these.
As a relief to the torture which such a state of tension ends in causing, the mind at length, if it cannot abandon itself to hope, embraces even despair.
About five o'clock Miss Morton was startled by an
exceeding bitter cry. Grace was sitting upon the
sofa. " Oh, Miss Morton ! " she cried, bursting
into tears which before she had not been able to
shed, " he is dead ! "

" Grace ! Grace ! what do you mean ? "

"He is dead, I know he is dead!" wailed the girl; and then she explained that while from moment to moment she had sent up prayers for him, every breath a cry to God, she suddenly had been unable to pray more, and this she felt was a sign that petition for his life was now vain. Miss Morton strove to convince her that this was but an effect of overwrought nerves, but with slight success.

In the early evening Mr. Morton returned with the latest news the telegraph had brought. The full scope of the result was not yet known. The advantage had probably remained with the National forces, although the struggle had been one of those close and stubborn ones, with scanty laurels for the victors, to be expected when men of one race meet in battle. The losses on both sides had been enormous, and the report was confirmed that Philip's division had been badly cut up.

The parsonage was but one of thousands of homes in the land where no lamps were lighted that evening, the members of the household sitting together in the dark, — silent, or talking in low tones of the far-away star-lighted battlefield, the anguish of the wounded, the still heaps of the dead.

Nevertheless, when at last Grace went home she was less entirely despairing than in the afternoon. Mr. Morton, in his calm, convincing way, had shown her the groundlessness of her impression that Philip was certainly dead, and had enabled her again to entertain hope. It no longer rose, indeed, to the height of a belief that he had escaped wholly scathless. In face of the terrible tidings, that would have been too presumptuous. But perhaps he had been only wounded. Yesterday the thought would have been insupportable, but now she was eager to make this compromise with Providence. She was distinctly affected by the curious superstition that if we voluntarily concede something to fate, while yet the facts are not known, we gain a sort of equitable assurance against a worse thing. It was settled, she told herself, that she was not to be overcome or even surprised to hear that Philip was wounded, — slightly wounded. She was no better than other women, that he should be wholly spared.

The paper next morning gave many names of officers who had fallen, but Philip's was not among them. The list was confessedly incomplete; nevertheless, the absence of his name was reassuring. Grace went across the garden after breakfast to talk with Miss Morton about the news and the auspicious lack of news. Her friend's cheerful tone infused her with fresh courage. To one who has despaired, a very little hope goes to the head like wine to the brain of a faster, and, though still very tremulous, Grace could even smile a little now and was almost cheerful. Secretly already she was beginning to play false with fate, and, in

flat repudiation of her last night's compact, to
indulge the hope that her soldier had not been
even wounded. But this was only at the bottom
of her heart. She did not own to herself that she
really did it. She felt a little safer not to break
the bargain yet.

About eleven o'clock in the forenoon Mr. Morton
came in. His start and look of dismay on seeing
Grace indicated that he had expected to find his
sister alone. He hastily attempted to conceal an
open telegram which he held in his hand, but it
was too late. Grace had already seen it, and whatever the tidings it might contain, there was no
longer any question of holding them back or ex-
tenuating them. Miss Morton, after one look at
her brother's face, silently came to the girl's side
and put her arms around her waist. " Christ, our
Saviour," she murmured, " for thy name's sake,
help her now." Then the minister said : —

"Try to be brave, try to bear it worthily of him;
for, my poor little girl, your sacrifice has been
accepted. He fell in a charge at the head of his
men."

V

Philip's body was brought home for burial, and
the funeral was a great event in the village. Business of all kinds was suspended, and all the people
united in making of the day a solemn patriotic fes-
tival. Mr. Morton preached the funeral sermon.

"Oh, talk about the country," sobbed Grace, when he asked her if there was anything in particular she would like him to speak of.

" For pity's sake don't let me feel sorry now that I gave him up for the Union. Don't leave me now to think it would have been better if I had not let him go."

So he preached of the country, as ministers sometimes did preach in those days, making it very plain that in a righteous cause men did well to die for their native land and their women did well to give them up. Expounding the lofty wisdom of self-sacrifice, he showed how truly it was said that " whosoever will save his life shall lose it : and whosoever will lose his life . . . shall find it," and how none make such rich profit out of their lives as the heroes who seem to throw them away.

They had come, he told the assembled people, to mourn no misadventure, no misfortune ; this dead soldier was not pitiable. He was no victim of a tear-compelling fate. No broken shaft typified his career. He was rather one who had done well for himself, a wise young merchant of his blood, who having seen a way to barter his life at incredible advantage, at no less a rate indeed than a man's for a nation's, had not let slip so great an opportunity.

So he went on, still likening the life of a man to the wares of a shopkeeper, worth to him only what they can be sold for and a loss if overkept, till those who listened began to grow ill at ease in presence of that flag-draped coffin, and were vaguely troubled because they still lived.

Then he spoke of those who had been bereaved. This soldier, he said, like his comrades, had staked for his country not only his own life but the earthly happiness of others also, having been fully empowered by them to do so. Some had staked with their own lives the happiness of parents, some that of wives and children, others maybe the hopes of maidens pledged to them. In offering up their lives to their country they had laid with them upon the altar these other lives which were bound up with theirs, and the same fire of sacrifice had consumed them both. A few days before, in the storm of battle, those who had gone forth had fulfilled their share of the joint sacrifice. In a thousand homes, with tears and the anguish of breaking hearts, those who had sent them forth were that day fulfilling theirs. Let them now in their extremity seek support in the same spirit of patriotic devotion which had upheld their heroes in the hour of death. As they had been lifted above fear by the thought that it was for their country they were dying, not less should those who mourned them find inspiration in remembering it was for the nation's sake that their tears were shed, and for the country that their hearts were broken. It had been appointed that half in blood of men and half in women's tears the ransom of the people should

be paid, so that their sorrow was not in vain, but
for the healing of the nation.

It behooved these, therefore, to prove worthy of
their high calling of martyrdom, and while they
must needs weep, not to weep as other women
wept, with hearts bowed down, but rather with
uplifted faces, adopting and ratifying, though it
might be with breaking hearts, this exchange they
had made of earthly happiness for the life of their
native land. So should they honor those they
mourned, and be joined with them not only in sacrifice but in the spirit of sacrifice.

So it was in response to the appeal of this
stricken girl before him that the minister talked
of the country, and to such purpose was it that the
piteous thing she had dreaded, the feeling, now
when it was forever too late, that it would have
been better if she had kept her lover back, found
no place in her heart. There was, indeed, had she
known it, no danger at all that she would be left
to endure that, so long as she dreaded it, for the
only prayer that never is unanswered is the prayer
to be lifted above self. So to pray and so to wish
is but to cease to resist the divine gravitations ever
pulling at the soul. As the minister discoursed of
the mystic gain of self-sacrifice, the mystery of
which he spoke was fulfilled in her heart. She
appeared to stand in some place overarching life
and death, and there was made partaker of an exultation whereof if religion and philosophy might

but catch and hold the secret, their ancient quest were over.

Gazing through streaming eyes upon the coffin of her lover, she was able freely to consent to the sacrifice of her own life which he had made in giving up his own.

THE OLD FOLKS' PARTY

"AND now what shall we do next Wednesday evening?" said Jessie Hyde, in a business-like tone. "It is your turn, Henry, to suggest."

Jessie was a practical, energetic young lady, whose blue eyes never relapsed into the dreaminess to which that color is subject. She furnished the "go" for the club. Especially she furnished the "go" for Henry Long, who had lots of ideas, but without her to stir him up was as dull as a flint without a steel.

There were six in the club, and all were present to-night in Jessie's parlor. The evening had been given to a little music, a little dancing, a little card-playing, and a good deal of talking. It was near the hour set by the club rule for the adjournment of its reunions, and the party had drawn their chairs together to consult upon the weekly recurring question, what should be done at the next meeting by way of special order of amusement. The programmes were alternately reading, singing, dancing, whist; varied with evenings of miscellaneous sociality like that which had just passed. The members took turns in suggesting recreations. To-night it was Henry Long's turn, and to him accordingly the eyes of the group turned at Jessie's question.

"Let's have an old folks' party," was his answer.

Considering that all of the club were yet at ages when they celebrated their birthdays with the figure printed on the cake, the suggestion seemed sufficiently irrelevant.

"In that case," said Frank Hays, "we shall have to stay at home."

Frank was an alert little fellow, with a jaunty air, to whom, by tacit consent, all the openings for jokes were left, as he had a taste that way.

"What do you mean, Henry?" inquired George Townsley, a thick-set, sedate young man, with an intelligent, but rather phlegmatic look.

"My idea is this," said Henry, leaning back in his chair, with his hands clasped behind his head, and his long legs crossed before him. "Let us dress up to resemble what we expect to look like fifty years hence, and study up our demeanor to correspond with what we expect to be and feel like at that time, and just call on Mary next Wednesday evening to talk over old times, and recall what we can, if anything, of our vanished youth, and the days when we belonged to the social club at C——."

The others seemed rather puzzled in spite of the explanation. Jessie sat looking at Henry in a brown study as she traced out his meaning.

"You mean a sort of ghost party," said she finally; "ghosts of the future, instead of ghosts of the past."

"That's it exactly," answered he. "Ghosts of the future are the only sort worth heeding. Apparitions of things past are a very unpractical sort of demonology, in my opinion, compared with apparitions of things to come."

"How in the world did such an odd idea come into your head?" asked pretty Nellie Tyrrell, whose dancing black eyes were the most piquant of interrogation points, with which it was so delightful to be punctured that people were generally slow to gratify her curiosity.

"I was beginning a journal this afternoon," said Henry, "and the idea of Henry Long, ætat. seventy, looking over the leaves, and wondering about the youth who wrote them so long ago, came up to my mind."

Henry's suggestion had set them all thinking, and the vein was so unfamiliar that they did not at once find much to say.

"I should think," finally remarked George, "that such an old folks' party would afford a chance for some pretty careful study, and some rather good acting."

"Fifty years will make us all not far from seventy. What shall we look like then, I wonder?" musingly asked Mary Fellows.

She was the demurest, dreamiest of the three

girls ; the most of a woman, and the least of a talker. She had that poise and repose of manner which are necessary to make silence in company graceful.

" We may be sure of one thing, anyhow, and that is, that we shall not look and feel at all as we do now," said Frank. " I suppose," he added, " if, by a gift of second sight, we could see to-night, as in a glass, what we shall be at seventy, we should entirely fail to recognize ourselves, and should fall to disputing which was which."

" Yes, and we shall doubtless have changed as much in disposition as in appearance," added Henry. " Now, for one, I 've no idea what sort of a fellow my old man will turn out. I don't believe people can generally tell much better what sort of old people will grow out of them than what characters their children will have. A little better, perhaps, but not much. Just think how different sets of faculties and tastes develop and decay, come into prominence and retire into the background, as the years pass. A trait scarcely noticeable in youth tinges the whole man in age."

" What striking dramatic effects are lost because the drama of life is spun out so long instead of having the ends brought together," observed George. " The spectators lose the force of the contrasts because they forget the first part of every rôle before the latter part is reached. One fails in consequence to get a realizing sense of the sublime inconsistencies of every lifetime."

"That difficulty is what we propose, in a small way, to remedy next Wednesday night," replied Henry.

Mary professed some scruples. It was so queer, she thought it must be wrong. It was like tempting Providence to take for granted issues in his hands, and masquerade with uncreated things like their own yet unborn selves. But Frank reminded her that the same objection would apply to any arrangement as to what they should do next week.

"Well, but," offered Jessie, "is it quite respectful to make sport of old folks, even if they are ourselves?"

"My conscience is clear on that point," said Frank. "It's the only way we can get even with them for the deprecating, contemptuous way in which they will allude to us over their snuff and tea, as callow and flighty youth, if indeed they deign to remember us at all, which is n't likely."

"I'm all tangled up in my mind," said Nellie, with an air of perplexity, "between these old people you are talking about and ourselves. Which is which? It seems odd to talk of them in the third person, and of ourselves in the first. Are n't they ourselves too?"

"If they are, then certainly we are not," replied Henry. "You may take your choice.

"The fact is," he added, as she looked still

more puzzled, "there are half a dozen of each one of us, or a dozen if you please, one in fact for each epoch of life, and each slightly or almost wholly different from the others. Each one of these epochs is foreign and inconceivable to the others, as ourselves at seventy now are to us. It's as hard to suppose ourselves old as to imagine swapping identities with another. And when we get old it will be just as hard to realize that we were ever young. So that the different periods of life are to all intents and purposes different persons, and the first person of grammar ought to be used only with the present tense. What we were, or shall be, or do, belongs strictly to the third person."

"You would make sad work of grammar with that notion," said Jessie, smiling.

"Grammar needs mending just there," replied Henry. "The three persons of grammar are really not enough. A fourth is needed to distinguish the ego of the past and future from the present ego, which is the only true one."

"Oh, you're getting altogether too deep for me," said Jessie. "Come, girls, what in the world are we going to get to wear next Wednesday?"

"Sure enough!" cried they with one accord, while the musing look in their eyes gave place to a vivacious and merry expression.

"My mother isn't near as old as we're going to be. Her things won't do," said Nellie.

"Nor mine," echoed Jessie; "but perhaps Mary's grandmother will let us have some of her things."

"In that case," suggested Frank, "it will be only civil to invite her to the party."

"To be sure, why not?" agreed Jessie. "It is to be an 'old folks'' party, and her presence will give a reality to the thing."

"I don't believe she'll come," said George. "You see being old is dead earnest to her, and she won't see the joke."

But Mary said she would ask her anyway, and so that was settled.

"My father is much too large in the waist for his clothes to be of any service to me," said George lugubriously.

But Frank reminded him that this was a hint as to his get-up, and that he must stuff with pillows that the proverb might be fulfilled, "Like father like son."

And then they were rather taken aback by Henry's obvious suggestion that there was no telling what the fashion in dress would be in A. D. 1925, "even if," he added, "the scientists leave us any A. D. by that time," though Frank remarked here that A. D. would answer just as well as *Anno Darwinis*, if worst came to worst. But it was decided that there was no use trying after prophetical accuracy in dress, since it was out of the question, and even if attainable would not suggest age to their own minds as would the elderly weeds which they were accustomed to see.

"It's rather odd, is n't it," said Jessie gravely, "that it did n't occur to anybody that in all probability not over one or two of us at most will be alive fifty years hence."

"Let's draw lots for the two victims, and the rest of us will appear as ghosts," suggested Frank grimly.

"Poor two," sighed Nellie. "I'm sorry for them. How lonely they will be. I'm glad I have n't got a very good constitution."

But Henry remarked that Jessie might have gone further and said just as truly that none of them would survive fifty years, or even ten.

"We may, some of us, escape the pang of dying as long as that," said he, "but that is but a trifle, and not a necessary incident of death. The essence of mortality is change, and we shall be changed. Ten years will see us very different persons. What though an old dotard calling himself Henry Long is stumping around fifty years hence, what is that to me? I shall have been dead a half century by that time."

"The old gentleman you speak so lightly of will probably think more tenderly of you than you do of him," said Jessie.

"I don't believe it," answered Henry. "In fact, if we were entirely true to nature next Wednesday, it would spoil the fun, for we probably should not, if actually of the age we pretend, think of our youth once a year, much less meet to talk it over."

"Oh, I don't think so," protested Nellie. "I'm sure all the story-books and poetry say that old folks are much given to reviewing their youth in a pensive, regretful sort of way."

"That's all very pretty, but it's all gammon in my opinion," responded Henry. "The poets are young people who know nothing of how old folks feel, and argue only from their theory of the romantic fitness of things. I believe that reminiscence takes up a very small part of old persons' time. It would furnish them little excitement, for they have lost the feelings by which their memories would have to be interpreted to become vivid. Remembering is dull business at best. I notice that most persons, even of eventful lives, prefer a good novel to the pleasures of recollection. It is really easier to sympathize with the people in a novel or drama than with our past selves. We lose a great source of recreation just because we can't recall the past more vividly."

"How shockingly Henry contradicts to-night," was the only reply Nellie deigned to this long speech.

"What shall we call each other next Wednesday?" asked Mary. "By our first names, as now?"

"Not if we are going to be prophetically accu-

rate," said Henry. "Fifty years hence, in all
probability, we shall, most of us, have altogether
forgotten our present intimacies and formed others,
quite inconceivable now. I can imagine Frank
over there, scratching his bald head with his spectacle tips, and trying to recall me. 'Hen. Long,
Hen. Long, — let me think; name sounds familiar,
and yet I can't quite place him. Did n't I know
him at C——, or was it at college? Bless me, how
forgetful I 'm growing!'"

They all laughed at Henry's bit of acting. Perhaps it was only sparkles of mirth, but it might
have been glances of tender confidence that shot
between certain pairs of eyes betokening something
that feared not time. This is in no sort a love
story, but such things can't be wholly prevented.

The girls, however, protested that this talk about
growing so utterly away from each other was too
dismal for anything, and they would n't believe it
anyhow. The old-fashioned notions about eternal
constancy were ever so much nicer. It gave them
the cold shivers to hear Henry's ante-mortem dis-
section of their friendship, and that young man
was finally forced to admit that the members of
the club would probably prove exceptions to the
general rule in such matters. It was agreed, therefore, that they should appear to know each other at
the old folks' party.

"All you girls must, of course, be called 'Mrs.'
instead of 'Miss,'" suggested Frank, "though you

will have to keep your own names, that is, unless you prefer to disclose any designs you may have upon other people's; " for which piece of imperti- nence Nellie, who sat next him, boxed his ears, — for the reader must know that these young people were on a footing of entire familiarity and long intimacy.

" Do you know what time it is ? " asked Mary, who, by virtue of the sweet sedateness of her dis- position, was rather the monitress of the company.

" It 's twelve o'clock, an hour after the club's curfew."

" Well," remarked Henry, rousing from the fit of abstraction in which he had been pursuing the subject of their previous discussion, " it was to be expected we should get a little mixed as to chrono- logy over such talk as this."

" With our watches set fifty years ahead, there 'll be no danger of overstaying our time next Wednes- day, anyhow," added Frank.

Soon the girls presented themselves in readiness for outdoors, and, in a pleasant gust of good-bys and parting jests, the party broke up.

" Good-by for fifty years," Jessie called after them from the stoop, as the merry couples walked away in the moonlight.

The following week was one of numerous consul- tations among the girls. Grandmother Fellows's wardrobe was pretty thoroughly rummaged under that good-natured old lady's superintendence, and many were the queer effects of old garments upon young figures which surprised the steady-going mirror in her quiet chamber.

"I'm afraid I can never depend on it again," said Mrs. Fellows.

She had promised to be at the party.

"She looked so grave when I first asked her," Mary explained to the girls, "that I was sorry I spoke of it. I was afraid she thought we wanted her only as a sort of convenience, to help out our pantomime by the effect of her white hair. But in a minute she smiled in her cheery way, and said, as if she saw right through me : 'I suppose, my child, you think being old a sort of misfortune, like being hunchbacked or blind, and are afraid of hurting my feelings, but you need n't be. The good Lord has made it so that at whichever end of life we are, the other end looks pretty uninteresting, and if it won't hurt your feelings to have somebody in the party who has got through all the troubles you have yet before you, I should be glad to come.' That was turning the tables for us pretty neatly, eh, girls ? "

The young ladies would not have had the old lady guess it for worlds, but truth compels me to own that all that week they improved every opportunity furtively to study Mrs. Fellows's gait and manner, with a view to perfecting their parts.

Frank and George met a couple of times in Henry's room to smoke it over and settle details,

and Henry called on Jessie to arrange several con-
certed features of the programme, and for some
other reasons for aught I know.

As each one studied his or her part and strove
in imagination to conceive how they would act and
feel as old men and old women, they grew more
interested, and more sensible of the mingled pathos
and absurdity of the project, and its decided general effect of queerness. They all set themselves
to make a study of old age in a manner that had
never occurred to them before, and never does
occur to most people at all. Never before had
their elderly friends received so much attention at
their hands.

In the prosecution of these observations they
were impressed with the entire lack of interest generally felt by people in the habits and manners of
persons in other epochs of life than their own. In
respect of age, as in so many other respects, the
world lives on flats, with equally little interest in
or comprehension of the levels above or below
them. And a surprising thing is that middle age
is about as unable to recall and realize youth as to
anticipate age. Experience seems to go for nothing
in this matter.

They thought they noticed, too, that old people
are more alike than middle-aged people. There is
something of the same narrowness and similarity
in the range of their tastes and feelings that is
marked in children. The reason they thought to

be that the interests of age have contracted to about the same scope as those of childhood before it has expanded into maturity. The skein of life is drawn together to a point at the two ends and spread out in the middle. Middle age is the period of most diversity, when individuality is most pronounced. The members of the club observed with astonishment that, however affectionately we may regard old persons, we no more think of becoming like them than of becoming negroes. If we catch ourselves observing their senile peculiarities, it is in a purely disinterested manner, with a complete and genuine lack of any personal concern, as with a state to which we are coming.

They could not help wondering if Henry were not right about people never really growing old, but just changing from one personality to another. They found the strange inability of one epoch to understand or appreciate the others, hard to reconcile with the ordinary notion of a persistent identity.

Before the end of the week, the occupation of their minds with the subject of old age produced a singular effect. They began to regard every event and feeling from a double standpoint, as present and as past, as it appeared to them and as it would appear to an old person.

Wednesday evening came at last, and a little before the hour of eight, five venerable figures, more or less shrouded, might have been seen making their way from different parts of the village toward the Fellows mansion. The families of the members of the club were necessarily in the secret, and watched their exit with considerable laughter from behind blinds. But to the rest of the villagers it has never ceased to be a puzzle who those elderly strangers were who appeared that evening and were never before or since visible. For once the Argus-eyed curiosity of a Yankee village, compared with which French or Austrian police are easy to baffle, was fairly eluded.

Eight o'clock was the hour at which the old folks' party began, and the reader will need a fresh introduction to the company which was assembled at that time in Mary Fellows's parlor. Mary sat by her grandmother, who from time to time regarded her in a half-puzzled manner, as if it required an effort of her reasoning powers to reassure her that the effect she saw was an illusion. The girl's brown hair was gathered back under a lace cap, and all that appeared outside it was thickly powdered. She wore spectacles, and the warm tint of her cheeks had given place to the opaque saffron hue of age. She sat with her hands in her lap, their fresh color and dimpled contour concealed by black lace half-gloves. The fullness of her young bosom was carefully disguised by the arrangement of the severely simple black dress she wore, which was also in other respects studiously adapted to conceal, by its stiff and angular lines, the luxuriant contour of her figure. As she rose and advanced to welcome Henry and Jessie, who were the last to arrive, it was with a striking imitation of the tremulously precipitate step of age.

Jessie, being rather taller than the others, had affected the stoop of age very successfully. She wore a black dress spotted with white, and her whitened hair was arranged with a high comb. She was the only one without spectacles or eye-glasses. Henry looked older and feebler than any of the company. His scant hair hung in thin and long white locks, and his tall, slender figure had gained a still more meagre effect from his dress, while his shoulders were bowed in a marked stoop; his gait was rigid and jerky. He assisted himself with a gold-headed cane, and sat in his chair leaning forward upon it.

George, on the other hand, had followed the hint of his father's figure in his make-up, and appeared as a rubicund old gentleman, large in the waist, bald, with an apoplectic tendency, a wheezy asthmatic voice, and a full white beard.

Nellie wore her hair in a row of white curls on each side of her head, and in every detail of her dress and air affected the coquettish old lady to perfection, for which, of course, she looked none the younger. Her cheeks were rouged to go with that style.

Frank was the ideal of the sprightly little old gentleman. With his brisk air, natty eye-glasses, cane and gloves, and other items of dress in the most correct taste, he was quite the old beau. His white hair was crispy, brushed back, and his snowy mustache had rather a rakish effect.

Although the transformation in each case was complete, yet quite enough of the features, expression, or bearing was apparent through the disguise to make the members of the party entirely recognizable to each other, though less intimate acquaintances would perhaps have been at first rather puzzled. At Henry's suggestion they had been photographed in their costumes, in order to compare the ideal with the actual when they should be really old.

"It is n't much trouble, and the old folks will enjoy it some day. We ought to consider them a little," Henry had said, meaning by "the old folks" their future selves.

It had been agreed that, in proper deference to the probabilities, one, at least, of the girls ought to illustrate the fat old lady. But they found it impossible to agree which should sacrifice herself, for no one of the three could, in her histrionic enthusiasm, quite forget her personal appearance. Nellie flatly refused to be made up fat, and Jessie as flatly, while both the girls had too much reverence for the sweet dignity of Mary Fellows's beauty to consent to her taking the part, and so the idea was given up.

It had been a happy thought of Mary's to get her two younger sisters, girls of eleven and sixteen, to be present, to enhance the venerable appearance of the party by the contrast of their bloom and freshness.

" Are these your little granddaughters ? " inquired Henry, benevolently inspecting them over the tops of his spectacles as he patted the elder of the two on the head, a liberty she would by no means have allowed him in his proper character, but which she now seemed puzzled whether to resent or not.

" Yes," replied Mary, with an indulgent smile. " They wanted to see what an old folks' party was like, though I told them they would n't enjoy it much. I remember I thought old people rather dull when I was their age."

Henry made a little conversation with the girls, asking them the list of fatuous questions by which adults seem fated to illustrate the gulf between them and childhood in the effort to bridge it.

" Annie, dear, just put that ottoman at Mrs. Hyde's feet," said Mary to one of the little girls. " I 'm so glad you felt able to come out this evening, Mrs. Hyde ! I understood you had not enjoyed good health this summer."

" I have scarcely been out of my room since spring, until recently," replied Jessie. " Thank you, my dear " (to the little girl) ; " but Dr. Sanford has done wonders for me. How is your health now, Mrs. Fellows ? "

" I have not been so well an entire summer in ten years. My daughter, Mrs. Tarbox, was saying the other day that she wished she had my strength. You know she is quite delicate," said Mary.

"Speaking of Dr. Sanford," said Henry, looking at Jessie, "he is really a remarkable man. My son has such confidence in him that he seemed quite relieved when I had passed my grand climacteric and could get on his list. You know he takes no one under sixty-three. By the way, governor," he added, turning around with some ado, so as to face George, "I heard he had been treating your rheumatism lately. Has he seemed to reach the difficulty?"

"Remarkably," replied George, tenderly stroking his right knee in an absent manner. "Why, don't you think I walked half the way home from my office the other day when my carriage was late?"

"I wonder you dared venture it," said Jessie, with a shocked air. "What if you had met with some accident!"

"That's what my son said," answered George. "He made me promise never to try such a thing again; but I like to show them occasionally that I'm good for something yet."

He said this with a "he, he," of senile complacency, ending in an asthmatic cough, which caused some commotion in the company. Frank got up and slapped him on the back, and Mary sent Annie for a glass of water.

George being relieved, and quiet once more restored, Henry said to Frank: —

" By the way, doctor, I want to congratulate you
on your son's last book. You must have helped
him to the material for so truthful a picture of
American manners in the days when we were
young. I fear we have not improved much since
then. There was a simplicity, a naturalness in
society fifty years ago, that one looks in vain for
now. There was, it seems to me, much less regard
paid to money, and less of morbid social ambition.
Don't you think so, Mrs. Tyrrell ? "

" It 's just what I was saying only the other
day," replied Nellie. " I 'm sure I don't know
what we 're coming to nowadays. Girls had some
modesty when I was young," and she shook her
head with its rows of white curls with an air of
mingled reprobation and despair.

" Did you attend Professor Merryweather's lecture last evening, Mrs. Hyde ? " asked Frank, adjusting his eye-glasses and fixing Jessie with that
intensity of look by which old persons have to make
up for their failing eyesight. " The hall was so
near your house, I did n't know but you would feel
like venturing out."

" My daughters insisted on my taking advantage
of the opportunity, it is so seldom I go anywhere
of an evening," replied Jessie, " and I was very
much interested, though I lost a good deal owing
to the carrying on of a young couple in front of
me. When I was a girl, young folks did n't do
their courting in public."

Mary had not heard of the lecture, and Frank explained that it was one of the ter-semi-centennial course on American society and politics fifty years ago.

"By the way," remarked George, "did you observe what difficulty they are having in finding enough survivors of the civil war to make a respectable squad. The papers say that not over a dozen of both armies can probably be secured, and some of the cases are thought doubtful at that."

"Is it possible!" said Henry. "And yet, too, it must be so ; but it sounds strangely to one who remembers as if it were yesterday seeing the grand review of the Federal armies at Washington just after the war. What a host of strong men was that, and now scarcely a dozen left. My friends, we are getting to be old people. We are almost through with it."

Henry sat gazing into vacancy over the tops of his spectacles, while the old ladies wiped theirs and sniffed and sighed a little. Finally Jessie said : —

"Those were heroic days. My little grand-daughters never tire of hearing stories about them. They are strong partisans, too. Jessie is a fierce little rebel and Sam is an uncompromising Unionist, only they both agree in denouncing slavery."

"That reminds me," said Frank, smiling, "that our little Frankie came to me yesterday with a black eye he got for telling Judge Benson's little boy that people of his complexion were once slaves.

He had read it in his history, and appealed to me to know if it was n't true."

"I 'm not a bit surprised that the little Benson boy resented the imputation," said George. "I really don't believe that more than half the people would be certain that slavery ever existed here, and I 'm sure that it rarely occurs to those who do know it. No doubt that company of old slaves at the centennial — that is, if they can find enough survivors — will be a valuable historical reminder to many."

"Dr. Hays," said Nellie, "will you settle a question between Mrs. Hyde and myself ? Were you in C——, it was then only a village, along between 1870 and '80, about forty or fifty years ago?"

"No — and yet, come to think — let me see — when did you say?" replied Frank doubtfully.

"Between 1870 and '80, as nearly as we can make out, probably about the middle of the decade," said Nellie.

"I think I was in C—— at about that time. I believe I was still living with my father's family."

"I told you so," said Nellie to Jessie, and, turning again to Frank, she asked: —

"Do you remember anything about a social club there?"

"I do," replied Frank, with some appearance of interest. "I recall something of the sort quite distinctly, though I suppose I have n't thought of it for twenty years. How did you ever hear of it, Mrs. Hyde?"

" Why, I was a member," replied she briskly, "and so was Mrs. Tyrrell. We were reminded of it the other day by a discovery Mrs. Tyrrell made in an old bureau drawer of a photograph of the members of the club in a group, taken probably all of fifty years ago, and yellow as you can imagine. There was one figure that resembled you, doctor, as you might have looked then, and I thought, too, that I recalled you as one of the members; but Mrs. Tyrrell could not, and so we agreed to settle the matter by appealing to your own recollection."

" Yes, indeed," said Frank, " I now recall the club very perfectly, and it seems to me Governor Townsley was also in it."

" Yes, I think I was a member," assented George, " though my recollections are rather hazy."

Mary and Henry, being appealed to, failed to remember anything about the club, the latter suggesting that probably it flourished before he came to C——. Jessie was quite sure she recalled Henry, but the others could not do so with much positiveness.

" I will ask Mrs. Long when I get home," said Henry. " She has always lived at C——, and is great for remembering dates. Let's see; what time do you think it was ? "

" Mrs. Tyrrell and I concluded it must have been between 1873 and 1877," said Jessie; adding

slyly, " for she was married in 1877. Mrs. Tyrrell,
did you bring that old photograph with you? It
might amuse them to look at it."

Nellie produced a small picture, and, adjusting
their spectacles and eye-glasses, they all came forward to see it. A group of six young people was
represented, all in the very heyday of youth. The
spectators were silent, looking first at the picture,
and then at each other.

" Can it be," said Frank, " that these were ever
our pictures? I hope, Mrs. Tyrrell, the originals
had the forethought to put the names on the back,
that we may be able to identify them."

" No," said she, " we must guess as best we can.
First, who is that? " pointing to one of the figures.

" That must be Mrs. Hyde, for she is taller than
the others," suggested Grandma Fellows.

" By the same token, that must be Mrs. Tyrrell,
for she is shorter," said Jessie ; " though, but for
that, I don't see how we could have told them
apart."

" How oddly they did dress in those days! "
said Mary.

" Who can that be? " asked Frank, pointing to
the finest-looking of the three young men. " If that
is one of us, there was more choice in our looks
than there is now, — eh, Townsley ? "

" No doubt," said George, " fifty years ago
somebody's eye scanned those features with a very
keen sense of proprietorship. What a queer feel-

ing it would have given those young things to have
anticipated that we should ever puzzle over their
identities in this way!"

They finally agreed on the identity of Jessie,
Nellie, and Frank, and of George also, on his as-
suring them that he was once of slender figure.
This left two figures which nobody could recognize, though Jessie insisted that the gentleman was
Henry, and Mary thought the other young lady
was a Miss Fellows, a girl of the village, who, she
explained, had died young many, many years ago.

"Don't you remember her?" she asked them,
and her voice trembled with a half-genuine sort of
self-pity, as if, for a moment, she imagined herself
her own ghost.

"I recall her well," said Frank; "tall, grave,
sweet, I remember she used to realize to me the
abstraction of moral beauty when we were studying Paley together."

"I don't know when I have thought so much
of those days as since I received cards for your
golden wedding, Judge," said Nellie to Henry,
soon after. "How many of those who were
present at your wedding will be present at your
golden wedding, do you suppose?"

"Not more than two or three," replied Henry,
"and yet the whole village was at the wedding."

"Thank God," he said a moment after, "that
our friends scatter before they die. Otherwise
old people like us would do nothing but attend

funerals during the last half of our lives. Parting
is sad, but I prefer to part from my friends while
they are yet alive, that I may feel it less when
they die. One must manage his feelings or they
will get the better of him."

"It is a singular sensation," said George, "to
outlive one's generation. One has at times a
guilty sense of having deserted his comrades. It
seems natural enough to outlive any one contem-
porary, but unnatural to survive them as a mass,
— a sort of risky thing, fraught with the various
vague embarrassments and undefined perils threatening one who is out of his proper place. And
yet one does n't want to die, though convinced he
ought to, and that 's the cowardly misery of it."

"Yes," said Henry, "I had that feeling pretty
strongly when I attended the last reunion of our
alumni, and found not one survivor within five
classes of me. I was isolated. Death had got
into my rear and cut me off. I felt ashamed and
thoroughly miserable."

Soon after, tea was served. Frank vindicated
his character as an old beau by a tottering alacrity
in serving the ladies, while George and Henry, by
virtue of their more evident infirmity, sat still and
allowed themselves to be served. One or two
declined tea as not agreeing with them at that
hour.

The loquacious herb gave a fresh impulse to the
conversation, and the party fell to talking in a

broken, interjectory way of youthful scenes and experiences, each contributing some reminiscence, and the others chiming in and adding scraps, or perhaps confessing their inability to recall the occurrences.

"What a refinement of cruelty it is," said Henry at last, "that makes even those experiences which were unpleasant 'or indifferent when passing look so mockingly beautiful when hopelessly past."

"Oh, that's not the right way to look at it, Judge," broke in Grandma Fellows, with mild reproof. "Just think rather how dull life would be, looking forward or backward, if past or coming experiences seemed as uninteresting as they mostly are when right at hand."

"Sweet memories are like moonlight," said Jessie musingly. "They make one melancholy, however pleasing they may be. I don't see why, any more than why moonlight is so sad, spite of its beauty; but so it is."

The fragile tenure of the sense of personal identity is illustrated by the ease and completeness with which actors can put themselves in the place of the characters they assume, so that even their instinctive demeanor corresponds to the ideal, and their acting becomes nature. Such was the experience of the members of the club. The occupation of their mind during the week with the study of their assumed characters had produced an impression that had been deepened to an astonishing degree by the striking effect of the accessories of costume and manner. The long-continued effort to project themselves mentally into the period of old age was assisted in a startling manner by the illusion of the senses produced by the decrepit figures, the sallow and wrinkled faces, and the white heads of the group.

Their acting had become spontaneous. They were perplexed and bewildered as to their identity, and in a manner carried away by the illusion their own efforts had created. In some of the earlier conversation of the evening there had been occasional jests and personalities, but the talk had now become entirely serious. The pathos and melancholy of the retrospections in which they were indulging became real. All felt that if it was acting now, it was but the rehearsal of a coming reality. I think some of them were for a little while not clearly conscious that it was not already reality, and that their youth was not forever vanished. The sense of age was weighing on them like a nightmare. In very self-pity voices began to tremble and bosoms heaved with suppressed sobs.

Mary rose and stepped to the piano. It indicated how fully she had realized her part that, as she passed the mirror, no involuntary start testified to surprise at the aged figure it reflected. She played in a minor key an air to the words of Tennyson's matchless piece of pathos, —

"The days that are no more,"

accompanying herself with a voice rich, strong, and sweet. By the time she had finished, the girls were all crying.

Suddenly Henry sprang to his feet, and, with the strained, uncertain voice of one waking himself from a nightmare, cried : —

"Thank God, thank God, it is only a dream," and tore off the wig, letting the brown hair fall about his forehead. Instantly all followed his example, and in a moment the transformation was effected. Brown, black, and golden hair was flying free ; rosy cheeks were shining through the powder where handkerchiefs had been hastily applied, and the bent and tottering figures of a moment ago had given place to broad-shouldered men and full-breasted girls. Henry caught Jessie around the waist, Frank Nellie, and George Mary, and with one of the little girls at the piano, up and down the room they dashed to the merriest of waltzes in the maddest round that ever was danced. There was a reckless abandon in their glee, as if the lust of life, the glow and fire of youth, its glorious freedom, and its sense of boundless wealth, suddenly set free, after long repression, had intoxicated them with its strong fumes. It was such a moment as their lifetime would not bring again.

It was not till, flushed and panting, laughing and exhausted, they came to a pause, that they thought of Grandma Fellows. She was crying, and yet smiling through her tears.

"Oh, grandma," cried Mary, throwing her arms around her, and bursting into tears, "we can't take you back with us. Oh, dear."

And the other girls cried over her, and kissed her in a piteous, tender way, feeling as if their hearts would break for the pity of it. And the young men were conscious of moisture about the eyes as they stood looking on.

But Grandma Fellows smiled cheerily, and said: —

"I'm a foolish old woman to cry, and you must n't think it is because I want to be young again. It's only because I can't help it."

Perhaps she could n't have explained it better.

THE COLD SNAP

In the extremes of winter and summer, when
the weather is either extraordinarily cold or hot, I
confess to experiencing a peculiar sense of help-
lessness and vague uneasiness. I have a feeling
that a trifling additional rise or fall of temperature, such as might be caused by any slight hitch
in the machinery of the universe, would quite
crowd mankind out of existence. To be sure, the
hitch never has occurred, but what if it should?
Conscious that I have about reached the limit of
my own endurance, the thought of the bare con-
tingency is unpleasant enough to cause a feeling
of relief, not altogether physical, when the rising
or falling mercury begins to turn. The consciousness how wholly by sufferance it is that man exists
at all on the earth is rather forcibly borne in
upon the mind at such times. The spaces above
and below zero are indefinite.

I have to take my vacations as the fluctuations
of a rather exacting business permit, and so it
happened that I was, with my wife, passing a fortnight in the coldest part of winter at the family
homestead in New England. The ten previous
days had been very cold, and the cold had " got

into the house," which means that it had so penetrated and chilled the very walls and timbers that
a cold day now took hold of us as it had not earlier in the season. Finally there came a day that
was colder than any before it. The credit of discovering and first asserting that it was the coldest
day of the season is due to myself, — no slight distinction in the country, where the weather is always a more prominent topic than in the city, and
the weather-wise are accordingly esteemed. Every
one hastened to corroborate this verdict with some
piece of evidence. Mother said that the frost had
not gone off the kitchen window nearest the stove
in all the day, and that was a sign. The sleighs and
sledges as they went by in the road creaked on the
snow, so that we heard them through the double
windows, and that was a sign; while the teamsters
swung their benumbed arms like the sails of a wind-
mill to keep up the circulation, and the frozen
vapor puffed out from the horses' nostrils in a manner reminding one of the snorting coursers in sen-
sational pictures. The schoolboys on their way
from school did not stop to play, and that was a
sign. No women had been seen on the street since
noon. Young men, as they hurried past on the
peculiar high-stepping trot of persons who have
their hands over their ears, looked strangely anti-
quated with their mustaches and beards all grizzled
with the frost.

Toward dusk I took a short run to the post-office. I was well wrapped up, but that did not prevent me from having very singular sensations before I got home. The air, as I stepped out from cover, did not seem like air at all, but like some almost solid medium, whose impact was like a blow. It went right through my overcoat at the first assault, and nosed about hungrily for my little spark of vital heat. A strong wind with the flavor of glaciers was blowing straight from the pole. How inexpressibly bleak was the aspect of the leaden clouds that were banked up around the horizon! I shivered as I looked at the sullen masses. The houses seemed little citadels against the sky. I had not taken fifty steps before my face stiffened into a sort of mask, so that it hurt me to move the facial muscles. I came home on an undignified run, experiencing a lively sense of the inadequacy of two hands to protect two ears and a nose. Did the Creator intend man to inhabit high latitudes?

At nightfall father, Bill, and Jim, the two latter being my younger brothers, arrived from their offices, each in succession declaring, with many "whews" and "ughs," that it was by all odds the coldest night yet. Undeniably we all felt proud of it, too. A spirited man rather welcomes ten or fifteen degrees extra, if so be they make the temperature superlatively low; while he would very likely grumble at a much less positive chilliness coupled with the disheartening feeling that he was

enduring nothing extraordinary. The general exaltation of spirit and suspension of the conventionalities for the time being, which an extraordinarily hot or cold snap produces in a community,
especially in the country, is noteworthy. During
that run of mine to the post-office every man I met
grinned confidentially, as if to say, " We 're hearty
fellows to stand it as we do." We regarded each
other with an increase of mutual respect. That
sense of fellowship which springs up between those
associated in an emergency seemed to dispense with
ordinary formalities, and neighbors with whom I
had not a bowing acquaintance fairly beamed on
me as we passed.

After tea Ella (Ella was a sister) got the evening paper out of somebody's overcoat, and was
running it over in the dainty, skimming fashion
peculiar to the gentler sex when favoring the press
with their attention. It reminds one of sea-birds
skimming the water, and anon diving for a tidbit.
She read aloud : " Old Prob. reports another cold
wave on the way East. It will probably reach the
New England States this evening. The thermo-
meters along its course range from 40° below zero
at Fort Laramie, to 38° in Omaha, 31° in Chicago,
and 30° in Cleveland. Numerous cases of death
by freezing are reported. Our readers will do well
to put an extra shovelful on the furnace overnight."

" Don't forget that, Jim," said father.

A gentleman friend called to take Ella out to a concert or something of the sort. Her mother was for having her give it up on account of the cold. But it so happens that young people, who, having life before them, can much better afford than their elders to forego particular pleasures, are much less resigned to doing so. The matter was compromised by piling so many wraps upon her that she protested it was like being put to bed. But, before they had been gone fifteen minutes, they were back again, half frozen. It had proved so shockingly cold they had not dared to keep on, and persuaded themselves accordingly that the entertainment had probably been postponed. The streets were entirely deserted ; not even a policeman was visible, and the chilled gas in the street lamps gave but a dull light.

Ella proposed to give us our regular evening treat of music, but found the corner of the room where the melodeon stood too cold. Generally the room is warm in every part, and Jim got upbraided for keeping a poor fire. But he succeeded in proving that it was better than common ; the weather was the matter. As the evening wore on, the members of the family gradually edged around the register, finally radiating from it as a centre like the spokes of a wheel, of which the collected feet of the group made the hub.

My wife is from the Southern States, and the huge cold of the North had been a new and rather

terrifying experience to her. She had been growing nervous all the evening, as the signs and por-
tents of the weather accumulated. She was really
half frightened.

" Are n't you afraid it will get so cold it will
never be able to get warm again, — and then what
would become of us ? " she asked.

Of course we laughed at her, but I think her
fears infected me with a slight, vague anxiety, as
the evidences of extraordinary and still increasing
cold went on multiplying. I had so far gotten
over my bravado earlier in the evening that I
should have been secretly relieved if the thermo-
meter had taken a turn.

At length, one by one, the members of the
family, with an anticipatory shiver over the register, went to their rooms, and were doubtless in bed
in the shortest possible time, and I fear without
saying their prayers. Finally my wife suggested
that we had better go before we got too cold to
do so.

The bedroom was shockingly cold. Going to
bed is a test of character. I pride myself on the
fact that generally, even when my room is cold, I
can, with steady nerve and resolute hand, remove
the last habiliment, and without undignified pre-
cipitation reach for and indue the nocturnal garment. I admit, however, that on this occasion I
gave way to a weak irresolution at the critical
instant and shivered for some moments in con-

stantly increasing demoralization, before I could make up my mind to the final change. Then ensued the slow and gradual conquest of the frozen bed to a tolerable warmth, a result attained only by clever strategic combinations of bedclothes and the most methodical policy. As I lay awake, I heard the sides of the house crack in the cold. "What," said I to myself with a shiver, "should I do if anything happened that required me to get up and dress again?" It seemed to me I should be capable of letting a man die in the next room for need of succor. Being of an imaginative temperament, not to feel prepared for possible contingencies is for me to feel guilty and miserable. The last thing I remember before dropping off to sleep was solemnly promising my wife never to trust ourselves North another winter. I then fell asleep and dreamed of the ineffable cold of the interstellar spaces, which the scientific people talk about.

The next thing I was sensible of was a feeling of the most utter discomfort I ever experienced. My whole body had become gradually chilled through. I could feel the flesh rising in goose pimples at every movement. What has happened? was my first thought. The bedclothes were all there, four inches of them, and to find myself shivering under such a pile seemed a reversal of the laws of nature. Shivering is an unpleasant operation at best and at briefest; but when one

has shivered till the flesh is lame, and every quiver
is a racking, aching pain, that is something quite
different from any ordinary shivering. My wife
was awake and in the same condition. What did
I ever bring her to this terrible country for? She
had been lying as still as possible for an hour or
so, waiting till she should die or something; and
feeling that if she stirred she should freeze, as
water near the freezing point crystallizes when
agitated. She said that when I had disturbed the
clothes by any movement, she had felt like hating
me. We were both almost scared, it must be confessed. Such an experience had never been ours
before. In voices muffled by the bedclothes we
held dismal confab, and concluded that we must
make our way to the sitting-room and get over the
register.

I have had my share of unpleasant duties to face
in my life. I remember how I felt at Spottsylvania
when I stepped up and out from behind a breast-
work of fence rails, over which the bullets were
whistling like hailstones, to charge the enemy.
Worse still, I remember how I felt at one or two
public banquets when I rose from my seat to reply
to a toast, and to meet the gaze of a hundred expectant faces with an overpowering consciousness
of looking like a fool, and of total inability to do or
say anything which would not justify the presumption. But never did an act of my life call for so
much of sheer will-power as stepping out of that

comfortless bed into that freezing room. It is a general rule in getting up winter mornings that the air never proves so cold as was anticipated while lying warm in bed. But it did this time, probably because my system was deprived of all elasticity and power of reaction by being so thoroughly chilled. Hastily donning in the dark what was absolutely necessary, my poor wife and myself, with chattering teeth and prickly bodies, the most thoroughly demoralized couple in history, ran downstairs to the sitting-room.

Much to our surprise, we found the gas lighted and the other members of the family already gathered there, huddling over the register. I felt a sinking at the heart as I marked the strained, anxious look on each face, a look that asked what strange thing had come upon us. They had been there, they said, for some time. Ella, Jim, and Bill, who slept alone, had been the first to leave their beds. Then father and mother, and finally my wife and I, had followed. Soon after our arrival there was a fumbling at the door, and the two Irish girls, who help mother keep house, put in their blue, pinched faces. They scarcely waited an invitation to come up to the register.

The room was but dimly lighted, for the gas, affected by the fearful chill, was flowing slowly and threatened to go out. The gloom added to the depressing effect of our strange situation. Little was said. The actual occurrence of strange and

unheard-of events excites very much less wonder-
ment than the account of them written or re-
hearsed. Indeed, the feeling of surprise often
seems wholly left out of the mental experience of
those who undergo or behold the most prodigious
catastrophes. The sensibility to the marvelous
is the one of our faculties which is, perhaps, the
soonest exhausted by a strain. Human nature
takes naturally to miracles, after all. " What can
it mean ? " was the inquiry a dozen times on the
lips of each one of us, but beyond that, I recall
little that was said. Bill, who was the joker of the
family, had essayed a jest or two at first on our
strange predicament, but they had been poorly received. The discomfort was too serious, and the
extraordinary nature of the visitation filled every
mind with nameless forebodings and a great, un-
formed fear.

We asked each other if our neighbors were all
in the same plight with ourselves. They must be,
of course, and many of them far less prepared to
meet it. There might be whole families in the
last extremity of cold right about us. I went to
the window, and with my knife scraped away the
rime of frost, an eighth of an inch thick, which
obscured it, till I could see out. A whitish-gray
light was on the landscape. Every object seemed
still, with a quite peculiar stillness that might be
called intense. From the chimneys of some of the
houses around thick columns of smoke and sparks

were pouring, showing that the fires were being crowded below. Other chimneys showed no smoke at all. Here and there a dull light shone from a window. There was no other sign of life anywhere. The streets were absolutely empty. No one suggested trying to communicate with other houses. This was a plight in which human concourse could avail nothing.

After piling all the coal on the furnace it would hold, the volume of heat rising from the register was such as to singe the clothes of those over it, while those waiting their turn were shivering a few feet off. The men of course yielded the nearest places to the women, and, as we walked briskly up and down in the room, the frost gathered on our mustaches. The morning, we said, would bring relief, but none of us fully believed it, for the strange experience we were enduring appeared to imply a suspension of the ordinary course of nature.

A number of cats and dogs, driven from their accustomed haunts by the intense cold, had gathered under the windows, and there piteously moaned and whined for entrance.

Swiftly it grew colder. The iron casing of the register was cold in spite of the volume of heat pouring through it. Every point or surface of metal in the room was covered with a thick coating of frost. The frost even settled upon a few filaments of cobweb in the corners of the room which had escaped the housemaid's broom, and which now shone like hidden sins in the day of judgment. The door-knob, mop-boards, and wooden casings of the room glistened. We were so chilled that woolen was as cold to the touch as wood or iron. There being no more any heat in our bodies, the non-conducting quality of a substance was no appreciable advantage. To avoid the greater cold near the floor, several of our number got upon the tables, presenting, with their feet tucked under them, an aspect that would have been sufficiently laughable under other circumstances. But, as a rule, fun does not survive the freezing point. Every few moments the beams of the house snapped like the timbers of a straining ship, and at intervals the frozen ground cracked with a noise like cannon, — the hyperborean earthquake.

A ruddy light shone against the windows. Bill went and rubbed away the ice. A neighbor's house was burning. It was one of those whose chimneys were vomiting forth sparks when I had looked out before. There was promise of an extensive conflagration. Nobody appeared in the streets, and, as there were intervening houses, we could not see what became of the inmates. The very slight interest which this threatening conflagration aroused in our minds was doubtless a mark of the already stupefying effect of the cold. Even our voices had become weak and altered.

The cold is a sad enemy to beauty. My poor

wife and Ella, with their pinched faces, strained, aching expression, red, rheumy eyes and noses, and blue or pallid cheeks were sad parodies on their comely selves. Other forces of nature have in them something the spirit of man can sympathize with, as the wind, the waves, the sun ; but there is something terribly inhuman about the cold. I can imagine it as a congenial principle brooding over the face of chaos in the æons before light was.

Hours had passed, it might have been years, when father said, " Let us pray." He knelt down, and we all mechanically followed his example, as from childhood up we had done at morning and evening. Ever before, the act had seemed merely a fit and graceful ceremony, from which no one had expected anything in particular to follow, or had experienced aught save the placid reaction that commonly results from a devotional act. But now the meaning so long latent became eloquent. The morning and evening ceremony became the sole resource in an imminent and fearful emergency. There was a familiar strangeness about the act under these circumstances which touched us all. With me, as with most, something of the feeling implied in the adage, " Familiarity breeds contempt," had impaired my faith in the practical efficacy of prayer. How could extraordinary results be expected from so common an instrumentality, and especially from so ordinary and every-day a thing as family prayer? Our faith in the present instance was also not a little lessened by the peculiar nature of the visitation. In any ordinary emergency God might help us, but we had a sort of dim apprehension that even He could not do anything in such weather. So far as humbleness was concerned, there was no lack of that. There are some inflictions which, although terrible, are capable of stirring in haughty human hearts a rebellious indignation. But to cold succumb soul and mind. It has always seemed to me that cold would have broken down Milton's Satan. I felt as if I could grovel to be vouchsafed a moment's immunity from the gripe of the savage frost.

Owing to the sustaining power there is in habit, the participation in family devotions proved strengthening to us all. In emergencies, we get back from our habits the mental and moral vigor that first went to their formation, and has since remained on interest.

It is not the weakest who succumb first to cold, as was strikingly proved in our experience. The prostration of the faculties may be long postponed by the power of the will. All assaults on human nature, whether of cold, exhaustion, terror, or any other kind, respect the dignity of the mind, and await its capitulation before finally storming the stronghold of life. I am as strong in physique as men average, but I gave out before my mother. The voices of mother and Bill, as they took counsel for our salvation, fell on my ears like an idle sound. This was the crisis of the night.

The next thing I knew, Bill was urging us to eat some beefsteak and bread. The former, I afterward learned, he had got out of the pantry and cooked over the furnace fire. It was about five o'clock, and we had eaten nothing for nearly twelve hours. The general exhaustion of our powers had prevented a natural appetite from making itself felt, but mother had suggested that we should try food, and it saved us. It was still fearfully cold, but the danger was gone as soon as we felt the reviving effect of the food. An ounce of food is worth a pound of blankets. Trying to warm the body from the outside is working at a tremendous disadvantage. It was a strange picnic as, perched on chairs and tables in the dimly lighted room, we munched our morsels, or warmed the frozen bread over the register. 'After this, some of us got a little sleep.

I shall never forget my sensations when, at last, I looked out at the eastern window and saw the rising sun. The effect was indeed peculiarly splendid, for the air was full of particles of ice, and the sun had the effect of shining through a mist of diamond dust. Bill had dosed us with whiskey, and perhaps it had got into our heads, for I shouted, and my wife cried. It was, at the end of the weary night, like the first sight of our country's flag when returning from a foreign world.

TWO DAYS' SOLITARY IMPRISONMENT

MR. JOSEPH KILGORE was suffering from one
of those spring influenzas which make a man feel
as if he were his own grandfather. His nose had
acquired the shape of a turnip and the complexion
of a beet. All his bones ached as if he had been
soundly thrashed, and his eyes were weak and
watery. Your deadly disease is oftener than not
a gentleman who takes your life without mauling
you, but the minor diseases are mere bruisers who
just go in for making one as uncomfortable and
unpresentable as possible. Mr. Kilgore's influenza
had been coming on for several days, and when he
woke up this particular morning and heard the
rain dripping on the piazza-roof just under his bed-
room-window, he concluded, like a sensible man,
that he would stay at home and nurse himself over
the fire that day, instead of going to the office. So
he turned over and snoozed for an hour or two,
luxuriating in a sense of aches and pains just pronounced enough to make the warmth and softness
of the bed delightful.

Toward noon, the edge of this enjoyment becoming dulled, he got up, dressed, and came downstairs to the parlor, where his brother's wife (he

was a bachelor, living with a married brother) had considerately kindled up a coal-fire in the grate for his benefit.

After lying off in the rocking-chair till past dinner-time, he began to feel better and consequently restless. Concluding that he would like to read, he went rummaging about the bookcases for a likely-looking novel. At length he found in the upper shelf of a closet a book called "Rôles of a Detective," containing various thrilling accounts of crimes and the entanglement of criminals in the meshes of law and evidence.

One story in particular made a strong impression on his mind. It was a tale of circumstantial evidence, and about how it very nearly hung an innocent man for a murder which he had no thought of committing. It struck Joseph rather forcibly that this victim of circumstantial evidence was as respectable and inoffensive a person as himself, and probably had never any more thought of being in danger from the law. Circumstances had set their trap for him while he was quite unconscious of peril, and he only awoke to find himself in the toils. And from this he went on to reflect upon the horrible but unquestionable fact that every year a certain proportion, and perhaps a very considerable proportion, of those who suffered the penalties of the law, and even the death-penalty, are innocent men, — victims of false or mistaken evidence. No man, however wise or virtuous, can be sure that he will not be taken in this fearful conscription of victims to the blind deity of justice. "None can tell," thought Joseph, with a shudder, "that the word he is saying, the road he is turning, the appointment he is making, or whatever other innocent act he is now engaged in, may not prove the last mesh in some self-woven death-net, the closing link in some damning chain of evidence whose devilish subtlety shall half convince him that he must be guilty as it wholly convinces others."

Timidity is generally associated with imaginativeness, if not its result, and Joseph, although he concealed the fact pretty well under the mask of reticence, was constitutionally very timid. He had an unprofitable habit of taking every incident of possible embarrassment or danger that occurred to his mind as the suggestion for imaginary situations of inconvenience or peril, which he would then work out, fancying how he would feel and what he would do, with the utmost elaboration, and often with really more nervous excitement than he would be likely to experience if the events supposed should really occur. So now, and all the more because he was a little out of sorts, the suggestions of this story began to take the form in his mind of an imaginary case of circumstantial evidence of which he was the victim. His fancy worked up the details of a fictitious case against himself, which he, although perfectly innocent, could meet with nothing more than his bare denial.

He imagined the first beginnings of suspicion ;
he saw it filming the eyes of his acquaintances,
then of his friends, and at last sicklying over the
face even of his brother Silas. In fancy he made
frantic attempts to regain the confidence of his
friends, to break through the impalpable, impene-
trable barrier which the first stir of suspicion had
put between their minds and his. He cried, he
begged, he pleaded. But in vain, all in vain. Suspicion had made his appeals and adjurations sound
even to his friends as strange and meaningless as
the Babel-builders' words of a sudden became to
each other. The yellow badge of suspicion once
upon him, all men kept afar, as if he were a fever-
ship in quarantine. No solitary imprisonment in a
cell of stone could so utterly exclude him from the
fellowship of men as the invisible walls of this dun-
geon of suspicion. And at last he saw himself giving up the hopeless struggle, yielding to his fate
in dumb despair, only praying that the end might
come speedily, perhaps even reduced to the abjectness of confessing the crime he had not committed,
in order that he might at least have the pity of
men, since he could not regain their confidence.
And so strongly had this vision taken hold on him
that his breath came irregularly, and his forehead
was damp as he drew his hand across it.

As has been intimated, it was Mr. Joseph Kilgore's very bad habit to waste his nervous tissue
in the conscientiously minute elaboration of such

painful imaginary situations as that above described, and in his present experience there was
nothing particularly novel or extraordinary for
him. It was the occurrence of a singular coincidence between this internal experience and a wholly
independent course of actual events, which made
that waking nightmare the beginning of a somewhat remarkable comedy, or, more properly, a
tragedy, of errors. For, as Joseph lay back in his
chair, in a state of nervous exhaustion and moral
collapse, the parlor-door was thrown open, and
Mrs. Silas Kilgore, his sister-in-law, burst into the
room. She was quite pale, and her black eyes
were fixed on Joseph's with the eager intensity, as
if seeking moral support, noticeable in those who
communicate startling news which they have not
had time to digest.

The effect of this apparition upon Joseph in his
unstrung condition may be readily imagined. He
sprang up, much paler than Mrs. Kilgore, his lips
apart, and his eyes staring with the premonition of
something shocking. These symptoms of extraordinary excitement even before she had spoken, and
this air as if he had expected a shocking revelation, recurred to her mind later, in connection with
other circumstances, but just now she was too full
of her intelligence to dwell on anything else.

" A man was murdered in our barn last night.
They 've found the body ! " she exclaimed.

As the meaning of her words broke on him, Jo-

seph was filled with that sort of mental confusion
which one experiences when the scene or circumstances of a dream recur in actual life. Was he
still dreaming that ghostly vision of suspicion and
the death-trap of circumstances? Was this a mere
continuation of it? No, he was awake; his sister-
in-law standing there, with pallid face and staring
eyes, was not an apparition. The horrid, fatal
reality which he had been imagining was actually
upon him.

"I did not do it!" dropped from his ashen lips.

"You do it? Are you crazy? Who said anything about your doing it?" cried the astounded
woman.

The ring of genuine amazement in her voice was
scarcely needed to recall Joseph to the practical
bearing of his surroundings, and break the spell of
superstitious dread. The sound of his own words
had done it. With a powerful effort he regained
something like self-control, and said, with a forced
laugh: —

"What an absurd thing for me to say! I don't
know what I could have been thinking of. Very
odd, was it not? But, dear me! a man murdered
in our barn? You don't tell me! How terrible!"

His constrained, overdone manner was not calculated to abate Mrs. Kilgore's astonishment, and
she continued to stare at him with an expression
in which a vague terror began to appear. There
are few shorter transitions than that from panic to

anger. Seeing that her astonishment at his reception of the news increased rather than diminished, he became exasperated at the intolerable position in which he was placed. His face, before so pale, flushed with anger.

" Damnation! What are you staring at me that way for?" he cried fiercely.

Mrs. Kilgore gave a little cry, half of indignation, half of fright, and went out of the room, shutting the door after her.

Joseph had ample opportunity to review the situation before he was again disturbed, which, indeed, was not till some hours later, at dusk, when Silas came home, and the tea-table was set. Silas had been promptly summoned from his shop when the discovery of the body was made, and had been busy all the afternoon with the police, the coroner, and the crowds of visitors to the scene of the tragedy.

The conversation at the tea-table ran entirely upon the various incidents of the discovery, the inquest, and the measures of the police for the apprehension of the criminal. Mrs. Kilgore was so full of questions that she scarcely gave Silas time to answer, and Joseph flattered himself that his comparative silence was not noticeable. Nevertheless, as they rose from the table, Silas remarked: —

" You don't seem much interested in our murder, Joseph; you have n't asked the first question about it."

Mrs. Kilgore was just leaving the room, and she turned her head to see how he would answer. But he, too, turned off the matter by saying something about Maria's loquaciousness having left him no chance. After tea the little family circle was gathered in the parlor. Mrs. Kilgore was sewing; Silas read the newspaper, and Joseph sat up by the fire. From time to time, as he glanced around, he caught Mrs. Kilgore's eyes studying him very intently. Her manner indicated that her indignation at his behavior and language earlier in the afternoon had been quite neutralized by her curiosity as to its cause.

" There 's nothing in the paper to-night but the murder, and I know that already," exclaimed Silas, finally. " Maria, where 's there something to read? Hullo! what 's this?"

He had taken up from the table the story of circumstantial evidence which Joseph had been reading that morning.

" Why, Maria, here 's that murder-book you would n't let me finish last summer for fear I 'd murder you some night. Who on earth hunted up that book of all books, to-day of all days?"

" I did," replied Joseph, clearing his throat, in order to speak with a natural inflection.

" You did?" exclaimed Silas.

" You must have looked the house over to find it, for I hid it carefully," said Mrs. Kilgore, looking sharply at him. " What made you so anxious to get it?"

" I was not particularly anxious. I was merely looking for something to read," said Joseph, making a pretense of yawning, as if the matter was a very trivial one.

" I suppose the murder brought it to his mind," said Silas.

" Why, no ! " exclaimed Mrs. Kilgore quickly. " You must have been reading it before the murder. Now that I remember, I saw it in your hands."

" Before the murder, were you, Joseph ? Why, that's almost enough to make one feel superstitious," said Silas, turning around in his chair, so as to look fairly at him.

Joseph had half a mind to make a clean breast of the matter then and there, and explain to them how curiously the reading of that book had affected him. But he reflected that Silas was rather unimaginative, and would probably be more mystified than enlightened by his explanation.

" I do believe it was reading that book which made you act so queerly when I brought you in the news of the murder," pursued Mrs. Kilgore.

" How is that ? How did he act queerly ? " asked Silas.

" I am not aware that I acted queerly at all," said Joseph doggedly.

He knew well enough he had acted queerly, and did not mean to deny that; but, as children and confused persons often do, he answered to the underlying motive rather than the language. He only thought of denying the inference of suspicion that her words seemed to him to suggest. But to Mrs. Kilgore he very naturally seemed to be prevaricating.

" Why, Joseph ! " said she, in a raised voice, and with a slight asperity ; " you know how you jumped up, looking like a ghost, the moment I opened the door, and the first thing you said after I 'd told you that they 'd found a murdered man in the barn, was — Why, Joseph, what 's the matter ? "

But I must go back a little. When the conversation turned on the book and Joseph's connection with it, a minute or so previous, Silas had quite naturally glanced over at his brother, and, as the talk went on, his glance had become a somewhat concentrated gaze, although expressive of nothing but the curiosity and slight wonder which the circumstances suggested. It would not do to have Silas think that he avoided his eyes, and so Joseph had, as soon as he felt this gaze, turned his own face rather sharply toward it. He had meant merely to meet his brother's look in a natural and unaffected manner. But, although never more sensible of just what such a manner would be, he was utterly unable to compass it. He was perfectly aware that the expression of his eyes was much too serious and challenging, — and yet he could not, for the soul of him, modify it. Nor did he dare to withdraw his gaze after it had once met his brother's, although knowing that it was fast becoming a fierce stare, and perceiving that Silas had already noticed something peculiar in it. For to drop his eyes would be utter discomfiture and rout. As Mrs. Kilgore alluded to his queer demeanor when she told him the news, his face began to flush with the anticipation of the revelation that was coming at this most unfavorable moment, even while his eyes were locked with the already startled ones of Silas. As she went on, the flush covered the lower part of his face, and rose like a spring-tide up his cheeks, and lent a fierce, congested glare to his eyes. He felt how woeful and irretrievable a thing it would be for him just then to lose his countenance, and at the thought the flush burned deeper and merged higher. It overspread his high, bald, intellectual forehead, and incarnadined his sconce up to the very top of it. At this moment it was that Mrs. Kilgore broke off her narrative with the exclamation, " Why, Joseph, what's the matter ? "

At her words it seemed as if every drop of blood in his body poured into his face. He could endure it no longer. He rose abruptly, strode out of the parlor, and went to his room, although it was but eight o'clock, and he had no fire there. If he had staid another moment he must have brained Silas and his wife with the poker, such an ungovernable anger boiled up in him with the sense of his causeless, shameful discomfiture.

As Joseph left the parlor the eyes of Silas and

his wife met each other, — his dull with bewilderment and terror at a spectral fear ; hers keen with a definite suspicion. But even her loquacity was subdued by a real fright. She had nothing to say. Her sensation was like that of one who, hunting a hare, stumbles upon a wolf. She had been both offended and made curious by Joseph's demeanor that afternoon, but the horrid idea that within a moment had been suggested to both their minds had so little occurred to her as a serious possibility that she was even on the point of rallying Joseph on it before her husband. Some time after he had left the parlor Silas asked, with averted face : —

" What was it that he said when you told him the news ? " and then she repeated his words.

And Joseph, sitting wild-eyed upon his bed in the darkness in the room above, red no longer, but pale as death, heard the murmur of the voices, and knew that she was telling him. No one of the household slept much that night, except Mrs. Kilgore. Whenever she awoke she heard her husband tossing restlessly, but she dared not ask him what was the matter. In vain did Silas rehearse to himself all through the night-hours how petty were the trifles in Joseph's demeanor which had disturbed him. They were of the sort of trifles which create that species of certainty known as moral certainty, — the strongest of all in the mind it occupies, although so incapable of being communicated to others. It mattered little how much evidence there

was, if it sufficed to lodge the faintest trace of suspicion in his mind.   For, like some poisons, an
atom of suspicion is as fatal as the largest quantity.
Nay, perhaps, even more surely so, for against
great suspicion the mind often takes arms and
makes valiant head ; but a little doubt, by its timid
and hesitant demeanor, disarms opposition, and is
readily entertained.   And all that night, lying
awake, and knowing that Silas was sleepless just
the other side of the partition, and that the fungus
of suspicion was moment by moment overgrowing
his mind, he could hardly wait for morning, but
would fain have rushed, even now in the darkness,
to his bedside to cry : "I did not do it !   Believe
me, brother, I did not do it !"

In the morning, however, the sun shone brightly
into his room, and last night's events and misunderstandings seemed like a bad dream.   He went
downstairs almost cheery.   He did not find Silas,
but Mrs. Kilgore was about.   He was rather
startled to observe the entire change in her demeanor.   Yesterday she was constantly following
him up with her sharp black eyes and brisk questions and exclamations, but now she seemed frightened, acted in a constrained manner, and avoided
his eyes.

" Where is Silas ?" he asked, as they sat down
to table.

" He said that there was something he must see
to at the shop before work began, so he had an

early breakfast," replied Mrs. Kilgore, with her eyes on her plate.

Had she been looking up, she would have seen a piteous constriction in the muscles of Joseph's face. His heart was sick, and all his regained courage sank away. It was no bad dream. Silas was afraid to meet him. He left his meal untasted, and went to the office. A dozen acquaintances stopped him on his way down-street to ask about the murder ; and all day long somebody was dropping in to pester him on the same subject. He told them with a dull, abstracted air all the fresh details he knew, but felt all the time as if he cheated each auditor of the vital part of the matter, in that he failed to shout after him : —

" Silas suspects me of it ! "

Silas had, indeed, left the house early for the purpose of avoiding his brother. He was in a condition of mind and nerve in which he did not dare to meet him. At tea the brothers met for the first time since the night previous. There was a constraint between them like that between strangers, but stronger and more chilling far than ever that is. There is no chill like that which comes between friends, and the nearer the friends the more deathly the cold. Silas made a little effort to speak of business-matters, but could not keep it up, and soon a silence settled over the party, only broken by the words of table-service. Mrs. Kilgore sat pale and frightened all through the meal without venturing a single phrase, and scarcely looking up from her plate.

The silence was of that kind which all felt to be more expressive than the loudest, most explicit language could be, — more merciless than any form of verbal accusation. Such silence is a terribly perfect medium, in which souls are compelled to touch each other, resent as they may the contact. Several times Joseph was on the point of rising and rushing from the table. How many more such meals could he stand or could they stand? All of them recognized that the situation had become perceptibly more serious and more pronounced on account of that silent tea-table.

There was in particular not the slightest allusion made by any one to the murder, which, seeing that it had happened but yesterday, and would naturally still have been an engrossing topic, was an omission so pointed as to be an open charge of guilt. There is such a thing as emphasizing a topic by suppressing it, as letters are sunk into stone. The omission impressed Silas as it did Joseph, but, regarding it from his point of view, it did not occur to him but that Joseph was the one solely responsible for it. He, Silas, had refrained from reference to it because his suspicions in regard to Joseph made the topic unendurable. But he could not imagine that Joseph could have had any other motive for his silence on the subject but a guilty conscience, — some secret knowledge of the crime. Thus regarded,

it was a terrible confirmation. That a perception
that he was suspected might cause an innocent
man to act very much as if he were conscious of
guilt did not occur to Silas, as, perhaps, it would
have failed to occur to most persons in just his
position.

After leaving the tea-table the brothers went together into the parlor, according to the family custom. They took their accustomed seats on opposite
sides of the fireplace, but there was no conversation.
A veil was between them. Both were thinking of
the same thing, — thinking of it intensely, — and
each knew that the other was thinking of it, and
yet neither for worlds could have commanded the
courage to speak of it. The suspicion had grown
definite in Silas's mind, and yet, whenever he
brought himself to the point of putting it in words,
it suddenly seemed impossible, cruel, and absurd.
But if Silas found it impossible to speak, far more
so it seemed to Joseph.

To charge another with suspecting us is half to
confess ourselves worthy of suspicion. It is demoralizing, — it is to abandon the pride of conscious
rectitude. To deny an accusation is to concede to
it a possibility, a color of reason ; and Joseph
shrank with unutterable repugnance from that.
He felt that he could be torn limb from limb sooner
than betray by a word that he recognized the existence of suspicion so abominable. Besides, of what
avail would be a denial without evidence to dis-

prove a suspicion which had arisen without evidence? It was a thing too impalpable to contend with. As well fight a fog as seek to destroy by mere denial suspicion so vague, unsubstantial, and subtile, as that which enveloped him. Silas would, of course, eagerly accept his denial; he well knew how he would spring to his side, how warm and firm would be his hand-clasp, and how great, perhaps, his momentary relief. But he was, after all, but human, and no man can control his doubts. Silas would still be unable, when he thought the matter over, to help the feeling that there was, after all, something very strange about his conduct from first to last. It is the subtiler nature of doubt to penetrate the heart more profoundly than confidence, and to underlie it. No generous St. George of faith can reach the nether den where it lurks. Or, rather, is it like the ineradicable witch-grass which, though it be hewed off at the surface, still lives at the root, and springs forth luxuriantly again at the first favoring season?

Moreover, Joseph hoped that some circumstance, the detection of the murderer, or a healthier moral tone, might dissipate the cloud of suspicion between them, and then it would be far better not to have spoken, for, once put in words, the hateful thing would ever remain a mutual memory, never again to be denied, and which might come up to their minds whenever they looked each other in the eye thereafter. And so the brothers sat opposite each other in silence, their faces growing grayer as the clock ticked.

" The weather is growing cooler again," said Joseph, at last, rising to go to his room.

It was at least two hours before his usual bed-time, but he could sit there no longer.

" Yes, I think we shall have a frost," replied Silas, and the brothers parted.

After Joseph had gone, Mrs. Kilgore came into the parlor and sat down with some sewing. She waited for her husband to speak and tell her if Joseph had said anything. But he sat there staring at the wall, and took no notice of her. Although she knew so well what had been preying upon his mind since last evening, yet he had not once referred to the matter, and she had not dared to do so. It was hard for a talkative little lady like her to understand this reticence about a matter so deeply felt. She could not comprehend that there may be griefs so ghastly that we dare not lift from them the veil of silence. She wanted to " talk it over " a little. She felt that would do Silas good, because she knew it would be a relief to her. Nor was she insensible to the gratification it would afford her vanity to discuss so serious a matter with her husband, whose general tone with her was one of jest and pleasantry, to the disparagement of her intellectual powers, as she thought. So, after glancing up several times timidly at Silas's still set profile, she said, in a weighty little voice : —

" Don't you think Joseph behaves very strangely about the murder ? "   Her words seemed to be several seconds in making an impression on Silas's mind, and then he slowly turned his face full upon her.   It was a terrible look.   The squared jaw, the drawn lips, the dull, distant stare, repulsed her as one might repulse a stranger intermeddling with a bitter private grief.   Who was she, to come between him and his brother ?   He did not seem to think it worth while to say anything to explain so eloquent a glance, but immediately faced about again, as if dismissing the interruption from his mind.   Mrs. Kilgore did not try to make any more conversation, but went to her bedroom and cried herself to sleep.

But Silas sat in his chair in the parlor, and took no note of the hours till the lamp spluttered and went out.   All through the evening, in Joseph's room, which was directly above, he had heard him walking to and fro, to and fro, sitting down awhile, and then starting again ; and if the pacing had not finally come to an end, Silas could not have gone to bed, for his heart went out to his brother wrestling there alone with his dreadful secret, and he could not rest till he thought that he, too, was at rest.

Indeed, for the very reason that Joseph was so dear to him, and he felt nothing could change that, he actually hesitated the less to admit these horrible suspicions.   Love is impatient of uncertainty,

and would rather presume the guilt of a friend
from its longing to pour itself out in pity and tenderness, than restrain itself while judgment scru-
tinizes evidence and decides by a straw's weight.

A practical reflection, moreover, had occurred to
Silas.

If Joseph had really — he did not dare to say to
himself what — then it was of the utmost importance that they should quickly understand each
other, so as to take steps to place him in safety.
His desire to share Joseph's horrible secret was
like the feeling with which one would fain uncover
a friend's loathsome disease in order to help him.
Before he went to sleep that night he resolved,
therefore, that he would win his confidence by letting him see in every possible way, short of actual
words, that he suspected the true state of things,
and that Joseph might still confide in him as a
faithful brother who would stand by him in the
worst emergency.

On first meeting him the following morning
he began to carry out this project so worthy of
fraternal devotion. He sought occasion to shake
hands with Joseph, and gave a meaning pressure to
his clasp. At breakfast he was the only one who
talked, and endeavored by his manner to let Joseph understand that he perfectly comprehended
the situation, and was talking to cover his embarrassment and prevent Mrs. Kilgore from suspecting
anything. Several times also he managed to catch

his brother's eye, and give him a glance implying sympathy and mutual understanding. This demeanor added the last touch to Joseph's exasperation.

Evading Silas's evident intention of walking down-street, he got away alone, and took both dinner and tea at a restaurant, to put off meeting his brother and sister-in-law as long as possible. He lingered long over his tea in the darkest, loneliest corner of the eating-house, for the prospect, no longer to be avoided, of returning home to confront his sister-in-law's frightened face and Silas's pathetic glances appeared intolerable. Wild ideas of flying from the city and returning never, or not until the truth about the murder had come to light, occurred to him. He even began to arrange what sort of a letter he should write to Silas. But men of forty, especially of Joseph's temperament, who have moved in the same business and domestic ruts all their lives, do not readily make up their minds to bold steps of this sort. To endure 'suffering or inconvenience is more natural than to change their settled habits. So it all ended in his going home at about eight o'clock, and being greatly relieved to find some callers there.

All three of this strangely stricken family, indeed, shared that feeling. It was such a rest from the nervous strain whenever either or both were left alone with Joseph! The earnestness with which Mrs. Kilgore pressed her guests to stay a little longer was so unusual and apparently uncalled for that I fancy Mr. and Mrs. Smith had a vague suspicion that they were being made game of. But they would have been disabused of that impression could they have appreciated the sinking of heart with which their hosts heard the front-door close, and realized that they were again left to themselves. Only one thing had occurred to mar the relief which the call had afforded. The topic of the murder had been exhausted before Joseph entered, but, just as she was leaving, Mrs. Smith made a return to it, saying : —

" Mrs. Kilgore, I was telling my husband I should think you must be scared to be in the house, for fear the murderer might still be hanging around."

Mrs. Kilgore shuddered, and cast an instantaneous, wholly involuntary glance at Joseph. Her husband intercepted it, and, catching his eye, she saw an expression in it as if he could strangle her for what was really only the fault of her nerves. She stammered something, and the bustle of the retiring guests covered her confusion well enough.

Unfortunately, Joseph, too, had caught that sudden, terrified glance of his sister-in-law's at him, and it affected him more than anything that had occurred in either of the two days since the murder. As the guests took their leave, his head dropped on his breast, and his arms fell by the sides of his chair. Mr. Kilgore wanted to send his wife from the room, but his voice stuck in his throat, his tongue refused to move. They waited a moment, and then Joseph said : —

"Send for the police! For God's sake, take me out of this! I can't stand it any longer!"

It was not yet nine o'clock, and a boy came by in the street crying: —

"Extra! The Kilgore barn murderer captured! Full confession!"

Although the words were perfectly audible through the lowered windows to all in the room, Mrs. Kilgore was the only one who took any mental cognizance of them. Nor did either of the men, who sat there like stones, take note of her as she left the room. A minute later they heard her scream, and she ran back with the open paper in her hands.

"He did not do it! He is crazy! They have found the murderer!"

Silas fixed an incredulous, questioning stare upon his wife, and then turned quickly toward his brother. As for Joseph, at first and for several moments, he gave no sign that he had heard at all. Then he slowly raised his eyes to his brother's face with a deliberate, cruel gaze of contemptuous sarcasm and cold aversion. The first effect of this great relief was to flood his mind with bitter wrath at those who had done him the great wrong from which, no thanks to them, he had been rescued.

Mrs. Kilgore hastily read aloud, in a breathless

voice, the newspaper account. It seemed that two tramps had taken refuge in the barn from the storm that had raged the night of the murder, and getting into some quarrel before morning, one had stabbed the other and fled, only to be captured two days later and confess everything. When Mrs. Kilgore ceased reading, Joseph said : —

"It must be a great disappointment for you that they are not going to hang me for it. I sincerely condole with you."

Mrs. Kilgore cried, "Oh, don't!" and Silas made a gesture of deprecation, but both felt that Joseph had a right to revile them as he chose, and they had no right to complain. But he, even while he could not deny himself the gratification of a little cruel reproach, knew that they were not to be blamed, that they had been as much the victims of a fatality as himself, and that this was one of those peculiarly exasperating wrongs which do not leave the sufferer even the satisfaction of being angry. Soon he got up and walked across the room, stretched himself, drew his hand over his forehead, and said : —

"I feel as if I had just been dug up after being buried alive."

At this sign of returning equanimity, Silas took courage and ventured to say : —

"I know we 've been a pair of crazy fools, Joe, but you 're a little to blame. What 's made you act so queerly ? You won't deny that you have acted so ? "

Joseph smiled, — one does n't appreciate the pure luxury of a smile until he has been deprived of it for a while, — lit a cigar, sat down with his legs over the arm of his arm-chair, — he had not indulged in an unconstrained posture for two days, — and told his side of the story. He explained how, thanks to that tale he was reading, and the ghastly reverie it suggested, his nerves were all on edge when Mrs. Kilgore burst in with a piece of news whose extraordinary coincidence with his train of thought had momentarily thrown him off his balance; and he tried to make them see that, after that first scene, all the rest was a logical sequence.

Mrs. Kilgore, by virtue of her finer feminine nervous organization, understood him so readily that he saw he had made a mistake in not unbosoming himself to her at first. But Silas evidently did not so easily take his idea.

" But why did n't you just tell us that you had n't done it, and end the misunderstanding at one blow ? " he asked.

" Why, don't you see," replied Joseph, " that to deny a thing before you are distinctly suspected of it is to suggest suspicion; while to deny it afterward, unless you have proof to offer, is useless ? "

" What should we have come to but for the capture of the real murderer ? " cried Mrs. Kilgore, with a shudder.

A SUMMER EVENING'S DREAM

It is a village street, with great elms on either side, while along the middle stands another row set in a narrow strip of grassy common, so that the street and roadway are in reality double. The dwellings on either side are not only widely parted by the broad street, but are still further isolated, each in its large garden of ancient fruit trees. It is four o'clock of a sunny August afternoon, and a quiet, Sabbath-like but for its lazy voluptuousness, broods over the scene. No carriage, or even pedestrian, has passed for an hour. The occasional voices of children at play in some garden, the latching of a gate far down the street, the dying fall of a drowsy chanticleer, are but the punctuation of the poem of summer silence that has been flowing on all the afternoon. Upon the tree-tops the sun blazes brightly, and between their stems are glimpses of outlying meadows, which simmer in the heat as if about to come to a boil. But the shadowed street offers a cool and refreshing vista to the eye, and a veritable valley of refuge to the parched and dusty traveler along the highway.

On the broad piazza of one of the quaint old-fashioned houses, behind a needless screen of climbing woodbine, two girls are whiling away the afternoon. One of them is lounging in a lazy rocking-chair, while the other sits more primly and is industriously sewing.

" I suppose you 'll be glad enough to see George when he comes to-night to take you back to the city? I 'm afraid you find it pretty dull here," said the latter, with an intonation of uneasy responsibility sufficiently attesting that the brilliant-looking girl opposite was a guest.

That young lady, when addressed, was indulging in a luxurious country yawn, an operation by no means to be hurried, but to be fully and lazily enjoyed in all its several and long-drawn stages, and as thus practiced a wonderfully calming and soporific relaxation wholly unknown to the fretted denizens of cities, whose yawn is one of irritation and not of rest. " I do so enjoy your Plainfield yawns, Lucy," she said when she had quite finished. " Were you saying that it was a little dull? Well, perhaps it is, but then the trees and things seem to be enjoying themselves so hugely that it would be selfish to make a fuss, even if it is n't exactly my kind of fun."

" Your kind of fun is due by the six-o'clock stage, I believe."

The other laughed and said, " I wish you would n't make another allusion to George. I think of him so much that I 'm ashamed, as it is.

I'm sure this is a very aggravating place for an
engaged girl to be at. One gets so dreadfully
sentimental with nothing to take up the mind,
especially with such monstrous moons as you have.
I got fairly frightened of the one last night. It
drew me out through my eyes like a big plaster."

" Mabel French! "

" I don't care; it did. That was just the
feeling."

There was no hurry about talking, for the rich,
mellow summer silence had a body to it that prevented pauses from seeming empty, and it might
have been half an hour afterward that Mabel
suddenly leaned forward, putting her face close
to the vine-trellis, and cried in a low voice,
" Who's that ? Do tell me! They're the very
first persons who have gone by this afternoon, I
do believe."

A pretty phaeton was slowly passing, containing
an elderly gentleman and lady.

" Oh, that is only Lawyer Morgan and old Miss
Rood," replied Lucy, just glancing up, and then
down again. " They go out driving once a week
regularly, and always at about this time in the
afternoon."

" They look like afternoon sort of people," said
Mabel. " But why does n't Lawyer Morgan take
out his wife ? "

" He has n't got any. Miss Rood comes nearest
to that. Oh, no, you need n't open your eyes;

there's not a properer old maid in town, or old
bachelor either, for that matter."

" Are they relatives ? "

" No, indeed."

" How long has this Platonic romance been
going on, pray ? "

" Oh, ever since they were young, — forty years,
perhaps. I only know by tradition, you see. It
began ages before my day. They say she was
very pretty once. Old Aunty Perkins remembers
that she was quite the belle of the village as a
girl. It seems strange, does n't it ? "

" Tell me the whole story," said Mabel, turning
round so as to face Lucy as the phaeton passed out
of sight.

" There's not much to tell. Mr. Morgan has
always lived here, and so has Miss Rood. He lives
alone with a housekeeper in that fine house at the
end of the street, and she entirely alone in that
little white house over there among the apple-trees.
All the people who knew them when they were
young are dead, gone away, or moved off. They
are relics of a past generation, and are really about
as much shut up to each other for sympathy as an
old married couple."

" Well, why on earth are n't they married ? "

" People hereabouts got tired of asking that full
thirty years ago," replied Lucy, with a little shrug.
" Even the gossips long since wore out the subject,
and I believe we have all of us forgotten that

there is anything peculiar about their relations. He calls on her two or three times a week, and takes her out driving on pleasant days ; escorts her to places of amusement or social gatherings when either of them cares to go, which is n't often ; and wherever they are, people take it for granted they will pair off together. He is never seen with any other lady."

" It 's very strange," said Mabel thoughtfully, "and I 'm sure it 's very romantic. Queer old couple ! I wonder how they really feel toward each other, and whether they would n't like to be married ? "

Awhile after she suddenly demanded, " Don't you think Miss Rood looks like me ? "

Lucy laughed at first, but upon closer inspection of the fair questioner admitted that there might be some such resemblance as the shriveled apples brought up from the cellar in spring bear to the plump, rosy-cheeked beauties that went down in October.

If Mr. Morgan and Miss Rood, as they rode past, had chanced to overhear Mabel's question why they had not married, it would have affected them very differently. He would have been startled by the novelty of an idea that had not occurred to him in twenty years, but the blush on her cheek would have been one of painful consciousness.

As boy and girl they had been each other's

chosen companion, and as young man and maiden their childish preference had bloomed into a reciprocal love. Thanks to the freedom and simplicity of village life, they enjoyed as lovers a constant and easy familiarity and daily association almost as complete in sympathy of mind and heart as anything marriage could offer. There were none of the usual obstacles to incite them to matrimony. They were never even formally engaged, so wholly did they take it for granted that they should marry. It was so much a matter of course that there was no hurry at all about it; and besides, so long as they had it to look forward to, the foreground of life was illuminated for them: it was still morning. Mr. Morgan was constitutionally of a dreamy and unpractical turn, a creature of habits and a victim of ruts; and as years rolled on he became more and more satisfied with these half-friendly, half-loverlike relations. He never found the time when it seemed an object to marry, and now, for very many years, the idea had not even occurred to him as possible; and so far was he from the least suspicion that Miss Rood's experience had not been precisely similar to his own, that he often congratulated himself on the fortunate coincidence.

Time cures much, and many years ago Miss Rood had recovered from the first bitterness of discovering that his love had become insensibly transformed into a very tender but perfectly peaceful friendship. No one but him had ever touched her heart, and she had no interest in life besides him. Since she was not to be his wife, she was glad to be his lifelong, tender, self-sacrificing friend. So she raked the ashes over the fire in her heart, and left him to suppose that it had gone out as in his. Nor was she without compensation in their friendship. It was with a delightful thrill that she felt how fully in mind and heart he leaned and depended upon her, and the unusual and romantic character of their relations in some degree consoled her for the disappointment of womanly aspirations by a feeling of distinction. She was not like other women: her lot was set apart and peculiar. She looked down upon her sex. The conventionality of women's lives renders their vanity peculiarly susceptible to a suggestion that their destiny is in any respect unique, — a fact that has served the turn of many a seducer before now.

To-day, after returning from his drive with Miss Rood, Mr. Morgan had walked in his garden, and as the evening breeze arose, it bore to his nostrils that first indescribable flavor of autumn which warns us that the soul of Summer has departed from her yet glowing body. He was very sensitive to these changes of the year, and, obeying an impulse that had been familiar to him in all unusual moods his life long, he left the house after tea and turned his steps down the street. As he stopped at Miss Rood's gate, Lucy, Mabel, and George

Hammond were under the apple-trees in the garden opposite.

"Look, Mabel! There's Mr. Morgan going to call on Miss Rood," said Lucy softly.

"Oh, do look, George!" said Mabel eagerly. "That old gentleman has been paying court to an old maid over in that little house for forty years. And to think," she added in a lower tone, intended for his private ear, "what a fuss you make about waiting six months!"

"Humph! You please to forget that it's easier to wait for some things than for others. Six months of my kind of waiting, I take it, require more patience than forty years of his — or any other man's," he added, with increased emphasis.

"Be quiet, sir!" replied Mabel, answering his look of unruly admiration with one of half pique. "I'm not a sugar-plum, that's not enjoyed till it's in the mouth. If you have n't got me now, you'll never have me. If being engaged is n't enough, you don't deserve to be married." And then, seeing the blank expression with which he looked down at her, she added with a prescient resignedness, "I'm afraid, dear, you'll be so disappointed when we're married, if you find this so tedious."

Lucy had discreetly wandered away, and of how they made it up there were no witnesses. But it seems likely that they did so, for shortly after they wandered away together down the darkening street.

Like most of the Plainfield houses, that at which Mr. Morgan turned in stood well back from the street. At a side window, still further sheltered from view by a syringa-bush at the house corner, sat a little woman with a small, pale face, the still attractive features perceptibly sharpened by years, of which the half-gray hair bore further testimony. The eyes, just now fixed absently upon the dusking landscape, were light gray and a little faded, while around the lips there were crow's-feet, especially when they were pressed together, as now, in an unsatisfied, almost pathetic look, evidently habitual to her face when in repose. There was withal something in her features that so reminded you of Mr. Morgan that any one conversant with the facts of his life-romance would have at once inferred — though by just what logic he might not be able to explain — that this must be Miss Rood. It is well known that long-wedded couples often gain at length a certain resemblance in feature and manner; and although these two were not married, yet their intimacy of a lifetime was perhaps the reason why her face bore when in repose something of that seer-like expression which communion with the bodiless shapes of memory had given to his.

The latching of the gate broke up her depressing reverie, and banished the pinched and pining look from her features. Among the neighbors Miss Rood was sometimes called a sour old maid, but

the face she kept for Mr. Morgan would never
have suggested that idea to the most ill-natured
critic.

He stopped at the window, near which the walk
passed to the doorway, and stood leaning on the
sill, — a tall, slender figure, stooping a little, with
smooth, scholarly face, and thin iron-gray hair. His
only noticeable feature was a pair of eyes whose
expression and glow indicated an imaginative temperament. It was pleasant to observe the relieved
restlessness in the look and manner of the two
friends, as if at the mere being in each other's
presence, though neither seemed in any haste to
exchange even the words of formal greeting.

At length she said, in a tone of quiet satisfaction, "I knew you would come, for I was sure this
deathly autumn's flavor would make you restless.
Is n't it strange how it affects the nerves of memory, and makes one sad with thinking of all the
sweet, dear days that are dead ? "

" Yes, yes," he answered eagerly ; " I can think
of nothing else. Do they not seem wonderfully
clear and near to-night ? To-night, of all nights
in the year, if the figures and scenes of memory
can be reëmbodied in visible forms, they ought to
become so to the eyes that strain and yearn for
them."

" What a fanciful idea, Robert ! "

" I don't know that it is ; I don't feel sure. Nobody understands the mystery of this Past, or what

are the conditions of existence in that world. These
memories, these forms and faces, that are so near,
so almost warm and visible that we find ourselves
smiling on the vacant air where they seem to be,
are they not real and living?"

"You don't mean you believe in ghosts?"

"I am not talking of ghosts of the dead, but of
ghosts of the past, — memories of scenes or persons, whether the persons are dead or not — of our
own selves as well as others. Why," he continued,
his voice softening into a passionate, yearning tenderness, "the figure I would give most to see just
once more is yourself as a girl, as I remember you
in the sweet grace and beauty of your maidenhood.
Ah, well! ah, well!"

"Don't!" she cried involuntarily, while her features contracted in sudden pain.

In the years during which his passion for her
had been cooling into a staid friendship, his imagination had been recurring with constantly increasing fondness and a dreamy passion to the memory
of her girlhood. And the cruelest part of it was
that he so unconsciously and unquestioningly assumed that she could not have identity enough
with that girlish ideal to make his frequent glowing references to it even embarrassing. Generally,
however, she heard and made no sign, but the suddenness of his outburst just now had taken her off
her guard.

He glanced up with some surprise at her ex-

clamation, but was too much interested in his subject to take much notice of it. "You know," he
said, "there are great differences in the distinctness with which we can bring up our memories.
Very well! The only question is, What is the
limit to that distinctness, or is there any? Since
we know there are such wide degrees in distinctness, the burden of proof rests on those who would
prove that those degrees stop short of any particular point. Don't you see, then, that it might be
possible to see them?" And to enforce his meaning he laid his hand lightly on hers as it rested on
the window-seat.

She withdrew it instantly from the contact, and
a slight flush tinged her sallow cheeks. The only
outward trace of her memory of their youthful
relations was the almost prudish chariness of her
person by which she indicated a sense of the line
to be drawn between the former lover and the present friend.

"Something in your look just now," he said, regarding her musingly, as one who seeks to trace
the lineaments of a dead face in a living one,
"reminds me of you as you used to sit in this very
window as a girl, and I stood just here, and we
picked out stars together. There! now it 's gone;"
and he turned away regretfully.

She looked at his averted face with a blank pite-
ousness which revealed all her secret. She would
not have had him see it for worlds, but it was a

relief just for a moment to rest her features in the sad cast which the muscles had grown tired in repressing. The autumn scent rose stronger as the air grew damp, and he stood breathing it in, and apparently feeling its influence like some Delphian afflatus.

"Is there anything, Mary, — is there anything so beautiful as that light of eternity that rests on the figures of memory? Who that has once felt it can care for the common daylight of the present any more, or take pleasure in its prosaic groups?"

"You'll certainly catch cold standing in that wet grass; do come in and let me shut the blinds," she said, for she had found cheerful lamplight the best corrective for his vagaries.

So he came in and sat in his special arm-chair, and they chatted about miscellaneous village topics for an hour. The standpoint from which they canvassed Plainfield people and things was a peculiarly outside one. Their circle of two was like a separate planet from which they observed the world. Their tone was like, and yet quite unlike, that in which a long-married couple discuss their acquaintances; for, while their intellectual intimacy was perfect, their air expressed a constant mutual deference and solicitude of approbation not to be confounded with the terrible familiarity of matrimony; and at the same time they constituted a self-sufficient circle, apart from the society around them, as man and wife cannot. Man and wife are

so far merged as to feel themselves a unit over
against society. They are too much identified to
find in each other that sense of support and countenance which requires a feeling of the exteriority
of our friend's life to our own. If these two should
marry, they would shortly find themselves impelled
to seek refuge in conventional relations with that
society of which now they were calmly independent.

At length Mr. Morgan rose and threw open the
blinds. The radiance of the full harvest-moon so
flooded the room that Miss Rood was fain to blow
out the poor lamp for compassion. "Let us take
a walk," he said.

The streets were empty and still, and they walked
in silence, spelled by the perfect beauty of the
evening. The dense shadows of the elms lent a
peculiarly rich effect to the occasional bars and
patches of moonlight on the street floor ; the white
houses gleamed among their orchards ; and here
and there, between the dark tree-stems, there were
glimpses of the shining surface of the broad outlying meadows, which looked like a surrounding
sea.

Miss Rood was startled to see how the witchery
of the scene possessed her companion. His face
took on a set, half-smiling expression, and he
dropped her arm as if they had arrived at the
place of entertainment to which he had been escorting her. He no longer walked with measured

pace, but glided along with a certain stealthiness, peering on this side and that down moony vistas and into shadow-bowers, as if half-expecting, if he might step lightly enough, to catch a glimpse of some sort of dream-people basking there.

Nor could Miss Rood herself resist the impression the moony landscape gave of teeming with subtle forms of life, escaping the grosser senses of human beings, but perceptible by their finer parts. Each cosy nook of light and shadow was yet warm from some presence that had just left it. The landscape fairly stirred with ethereal forms of being beneath the fertilizing moon-rays, as the earth-mould wakes into physical life under the sun's heat. The yellow moonlight looked warm as spirits might count warmth. The air was electric with the thrill of circumambient existence. There was the sense of pressure, of a throng. It would have been impossible to feel lonely. The pulsating sounds of the insect world seemed the rhythm to which the voluptuous beauty of the night had spontaneously set itself. The common air of day had been transmuted into the atmosphere of reverie and Dreamland. In that magic medium the distinction between imagination and reality fast dissolved. Even Miss Rood was conscious of a delightful excitement, a vague expectancy. Mr. Morgan, she saw, was moved quite beyond even his exaggerated habit of imaginative excitement. His wet, shining, wide-opened eyes

and ecstatic expression indicated complete abandonment to the illusions of the scene.

They had seated themselves, as the concentration of the brain upon imaginative activity made
the nerves of motion sluggish, upon a rude bench
formed by wedging a plank between two elms that
stood close together. They were within the shadow
of the trees, but close up to their feet rippled a lake
of moonlight. The landscape shimmering before
them had been the theatre of their fifty years of
life. Their history was written in its trees and
lawns and paths. The very air of the place had
acquired for them a dense, warm, sentient feeling,
to which that of all other places was thin and raw.
It had become tinctured by their own spiritual
emanations, by the thoughts, looks, words and
moods of which it had so long received the impression. It had become such vitalized air, surcharged
with sense and thought, as might be taken to make
souls for men out of.

Over yonder, upon the playground, yet lingered
the faint violet fragrance of their childhood. Beneath that elm a kiss had once touched the air with
a fire that still warmed their cheeks in passing.
Yonder the look of a face was cut on the viewless
air as on marble. Surely, death does but touch the
living, for the dead ever keep their power over us ;
it is only we who lose ours over them. Each vista
of leafy arch and distant meadow framed in some
scene of their youth-time, painted in the imperish-

able hues of memory that borrow from time an ever richer and more glowing tint. It was no wonder that to these two old people, sitting on the bench between the elms, the atmosphere before them, saturated with associations, dense with memories, should seem fairly quivering into material forms, like a distant mist turning to rain.

At length Miss Rood heard her companion say, in a whisper of tremulous exultation, "Do you know, Mary, I think I shall see them very soon."

" See whom ? " she asked, frightened at his strange tone.

" Why, see us, of course, as I was telling you," he whispered, — " you and me as we were young, — see them as I see you now. Don't you remember it was just along here that we used to walk on spring evenings ? We walk here no more, but they do evermore, beautiful, beautiful children. I come here often to lie in wait for them. I can feel them now ; I can almost, almost see them." His whisper became scarcely audible and the words dropped slowly. "I know the sight is coming, for every day they grow more vivid. It can't be long before I quite see them. It may come at any moment."

Miss Rood was thoroughly frightened at the intensity of his excitement, and terribly perplexed as to what she should do.

"It may come at any time ; I can almost see them now," he murmured. " A—h ! look ! " With parted lips and unspeakably intense eyes, as if his life were flowing out at them, he was staring across the moonlit paths before them to the point where the path debouched from the shadow.

Following his eyes, she saw what for a moment made her head swim with the thought that she too was going mad. Just issuing from the shadows, as if in answer to his words, were a young man and a girl, his arm upon her waist, his eyes upon her face. At the first glance Miss Rood was impressed with a resemblance to her own features in those of the girl, which her excitement exaggerated to a perfect reproduction of them. For an instant the conviction possessed her that by some impossible, indescribable, inconceivable miracle she was looking upon the resurrected figures of her girlish self and her lover.

At first Mr. Morgan had half started from his seat, and was between rising and sitting. Then he rose with a slow, involuntary movement, while his face worked terribly between bewilderment and abandonment to illusion. He tottered forward a few steps to the edge of the moonlight, and stood peering at the approaching couple with a hand raised to shade his eyes and a dazed, unearthly smile on his face. The girl saw him first, for she had been gazing demurely before her, while her lover looked only at her. At sight of the gray-haired man suddenly confronting them with a look of bedlam, she shrieked and started back in terror. Miss Rood, recalled to her senses, sprang forward, and catching Mr. Morgan's arm endeavored with gentle force to draw him away.

But it was too late for that. The young man, at first almost as much startled as his companion at the uncanny apparition, naturally experienced a revulsion of indignation at such an extraordinary interruption to his tête-à-tête, and stepped up to Mr. Morgan as if about to inflict summary chastisement. But perceiving that he had to do with an elderly man, he contented himself with demanding in a decidedly aggressive tone what the devil he meant by such a performance.

Mr. Morgan stared at him without seeing him, and evidently did not take in the words. He merely gasped once or twice, and looked as if he had fainted away on his feet. His blank, stunned expression showed that his faculties were momentarily benumbed by the shock. Miss Rood felt as if she should die for the pity of it as she looked at his face, and her heart was breaking for grief as she sought to mollify the young man with some inarticulate words of apology, meanwhile still endeavoring to draw Mr. Morgan away. But at this moment the girl, recovering from her panic, came up to the group and laid her hand on the young man's arm, as if to check and silence him. It was evident that she saw there was something quite unusual in the circumstances, and the look which she bent upon Mr. Morgan was one of sympathy and considerate interrogation. But Miss Rood

could see no way out of their awkward situation,
which grew more intolerable every moment as they
thus confronted each other. It was finally Mr.
Morgan's voice, quite firm, but with an indescribable sadness in the tones, which broke the silence :
"Young people, I owe you an apology, such as it
is. I am an old man, and the past is growing so
heavy that it sometimes quite overbalances me.
My thoughts have been busy to-night with the days
of my youth, and the spell of memory has been so
strong that I have not been quite myself. As you
came into view I actually entertained the incredible
idea for a moment that somehow I saw in you the
materialized memories of myself and another as we
once walked this same path."

The young man bowed, as Mr. Morgan ended, in
a manner indicating his acceptance of the apology,
although he looked both amazed and amused. But
the explanation had a very different effect upon the
girl at his side. As she listened, her eyes had filled
with tears, and her face had taken on a wonderfully
tender, pitiful smile. When he ended speaking,
she impulsively said, " I 'm so sorry we were not
what you thought us ! Why not pretend we are,
to-night at least ? We can pretend it, you know.
The moonlight makes anything possible ; " and then
glancing at Miss Rood, she added, as if almost
frightened, " Why, how much we look alike ! I 'm
not sure it is n't true, anyway."

This was, in fact, an unusually marked example

of those casual resemblances between strangers which are sometimes seen. The hair of the one was indeed gray and that of the other dark, but the eyes were of the same color by night, and the features, except for the greater fullness of the younger face, were cast in the same mould, while figure and bearing were strikingly similar, although daylight would doubtless have revealed diversities enough that moonlight refused to disclose.

The two women looked at each other with an expression almost of suspicion and fear, while the young man observed, "Your mistake was certainly excusable, sir."

"It will be the easier to pretend," said the girl, as with a half-serious, half-sportive imperiousness she laid her hand on Mr. Morgan's arm. "And now it is thirty years ago, and we are walking together." He involuntarily obeyed the slight pressure, and they walked slowly away, leaving the other two, after an embarrassed pause, to follow them.

For some time they walked in silence. He was deliberately abandoning himself to the illusion, supported as it was by the evidence of his senses, that he was wandering in some of the mysterious between-worlds which he had so often dreamed of, with the love of his youth in her youth-time charm. Did he really believe it to be so? Belief is a term quite irrelevant to such a frame as his, in which the reflective and analytical powers are for a time purposely held in abeyance. The circumstances of her introduction to him had dropped from his mind as irrelevant accidents, like the absurdities which occur in our sweetest and most solemn dreams without marring their general impression in our memories. Every glance he threw upon his companion, while on the one hand it shocked his illusion in that she seemed not likely to vanish away, on the other strengthened it with an indescribable thrill by the revelation of some fresh trait of face or figure, some new expression, that reproduced the Miss Rood of his youth. Not, indeed, that it is likely his companion was thus perfectly the double of that lady, although so much resembling her, but the common graces of maidenhood were in Mr. Morgan's mind the peculiar personal qualities of the only woman he had ever much known.

Of his own accord he would not have dared to risk breaking the charm by a word. But his companion — who, as is tolerably evident by this time, was Mabel French — had meanwhile formed a scheme quite worthy of her audacious temper. She had at once recognized both Mr. Morgan and Miss Rood, and had gone thus far from a mere romantic impulse, without definite intentions of any sort. But the idea now came into her head that she might take advantage of this extraordinary situation to try a match-making experiment, which instantly captivated her fancy. So she said, while ever so gently pressing his arm and looking up into his face with an arch smile (she was recognized as the best amateur actress in her set at home), " I wonder if the moon will be so mellow after we are married ? "

His illusion was rudely disturbed by the shock of an articulate voice, softly and low as she spoke, and he looked around with a startled expression that made her fear her rôle was ended. But she could not know that the eyes she turned to his were mirrors where he saw his dead youth. The two Miss Roods — the girl and the woman, the past and the present — were fused and become one in his mind. Their identity flashed upon him.

An artesian well sunk from the desert surface through the underlying strata, the layers of ages, strikes some lake long ago covered over, and the water welling up converts the upper waste into a garden. Just so at her words and her look his heart suddenly filled, as if it came from afar, with the youthful passion he had felt toward Miss Rood, but which, he knew not exactly when or how, had been gradually overgrown with the dullness of familiarity and had lapsed into an indolent affectionate habit. The warm, voluptuous pulse of this new feeling — new, and yet instantly recognized as old — brought with it a flood of youthful associations, and commingled the far past with the present in a confusion more complete and more intoxicating than ever. He saw double again. " Married ! " he murmured dreamily. " Yes, surely, we will be married."

And as he spoke, he looked at her with such a peculiar expression that she was a little frightened. It looked like a more serious business than she had counted on, and for a moment, if she could have cut and run, perhaps she would have done so. But she had a strain of the true histrionic artist about her, and with a little effort rose to the difficulty of the rôle. " Of course we will be married," she replied, with an air of innocent surprise. " You speak as if you had just thought of it."

He turned toward her as if he would sober his senses by staring at her, his pupils dilating and contracting in the instinctive effort to clear the mind by clearing the eyes.

But with a steady pressure on his arm she compelled him to walk on by her side. Then she said, in a soft, low voice, as if a little awed by what she were telling, while at the same time she nestled nearer his side, " I had such a sad dream last night, and your strange talk reminds me of it. It seemed as if we were old and white-haired and stooping, and went wandering about, still together, but not married, lonely and broken. And I woke up feeling you can't think how dreary and sad, — as if a bell had tolled in my ears as I slept ; and the feeling was so strong that I put my fingers to my face to find if it was withered ; and when I could not tell certainly, I got up and lit my lamp and looked in the glass ; and my face, thank God ! was fresh and young ; but I sat on my bed and cried to think of the poor old people I had left behind in my dream."

Mabel had so fallen into the spirit of her part that she was really crying as she ended. Her tears completed Mr. Morgan's mental confusion, and he absolutely did not know whom he was addressing or where he was himself, as he cried, "No, no, Mary! Don't cry! It shall not be; it shall never be."

Lightly withdrawing her hand from his arm, she glided like a sprite from his side, and was lost in the shadows, while her whispered words still sounded in his ear, "Good-by for thirty years!"

A moment after, three notes, clear as a bird's call, sounded from the direction whither she had vanished, and Miss Rood's companion, breaking off short a remark on the excessive dryness of the weather, bowed awkwardly and also disappeared among the shadows.

When Miss Rood laid her hand on Mr. Morgan's arm to recall him to the fact that they were now alone together, he turned quickly, and his eyes swept her from head to foot, and then rested on her face with an expression of intense curiosity and a wholly new interest, as if he were tracing out a suddenly suggested resemblance which overwhelmed him with emotion. And as he gazed, his eyes began to take fire from the faded features on which they had rested so many years in mere complacent friendliness, and she instinctively averted her face.

Long intimacy had made her delicately sensitive
to his moods, and when he drew her arm in his
and turned to walk, although he had not uttered
a word, she trembled with agitation.

" Mary, we have had an extraordinary experience to-night," he said. The old dreaminess in his
voice, as of one narcotized or in a trance, sometimes
a little forced, as of one trying to dream, to which
she had become accustomed, and of which in her
heart of hearts she was very weary, was gone. In
its place she recognized a resonance which still
further confused her with a sense of altered relations. His polarity had changed : his electricity
was no longer negative, but positive.

Her feminine instinct vaguely alarmed, she replied, " Yes, indeed, but it is getting late. Had n't
we better go in ? " What lent the unusual intonation of timidity to her voice? Certainly nothing
that she could have explained.

" Not quite yet, Mary," he answered, turning his
gaze once more fully upon her.

Her eyes dropped before his, and a moment after
fluttered up to find an explanation for their behavior, only to fall again in blind panic. For,
mingling unmistakably with the curiosity with
which he was still studying her features, was a new-
born expression of appropriation and passionate
complacency. Her senses whirled in a bewilderment that had a suffocating sweetness about it.
Though she now kept her eyes on the ground, she

felt his constant sidewise glances, and, desperately
seeking relief from the conscious silence that enveloped them like a vapor of intoxicating fumes,
she forced herself to utter the merest triviality she
could summon to her lips: " See that house." The
husky tones betrayed more agitation than the ruse
concealed.

He answered as irrelevantly as she had spoken,
" Yes, indeed, so it is." That was their only attempt at conversation.

For a half hour — it might have been much
more or much less — they walked in this way,
thrilling with the new magnetism that at once attracted and estranged them with an extraordinary
sense of strangeness in familiarity. At length they
paused under the little porch of Miss Rood's cot-
tage, where he commonly bade her good-evening
after their walks. The timidity and vague alarms
that had paralyzed her while they were walking
disappeared as he was about to leave her, and she
involuntarily returned his unusual pressure of her
hand.

A long time after, behold her still encircled in
his arms, not blushing, but pale and her eyes full
of a soft, astonished glow ! " Oh, Robert ! " was
all she had said after one first little gasp.

They never met George or Mabel again. Mrs.
Morgan learned subsequently that two young people from the city answering their description had
been guests at the opposite house, and had left

Plainfield the morning after the events hereinbefore set forth, and drew her conclusions accordingly. But her husband preferred to cherish the secret belief that his theory that memories might become visible had proved true in one instance at least.

POTTS'S PAINLESS CURE

" MUST you go up to that tiresome old college again to-night? "

Pouting lips and delicate brows fretted in pretty importunity over the troubled eyes enforced the pleading tones, and yet the young man to whom they were addressed found strength to reply : —

" I 'm afraid I can't get rid of it. I particularly promised Sturgis I would look in on him, and it won't do for me to cut my acquaintance with the class entirely just because I 'm having such a jolly time down here."

" Oh, no, you don't think it jolly at all, or you would n't be so eager to go away. I 'm sure I must be very dull company."

The hurt tone and pretended pique with which she said this were assuredly all that was needed to make the *petite* teaser irresistible. But the young man replied, regarding her the while with an admiration in which there was a singular expression of uneasiness : —

" Can't, Annie, 'pon honor. I 'm engaged, and you know —

> " ' I could not love thee, dear, so much,
> Loved I not honor more ! ' "

And transferring her hand to his lips he loosed its soft, lingering clasp and was gone, stopping at the gate to throw back a kiss to her as she stood in the porch, by way of amends for his hasty parting.

" George Hunt, you 're an infernal scamp ! "

These were the opprobrious words he muttered to himself as he passed out of earshot. The beneficent common law does not condemn a man merely on his own confession unless circumstances in evidence lend probability to his self-accusation. Before we coincide in Mr. Hunt's opinion of himself, let us therefore inquire into the circumstances.

He was in the last term of senior year at —— college. For the past year he had been boarding at the Giffords', and Annie and he had fallen in love. The fall on his part had been quite voluntary and deliberate. He had fallen in love because it was the correct thing for a young collegian, engaged in the study of the humanities, to be in love, and made him feel more like a man than smoking, drinking, or even sporting a stove-pipe hat and cane. Vanity aside, it was very jolly to have a fine, nice girl who thought no end of a fellow, to walk, talk, and sing with, and to have in mind when one sang the college songs about love and wine with the fellows. And it gave him also a very agreeable sense of superior experience as he mingled in their discussions of women and the tender passion.

But withal he was a conscientious, kind-hearted

young fellow enough, and had suffered occasional qualms of conscience when little words or incidents had impressed him with the knowledge that Annie's love for him was a more serious matter than his for her. He felt that by insisting on exchanging the pure gold of her earnest affection for the pinchbeck of his passing fancy, she was making a rogue of him. He should be in no position to marry for years, nor did he want to ; and if he had wanted to, though he felt terribly hard-hearted when he owned it to himself, his feeling toward Annie was not quite so deep as to be a real wish to marry her. As his last year in college approached its end, he had thought more and more of these things, and had returned from his last vacation determined to begin to draw gradually away from her, and without any shock to bring their relations back to the footing of friendship. The idea seemed a very plausible one, but it is scarcely necessary to state that, living in the same house, and frequently alone with her, it took about a week and a few dozen reproachful glances from grieving eyes to melt this artificial ice with a freshet of affection, and when, a couple of months later, he calmly reviewed the situation, he found himself involved perceptibly deeper than ever, on account of the attempt at extrication.

Only two or three weeks of the term remained, and it was too late to repeat the unsuccessful experiment. He had tried his best and failed, and nothing remained but to be as happy as possible with her in the short time left. Then she must get over her disappointment as other girls did in like cases. No doubt some woman would hurt his feelings some day, and so make it square. He took much satisfaction in this reflection. But such cynical philosophy did not lull his conscience, which alternately inspired his manner with an unwonted demonstrativeness and tenderness, and again made him so uncomfortable in her presence that he was fain to tear himself away and escape from her sight on any pretext. Her tender glances and confiding manner made him feel like a brute, and when he kissed her he felt that it was the kiss of a Judas. Such had been his feelings this evening, and such were the reflections tersely summed up in that ejaculation, —

" George Hunt, you 're an infernal scamp ! "

On arriving at Sturgis's room, he found it full of tobacco smoke, and the usual crowd there, who hailed him vociferously. For he was one of the most popular men in college, although for a year or so he had been living outside the buildings. Several bottles stood on the tables, but the fellows had as yet arrived only at the argumentative stage of exhilaration, and it so happened that the subject under discussion at once took Hunt's close attention. Mathewson had been reading the first volume of Goethe's autobiography, and was indulging in some strictures on his course in jilting Frederica and leaving the poor girl heartbroken.

"But, man," said Sturgis, "he did n't want to marry her, and seeing he did n't, nothing could have been crueler to her, to say nothing of himself, than to have done so."

"Well, then," said Mathewson, "why did he go and get her in love with him?"

"Why, he took his risk and she hers, for the fun of the game. She happened to be the one who paid for it, but it might just as well have been he. Why, Mat, you must see yourself that for Goethe to have married then would have knocked his art-life into a cocked hat. Your artist has just two great foes, — laziness and matrimony. Each has slain its thousands. Hitch Pegasus to a family cart and he can't go off the thoroughfare. He must stick to the ruts. I admit that a bad husband may be a great artist; but for a good husband, an uxorious, contented husband, there 's no chance at all."

"You are neither of you right, as usual," said little Potts, in his oracular way.

When Potts first came to college, the fellows used to make no end of fun of the air of superior and conclusive wisdom with which he assumed to lay down the law on every question, this being the more laughable because he was such a little chap. Potts did not pay the least attention to the jeers, and finally the jeerers were constrained to admit that if he did have an absurdly pretentious way of talking, his talk was unusually well worth listening to, and the result was that they took him at his own valuation, and, for the sake of hearing what he had to say, quietly submitted to his assumption of authority as court of appeal. So when he coolly declared both disputants wrong, they manifested no resentment, but only an interest as to what he was going to say, while the other fellows also looked up curiously.

" It would have been a big mistake for Goethe to have married her," pursued Potts, in his deliberate monotone, " but he was n't justified on that account in breaking her heart. It was his business, having got her in love with him, to get her out again and leave her where she was."

" Get her out again ? " demanded Mathewson. " How was he to do that ? "

" Humph ! " grunted Potts. " If you have n't found it much easier to lose a friend than to win one, you 're luckier than most. If you asked me how he was to get her in love with him, I should have to scratch my head, but the other thing is as easy as unraveling a stocking."

" Well, but, Potts," inquired Sturgis, with interest, " how could Goethe have gone to work, for instance, to disgust Frederica with him ? "

" Depends on the kind of girl. If she is one of your high-steppers as to dignity and sense of honor, let him play mean and seem to do a few dirty tricks. If she 's a stickler for manners and good taste, let him betray a few traits of boorishness or Philistinism ; or if she has a keen sense of the ridiculous, let him make an ass of himself. I should say the last would be the surest cure and leave least of a sore place in her feelings, but it would be hardest on his vanity. Everybody knows that a man would ' rather seem a scamp than a fool.' "

" I don't believe there 's a man in the world who would play the voluntary fool to save any woman's heart from breaking, though he might manage the scamp," remarked Mathewson. " And anyhow, Potts, I believe there 's no girl who would n't choose to be jilted outright, rather than be juggled out of her affections that way."

" No doubt she would say so, if you asked her," replied the imperturbable Potts. " A woman always prefers a nice sentimental sorrow to a fancy-free state. But it is n't best for her, and looking out for her good, you must deprive her of it. Women are like children, you know, our natural wards."

This last sentiment impressed these beardless youths as a clincher, and there was a pause. But Mathewson, who was rather strong on the moralities, rallied with the objection that Potts's plan would be deceit.

" Well, now, that 's what I call cheeky," replied its author, with a drawl of astonishment. " I suppose it was n't deceit when you were prancing around in your best clothes both literally and figuratively, trying to bring your good points into such absurd prominence as to delude her into the idea

that you had no bad ones. Oh, no, it's only deceit
when you appear worse than you are, not when
you try to appear better. Strikes me that when
you 've got a girl into a fix, it won't do at that time
of day to plead your conscience as a reason for not
getting her out of it. Seeing that a man is generally ready to sacrifice his character in reality to
his own interests, he ought to be willing to sacrifice it in appearance to another's."

Mathewson was squelched, but Sturgis came to
his relief with the suggestion : —

" Would n't a little genuine heartache, which I
take it is healthy enough, if it is n't pleasant, be
better for her than the cynical feeling, the disgust
with human nature, which she would experience
from finding her ideal of excellence a scamp or a
fool ? "

The others seemed somewhat impressed, but
Potts merely ejaculated, —

" Bosh ! " Allowing a brief pause for this ejaculation to do its work in demoralizing the opposition he proceeded. " Sturgis, you remember
' Midsummer Night's Dream,' and how Titania, on
the application of Puck's clarifying lotion to her
eyes, perceives that in Bottom she has loved an
ass. Don't you suppose Titania suffered a good
deal from the loss of her ideal ? "

There was a general snicker at Sturgis's expense.

" Well, now," continued Potts gravely, " a wo-

man who should fall in love with one of us fellows
and deem him a hero would be substantially in
Titania's plight when she adored Bottom, and
about as much an object of pity when her hero
disclosed an asininity which would be at least as
near to being his real character as the heroism she
ascribed to him."

" That 's all very well," said Merril dryly, " but
it strikes me that it 's middling cheeky for you
fellows to be discussing how you 'll jilt your sweethearts with least expense to their feelings, when
the chances are that if you should ever get one,
you 'll need all your wits to keep her from jilting
you."

" You are, as usual, trivial and inconsequential
this evening, Merril," replied Potts, when the
laughter had subsided. " Supposing, as you suggest, that we shall be the jilted and not the jilters,
it will be certainly for our interest that the ladies
should spare our feelings by disenchanting us, —
saying, as it were, the charm backward that first
charmed us. He who would teach the ladies the
method and enlist their tender hearts in its behalf
would be, perhaps, the greatest benefactor his
much-jilted and heart-sore sex ever had. Then,
indeed, with the heart - breakers of both sexes
pledged to so humane a practice, there would be
no more any such thing as sorrow over unrequited
affections, and the poets and novelists would beg
their bread."

"That is a millennial dream, Potts," responded
Merril. "You may possibly persuade the men to
make themselves disagreeable for pity's sake, but
it is quite too much to expect that a woman would
deliberately put herself in an unbecoming light,
if it were to save a world from its sins."

"Perhaps it is," said Potts pensively; "but
considering what perfectly inexhaustible resources
of disagreeableness there are in the best of us and
the fairest of women, it seems a most gratuitous
cruelty that any heart should suffer when a very
slight revelation would heal its hurt. We can't
help people suffering because we are so faulty and
imperfect, but we might at least see that nobody
ever had a pang from thinking us better than we
are."

"Look at Hunt!" said Sturgis. "He doesn't
open his mouth, but drinks in Potts's wisdom as
eagerly as if he didn't know it was a pump that
never stops."

There was a general laugh among those who
glanced up in time to catch the expression of close
attention on Hunt's face.

"Probably he's deliberating on the application
of the Potts patent painless cure to some recent
victim of that yellow mustache and goatee," suggested Merril, with the envy of a smooth-faced
youth for one more favored.

Hunt, whose face had sprung back like a steel-
trap to its usual indifferent expression, smiled non-

chalantly at Merril's remark. One whose reticent
habit makes his secrets so absolutely secure as
Hunt's private affairs always were is stirred to
amusement rather than trepidation by random
guesses which come near the truth.

" If I were situated as Merril flatteringly suggests, I should enjoy nothing better than such an
experiment," he replied deliberately. " It would
be quite a novel sensation to revolutionize one's
ordinary rule of conduct so as to make a point of
seeming bad or stupid. There would be as much
psychology in it as in an extra term, at least. A
man would find out, for instance, how much there
was in him besides personal vanity and love of
approbation. It would be a devilish small residue
with most of us, I fancy."

The talk took a new turn, and the fun grew fast
and furious around Hunt, who sat puffing his pipe,
absorbed in contemplation. At about half-past
nine, when things were getting hilarious, he beat
a retreat, followed by the reproaches of the fellows. He was determined to administer the first
dose of Potts's painless cure to his interesting patient that very evening, if she had not already
retired. He was in high good humor. Potts was
a brick ; Potts was a genius. How lucky that he
had happened to go up to college that night ! He
felt as if an incubus were lifted off his mind. No
more pangs of conscience and uncomfortable sense
of being a mean and cruel fellow, for him. Annie

should be glad to be rid of him before he had
ended with her. She should experience a heartfelt relief, instead of a broken heart, on his departure. He could n't help chuckling. He had such
confidence in his nerve and his reticent habit that
his confidence and ability to carry out the scheme
were undoubting, and at its first suggestion he had
felt almost as much relief as if he had already
executed it.

On arriving home, he found Annie sewing alone
in the parlor, and a little offish in manner by way
of indicating her sense of his offense in leaving her
to spend the evening alone.

"Really, Annie," he said, as he sat down and
unfolded the evening paper, " I try to give you all
the time I can spare. If, instead of sulking, you
had taken a piece of paper and calculated how
many hours this week I have managed to give you
my company, you would scarcely have felt like
repining because you could n't see me for an hour
or two this evening."

That was the first gun of the campaign. She
looked up in blank surprise, too much astonished,
for the moment, to be indignant at such a vulgarly
conceited remark from him. Without giving her
time to speak, he proposed to read the newspaper
aloud, and at once began, making a point of selecting the dullest editorials and the flattest items and
witticisms, enlivening them with occasional comments of studied insipidity, and one or two stories,

of which he carefully left out the " nubs." He
was apparently making an unusual effort all the
while to be entertaining, and Annie, finding no
opening for expressing her vexation, finally ex-
cused herself and went upstairs, with no very
angelic expression of countenance.

" Pretty well for a beginning," was Hunt's muttered comment as he laid down the paper.

At breakfast Mr. Gifford asked him : —

" Shall I give you some tongue ? "

Looking around with the air of one saying a
good thing, he replied : —

" Thank you, I have enough of my own."

The silence was painful. Mr. Gifford looked
as if he had lost a near friend. Mrs. Gifford at
length, remembering that Hunt was a guest, forced
a momentary, ghastly smile. Annie was looking
melancholy enough before, but a slight compres-
sion of the lips indicated that she had received the
full effect. Certain degrees of badness in jokes
stamp the joker as a natural inferior in the eyes
of even the most rabid of social levelers. Scarcely
any possible exhibition of depravity gives quite
the sickening sense of disappointment in the per-
petrator imparted by a genuinely bad or stale
joke. Two or more similar sensations coming near
together are multiplied by mutual reverberations
so as to be much more impressive than if they
occurred at considerable intervals. Hunt's tongue
joke not only retroacted to deepen the impression

of vulgarity which his last evening's performance had given Annie, but in turn was made to appear a far more significant indication of his character on account of its sequence to that display.

That evening he made her a little present, having selected as a gift a book of the day of which he had chanced to overhear her express to a third person a particularly cordial detestation. It was decidedly the best book of the year, he said ; he had read it himself. She was obliged to thank him for it, and even to tell one or two polite fibs, which wrenched her terribly, and the memory of which lent a special spite to the vehemence with which she threw the book into a corner on reaching her room. Then she went remorsefully and picked it up again, and after holding it awhile irresolutely, proceeded to hide it away in a far corner of one of the least used drawers of her bureau.

Not sleeping very well that night, she came downstairs next morning just as Hunt was leaving. He kissed his hand to her and called out " Aw revore." At first she was merely puzzled, and smiled, and then it occurred to her that it was doubtless the barbarous way he pronounced *au revoir*, and the smile gave place to an expression of slight nausea. As Hunt well knew, her pet aversion was people who lugged mispronounced French phrases into their conversation under the impression that they imparted a piquant and graceful effect. It was a touch of vulgarity which

inspired her with a violent contempt absurdly
disproportioned to the gravity of the offense. It
had always been a cherished theory of hers that
there were certain offenses in manners which were
keys to character. If persons committed them, it
implied an essential strain of vulgarity in their
dispositions. Judged by this theory, where would
her lover come out?

Hunt managed to get into a political discussion
with Mr. Gifford at table that noon, talking in
a rather supercilious tone, and purposely making
several bad blunders, which Mr. Gifford corrected
rather pointedly. Annie could not help observing
that her lover's conceit and ignorance of the subjects discussed seemed about equal.

" How do you like your book ? " he asked that
evening.

She murmured something confusedly.

" Have n't begun it yet ? " he inquired in surprise. " Well, when once you do, I 'm sure you 'll
not lay it down till it 's finished. And, by the
way, your judgment in literary matters is so good,
I 'd like to get your opinion on the essay I 'm getting up for Commencement. I think it 's rather
the best thing I 've written."

He proceeded to read what purported to be a
sketch of its argument, which proved to be so flat
and vapid that Annie blushed with shame for his
mental poverty, and was fain to cover her chagrin
with a few meaningless comments.

Her mind was the theatre of a struggle between disgust and affection, which may be called ghastly. Had he been openly wicked, she would have known how to give a good account of all disloyal suggestions to desert or forget him. But what could she do against such a cold, creeping thing as this disgust and revulsion of taste, which, like the chills of incipient fever, mingled with every rising pulse of tender feeling? Finally, out of her desperation, she concluded that the fault must be with her; that she was fickle, while he was true. She tried hard to despise herself, and determined to fight down her growing coldness, and reciprocate as it deserved the affection with which he was so lavish. The result of these mental exercises was to impart a humility and constrained cordiality to her air very opposite to its usual piquancy and impulsiveness, and, by a sense of her own shortcomings, to distract her mind from speculation, which she might otherwise have indulged, over the sudden development of so many unpleasant qualities in her lover. Though, indeed, had her speculations been never so active and ingenious, the actual plan on which Hunt was proceeding would probably have lain far beyond the horizon of her conjecture.

Meanwhile, Hunt was straitened for time; only eight or ten days of the term were left, and in that time he must effect Annie's cure, if at all. A slow cure would be much more likely to prove a sure

one, but he must do the best he could in the time
he had. And yet he did not dare to multiply
startling strokes, for fear of bewildering instead
of estranging her, and, possibly, of suggesting suspicion. Stimulated by the emergency, he now
began to put in some very fine work, which, although it may not be very impressive in description, was probably more effective than any other
part of his tactics. Under guise of appearing
particularly attentive and devoted, he managed to
offend Annie's taste and weary her patience in
every way that ingenuity could suggest. His very
manifestations of affection were so associated with
some affectation or exhibition of bad taste, as always to leave an unpleasant impression on her
mind. He took as much pains to avoid saying
tolerably bright or sensible things in his conversation as people generally do to say them. In
all respects he just reversed the rules of conduct
suggested by the ordinary motive of a desire to
ingratiate one's self with others.

And by virtue of a rather marked endowment
of that delicate sympathy with others' tastes and
feelings which underlies good manners, he was
able to make himself far more unendurable to
Annie than a less sympathetic person could have
done. Evening after evening she went to her
room feeling as if she were covered with pin-pricks,
from a score of little offenses to her fastidious
taste which he had managed to commit. His

thorough acquaintance with her, and knowledge of her æsthetic standards in every respect, enabled him to operate with a perfect precision that did not waste a stroke.

It must not be supposed that it was altogether without sharp twinges of compunction, and occasional impulses to throw off his disguise and enjoy the bliss of reconciliation, that he pursued this cold-blooded policy. He never could have carried it so far, had he not been prepared by a long and painful period of self-reproach on account of his entanglement. It was, however, chiefly at the outset that he had felt like weakening. As soon as she ceased to seem shocked or surprised at his disclosures of insipidity or conceit, it became comparatively easy work to make them. So true is it that it is the fear of the first shocked surprise of others, rather than of their deliberate reprobation, which often deters us from exhibitions of unworthiness.

In connection with this mental and moral masquerade, he adopted several changes in his dress, buying some clothes of very glaring patterns, and blossoming out in particularly gaudy neckties and flashy jewelry. Lest Annie should be puzzled to account for such a sudden access of depravity, he explained that his mother had been in the habit of selecting some of his lighter toilet articles for him, but this term he was trying for himself. Did n't she think his taste was good? He also slightly changed the cut of his hair and whiskers, to affect a foppish air, his theory being that all these external alterations would help out the effect of being a quite different person from the George Hunt with whom she had fallen in love.

Lou Roberts was Annie's confidante, older than she, much more dignified, and of the reticent sort to which the mercurial and loquacious naturally tend to reveal their secrets. She knew all that Annie knew, dreamed, or hoped about Hunt; but had never happened to meet him, much to the annoyance of Annie, who had longed inexpressibly for the time when Lou should have seen him, and she herself be able to enjoy the luxury of hearing his praises from her lips. One evening it chanced that Lou called with a gentleman while Hunt had gone out to rest himself, after some pretty arduous masquerading, by a little unconstrained intercourse with the fellows up at college. As he returned home, at about half-past nine, he heard voices through the open windows, and guessed who the callers were.

As he entered the room, despite the disenchanting experiences of the past week, it was with a certain pretty agitation that Annie rose to introduce him, and she looked blank enough when, without waiting for her offices, he bowed with a foppish air to Lou and murmured a salutation.

" What, are you acquainted already ? " exclaimed Annie.

" I certainly did not know that we were," said Lou coldly, not thinking it possible that this flashily dressed youth, with such an enormous watch-chain and insufferable manners, could be Annie's hero.

" Ah, very likely not," he replied carelessly, adding with an explanatory smile that took in all the group: " Ladies' faces are so much alike that, 'pon my soul, unless there is something distinguished about them, I don't know whether I know them or not. I depend on them to tell me; fortunately they never forget gentlemen."

Miss Roberts's face elongated into a freezing stare. Annie stood there in a sort of stupor till Hunt said briskly: —

" Well, Annie, are you going to introduce this lady to me? "

As she almost inaudibly pronounced their names, he effusively extended his hand, which was not taken, and exclaimed: —

" Lou Roberts! is it possible? Excuse me if I call you Lou. Annie talks of you so much that I feel quite familiar."

" Do you know, Miss Roberts," he continued, seating himself close beside her, " I'm quite prepared to like you? "

" Indeed! " was all that young lady could manage to articulate.

" Yes," continued he, with the manner of one giving a flattering reassurance, " Annie has told me so much in your favor that, if half is true, we shall get on together excellently. Such girl friendships as yours and hers are so charming."

Miss Roberts glanced at Annie, and seeing that her face glowed with embarrassment, smothered her indignation, and replied with a colorless " Yes."

" The only drawback," continued Hunt, who manifestly thought he was making himself very agreeable, " is that such bosom friends always tell each other all their affairs, which of course involve the affairs of all their friends also. Now I suppose," he added, with a knowing grin and something like a wink, " that what you don't know about me is n't worth knowing."

" You ought to know, certainly," said Miss Roberts.

" Not that I blame you," he went on, ignoring her sarcasm. " There 's no confidence betrayed, for when I 'm talking with a lady, I always adapt my remarks to the ears of her next friend. It prevents misunderstandings."

Miss Roberts made no reply, and the silence attracted notice to the pitiable little dribble of forced talk with which Annie was trying to keep the other gentleman's attention from the exhibition Hunt was making of himself. The latter, after a pause long enough to intimate that he thought it was Miss Roberts's turn to say something, again took up the conversation, as if bound to be entertaining at any cost.

"Annie and I were passing your house the other day. What a queer little box it is! I should think you'd be annoyed by the howlings of that church next door. The —— are so noisy."

"I am a —— myself," said Miss Roberts, regarding him crushingly.

Hunt, of course, knew that, and had advisedly selected her denomination for his strictures. But he replied as if a little confused by his blunder:—

"I beg your pardon. You don't look like one."

"How do they usually look?" she asked sharply.

"Why, it is generally understood that they are rather vulgar, I believe, but you, I am sure, look like a person of culture." He said this as if he thought he were conveying a rather neat compliment. Indignant as she was, Miss Roberts's strongest feeling was compassion for Annie, and she bit her lips and made no reply.

After a moment's silence, Hunt asked her how she liked his goatee. It was a new way of cutting his whiskers, and young ladies were generally close observers and therefore good judges of such matters. Annie, finding it impossible to keep up even the pretense of talking any longer, sat helplessly staring at the floor, and waiting in nerveless despair for what he would say next, fairly hating Lou because she did not go.

"What's come over you, Annie?" asked Hunt briskly. "Are you talked out so soon? I suppose she is holding back to give you a chance to make my acquaintance, Miss Roberts, or do let me call you Lou. You must improve your opportunity, for she will want to know your opinion of me. May I hope it will prove not wholly unfavorable?" This last was with a killing smile.

"I had no idea it was so late. We must be going," said Miss Roberts, rising. She had been lingering, in the hope that something would happen to leave a more pleasant impression of Hunt's appearance, but seeing that matters were drifting from bad to worse, she hastened to break off the painful scene. Annie rose silently without saying a word, and avoided Lou's eyes as she kissed her good-by.

"Must you go?" Hunt said. "I'm sure you would not be in such haste if you knew how rarely it is that my engagements leave me free to devote an evening to the ladies. You might call on Annie a dozen times and not meet me."

As soon as the callers had gone, Hunt picked up the evening paper and sat down to glance it over, remarking lightly as he did so: —

"Rather nice girl, your friend, though she does n't seem very talkative."

Annie made no reply, and he looked up.

"What on earth are you staring at me in such an extraordinary manner for?"

Was he then absolutely unconscious of the figure he had made of himself?

" You are not vexed because I went out and left you in the early part of the evening? " he said anxiously.

" Oh, no, indeed," she wearily replied.

She sat there with trembling lip and a red spot in each cheek, looking at him as he read the paper unconcernedly, till she could bear it no longer, and then silently rose and glided out of the room. Hunt heard her running upstairs as fast as she could, and closing and locking her chamber door.

Next day he did not see her till evening, when she was exceedingly cold and distant, and evidently very much depressed. After bombarding her with grieved and reproachful glances for some time, he came over to her side, they two having been left alone, and said, with affectionate raillery : —

" I 'd no idea you were so susceptible to the green-eyed monster."

She looked at him, astonished quite out of her reserve.

" What on earth do you mean ? "

" Oh, you need n't pretend to misunderstand," he replied, with a knowing nod. " Don't you suppose I saw how vexed you were last night when your dear friend Miss Roberts was trying to flirt with me? But you need n't have minded so much. She is n't my style at all."

There was something so perfectly maddening in this cool assumption that her bitter chagrin on his account was a fond jealousy, that she fairly choked

with exasperation, and shook herself away from
his caress as if a snake had stung her. Her thin
nostrils vibrated, her red lips trembled with scorn,
and her black eyes flashed ominously. He had
only seen them lighten with love before, and it
was a very odd sensation to see them for the first
time blazing with anger, and that against himself.
Affecting an offended tone, he said : —

" This is really too absurd, Annie," and left the
room as if in a pet, just in time to escape the outburst he knew was coming. She sat in the parlor
with firm-set lips till quite a late hour that evening, hoping that he would come down and give
her a chance to set him right with an indignant
explanation. So humiliating to her did his misunderstanding seem, that it was intolerable he should
retain it a moment longer, and she felt almost
desperate enough to go and knock at his door
and correct it. Far too clever a strategist to risk
an encounter that evening, he sat in his room
comfortably smoking and attending to arrears of
correspondence, aware that he was supposed by
her to be sulking desperately all the while. He
knew that her feeling was anger and not grief, and
while, had it been the latter, he would have been
thoroughly uncomfortable from sympathy, he only
chuckled as he figured to himself her indignation.
At that very moment, she was undoubtedly clench-
ing her pretty little fists, and breathing fast with
impotent wrath, in the room below. Ah, well, let

her heart lie in a pickle of good strong disgust
overnight, and it would strike in a good deal more
effectually than if she were allowed to · clear her
mind by an indignant explanation on the spot.

The following day he bore himself toward her
with the slightly distant air of one who considers
himself aggrieved, and attempted no approaches.
In the evening, which was her first opportunity,
she came to him and said in a tone in which, by
this time, weariness and disgust had taken the
place of indignation : —

"You were absurdly mistaken in thinking that
Miss Roberts was trying to flirt " —

"Bless your dear, jealous heart!" interrupted
Hunt laughingly, with an air of patronizing affection. "I'd no idea you minded it so much.
There, there ! Let's not allude to this matter
again. No, no! not another word!" he gayly insisted, putting his hand over her mouth as she was
about to make another effort to be heard.

He was determined not to hear anything, and
she had to leave it so. It was with surprise that
she observed how indifferently she finally acqui-
esced in being so cruelly misunderstood by him.
In the deadened state of her feelings, she was not
then able to appreciate the entire change in the
nature of her sentiments which that indifference
showed. Love, though rooted in the past, depends
upon the surrounding atmosphere for the breath of
continued life, and he had surrounded her with the

stifling vapors of disgust until her love had succumbed and withered. She found that his exhibitions of conceit and insipidity did not affect her
in the same way as before. Her sensations were
no longer sharp and poignant, but chiefly a dull
shame and sense of disgrace that she had loved
him. She met his attentions with a coldly passive
manner, which gave him the liveliest satisfaction.
The cure was succeeding past all expectation; but
he had about time for one more stroke, which
would make a sure thing of it. He prepared the
way by dropping hints that he had been writing
some verses of late; and finally, with the evident
idea that she would be flattered, gave out that his
favorite theme was her own charms, and that she
might, perhaps, before long receive some tributes
from his muse. Her protests he laughed away as
the affectations of modesty.

Now Hunt had never actually written a line of
verse in his life, and had no intention of beginning.
He was simply preparing a grand move. From the
poet's corner of rural newspapers, and from comic
collections, he clipped several specimens of the crud-
est sort of sentimental trash in rhyme. These he
took to the local newspaper, and arranged for their
insertion at double advertising rates. A few days
later, he bustled into the parlor, smirking in his
most odious manner, and, coming up to Annie,
thrust an open newspaper before her, marked in
one corner to call attention to several stanzas

" Written for the ' Express.'
" To A——E G——D."

With sinking of heart she took the paper, after
ineffectually trying to refuse it, and Hunt sat down
before her with a supremely complacent expression,
to await her verdict. With a faint hope that the
verses might prove tolerable, she glanced down the
lines. It is enough to say that they were the very
worst which Hunt, after great industry, had been
able to find; and there he was waiting, just the
other side the paper, in a glow of expectant vanity,
to receive her acknowledgments.

" Well, what do you think of it? You need n't
try to hide your blushes. You deserve every word
of it, you know, Miss Modesty," he said gayly.

" It 's very nice," replied Annie, making a desperate effort.

" I thought you 'd like it," he said, with self-
satisfied assurance. " It 's queer that a fellow can't
lay on the praise too thick to please a woman. By
the way, I sent around a copy to Miss Roberts,
signed with my initials. I thought you 'd like to
have her see it."

This last remark he called out after her as she
was leaving the room, and he was not mistaken in
fancying that it would complete her demoralization. During the next week or two he several
times brought her copies of the local paper containing equally execrable effusions, till finally she
mustered courage to tell him that she would rather

he would not publish any more verses about her.
He seemed rather hurt at this, but respected her
feelings, and after that she used to find, hid in her
books and music, manuscript sonnets which he had
laboriously copied out of his comic collections.   It
was considerable trouble, but on the whole he was
inclined to think it paid, and it did, especially
when he culminated by fitting music to several of
the most mawkish effusions, and insisting on her
playing and singing them to him.   As the poor
girl, who felt that out of common politeness she
could not refuse, toiled wearily through this martyrdom, writhing with secret disgust at every line,
Hunt, lolling in an easy-chair behind her, was generally indulging in a series of horrible grimaces
and convulsions of silent laughter, which sometimes left tears in his eyes, — to convince Annie,
when she turned around to him, that his sentiment
was at least genuine if vulgar.   Had she happened
on one of these occasions to turn a moment before
she did, the resulting tableau would have been
worth seeing.

Hunt had determined to both crown and cru-
cially test the triumph of Potts's cure in Annie's
case by formally offering himself to her.   He calculated of course that she was now certain to reject
him, and that was a satisfaction which he thought
he fairly owed her.   She would feel better for it,
he argued, and be more absolutely sure not to regard herself as in any sense jilted, and that would

make his conscience clearer. Yes, she should certainly have his scalp to hang at her girdle, for he believed, as many do, that next to having a man's heart a woman enjoys having his scalp, while many prefer it. Six weeks ago he would have been horrified at the audacity of the idea. His utmost ambition then was to break a little the force of her disappointment at his departure. But the unexpected fortune that had attended his efforts had advanced his standard of success, until nothing would now satisfy him but to pop the question and be refused.

And still, as the day approached which he had set for the desperate venture, he began to get very nervous. He thought he had a sure thing if ever a fellow had, but women were so cursedly unaccountable. Supposing she should take it into her head to accept him! No logic could take account of a woman's whimsies. Then what a pretty fix he would have got himself into, just by a foolhardy freak! But there was a strain of Norse blood in Hunt, and in spite of occasional touches of ague, the risk of the scheme had in itself a certain fascination for him. And yet he could n't help wishing he had carried out a dozen desperate devices for disgusting her with him, which at the time had seemed to him too gross to be safe from suspicion.

The trouble was that since he loved her no more he had lost the insight which love only gives into the feelings of another. Then her every touch and

look and word was eloquent to his senses as to the
precise state of her feeling toward him, but now
he was dull and insensitive to such direct intuition.
He could not longer feel, but could only argue as
to how she might be minded toward him, and this it
was which caused him so much trepidation, in spite
of so many reasons why he should be confident of
the result. Argument as to another's feelings is
such a wretched substitute for the intuition of sympathy.

Finally, on the evening before the day on which
he was to offer himself, the last of his stay at the
Giffords', he got into such a panic that, determined
to clinch the assurance of his safety, he asked her
to play a game of cards, and then managed that
she should see him cheat two or three times. The
recollection of the cold disgust on her face as he
bade her good-evening was so reassuring that he
went to bed and slept like a child, in the implicit
confidence that four horses could n't drag that girl
into an engagement with him the next day.

It was not till the latter part of the afternoon
that he could catch her alone long enough to trans-
act his little business with her. Anticipating, or
at least apprehending his design, she took the greatest pains to avoid meeting him, or to have her mother with her when she did. She would have given
almost anything to escape his offer. Of course she
could reject it, but fastidious persons do not like
to have unpleasant objects put on their plates, even

if they have not necessarily to eat them. But her special reason was that the scene would freshly bring up and emphasize the whole wretched history of her former infatuation and its miserable ending, — an experience every thought of which was full of shame and strong desire for the cleansing of forgetfulness. He finally cornered her in the parlor alone. As she saw him approaching and realized that there was no escape, she turned and faced him with her small figure drawn to its full height, compressed lips, pale face, and eyes that plainly said, "Now have it over with as soon as possible." One hand resting on the table was clenched over a book. The other, hanging by her side, tightly grasped a handkerchief.

"Do you know I've been trying to get a chance to speak with you alone all day?" he said.

"Have you?" she replied in a perfectly inexpressive tone.

"Can't you guess what I wanted to say?"

"I'm not good at conundrums."

"I see you will not help me," he went on, and then added quickly, "it's a short story; will you be my wife?"

As he said the words, he felt as the lion-tamer does when he puts his head in the lion's jaws. He expects to take it out again, but if the lion should take a notion — His suspense was, however, of the shortest possible duration, for instantly, like a reviving sprinkle on a fainting face, the words fell on his ear : —

"I thank you for the honor, but I'm sure we are not suited."

Annie had conned her answer on many a sleepless pillow, and had it by heart. It came so glibly, although in such a constrained and agitated voice, that he instantly knew it must have been long cut and dried.

It was now only left for him to do a decent amount of urging, and then acquiesce with dignified melancholy and go off laughing in his sleeve. What is he thinking of to stand there gazing at her downcast face as if he were daft?

A strange thing had happened to him. The sweet familiarity of each detail in the *petite* figure before him was impressing his mind as never before, now that he had achieved his purpose of putting it beyond the possibility of his own possession. The little hands he had held so often in the old days, conning each curve and dimple, reckoning them more his hands than were his own, and far more dearly so; the wavy hair he had kissed so fondly and delighted to touch; the deep dark eyes under their long lashes, like forest lakes seen through environing thickets, eyes that he had found his home in through so long and happy a time, — why, they were his! Of course he had never meant to really forfeit them, to lose them, and let them go to anybody else. The idea was preposterous, — was laughable. It was indeed the first time it had occurred to him in that light. He had only thought of her as losing him; scarcely at all of himself as losing her. During the whole time he had been putting himself in her place so constantly that he had failed sufficiently to fully canvass the situation from his own point of view. Wholly absorbed in estranging her from him, he had done nothing to estrange himself from her.

It was rather with astonishment and even an appreciation of the absurd, than any serious apprehension, that he now suddenly saw how he had stultified himself, and come near doing himself a fatal injury. For knowing that her present estrangement was wholly his work, it did not occur to him but that he could undo it as easily as he had done it. A word would serve the purpose and make it all right again. Indeed, his revulsion of feeling so altered the aspect of everything that he quite forgot that any explanation at all was necessary, and, after gazing at her for a few moments while his eyes, wet with a tenderness new and deliciously sweet, roved fondly from her head to her little slipper, doating on each feature, he just put out his arms to take her with some old familiar phrase of love on his lips.

She sprang away, her eye flashing with anger.

He looked so much taken aback and discomfited that she paused in mere wonder, as she was about to rush from the room.

"Annie, what does this mean?" he stammered.

"Oh, yes, — why, — my darling, don't you know,

— did n't you guess, — it was all a joke, — a stupid joke? I 've just been pretending."

It was not a very lucid explanation, but she understood, though only to be plunged in greater amazement.

" But what for?" she murmured.

" I did n't know I loved you," he said slowly, as if recalling with difficulty, and from a great distance, his motives, "and I thought it was kind to cure you of your love for me by pretending to be a fool. I think I must have been crazy, don't you?" and he smiled in a dazed, deprecating way.

Her face from being very pale began to flush. First a red spot started out in either cheek; then they spread till they covered the cheeks; next her forehead took a roseate hue, and down her neck the tide of color rushed, and she stood there before him a glowing statue of outraged womanhood, while in the midst her eyes sparkled with scorn.

" You wanted to cure me," she said at last, in slow, concentrated tones, " and you have succeeded. You have insulted me as no woman was ever insulted before."

She paused as if to control herself; for her voice trembled with the last words. She shivered, and her bosom heaved once or twice convulsively. Her features quivered; scorching tears of shame rushed to her eyes, and she burst out hysterically: —

" For pity's sake never let me see you again !"

And then he found himself alone.

A LOVE STORY REVERSED

I

THE golden hands of the parlor clock point glimmeringly to an hour after midnight, and the house is still. The gas is turned almost out, but the flickering of the dying sea-coal fire in the grate fitfully illumines the forms and faces of two young women, who are seated before it, talking earnestly in low tones. It is apparent from their costumes that they have been spending the evening out.

The fair girl in the low chair, gazing pensively into the fire, is Maud Elliott, the daughter of the house. Not generally called handsome, her features are good and well balanced, and her face is altogether a sweet and wholesome one. She is rather tall, and the most critical admit that she has a fine figure. Her eyes are blue, and their clear, candid expression indicates an unusually sincere and simple character. But, unfortunately, it is only her friends who are fully conversant with the expression of her eyes, for she is very shy. Shyness in little people is frequently piquant, but its effect in girls of the Juno style is too often that of awkwardness. Her friends call Maud Elliott stately; those who do not like her call her stiff;

while indifferent persons speak of her as rather too
reserved and dignified in manner to be pleasing.
In fact, her excess of dignity is merely the cloak
of her shyness, and nobody knows better than she
that there is too much of it. Those who know her
at all well know that she is not dull, but with mere
acquaintances she often passes for that. Only her
intimate friends are aware what wit and intelligence, what warmth and strength of feeling, her
coldness when in company conceals.

No one better understands this, because no one
knows her better or has known her longer, than
her present companion before the fire, Lucy Merritt. They were roommates and bosom friends at
boarding-school; and Lucy, who recently has been
married, is now on her first visit to her friend since
that event. She is seated on a hassock, with her
hands clasped over her knees, looking up at Maud,
— an attitude well suited to her *petite* figure. She
is going home on the morrow, or rather on the
day already begun; and this fact, together with
the absorbing nature of the present conversation,
accounts for the lateness of the session.

" And so, Maud," she is saying, while she regards
her friend with an expression at once sympathetic
and amused, — " and so that is what has been making your letters so dismal lately. I fancied that
nothing less could suggest such melancholy views
of life. The truth is, I came on this visit as much
as anything to find out about him. He is a good-
looking fellow, certainly; and, from what little

chance I had to form an opinion to-night, seems
sensible enough to make it quite incredible that he
should not be in love with such a girl in a thousand as you. Are you quite sure he is n't?"

"You had a chance to judge to-night," replied
Maud, with a hard little laugh. "You overheard
our conversation. 'Good-evening, Miss Elliott;
jolly party, is n't it?' That was all he had to say
to me, and quite as much as usual. Of course we
are old acquaintances, and he 's always pleasant
and civil: he could n't be anything else; but he
wastes mighty little time on me. I don't blame
him for preferring other girls' society. He would
show very little taste if he did not enjoy Ella
Perry's company better than that of a tongue-tied
thing like me. She is a thousand times prettier
and wittier and more graceful than I am."

"Nonsense," exclaimed Lucy. "She is a flirt
and a conceited little minx. She is not to be mentioned the same day with you; and he would think
so, if he could only get to know you. But how in
the world is he ever going to? Why, you seem to
be shyer than ever, poor dear. You were actually
distant, almost chilling, in your manner towards
him to-night, although I know you did n't mean
to be."

"I know it. Don't I know it!" groaned Maud.
"I always am shyer and stiffer with him than with
any one else. O Lucy! you can't guess what a
dreadful thing it is to be shy. It is as if you were

surrounded by a fog, which benumbs you, and chills all who approach you. I dare say he thinks that I actually dislike him. I could not blame him if he did. And I can't help it. I could never make him understand anything else, unless I told him in so many words."

The tears filled her eyes as she spoke, and hung heavy on the lashes. Lucy took one of her hands in both of hers, and pressed and stroked it caressingly.

"I know you could n't, poor dear, I know you could n't," she said ; "and you cannot tell him in so many words because, forsooth, you are a woman. I often think, Maud, what a heap of trouble would be saved if women, when they cannot make themselves understood in other ways, were allowed to speak out as men do, without fear or reproach. Some day they will, when the world gets wiser, — at least I think so. Why should a woman have to hide her love, as if it were a disgraceful secret? Why is it any more a disgrace to her than to a man ?"

"I can't quite see what good it would do me," said Maud, "even if women could 'speak out,' as you say. If a man did n't care for one already, I can't see how it would make him know that one cared for him. I should think she would prefer to keep her secret."

"That is n't what men do," replied Lucy. "If they have such a secret, they tell it right away, and

that is why they succeed. The way half the women
are induced to fall in love is by being told the men
are in love with them ; you know that."

"But men are different," suggested Maud.

"Not a bit of it : they 're more so, if anything,"
was the oracular response of the young wife.
"Possibly there are men," she continued, — "the
story-tellers say so, anyhow, — who are attracted
by repulsion and warmed by coldness, who like resistance for the pleasure of overcoming it. There
must be a spice of the tyrant in such men. I
would n't want to marry one of them. Fortunately, they 're not common. I 've noticed that
love, like lightning, generally takes the path of
least resistance with men as well as women. Just
suppose now, in your case, that Mr. Burton had
followed us home, and had overheard this conversation from behind that door."

"No, no," she added laughing, as Maud looked
around apprehensively ; "he is n't there. But if
he had been there and had overheard you own that
you were pining for him, what a lucky chance it
would have been! If he, or any other man, once
knew that a magnificent girl like you had done him
the honor to fall in love with him, half the battle
would be won, or I 'm no judge of men. But such
lucky eavesdropping only happens in stories and
plays ; and for lack of it this youth is in a fair way
to marry a chit of a girl who does not think half
so much of him as you do, and of whom he will

never think a quarter what he would of you. He is not, probably, entirely stupid either. All he wants, very likely, is just a hint as to where his true happiness lies : but, being a woman, you can't give it in words; and, being Maud Elliott, you can't give it in any other way, if you died for it. Really, Maud, the canon which makes it a woman's duty to be purely passive in love is exasperating, especially as it does not represent what anybody really believes, but only what they pretend to believe. Everybody knows that unrequited love comes as often to women as to men. Why, then, should n't they have an equal chance to seek requital ? Why have not they the same right to look out for the happiness of their lives by all honorable means that men have? Surely it is far more to them to marry the men they love than to a man to marry any particular woman. It seems to me that making suitable matches is not such an easy matter that society can afford to leave the chief part of it to the stupider sex, giving women merely the right of veto. To be sure, even now women who are artful enough manage to evade the prohibition laid on their lips and make their preference known. I am proud to say that I have a royal husband, who would never have looked my way if I had not set out to make him do so ; and if I do say it, who should n't, I flatter myself he has a better wife than he could have picked out without my help. There are plenty of women who can say the same thing ; but, unluckily, it is the best sort of women, girls like you, — simple, sincere, noble, without arts of any sort, — who can't do this. On them the etiquette that forbids women to reveal their hearts except by subterfuge operates as a total disability. They can only sit with folded hands, looking on, pretending not to mind, while their husbands are run away with by others."

Maud took up the poker and carefully arranged the coals under the grate in a heap. Then she said : " Suppose a girl did what you 've been speaking of. I mean, suppose she really said such a thing to a man, — said that she cared for him, or anything like that, — what do you suppose he would think of her? Don't you fancy she would be in danger of making him think very cheaply of her ? "

" If she thought he were that kind of a man," replied Lucy, " I can't understand her ever falling in love with him. Of course, I 'm not saying that he would necessarily respond by falling in love with her. She would have to take her chance of that ; but I 'm sure, if he were a gentleman, she need have no fear of his thinking unworthily of her. If I had spoken to Dick in that way, even if he had never wanted to marry me, I know he would have had a soft spot for me in his heart all the rest of his life, out of which even his wife would not have quite crowded me. Why, how do we think of men whom we have refused ? Do we

despise them? Do we ridicule them? Some girls
may, but they are not ladies. A low fellow might
laugh at a woman who revealed a fondness for him
which he did not return; but a gentleman, never.
Her secret would be safe with him."

"Girls!" It was the voice of Mrs. Elliott speaking from the upper hall. "Do you know how late
it is? It is after one o'clock."

"I suppose we might as well go to bed," said
Lucy. "There's no use sitting up to wait for
women to get their rights. They won't get them
to-night, I dare say; though, mark my word, some
day they will."

"This affair of yours may come out all right
yet," she said hopefully, as they went upstairs together. "If it does not, you can console yourself
with thinking that people in general, and especially
girls, never know what is good for them till afterward. Do you remember that summer I was at
the beach, what a ninny I made of myself over
that little Mr. Parker? How providential it was
for me that he did not reciprocate. It gives me
the cold shivers when I think what might have
become of me if he had proposed."

At the door of her room Lucy said again: "Remember, you are to come to me in New York for a
long visit soon. Perhaps you will find there are
other people in the world then."

Maud smiled absently, and kissed her good-night.
She seemed preoccupied, and did not appear to

have closely followed what her lively friend was saying.

The following afternoon, as she was walking home after seeing Lucy on the cars, she met a gentleman who lifted his hat to her. It was Arthur Burton. His office was on the one main street of the small New England city which is the scene of these events, and when out walking or shopping Maud often met him. There was therefore nothing at all extraordinary in the fact of their meeting. What was extraordinary was its discomposing effect upon her on this particular afternoon. She had been absorbed a moment before in a particularly brown study, taking no more notice of surrounding objects and persons than was necessary to avoid accidents. On seeing him she started perceptibly, and forthwith became a striking study in red. She continued to blush so intensely after he had passed that, catching sight of her crimson cheeks in a shop window, she turned down a side street and took a quieter way home.

There was nothing particularly remarkable about Arthur Burton. Fortunately there does not need to be anything remarkable about young men to induce very charming girls to fall in love with them. He was just a good-looking fellow, with agreeable manners and average opinions. He was regarded as a very promising young man, and was quite a favorite among the young ladies. If he noticed Maud's confusion on meeting him, he certainly did

not think of associating it in any way with himself.
For although they had been acquaintances these
many years, and belonged to the same social set,
he had never entertained the first sentimental fancy
concerning her. So far as she had impressed him
at all, it was as a thoroughly nice girl, of a good
family, not bad-looking, but rather dull in society,
and with very little facility in conversation; at
least he had always found it hard to talk with her.

Ten days or a fortnight after Lucy Merritt's departure there was a little party at Ella Perry's, and
both Arthur Burton and Maud were present. It
was the custom of the place for the young men to
escort the girls home after evening entertainments,
and when the couples were rightly assorted, the walk
home was often the most agreeable part of the
evening. Although they were not engaged, Arthur
imagined that he was in love with Ella Perry, and
she had grown into the habit of looking upon him
as her particular knight. Towards the end of the
evening he jestingly asked her whom he should go
home with, since he could not that evening be her
escort.

"Maud Elliott," promptly suggested Ella, selecting the girl of those present in her opinion least
likely to prove a diverting companion. So it
chanced that Arthur offered his company to Maud.

It struck him, as she came downstairs with her
wraps on, that she was looking remarkably pale.
She had worn a becoming color during the even-

ing, but she seemed to have lost it in the dressing-room. As they walked away from the house Arthur began, to the best of his ability, to make himself agreeable, but with very poor success. Not only was Maud, as usual, a feeble contributor of original matter, but her random answers showed that she paid little attention to what he was saying. He was mentally registering a vow never again to permit himself to be committed to a tête-à-tête with her, when she abruptly broke the silence which had succeeded his conversational efforts. Her voice was curiously unsteady, and she seemed at first to have some difficulty in articulating, and had to go back and repeat her first words. What she said was: —

" It was very good in you to come home with me to-night. It is a great pleasure to me."

" You 're ironical this evening, Miss Elliott," he replied, laughing, and the least bit nettled.

It was bore enough doing the polite to a girl who had nothing on her mind without being gibed by her to boot.

" I 'm not ironical," she answered. " I should make poor work at irony. I meant just what I said."

" The goodness was on your part in letting me come," he said, mollified by the unmistakable sincerity of her tone, but somewhat embarrassed withal at the decidedly flat line of remark she had chosen.

" Oh, no," she replied; " the goodness was not
on my side. I was only too glad of your company,
and might as well own it. Indeed, I will confess
to telling a fib to one young man who offered to
see me home, merely because I hoped the idea of
doing so would occur to you."

This plump admission of partiality for his society
fairly staggered Arthur. Again he thought, " She
must be quizzing me; " and, to make sure, stole
a sidelong glance at her. Her eyes were fixed
straight ahead, and the pallor and the tense expression of her face indicated that she was laboring under strong excitement. She certainly did
not look like one in a quizzing mood.

" I am very much flattered," he managed to say.

" I don't know whether you feel so or not," she
replied. " I'm afraid you don't feel flattered at
all, but I — I wanted to — tell you."

The pathetic tremor of her voice lent even
greater significance to her words than in themselves they would have conveyed.

She was making a dead set at him. There was
not a shadow of doubt any longer about that. As
the full realization of his condition flashed upon
him, entirely alone with her and a long walk before them, the strength suddenly oozed out of his
legs, he felt distinctly cold about the spine, and
the perspiration started out on his forehead. His
tongue clung to the roof of his mouth, and he could
only abjectly wonder what was coming next. It

appeared that nothing more was coming. A dead
silence lasted for several blocks. Every block
seemed to Arthur a mile long, as if he were walking in a hasheesh dream. He felt that she was expecting him to say something, to make some sort
of response to her advances; but what response,
in Heaven's name, could he make! He really
could not make love. He had none to make ; and
had never dreamed of making any to Maud Elliott,
of all girls. Yet the idea of letting her suppose
him such an oaf as not to understand her, or not to
appreciate the honor a lady's preference did him,
was intolerable. He could not leave it so.

Finally, with a vague idea of a compromise between the impossible alternative of making love to
her, which he could n't, and seeming an insensible
boor, which he would n't, he laid his disengaged
hand upon hers as it rested on his arm. It was
his intention to apply to it a gentle pressure, which,
while committing him to nothing, might tend to
calm her feelings and by its vaguely reassuring
influence help to stave off a crisis for the remainder
of their walk. He did not, however, succeed in
carrying out the scheme ; for at the moment of
contact her hand eluded his, as quicksilver glides
from the grasp. There was no hint of coquettish
hesitation in its withdrawal. She snatched it
away as if his touch had burned her ; and although
she did not at the same time wholly relinquish
his arm, that was doubtless to avoid making the

situation, on the street as they were, too awkward.

A moment before only concerned to evade her apparent advances, Arthur found himself in the position of one under rebuke for offering an unwarranted familiarity to a lady. There was no question that he had utterly misconstrued her previous conduct. It was very strange that he could have been such a fool; but he was quite too dazed to disentangle the evidence just then, and there was no doubt about the fact.

"Pardon me," he stammered, too much overcome with confusion and chagrin to be able to judge whether it would have been better to be silent.

The quickness with which the reply came showed that she had been on the point of speaking herself.

"You need not ask my pardon," she said. Her tones quivered with excitement and her utterance was low and swift. " I don't blame you in the least, after the way I have talked to you to-night. But I did not mean that you should think lightly of me. I have said nothing right, nothing that I meant to. What I wanted to have you understand was that I care for you very much." Her voice broke here, but she caught her breath and went right on. "I wanted you to know it somehow, and since I could not make you know it by ways clever girls might, I thought I would tell

you plainly. It really amounts to the same thing;
don't you think so? and I know you 'll keep my
secret. You need n't say anything. I know you 've
nothing to say and may never have. That makes
no difference. You owe me nothing merely because I care for you. Don't pity me. I 'm not
so much ashamed as you 'd suppose. It all seems
so natural when it 's once said. You need n't be
afraid of me. I shall never say this again or
trouble you at all. Only be a little good to me;
that 's all."

She delivered this little speech almost in one
breath, with headlong, explosive utterance, as if it
were something she had to go through with, cost
what it might, and only wanted somehow to get
out the words, regardless, for the time, of their
manner or effect. She ended with an hysterical
sob, and Arthur felt her hand tremble on his arm
as she struggled with an emotion that threatened
to overcome her. But it was over almost instantly;
and without giving him a chance to speak, she
exclaimed, with an entire alteration of tone and
manner : —

"Did you see that article in the ' Gazette ' this
morning about the craze for collecting pottery
which has broken out in the big cities? Do you
suppose it will reach here? What do you think
of it?"

Now it was perfectly true, as she had told him,
that Arthur had nothing whatever to say in re-

sponse to the declaration she had made; but all the same it is possible, if she had not just so abruptly diverted the conversation, that he would then and there have placed himself and all his worldly goods at her disposal. He would have done this, although five minutes before he had had no more notion of marrying her than the Emperor of China's daughter, merely because every manly instinct cried out against permitting a nice girl to protest her partiality for him without meeting her half-way. Afterward, when he realized how near he had come to going over the verge of matrimony, it was with such reminiscent terror as chills the blood of the awakened sleep-walker looking up at the dizzy ridge-pole he has trodden with but a hair's breadth between him and eternity.

During the remainder of the way to Maud's door the conversation upon pottery, the weather, and miscellaneous topics was incessant, — almost breathless, in fact. Arthur did not know what he was talking about, and Maud probably no better what she was saying, but there was not a moment's silence. A stranger meeting them would have thought, " What a remarkably jolly couple ! "

" I 'm much obliged for your escort," said Maud, as she stood upon her doorstep.

" Not at all. Great pleasure, I 'm sure."

" Good-evening."

" Good-evening." And she disappeared within the door.

Arthur walked away with a slow, mechanical step. His fallen jaw, open mouth, and generally idiotic expression of countenance would have justified his detention by any policeman who might have met him, on suspicion of being a feeble-minded person escaped from custody. Turning the first corner, he kept on with the same dragging step till he came to a vacant lot. Then, as if he were too feeble to get any farther, he stopped and leaned his back against the fence. Bracing his legs before him so as to serve as props, he thrust his hands deep in his pockets, and raising his eyes appealingly to the stars, ejaculated, " Proposed to, by Jove!" A period of profound introspection followed, and then he broke forth: " Well, I'll be hanged!" emphasizing each word with a slow nod. Then he began to laugh, — not noisily; scarcely audibly, indeed; but with the deep, unctuous chuckle of one who gloats over some exquisitely absurd situation, some jest of many facets, each contributing its ray of humor.

Yet, if this young man had tremblingly confessed his love to a lady, he would have expected her to take it seriously.

Nevertheless, let us not be too severe with him for laughing. It was what the average young man probably would have done under similar circumstances, and it was particularly stated at the outset that there was nothing at all extraordinary about Arthur Burton. For the rest, it was not a wholly bad symptom. Had he been a conceited fellow, he very likely would not have laughed. He would have stroked his mustache and thought it quite natural that a woman should fall in love with him, and even would have felt a pity for the poor thing. It was, in fact, because he was not vain that he found the idea so greatly amusing.

On parting with Arthur, Maud rushed upstairs and locked herself in her room. She threw herself into the first chair she stumbled over in the dimly lighted apartment, and sat there motionless, her eyes fixed on the empty air with an expression of desperation, her hands clinched so tightly that the nails bit the palms. She breathed only at considerable intervals, with short, quick inhalations.

Yet the act which caused this extraordinary revulsion of feeling had not been the result of any sudden impulse. It was the execution of a deliberate resolve which had originated in her mind on the night of Lucy Merritt's departure, as she sat with her before the fire, listening to her fanciful talk about the advantages which might be expected to attend franker relations in love affairs between men and women. Deeply in love, and at the same time feeling that in the ordinary course of events she had nothing but disappointment to look forward to, she was in a state of mind just desperate enough to catch at the idea that if Arthur Burton knew of her love, there would be some chance of his returning it. It seemed to her that if he did not, she could be no worse off than she was already. She had brooded over the subject day and night ever since, considering from every point of view of abstract right or true feminine propriety the question whether a woman might, without real prejudice to her maidenly modesty, tell a man that she cared for him, without waiting for him to ask her to marry him. Her conclusion had been that there was no reason, apart from her own feelings, why any woman, who dared do it, should not; and if she thought her life's happiness dependent on her doing it, that she would be a weak creature who did not dare.

Her resolve once taken, she had only waited an opportunity to carry it out; and that evening, when Arthur offered to walk home with her, she felt that the opportunity had come. Little wonder that she came downstairs from the dressing-room looking remarkably pale, and that after they had started, and she was trying to screw up her courage to the speaking point, her responses to his conversational efforts should have been at random. It was terribly hard work, this screwing up her courage. All the fine arguments which had convinced her that her intended course was justifiable and right had utterly collapsed. She could not recall one of them. What she had undertaken to do seemed shocking, hateful, immodest, scandalous, impossible. But there was a bed-rock of determination to her character; and a fixed, dogged resolve to do the thing she had once made up her mind to, come what might, had not permitted her to draw back. Hardly knowing what she was about, or the words she was saying, she had plunged blindly ahead. Somehow she had got through with it, and now she seemed to herself to be sitting amidst the ruins of her womanhood.

It was particularly remarked that Arthur Burton's laughter, as he leaned against the fence a square away in convulsions of merriment, was noiseless, but it was perfectly audible to Maud, as she sat in the darkness of her chamber. Nay, more: although his thoughts were not uttered at all, she overheard them, and among them some which the young man, to do him justice, had the grace not to think.

The final touch to her humiliation was imparted by the reflection that she had done the thing so stupidly, — so blunderingly. If she must needs tell a man she loved him, could she not have told him in language which at least would have been forcible and dignified? Instead of that, she had begun with mawkish compliments, unable in her excitement to think of anything else, and ended with an incoherent jumble that barely escaped being hysterical. He would think that she was as lacking in sense as in womanly self-respect. At last she turned up the gas, for very shame avoiding a glimpse of herself in the mirror as she did so, and bathed her burning cheeks.

II

Meanwhile Arthur had reached home and was likewise sitting in his room, thinking the matter over from his point of view, with the assistance of a long-stemmed pipe. But instead of turning the gas down, as Maud had done, he had turned it up, and, having lighted all the jets in the room, had planted his chair directly in front of the big looking-glass, so that he might enjoy the reflection of his own amusement and be doubly entertained.

By this time, however, amazement and amusement had passed their acute stages. He was considering somewhat more seriously, but still with frequent attacks of mirth, the practical aspects of the predicament in which Maud's declaration had placed him; and the more he considered it, the more awkward as well as absurd that predicament appeared. They had the same acquaintances, went to the same parties, and were very likely to meet whenever they went out of an evening. What if she should continue to pursue him? If she did, he either would have to cut society, which had promised to be unusually lively that winter, or provide himself with a chaperon for protection. For the first time in his life he was in a position to appreciate the courage of American girls, who, without a tremor, venture themselves, year in and year out, in the company of gentlemen from whom they are exposed at any time to proposals of a tender nature. It was a pity if he could not be as brave as girls who are afraid of a mouse. Doubtless it was all in getting used to it.

On reflection, he should not need a chaperon. Had she not assured him that he need not be afraid of her, that she would never repeat what she had said, nor trouble him again? How her arm trembled on his as she was saying that, and how near she came to breaking down! And this was Maud Elliott, the girl with whom he had never ventured to flirt with as with some of the others, because she was so reserved and distant. The very last girl anybody would expect such a thing from! If it had been embarrassing for him to hear it, what must it have cost such a girl as Maud Elliott to say it! How did she ever muster the courage?

He took the pipe from his mouth, and the expression of his eyes became fixed, while his cheeks reddened slowly and deeply. In putting himself in Maud's place, he was realizing for the first time how strong must have been the feeling which had nerved her to such a step. His heart began to beat rather thickly. There was something decidedly intoxicating in knowing that one was regarded in such a way by a nice girl, even if it were impossible, as it certainly was in this case, to reciprocate the feeling. He continued to put himself mentally in Maud's place. No doubt she was also at that moment sitting alone in her chamber, thinking the matter over as he was. She was not laughing, however, that was pretty certain; and it required no clairvoyant's gift for him to be sensible that her chief concern must be as to what he might be at that moment thinking about her. And how had he been thinking about her?

As this question came up to his mind, he saw himself for a moment through Maud's eyes, sitting there smoking, chuckling, mowing like an idiot before the glass because, forsooth, a girl had put herself at his mercy on the mistaken supposition that he was a gentleman. As he saw his conduct in this new light, he had such an access of self-contempt that, had it been physically convenient, it would have been a relief to kick himself. What touching faith she had shown in his ability to take a generous, high-minded view of what she had done, and here he had been guffawing over it like a corner loafer. He would not, for anything in the world, have her know how he had behaved. And she should not. She should never know that he was less a gentleman than she believed him.

She had told him, to be sure, that he owed her nothing because she loved him; but it had just struck him that he owed her at least, on that account, a more solicitous respect and consideration than any one else had the right to expect from him.

There were no precedents to guide him, no rules of etiquette prescribing the proper thing for a young man to do under such circumstances as

these. It was a new problem he had to work out,
directed only by such generous and manly instincts
as he might have. Plainly the first thing, and in
fact the only thing that he could do for her, seeing
that he really could not return her affection, was to
show her that she had not forfeited his esteem.

At first he thought of writing her a note and as-
suring her, in a few gracefully turned sentences,
of his high respect in spite of what she had done.
But somehow the gracefully turned sentences did
not occur to his mind when he took up his pen,
and it did occur to him that to write persons that
you still respect them is equivalent to intimating
that their conduct justly might have forfeited your
respect. Nor would it be at all easier to give such
an assurance by word of mouth. In fact, quite
the reverse. The meaning to be conveyed was too
delicate for words. Only the unspoken language
of his manner and bearing could express it without
offense. It might, however, be some time before
chance brought them together in society, even if
she did not, for a while at least, purposely avoid
him. Meantime, uncertain how her extraordinary
action had impressed him, how was she likely to
enjoy her thoughts ?

In the generous spirit bred of his new contrition,
it seemed to him a brutal thing to leave her weeks
or even days in such a condition of mind as must
be hers. Inaction on his part was all that was
required to make her position intolerable. Inac-

tion was not therefore permissible to him. It was
a matter in which he must take the initiative, and
there seemed to be just one thing he could do
which would at all answer the purpose. A brief
formal call, with the conversation strictly limited
to the weather and similarly safe subjects, would
make it possible for them to meet thereafter in society without too acute embarrassment. Had he
the pluck for this, the nerve to carry it through?
That was the only question. There was no doubt
as to what he ought to do. It would be an awkward call, to put it mildly. It would be skating
on terribly thin ice — a little thinner, perhaps, than
a man ever skated on before.

If he could but hit on some pretext, it scarcely
mattered how thin, — for of course it would not be
intended to deceive her, — the interview possibly
could be managed. As he reflected, his eyes fell
on a large volume, purchased in a fit of extravagance, which lay on his table. It was a profusely
illustrated work on pottery, intended for the victims of the fashionable craze on that subject, which
at the date of these events had but recently reached
the United States. His face lighted up with a
sudden inspiration, and taking a pen he wrote the
following note to Maud, dating it the next day: —

MISS ELLIOTT:

Our conversation last evening on the subject of
old china has suggested to me that you might be

interested in looking over the illustrations in the
volume which I take the liberty of sending with
this. If you will be at home this evening, I shall
be pleased to call and learn your impression.

ARTHUR BURTON.

The next morning he sent this note and the
book to Maud, and that evening called upon her.
To say that he did not twist his mustache rather
nervously as he stood upon the doorstep, waiting
for the servant to answer the bell, would be to
give him credit for altogether more nerve than he
deserved. He was supported by the consciousness
that he was doing something rather heroic, but he
very much wished it were done. As he was shown
into the parlor, Maud came forward to meet him.
She wore a costume which set off her fine figure to
striking advantage, and he was surprised to per-
ceive that he had never before appreciated what a
handsome girl she was. It was strange that he
should never have particularly observed before
what beautiful hands she had, and what a dazzling
fairness of complexion was the complement of her
red-brown hair. Could it be this stately maiden
who had uttered those wild words the night before?
Could those breathless tones, that piteous shame-
facedness, have been hers? Surely he must be the
victim of some strange self-delusion. Only the
deep blush that mantled her face as she spoke his
name, the quickness with which, after one swift

glance, her eyes avoided his, and the tremor of her hand as he touched it, fully assured him that he had not dreamed the whole thing.

A shaded lamp was on the centre-table, where also Arthur's book on pottery lay open. After thanking him for sending it and expressing the pleasure she had taken in looking it over, Maud plunged at once into a discussion of Sèvres, and Cloisonné, and Palissy, and tiles, and all that sort of thing, and Arthur bravely kept his end up. Any one who had looked casually into the parlor would have thought that old crockery was the most absorbing subject on earth to these young people, with such eagerness did they compare opinions and debate doubtful points. At length, however, even pottery gave out as a resource, especially as Arthur ceased, after a while, to do his part, and silences began to ensue, during which Maud rapidly turned the pages of the book or pretended to be deeply impressed with the illustrations, while her cheeks grew hotter and hotter under Arthur's gaze. He knew that he was a detestable coward thus to revel in her confusion, when he ought to be trying to cover it, but it was such a novel sensation to occupy this masterful attitude towards a young lady that he yielded basely to the temptation. After all, it was but fair. Had she not caused him a very embarrassing quarter of an hour the night before?

" I suppose I shall see you at Miss Oswald's

next Thursday," he said, as he rose to take his leave.

She replied that she hoped to be there. She accompanied him to the door of the parlor. There was less light there than immediately about the table where they had been sitting. " Good-evening," he said. " Good-evening," she replied ; and then, in a lowered voice, hardly above a whisper, she added, " I appreciate all that was noble and generous in your coming to-night." He made no reply, but took her hand and, bending low, pressed his lips to it as reverently as if she had been a queen.

Now Arthur's motive in making this call upon Maud, which has been described, had been entirely unselfish. Furthest from his mind, of all ideas, had been any notion of pursuing the conquest of her heart which he had inadvertently made. Nevertheless, the effect of his call, and that, too, even before it was made, — if this bull may be pardoned, — had been to complete that conquest as no other device, however studied, could have done.

The previous night Maud had been unable to sleep for shame. Her cheeks scorched the pillows faster than her tears could cool them ; and altogether her estate was so wretched that Lucy Merritt, could she have looked in upon her, possibly might have been shaken in her opinion as to the qualifications of women to play the part of men in love, even if permitted by society.

It had been hard enough to nerve herself to the point of doing what she had done in view of the embarrassments she had foreseen. An hour after she uttered those fatal words, her whole thinking was summed up in the cry, " If I only had not done it, then at least he would still respect me." In the morning she looked like one in a fever. Her eyes were red and swollen, her face was pallid but for a hard red spot in each cheek, and her whole appearance was expressive of bodily and mental prostration. She did not go down to breakfast, pleading a very genuine headache, and Arthur's note and the book on pottery were brought up to her. She guessed his motive in a moment. Her need gave her the clue to his meaning.

What was on Arthur's part merely a decent sort of thing to do, her passionate gratitude instantly magnified into an act of chivalrous generosity, proving him the noblest of men and the gentlest of gentlemen. She exaggerated the abjectness of the position from which his action had rescued her, in order to feel that she owed the more to his nobility. At any time during the previous night she gladly would have given ten years of her life to recall the confession that she had made to him ; now she told herself, with a burst of exultant tears, that she would not recall it if she could. She had made no mistake. Her womanly dignity was safe in his keeping. Whether he ever returned her love or not, she was not ashamed, but was glad, and always should be glad, that he knew she loved him.

As for Arthur, the reverence with which he bent over her hand on leaving her was as heartfelt as it was graceful. In her very disregard of conventional decorum she had impressed him the more strikingly with the native delicacy and refinement of her character. It had been reserved for her to show him how genuine a thing is womanly modesty, and how far from being dependent on those conventional affectations with which it is in the vulgar mind so often identified, with the effect of seeming as artificial as they.

When, a few evenings later, he went to Miss Oswald's party, the leading idea in his mind was that he should meet Maud there. His eyes sought her out the moment he entered the Oswald parlors, but it was some time before he approached her. For years he had been constantly meeting her, but he had never before taken special note of her appearance in company. He had a curiosity about her now as lively as it was wholly new. He took a great interest in observing how she walked and talked and laughed, how she sat down and rose up and demeaned herself. It gave him an odd but marked gratification to note how favorably she compared in style and appearance with the girls present. Even while he was talking with Ella Perry, with whom he believed himself in love, he was so busy making these observations that Ella dismissed him with the sarcastic advice to follow his eyes, which he presently proceeded to do.

Maud greeted him with a very fair degree of self-possession, though her cheeks were delightfully rosy. At first it was evidently difficult for her to talk, and her embarrassment betrayed uncertainty as to the stability of the conventional footing which his call of the other evening had established between them. Gradually, however, the easy, nonchalant tone which he affected seemed to give her confidence, and she talked more easily. Her color continued to be unusually though not unbecomingly high, and it took a great deal of skirmishing for him to get a glance from her eyes, but her embarrassment was no longer distressing. Arthur, indeed, was scarcely in a mood to notice that she did not bear her full part in the conversation. The fact of conversing on any terms with a young lady who had confessed to him what Maud had was so piquant in itself that it would have made talk in the deaf-and-dumb alphabet vivacious. All the while, as they laughed and talked together quite as any other two young people might do, those words of hers the other night: "I care for you very much," "Be a little good to me," were ringing in his ears. The reflection that by virtue of her confession of love she was his whenever he should wish to claim her, even though he never should claim her, was constantly in his mind, and gave him a sense of potential proprietorship which was decidedly heady.

" Arthur Burton seems to be quite fascinated. I never supposed that he fancied Maud Elliott before, did you? " said one of the young ladies, a little maliciously, to Ella Perry. Ella tossed her head and replied that really she had never troubled herself about Mr. Burton's fancies, which was not true. The fact is, she was completely puzzled as well as vexed by Arthur's attentions to Maud. There was not a girl in her set of whom she would not sooner have thought as a rival. Arthur had never, to her knowledge, talked for five minutes together with Maud before, and here he was spending half the evening in an engrossing tête-à-tête with her, to the neglect of his other acquaintances and of herself in particular. Maud was looking very well, to be sure, but no better than often before, when he had not glanced at her a second time. What might be the clue to this mystery? She remembered, upon reflection, that he had escorted Maud home from the party at her own house the week before, but that explained nothing. Ella was aware of no weapon in the armory of her sex capable of effecting the subjugation of a previously quite indifferent young man in the course of a ten-minutes' walk. If, indeed, such weapons there had been, Maud Elliott, the most reserved and diffident girl of her acquaintance, — " stiff and pokerish," Ella called her, — was the last person likely to employ them. It must be, Ella was forced to conclude, that Arthur was trying to punish her for snubbing him by devoting himself to Maud; and, having adopted this conclusion, the misguided damsel proceeded to flirt vigorously with a young man whom she detested.

In the latter part of the evening, when Arthur was looking again for Maud, he learned that she had gone home, a servant having come to fetch her. The result was that he went home alone, Ella Perry having informed him rather crushingly that she had accorded the honor of escorting herself to another. He was rather vexed at Ella's jilting him, though he admitted that she might have fancied she had some excuse.

A few days later he called on her, expecting to patch up their little misunderstanding, as on previous occasions. She was rather offish, but really would have been glad to make up, had he shown the humility and tractableness he usually manifested after their tiffs; but he was not in a humble frame of mind, and, after a brief and unsatisfactory call, took his leave. The poor girl was completely puzzled. What had come over Arthur? She had snubbed him no more than usual that night, and generally he took it very meekly. She would have opened her eyes very wide indeed if she had guessed what there had been in his recent experience to spoil his appetite for humble-pie.

It was not late when he left Ella, and as he passed Maud's house he could not resist the temptation of going in. This time he did not pretend

to himself that he sought her from any but entirely
selfish motives.   He wanted to remove the unplea-
santly acid impression left by his call on Ella by
passing an hour with some one whom he knew
would be glad to see him and not be afraid to let
him know it.   In this aim he was quite successful.   Maud's face fairly glowed with glad surprise
when he entered the room.   This was their second
meeting since the evening Arthur had called to
talk pottery, and the tacit understanding that her
tender avowal was to be ignored between them
had become so well established that they could
converse quite at their ease.   But ignoring is not
forgetting.   On the other hand, it implies a constant remembering ; and the mutual consciousness
between these young people could scarcely fail to
give a peculiar piquancy to their intercourse.

That evening was the first of many which the
young man passed in Maud's parlor, and the beginning of an intimacy which caused no end of
wonder among their acquaintances.   Had its real
nature been suspected, that wonder would have
been vastly increased.   For whereas they supposed
it to be an entirely ordinary love affair, except in
the abruptness of its development, it was, in fact,
a quite extraordinary variation on the usual social
relations of young men and women.

Maud's society had in fact not been long in
acquiring an attraction for Arthur quite independent of the peculiar circumstances under which he

had first become interested in her. As soon as she began to feel at ease with him, her shyness rapidly disappeared, and he was astonished to discover that the stiff, silent girl whom he had thought rather dull possessed culture and originality such as few girls of his acquaintance could lay claim to. His assurance beyond possibility of doubt that she was as really glad to see him whenever he called as she said she was, and that though his speech might be dull or his jests poor they were sure of a friendly critic, made the air of her parlor wonderfully genial. The result was that he fell into a habit whenever he wanted a little social relaxation, but felt too tired, dispirited, or lazy for the effort of a call on any of the other girls, of going to Maud. One evening he said to her just as he was leaving, "If I come here too much, you must send me home."

"I will when you do," she replied, with a bright smile.

"But really," he persisted, "I am afraid I bore you by coming so often."

"You know better than that," was her only reply, but the vivid blush which accompanied the words was a sufficient enforcement of them; and he was, at the bottom of his heart, very glad to think he did know better.

Without making any pretense of being in love with her, he had come to depend on her being in love with him. It had grown so pleasing to count on her loyalty to him that a change in her feelings would have been a disagreeable surprise. Getting something for nothing is a mode of acquisition particularly pleasing to mankind, and he was enjoying in some respects the position of an engaged man without any of the responsibilities.

But if in some respects he was in the position of an engaged man, in others he was farther from it than the average unengaged man. For while Maud and he talked of almost everything else under heaven, the subject of love was tabooed between them. Once for all Maud had said her say on that point, and Arthur could say nothing unless he said as much as she had said. For the same reason, there was never any approach to flirting between them. Any trifling of that sort would have been meaningless in an intimacy begun, as theirs had been, at a point beyond where most flirtations end.

Not only in this respect, but also in the singular frankness which marked their interchange of thought and opinion, was there something in their relation savoring of that of brother and sister. It was as if her confession of love had swept away by one breath the whole lattice of conventional affectations through which young men and women usually talk with each other. Once for all she had dropped her guard with him, and he could not do less with her. He found himself before long talking more freely to her than to any others of his acquaintance, and about more serious matters. They talked of their deepest beliefs and convictions, and he told her things that he had never told any one before. Why should he not tell her his secrets? Had she not told him hers? It was a pleasure to reciprocate her confidence if he could not her love. He had not supposed it to be possible for a man to become so closely acquainted with a young lady not a relative. It came to the point finally that when they met in company, the few words that he might chance to exchange with her were pitched in a different key from that used with the others, such as one drops into when greeting a relative or familiar friend met in a throng of strangers.

Of course, all this had not come at once. It was in winter that the events took place with which this narrative opened. Winter had meantime glided into spring, and spring had become summer. In the early part of June a report that Arthur Burton and Maud Elliott were engaged obtained circulation, and, owing to the fact that he had so long been apparently devoted to her, was generally believed. Whenever Maud went out she met congratulations on every side, and had to reply a dozen times a day that there was no truth in the story, and smilingly declare that she could not imagine how it started. After doing which, she would go home and cry all night, for Arthur was not only not engaged to her, but she

had come to know in her heart that he never
would be.

At first, and indeed for a long time, she was so
proud of the frank and loyal friendship between
them, such as she was sure had never before existed between unplighted man and maid, that she
would have been content to wait half her lifetime
for him to learn to love her, if only she were sure
that he would at last. But, after all, it was the
hope of his love, not his friendship, that had been
the motive of her desperate venture. As month
after month passed, and he showed no symptoms
of any feeling warmer than esteem, but always in
the midst of his cordiality was so careful lest he
should do or say anything to arouse unfounded
expectations in her mind, she lost heart and felt
that what she had hoped was not to be. She said
to herself that the very fact that he was so much
her friend should have warned her that he would
never be her lover, for it is not often that lovers
are made out of friends.

It is always embarrassing for a young lady to
have to deny a report of her engagement, especially when it is a report she would willingly have
true ; but what made it particularly distressing
for Maud that this report should have got about
was her belief that it would be the means of bringing to an end the relations between them. It
would undoubtedly remind Arthur, by showing
how the public interpreted their friendship, that

his own prospects in other quarters, and he might even think justice to her future, demanded the discontinuance of attentions which must necessarily be misconstrued by the world. The public had been quite right in assuming that it was time for them to be engaged. Such an intimacy as theirs between a young man and a young woman, unless it were to end in an engagement, had no precedent and belonged to no known social category. It was vain, in the long run, to try to live differently from other people.

The pangs of an accusing conscience completed her wretchedness at this time. The conventional proprieties are a law written on the hearts of refined, delicately nurtured girls; and though, in the desperation of unreciprocated and jealous love, she had dared to violate them, not the less did they now thoroughly revenge themselves. If her revolt against custom had resulted happily, it is not indeed likely that she would ever have reproached herself very seriously; but now that it had issued in failure, her self-confidence was gone and her conscience easily convicted her of sin. The outraged Proprieties, with awful spectacles and minatory, reproachful gestures, crowded nightly around her bed, the Titanic shade of Mrs. Grundy looming above her satellite shams and freezing her blood with a Gorgon gaze. The feeling that she had deserved all that was to come upon her deprived her of moral support.

Arthur had never showed that he thought
cheaply of her, but in his heart of hearts how
could he help doing so? Compared with the
other girls, serene and unapproachable in their
virgin pride, must she not necessarily seem bold,
coarse, and common? That he took care never to
let her see it only proved his kindness of heart.
Her sense of this kindness was more and more
touched with abjectness.

The pity of it was that she had come to love him
so much more since she had known him so well.
It scarcely seemed to her now that she could have
truly cared for him at all in the old days, and she
wondered, as she looked back, that the shallow
emotion she then experienced had emboldened her
to do what she had done. Ah, why had she done
it? Why had she not let him go his way? She
might have suffered then, but not such heart-break-
ing misery as was now in store for her.

Some weeks passed with no marked change in
their relations, except that a new and marked constraint which had come over Arthur's manner towards her was additional evidence that the end was
at hand. Would he think it better to say nothing,
but merely come to see her less and less frequently
and so desert her, without an explanation, which,
after all, was needless? Or would he tell her how
the matter stood and say good-by? She thought
he would take the latter course, seeing that they
had always been so frank with each other. She

tried to prepare herself for what she knew was coming, and to get ready to bear it. The only result was that she grew sick with apprehension whenever he did not call, and was only at ease when he was with her, in the moment that he was saying good-by without having uttered the dreaded words.

The end came during a call which he made on her in the last part of June. He appeared preoccupied and moody, and said scarcely anything. Several times she caught him furtively regarding her with a very strange expression. She tried to talk, but she could not alone keep up the conversation, and in time there came a silence. A hideous silence it was to Maud, an abyss yawning to swallow up all that was left of her happiness. She had no more power to speak, and when he spoke she knew it would be to utter the words she had so long expected. Evidently it was very hard for him to bring himself to utter them, — almost as hard as it would be for her to hear them. He was very tender-hearted she had learned already. Even in that moment she was very sorry for him. It was all her fault that he had to say this to her.

Suddenly, just as she must have cried out, unable to bear the tension of suspense any longer, he rose abruptly to his feet, uttering something about going and an engagement which he had almost forgotten. Hastily wishing her good-evening, with hurried steps he half crossed the room, hesitated, stopped, looked back at her, seemed to waver a

moment, and then, as if moved by a sudden decision, returned to her and took her gently by the
hand. Then she knew it was coming.

For a long moment he stood looking at her. She
knew just the pitifulness that was in his expression,
but she could not raise her eyes to his. She tried
to summon her pride, her dignity, to her support.
But she had no pride, no dignity, left. She had
surrendered them long ago.

"I have something to say to you," he said, in
a tone full of gentleness, just as she had known
he would speak. "It is something I have put off
saying as long as possible, and perhaps you have
already guessed what it is."

Maud felt the blood leaving her face; the room
spun around; she was afraid she should faint. It
only remained that she should break down now to
complete her humiliation before him, and apparently she was going to do just that.

"We have had a most delightful time the past
year," he went on; "that is, at least I have. I
don't believe the friendship of a girl was ever so
much to a man as yours has been to me. I doubt
if there ever was just such a friendship as ours has
been, anyway. I shall always look back on it as
the rarest and most charming passage in my life.
But I have seen for some time that we could not
go on much longer on the present footing, and to-
night it has come over me that we can't go on even
another day. Maud, I can't play at being friends

with you one hour more. I love you. Do you care
for me still? Will you be my wife?"

When it is remembered that up to his last words
she had been desperately bracing herself against
an announcement of a most opposite nature, it will
not seem strange that for a moment Maud had difficulty in realizing just what had happened. She
looked at him as if dazed, and with an instinct of
bewilderment drew back a little as he would have
clasped her. "I thought," she stammered — "I
thought — I" —

He misconstrued her hesitation. His eyes darkened and his voice was sharpened with a sudden
fear as he exclaimed, "I know it was a long time
ago you told me that. Perhaps you don't feel the
same way now. Don't tell me, Maud, that you
don't care for me any longer, now that I have
learned I can't do without you."

A look of wondering happiness, scarcely able
even yet to believe in its own reality, had succeeded
the bewildered incredulity in her face.

"O Arthur!" she cried. "Do you really mean
it? Are you sure it is not out of pity that you say
this? Do you love me after all? Would you
really like me a little to be your wife?"

"If you are not my wife, I shall never have
one," he replied. "You have spoiled all other
women for me."

Then she let him take her in his arms, and as
his lips touched hers for the first time he faintly

wondered if it were possible he had ever dreamed
of any other woman but Maud Elliott as his wife.
After she had laughed and cried awhile, she said :

" How was it that you never let me see you cared
for me ? You never showed it."

" I tried not to," he replied ; " and I would not
have shown it to-night, if I could have helped it. I
tried to get away without betraying my secret, but
I could not." Then he told her that when he found
he had fallen in love with her, he was almost angry
with himself. He was so proud of their friendship
that a mere love affair seemed cheap and common
beside it. Any girl would do to fall in love with ;
but there was not, he was sure, another in America
capable of bearing her part in such a rare and delicate companionship as theirs. He was determined
to keep up their noble game of friendship as long
as might be.

Afterward, during the evening, he boasted himself to her not a little of the self-control he had
shown in hiding his passion so long, a feat the
merit of which perhaps she did not adequately
appreciate.

" Many a time in the last month or two when
you have been saying good-by to me of an evening,
with your hand in mine, the temptation has been
almost more than I could withstand to seize you in
my arms. It was all the harder, you see, because
I fancied you would not be very angry if I did. In
fact, you once gave me to understand as much in

pretty plain language, if I remember rightly. Possibly you may recall the conversation. You took the leading part in it, I believe."

Maud had bent her head so low that he could not see her face. It was very cruel in him, but he deliberately took her chin in his hands, and gently but firmly turned her face up to his. Then, as he kissed the shamed eyes and furiously blushing cheeks, he dropped the tone of banter and said, with moist eyes, in a voice of solemn tenderness: —

"My brave darling, with all my life I will thank you for the words you spoke that night. But for them I might have missed the wife God meant for me."

DESERTED

"WHAT a glorious, all-satisfying country this Nevada desert would be, if one were only all eyes, and had no need of food, drink, and shelter! Would n't it, Miss Dwyer? Do you know, I 've no doubt that this is the true location of heaven. You see, the lack of water and vegetation would be no inconvenience to spirits, while the magnificent scenery and the cloudless sky would be just the thing to make them thrive."

"But what I can't get over," responded the young lady addressed, "is that these alkali plains, which have been described as so dreary and uninteresting, should prove to be in reality one of the most wonderfully impressive and beautiful regions in the world. What awful fibbers, or what awfully dull people, they must have been whose descriptions have so misled the public! It is perfectly unaccountable. Here I expected to doze all the way across the desert, while in fact I 've grudged my eyes time enough to wink ever since I left my berth this morning."

"The trouble is," replied her companion, "that persons in search of the picturesque, or with much eye for it, are rare travelers along this route. The

people responsible for the descriptions you complain of are thrifty business-men, with no idea that
there can be any possible attraction in a country
where crops can't be raised, timber cut, or ore dug
up.   For my part, I thank the Lord for the beautiful barrenness that has consecrated this great
region to loneliness.   Here there will always be a
chance to get out of sight and sound of the swarm-
ing millions who have already left scarcely stand-
ing-room for a man in the East.   I would n't give
much for a country where there are no wilder-
nesses left."

" But I really think it is rather hard to say in
just what the beauty of the desert consists," said
Miss Dwyer.   " It is so simple.   I scribbled two
pages of description in my note-book this morning,
but when I read them over, and then looked out
of the window, I tore them up.   I think the wonderfully fine, clear, brilliant air transfigures the
landscape and makes it something that must be
seen and can't be told.   After seeing how this
air makes the ugly sagebrush and the patches of
alkali and brown earth a feast to the eye, one can
understand how the light of heaven may make the
ugliest faces beautiful."

The pretty talker is sitting next the window of
palace-car No. 30 of the Central Pacific line, which
has already been her flying home for two days.
The gentleman who sits beside her professes to be
sharing the view, but it is only fair I should tell

the reader that under this pretense he is nefariously delighting in the rounded contour of his companion's half-averted face, as she, in unfeigned engrossment, scans the panorama unrolled before them by the swift motion of the car. How sweet and fresh is the bright tint of her cheek against the ghastly white background of the alkali-patches as they flit by! Still, it can't be said that he isn't enjoying the scenery too, for surely there is no such Claude-Lorraine glass to reflect and enhance the beauty of a landscape as the face of a *spirituelle* girl.

With a profound sigh, summing up both her admiration and that despair of attaining the perfect insight and sympathy imagined and longed for which is always a part of intense appreciation of natural beauty, Miss Dwyer threw herself back in her seat, and fixed her eyes on the car-ceiling with an expression as if she were looking at something at least as far away as the moon.

" I 'm going to make a statue when I get home," she said, — " a statue which will personify Nevada, and represent the tameless, desolate, changeless, magnificent beauty and the self-sufficient loneliness of the desert. I can see it in my mind's eye now. It will probably be the finest statue in the world."

" If you 'd as lief put your ideal into a painting, I will give you a suggestion that will be original if nothing else," he observed.

" What 's that ? "

" Why, having in view these white alkali-
patches that chiefly characterize Nevada, paint her
as a leper."

" That 's horrid ! You need n't talk to me any
more," she exclaimed emphatically.

With this sort of chatter they had beguiled the
time since leaving San Francisco the morning of
the day before. Acquaintances are indeed made
as rapidly on an overland train as on an ocean
steamship, but theirs had dated from the preceding
winter, during which they had often met in San
Francisco. When Mr. Lombard heard that Miss
Dwyer and Mrs. Eustis, her invalid sister, were
going East in April, he discovered that he would
have business to attend to in New York at about
that time; and oddly enough, — that is, if you
choose to take that view of it, — when the ladies
came to go, it turned out that Lombard had taken
his ticket for the selfsame train and identical
sleeping-car. The result of which was that he had
the privilege of handing Miss Dwyer in and out at
the eating-stations, of bringing Mrs. Eustis her
cup of tea in the car, and of sharing Miss Dwyer's
seat and monopolizing her conversation when he
had a mind to, which was most of the time. A
bright and congenial companion has this advantage
over a book, that he or she is an author whom you
can make discourse on any subject you please, instead of being obliged to follow an arbitrary selec-

tion by another, as when you commune with the printed page.

By way of peace-offering for his blasphemy in calling the Nevada desert a leper, Lombard had embezzled a couple of chairs from the smoking-room and carried them to the rear platform of the car, which happened to be the last of the train, and invited Miss Dwyer to come thither and see the scenery. Whether she had wanted to pardon him or not, he knew very well that this was a temptation which she could not resist, for the rear platform was the best spot for observation on the entire train, unless it were the cowcatcher of the locomotive.

The April sun mingled with the frosty air like whiskey with ice-water, producing an effect cool but exhilarating. As she sat in the door of the little passage leading to the platform, she scarcely needed the shawl which he wrapped about her with absurdly exaggerated solicitude. One of the most unmistakable symptoms of the lover is the absorbing and superfluous care with which he adjusts the wraps about the object of his affections whether the weather be warm or cold : it is as if he thought he could thus artificially warm her heart toward him. But Miss Dwyer did not appear vexed, pretending indeed to be oblivious of everything else in admiration of the spectacle before her.

The country stretched flat and bare as a table

for fifty miles on either side the track, — a distance looking in the clear air not over one fifth as great. On every side this great plain was circled by mountains, the reddish-brown sides of some of them bare to the summits, while others were robed in folds of glistening snow and looked like white curtains drawn part way up the sky. The whitey-gray of the alkali-patches, the brown of the dry earth, and the rusty green of the sagebrush filled the foreground, melting in the distance into a purple-gray. The wondrous dryness and clearness of the air lent to these modest tints a tone and dazzling brilliance that surprised the eye with a revelation of possibilities never before suspected in them. But the mountains were the greatest wonder. It was as if the skies, taking pity on their nakedness, had draped their majestic shoulders in imperial purple, while at this hour the westering sun tipped their pinnacles with gilt. In the distance half a dozen sand-spouts, swiftly-moving white pillars, looking like desert genii with too much "tanglefoot" aboard, were careering about in every direction.

But as Lombard pointed out the various features of the scene to his companion, I fear that his chief motive was less an admiration of Nature that sought sympathy than a selfish delight in making her eyes flash, seeing the color come and go in her cheeks, and hearing her charming unstudied exclamations of pleasure, — a delight not unmingled with complacency in associating himself in her mind with emotions of delight and admiration. It is appalling, the extent to which spoony young people make the admiration of Nature in her grandest forms a mere sauce to their love-making. The roar of Niagara has been notoriously utilized as a cover to unlimited osculation, and Adolphus looks up at the sky-cleaving peak of Mont Blanc only to look down at Angelina's countenance with a more vivid appreciation of its superior attractions.

It was delicious, Lombard thought, sitting there with her on the rear platform, out of sight and sound of everybody. He had such a pleasant sense of proprietorship in her! How agreeable — flatteringly so, in fact — she had been all day! There was nothing like traveling together to make people intimate. It was clear that she understood his intentions very well: indeed, how could she help it? He had always said that a fellow had shown himself a bungler at love-making if he were not practically assured of the result before he came to the point of the declaration. The sensation of leaving everything else so rapidly behind that people have when sitting on the rear platform of a train of cars makes them feel, by force of contrast, nearer to each other and more identified. How pretty she looked sitting there in the doorway, her eyes bent so pensively on the track behind as the car-wheels so swiftly reeled it off! He had tucked

her in comfortably. No cold could get to the
sweet little girl, and none ever should so long as
he lived to make her comfort his care.

One small gloved hand lay on her lap outside
the shawl. What a jolly little hand it was! He
reached out his own and took it, but, without even
a moment's hesitation for him to extract a flattering inference from, she withdrew it. Perhaps
something in his matter-of-course way displeased
her.

To know when it is best to submit to a partial
rebuff, rather than make a bad matter worse by
trying to save one's pride, is a rare wisdom. Still,
Lombard might have exercised it at another time.
But there are days when the magnetisms are all
wrong, and a person not ordinarily deficient in
tact, having begun wrong, goes on blundering like
a schoolboy. Piqued at the sudden shock to the
pleasant day-dream, in which he had fancied himself already virtually assured of this young lady, —
a day-dream which she was not really accountable
for spoiling, since she had not been privy to it, —
what should he do but find expression for his
mingled vexation and wounded affection by reminding her of a previous occasion on which she
had allowed him the liberty she now denied?
Doubtless helping to account for this lack of tact
was the idea that he should thus justify himself
for so far presuming just now. Not, of course,
that there is really any excuse for a young man's

forgetting that ladies have one advantage over Omniscience, in that not only are they privileged to remember what they please, but also to ignore what they see fit to forget.

"You have forgotten that evening at the California Theatre," was what this devoted youth said.

"I'm sure I don't know to what you refer, sir," she replied freezingly.

He was terrified at the distant accent of her voice. It appeared to come from somewhere beyond the fixed stars, and brought the chill of the interstellar spaces with it. He forgot in an instant all about his pique, vexation, and wounded pride, and was in a panic of anxiety to bring her back. In a moment more he knew that she would rise from her chair and remark that it was getting cold and she must go in. If he allowed her to depart in that mood, he might lose her forever. He could think of but one way of convincing her instantaneously of his devotion; and so what should he do but take the most inopportune occasion in the entire course of their acquaintance to make his declaration. He was like a general whose plan of battle has been completely deranged by an utterly unexpected repulse in a preliminary movement, compelling him to hurry forward his last reserves in a desperate attempt to restore the battle.

"What have I done, Miss Dwyer? Don't you know that I love you? Won't you be my wife?"

"No, sir," she said flatly, her taste outraged and her sensibilities set on edge by the stupid, blundering, hammer-and-tongs onset which from first to last he had made. She loved him, and had meant to accept him, but if she had loved him ten times as much she could n't have helped refusing him just then, under those circumstances, — not if she died for it. As she spoke, she rose and disappeared within the car. It is certainly to be hoped that the noise of the wheels, which out on the platform was considerable, prevented the recording angel from getting the full force of Lombard's ejaculation.

It is bad enough to be refused when the delicacy and respectfulness of the lady's manner make "No" sound so much like "Yes" that the rejected lover can almost persuade himself that his ears have deceived him. It is bad enough to be refused when she does it so timidly and shrinkingly and deprecatingly that it might be supposed she were the rejected party. It is bad enough to be refused when she expresses the hope that you will always be friends, and shows a disposition to make profuse amends in general agreeableness for the consummate favor which she is forced to decline you. Not to put too fine a point upon it, it is bad enough to be refused anyhow you can arrange the circumstances, but to be refused as Lombard had been, with a petulance as wounding to his dignity as was the refusal itself to his affections, is to take a bitter pill with an asafœtida coating.

In the limp and demoralized condition in which
he was left, the only clear sentiment in his mind
was that he did not want to meet her again just at
present. So he sat for an hour or more longer out
on the platform, and had become as thoroughly
chilled without as he was within when at dusk the
train stopped at a little three-house station for supper. Then he went into one of the forward day-
cars, not intending to return to the sleeping-car
till Miss Dwyer should have retired. When the
train reached Ogden the next morning, instead of
going on East he would take the same train back
to San Francisco, and that would be the end of
his romance. His engagement in New York had
been a myth, and with Miss Dwyer's " No, sir," the
only business with the East that had brought him
on this trip was at an end.

About an hour after leaving the supper-station,
the train suddenly stopped in the midst of the
desert. Something about the engine had become
disarranged, which it would take some time to put
right. Glad to improve an opportunity to stretch
their legs, many of the passengers left the cars and
were strolling about, curiously examining the sagebrush and the alkali, and admiring the ghostly
plain as it spread, bare, level, and white as an ice-
bound polar sea, to the feet of the far-off mountains.

Lombard had also left the car, and was walking
about, his hands in his overcoat pockets, trying to

clear his mind of the wreckage that obstructed its
working; for Miss Dwyer's refusal had come upon
him as a sudden squall that carries away the masts
and sails of a vessel and transforms it in a moment
from a gallant bounding ship to a mere hulk drifting in an entangled mass of débris.   Of course she
had a perfect right to suit herself about the kind
of a man she took for a husband, but he certainly
had not thought she was such an utter coquette.
If ever a woman gave a man reason to think himself as good as engaged, she had given him that
reason, and yet she refused him as coolly as she would
have declined a second plate of soup.   There must
be some truth, after all, in the rant of the poets
about the heartlessness and fickleness of women,
although he had always been used to consider it
the merest bosh.   Suddenly he heard the train
moving.   He was perhaps fifty yards off, and,
grumbling anathemas at the stupidity of the conductor, started to run for the last car.   He was
not quite desperate enough to fancy being left
alone on the Nevada desert with night coming on.
He would have caught the train without difficulty,
if his foot had not happened to catch in a tough
clump of sage, throwing him violently to the
ground.   As he gathered himself up, the train was
a hundred yards off, and moving rapidly.   To
overtake it was out of the question.

   "Stop! ho! stop!" he yelled at the top of his
lungs.   But there was no one on the rear platform

to see him, and the closed windows and the rattle
of the wheels were sufficient to render a much
louder noise than he could make inaudible to the
dozing passengers. And now the engineer pulled
out the throttle-valve to make up for lost time, and
the clatter of the train faded into a distant roar,
and its lights began to twinkle into indistinctness.

" Damnation ! "

A voice fell like a falling star : " Gentlemen do
not use profane language in ladies' company."

He first looked up in the air, as on the whole
the likeliest quarter for a voice to come from in
this desert, then around. Just on the other side
of the track stood Miss Dwyer, smiling, with a
somewhat constrained attempt at self-possession.
Lombard was a good deal taken aback, but in his
surprise he did not forget that this was the young
lady who had refused him that afternoon.

" I beg your pardon," he replied, with a stiff
bow ; " I did not suppose that there were any
ladies within hearing."

" I got out of the car supposing there was plenty
of time to get a specimen of sagebrush to carry
home," she explained ; " but when the cars started,
although I was but a little way off, I could not regain the platform ; " which, considering that she
wore a tie-back of the then prevalent fashion, was
not surprising.

" Indeed ! " replied Lombard, with the same formal manner.

"But won't the train come back for us?" she asked, in a more anxious voice.

"That will depend on whether we are missed. Nobody will miss me. Mrs. Eustis, if she has n't gone to bed, may miss you."

"But she has. She went to bed before I left the car, and is asleep by this time."

"That's unfortunate," was his brief reply, as he lit a cigar and began to smoke and contemplate the stars.

His services, so far as he could do anything for her, she should, as a lady, command, but if she thought that he was going to do the agreeable after what had happened a few hours ago, she was mightily mistaken.

There was a silence, and then she said, hesitatingly, "What are we going to do?"

He glanced at her. Her attitude and the troubled expression of her face, as well as her voice, indicated that the logic of the situation was overthrowing the jaunty self-possession which she had at first affected. The desert was staring her out of countenance. How his heart yearned toward her! If she had only given him a right to take care of her, how he would comfort her! what prodigies would he be capable of to succor her! But this rising impulse of tenderness was turned to choking bitterness by the memory of that scornful "No, sir." So he replied coldly, "I 'm not in the habit of being left behind in deserts, and I don't

know what it is customary to do in such cases. I
see nothing except to wait for the next train, which
will come along some time within twenty-four
hours."

There was another long silence, after which she
said, in a timid voice, " Had n't we better walk to
the next station ? "

At the suggestion of walking he glanced at her
close-fitting dress, and a sardonic grin slightly
twitched the corners of his mouth as he dryly answered, " It is thirty miles one way and twenty the
other to the first station."

Several minutes passed before she spoke again,
and then she said, with an accent almost like that
of a child in trouble and about to cry, " I 'm cold."

The strong, unceasing wind, blowing from snowy
mountain-caverns across a plain on which there
was not the slightest barrier of hill or tree to check
its violence, was indeed bitterly cold, and Lombard himself felt chilled to the marrow of his bones.
He took off his overcoat and offered it to her.

" No," said she, " you are as cold as I am."

" You will please take it," he replied, in a per-
emptory manner ; and she took it.

" At this rate we shall freeze to death before
midnight," he added, as if in soliloquy. " I must
see if I can't contrive to make some sort of a shelter with this sagebrush."

He began by tearing up a large number of bushes
by the roots. Seeing what he was doing, Miss

Dwyer was glad to warm her stiffened muscles by taking hold and helping ; which she did with a vigor that shortly reduced her gloves to shreds and filled her fingers with scratches from the rough twigs. Lombard next chose an unusually high and thick clump of brush, and cleared a small space three feet across in the centre of it, scattering twigs on the uncovered earth to keep off its chill.

"Now, Miss Dwyer, if you will step inside this spot, I think I can build up the bushes around us so as to make a sort of booth which may save us from freezing."

She silently did as he directed, and he proceeded to pile the brush which they had torn up on the tops of the bushes left standing around the spot where they were, thus making a circular wall about three feet high. Over the top he managed to draw together two or three bushes, and the improvised wigwam was complete.

The moonlight penetrated the loose roof sufficiently to reveal to each other the faces and figures of the two occupants as they sat in opposite corners, as far apart as possible, she cold and miserable, he cold and sulky, and both silent. And, as if to mock him, the idea kept recurring to his mind how romantic and delightful, in spite of the cold and discomfort, the situation would be if she had only said Yes, instead of No, that afternoon. People have odd notions sometimes, and it actually seemed to him that his vexation with her for destroying the pleasure of the present occasion was something quite apart from, and in addition to, his main grievance against her. It might have been so jolly, and now she had spoiled it. He could have boxed her pretty little ears.

She wondered why he did not try to light a fire, but she would n't ask him another thing, if she died. In point of fact, he knew the sagebrush would not burn. Suddenly the wind blew fiercer, there came a rushing sound, and the top and walls of the wigwam were whisked off like a flash, and as they staggered to their feet, buffeted by the whirling bushes, a cloud of fine alkali-dust enveloped them, blinding their eyes, penetrating their ears and noses, and setting them gasping, sneezing, and coughing spasmodically. Then, like a puff of smoke, the suffocating storm was dissipated, and when they opened their smarting eyes there was nothing but the silent, glorious desolation of the ghostly desert around them, with the snow-peaks in the distance glittering beneath the moon. A sand-spout had struck them, that was all, — one of the whirling dust-columns which they had admired all day from the car-windows.

Wretched enough before, both for physical and sentimental reasons, this last experience quite demoralized Miss Dwyer, and she sat down and cried. Now, a few tears, regarded from a practical, middle-aged point of view, would not appear to have greatly complicated the situation, but they threw Lombard into a panic. If she was going to cry, something must be done. Whether anything could be done or not, something *must* be done.

" Don't leave me," she cried hysterically, as he rushed off to reconnoitre the vicinity.

" I 'll return presently," he called back.

But five minutes, ten minutes, fifteen minutes passed, and he did not come back. Terror dried her tears, and her heart almost stopped beating. She had quite given him up for lost, and herself too, when with inexpressible relief she heard him call to her. She replied, and in a moment more he was at her side, breathless with running.

" I lost my bearings," he said. " If you had not answered me, I could not have found you."

" Don't leave me again," she sobbed, clinging to his arm.

He put his arms round her and kissed her. It was mean, base, contemptible, to take advantage of her agitation in that way, but she did not resist, and he did it again and again, — I forbear to say how many times.

" Is n't it a perfectly beautiful night ? " he exclaimed, with a fine gush of enthusiasm.

" Is n't it exquisite ? " she echoed, with a rush of sympathetic feeling.

" See those stars : they look as if they had just been polished," he cried.

" What a droll idea ! " she exclaimed gleefully. " But do see that lovely mountain."

Holding her with a firmer clasp, and speaking with what might be styled a fierce tenderness, he demanded, " What did you mean, miss, by refusing me this afternoon ? "

" What did you go at me so stupidly for ? I had to refuse," she retorted smilingly.

" Will you be my wife ? "

" Yes, sir ; I meant to be all the time."

The contract having been properly sealed, Lombard said, with a countenance curiously divided between a tragical expression and a smile of fatuous complacency, " There was a clear case of poetical justice in your being left behind in the desert to-night. To see the lights of the train disappearing, leaving you alone in the midst of desolation, gave you a touch of my feeling on being rejected this afternoon. Of all leavings behind, there 's none so miserable as the experience of the rejected lover."

" Poor fellow ! so he should n't be left behind. He shall be conductor of the train," she said, with a bewitching laugh.   His response was not verbal.

" How cold the wind is ! " she said.

" Shall I build you another wigwam ? "

" No ; let us exercise a little.   You whistle ' The Beautiful Blue Danube,' and we 'll waltz. This desert is the biggest, jolliest ball-room floor that ever was, and I dare say we shall be the first to waltz on it since the creation of the world. That will be something to boast of when we get home.

Come, let's dedicate the Great American Desert
to Terpsichore."

They stepped out from among the ruins of their
sagebrush booth upon a patch of hard, bare earth
close to the railroad track. Lombard puckered
his lips and struck up the air, and off they went
with as much enthusiasm as if inspired by a first-
class orchestra. Round and round, to and fro,
they swept until, laughing, flushed, and panting,
they came to a stop.

It was then that they first perceived that they
were not without a circle of appreciative spectators.
Sitting like statues on their sniffing, pawing ponies,
a dozen Piute Indians encircled them. Engrossed
with the dance and with each other, they had not
noticed them as they rode up, attracted from their
route by this marvelous spectacle of a pale-face
squaw and brave engaged in a solitary war dance
in the midst of the desert.

At sight of the grim circle of centaurs around
them Miss Dwyer would have fainted but for
Lombard's firm hold.

"Pretend not to see them; keep on dancing,"
he hissed in her ear. He had no distinct plan in
what he said, but spoke merely from an instinct of
self-preservation, which told him that when they
stopped, the Indians would be upon them. But
as she mechanically, and really more dead than
alive, obeyed his direction and resumed the dance,
and he in his excitement was treading on her feet

at every step, the thought flashed upon him that there was a bare chance of escaping violence, if they could keep the Indians interested without appearing to notice their presence. In successive whispers he communicated his idea to Miss Dyer : " Don't act as if you saw them at all, but do everything as if we were alone. That will puzzle them, and make them think us supernatural beings, or perhaps crazy: Indians have great respect for crazy people. It's our only chance. We will stop dancing now, and sing awhile. Give them a burlesque of opera. I'll give you the cues and show you how. Don't be frightened. I don't believe they'll touch us so long as we act as if we didn't see them. Do you understand? Can you do your part? "

" I understand ; I'll try," she whispered.

"Now," he said, and as they separated, he threw his hat on the ground, and, assuming an extravagantly languishing attitude, burst forth in a most poignant burlesque of a lovelorn tenor's part, rolling his eyes, clasping his hands, striking his breast, and gyrating about Miss Dwyer in the most approved operatic style. He had a fine voice and knew a good deal of music; so that, barring a certain nervousness in the performer, the exhibition was really not bad. In his singing he had used a meaningless gibberish varied with the syllables of the scale, but he closed by singing the words, " Are you ready now? Go ahead, then."

With that she took it up, and rendered the prima donna quite as effectively, interjecting " The Last Rose of Summer " as an aria in a manner that would have been encored in San Francisco. He responded with a few staccato notes, and the scene ended by their rushing into each other's arms and waltzing down the stage with abandon.

The Indians sat motionless on their horses, not even exchanging comments among themselves. They were evidently too utterly astonished by the goings on before them to have any other sentiment as yet beyond pure amazement. Here were two richly-dressed pale-faces, such as only lived in cities, out in the middle of an uninhabitable desert, in the freezing midnight, having a variety and minstrel show all to themselves, and, to make the exhibition the more unaccountable, without apparently seeing their auditors at all. Had they started up the show after being captured, Indian cunning would have recognized in it a device to save their lives, but the two had been at it before the party rode up, — had, in fact, first attracted attention by their gyrations, which were visible for miles out on the moony plain.

Lombard, without ever letting his eyes rest a moment on the Indians so as to indicate that he saw them, had still managed by looks askance and sweeping glances to keep close watch upon their demeanor, and noted with prodigious relief that his wild scheme was succeeding better than he had

dared to hope. Without any break in the entertainment he communicated his reassurance to Miss
Dwyer by singing, to the tune of "My Country,
't is of Thee," the following original hymn : —

> "We 're doing admir'blee —
> They 're heap much tickledee :
> Only keep on."

To which she responded, to the lugubrious air of
" John Brown's Body : " —

> "Oh, what do you s'pose they 'll go for to do,
> Oh, what do you s'pose they 'll go for to do,
> Oh, what do you s'pose they 'll go for to do,
> When we can sing no more ? "

A thing may be ridiculous without being amusing, and neither of these two felt the least inclina-
tion to smile at each other's poetry. After duly
joining in the chorus of " Glory, Hallelujah ! " Lombard endeavored to cheer his companion by words
adapted to the inspiriting air of " Rally Round the
Flag, Boys." This was followed by a series of
popular airs, with solos, duets, and choruses.

But this sort of thing could not go on forever.
Lombard was becoming exhausted in voice and
legs, and as for Miss Dwyer, he was expecting to
see her drop from moment to moment. Indeed, to
the air of " 'Way down upon the Swanee River "
she now began to sing : —

> "Oh, dear ! I can't bear up much longer :
> I 'm tired to death ;
> My voice 's gone all to pie-ee-ee-ces,
> My throat is very sore."

They must inevitably give out in a few minutes, and then he — and, terribly worse, she — would be at the mercy of these bestial savages, and this seeming farce would turn into most revolting tragedy. With this sickening conviction coming over him, Lombard cast a despairing look around the horizon to see if there were no help in their bitter extremity. Suddenly he burst forth, to the tune of " The Star-Spangled Banner : " —

> " Oh, say can you see,
>   Far away to the east,
>   A bright star that doth grow
>   Momentarily brighter ?
>   'Tis the far-flashing headlight
>   Of a railroad-train :
>   Ten minutes from now
>   We shall be safe and sound."

What they did in those ten minutes neither could tell afterward. The same idea was in both their minds, — that unless the attention of the Indians could be held until the train arrived, its approach would only precipitate their own fate by impelling the savages to carry out whatever designs of murder, insult, or capture they might have. Under the influence of the intense excitement of this critical interval it is to be feared that the performance degenerated from a high-toned concert and variety show into something very like a Howling-Dervish exhibition. But, at any rate, it answered its purpose until, after a period that seemed like a dozen eternities, the West-bound overland express with a

tremendous roar and rattle drew up beside them,
in response to the waving of Miss Dwyer's handkerchief and to Lombard's shouts.

Even had the Indians contemplated hostile intentions, — which they were doubtless in a condition
of too great general stupefaction to do, — the alacrity with which the two performers clambered
aboard the cars would probably have foiled their
designs. But as the train gathered headway once
more, Lombard could not resist the temptation of
venting his feelings by shaking his fist ferociously
at the audience which he had been so conscientiously trying to please up to that moment. It was
a gratification which had like to have cost him
dear. There was a quick motion on the part of
one of the Indians, and the conductor dragged
Lombard within the car just as an arrow struck
the door.

Mrs. Eustis had slept sweetly all night, and was
awakened the next morning an hour before the
train reached Ogden by the sleeping-car porter,
who gave her a telegram which had overtaken the
train at the last station. It read : —

Am safe and sound. Was left behind by your
train last night, and picked up by West-bound
express. Will join you at Ogden to-morrow morning.

JENNIE DWYER.

Mrs. Eustis read the telegram through twice

without getting the least idea from it. Then she
leaned over and looked down into Jennie's berth.
It had not been slept in. Then she began to
understand. Heroically resisting a tendency to
scream, she thus secured space for second thought,
and, being a shrewd woman of the world, ended by
making up her mind to tell no one about the matter. Evidently, Jennie had been having some decidedly unconventional experience, and the less
publicity given to all such passages in young ladies'
lives, the better for their prospects. It so happened that in the bustle attending the approach to
the terminus and the prospective change of cars
everybody was too busy to notice that any passengers were missing. At Ogden Mrs. Eustis left
the train and went to a hotel. The following
morning, a few minutes after the arrival of the
Central Pacific train, Jennie Dwyer walked into
her room, Lombard having stopped at the office to
secure berths for the three to Omaha by the Union
Pacific. After Jennie had given an outline account of her experiences, and Mrs. Eustis's equi-
librium had been measurably restored by proper
use of the smelling-salts, the latter lady remarked,
" And so Mr. Lombard was alone with you there
all night? It's very unfortunate that it should
have happened so."

" Why, I was thinking it very fortunate," replied Jennie, with her most childlike expression.
" If Mr. Lombard had not been there, I should

either have frozen to death, or by this time been celebrating my honeymoon as bride of a Piute chief."

"Nonsense, child! You know what I mean. People will talk; such unpleasant things will be said! I would n't have had it happen for anything. And when you were under my charge, too! Do hand me my salts."

"If people are going to say unpleasant things because I am out of an evening alone with Mr. Lombard," remarked Jennie, with a mischievous smile, "you must prepare yourself to hear a good deal said, my dear, for I presume this won't be the last time it will happen. We 're engaged to be married."

HOOKING WATERMELONS

THE train slackened, a brakeman thrust his head in at the door and shouted "Bah," — a mysterious formality observed on American trains as they enter towns, — and an elderly lady, two drummers, and a young man with a satchel got out, followed by the languid envy of the other passengers, who had longer or shorter penances of heat and dust before them. The train got under way again, while the knot of loafers about the station proceeded to eye the arrivals as judicially as if they were a committee of safety to protect the village from invasion by doubtful characters. The old lady, apparently laboring under some such impression, regarded them deferentially, as nervous travelers on arriving in strange places generally do regard everybody who seems to feel at home. The drummers briskly disappeared down the main street, each anxious to anticipate the other at the stores. The young man with the satchel, however, did not get away till he had shaken hands and exchanged a few good-natured inquiries with one of the loungers.

"Who's that, Bill?" asked one of the group, staring after the retreating figure with lazy curiosity.

" Why, did n't you know him ? Thought every-body knew him. That's Arthur Steele," replied the one who had shaken hands, in a tone of cordiality indicating that his politeness had left a pleasant impression on his mind, as Arthur Steele's politeness generally did.

" Who is he, anyhow ? " pursued the other.

" Why, he 's a Fairfield boy " (the brakeman pronounced it " Bah "), " born and brought up here. His folks allers lived right next to mine, and now he 's doin' a rushin' lawyer trade down New York, and I expect he 's just rakin' the stamps. Did yer see that diamond pin he wore ? "

" S'pose it 's genooine ? " asked a third loafer, with interest.

" Course it was. I tell you he 's on the make, and don't you forgit it. Some fellers allers has luck. Many 's the time he 'n' I 've been in swimmin' and hookin' apples together when we wuz little chaps," pursued Bill, in a tone implying a mild reproach at the deceitfulness of an analogy that after such fair promise in early life had failed to complete itself in their later fortunes.

" Why, darn it all, you know him, Jim," he continued, dropping the tone of pensive reminiscence into which he had momentarily allowed himself to fall. " That pretty gal that sings in the Baptis' choir is his sister."

After a space of silent rumination and jerking of peanut shells upon the track, the group broke up its session, and adjourned by tacit understanding till the next train was due.

Arthur Steele was half an hour in getting to his father's house, because everybody he met on the street insisted on shaking hands with him. Everybody in Fairfield had known him since he was a boy, and had seen him grow up, and all were proud of him as a credit to the village and one of its most successful representatives in the big outside world. The young man had sense and sentiment enough to feel that the place he held in the esteem of his native community was a thing to feel more just pride in than any station he could win in the city, and as he walked along hand-shaking with old friends on this side and that, it was about his idea of a triumphal entry.

There was the dear old house, and as he saw it his memory of it started out vividly in his mind as if to attest how faithfully it had kept each detail. It never would come out so clearly at times when he was far away and needed its comfort. He opened the door softly. The sitting-room was empty, and darkened to keep out the heat and flies. The latched door stood open, and, hearing voices, he tiptoed across the floor with a guileful smile and, leaning through the doorway, saw his mother and sister sitting by the cool, lilac-shaded window, picking over currants for tea, and talking tranquilly. Being a provident young man, he paused a minute to let the pretty, peaceful scene

impress itself upon his mind, to be remembered
afterward for the cheer of bleak boarding-house
Sunday afternoons. Then there was a sudden
glancing up, a cry of joyful consternation, and the
pan of currants rolled from Amy's lap like a
broken necklace of rubies across the uncarpeted
floor, while Arthur held mother and sister in a
double embrace. And when at length the kissing
had all been done, he established himself in his
familiar boyish attitude on the window-seat, kick-
ing his heels against the mopboard, with his
elbows on his knees, and the three talked away
steadily till the shop-bell rang, and Mrs. Steele
sprang up in a panic, exclaiming : " Father will be
here in five minutes, and the currants are on the
floor. Come, Amy, quick; we must pick some
more, and you shall help, Arthur."

But though he went out into the garden with
them readily enough, it was quite another thing to
make him pick currants, for he insisted on wandering all over the place and demanding what had
become of everything he missed, and the history
of everything new. And pretty soon Mr. Steele
also appeared in the garden, having found no one
in the house on reaching home. He had learned
on the street that Arthur had arrived, and came
out beaming. It was good to see the hearty affection with which the two shook hands.

The transition of the son from the pupilage of
childhood and youth to the independence of man-

hood is often trying to the filial relation. Neither party fully realizes that the old relation is at an end, or just what the new basis is, or when the change takes place. The absence of the son for two or three years at this period has often the best results. He goes a boy and returns a man; the old relation is forgotten by both parties, and they readily fall into the new one. So it had fared with Arthur and his father.

" You 've got a splendid lot of watermelons," said the former, as they arrived at the upper end of the ample garden in their tour of inspection.

" Yes," replied Mr. Steele, with a shrug; " only thus far they 've been stolen a little faster than they 've ripened."

" What made you plant them so near the fence ? "

" That was my blunder; but you see the soil is just the thing, better than lower down."

" Why don't you buy a bulldog ? "

" I think it 's more Christian to shoot a man outright than to set one of those devils on him. The breed ought to be extirpated."

" Put some ipecac in one or two. That 'll fetch 'em. I know how sick it made me once."

" I did; but more were stolen next night. I can't afford to medicate the whole village. Last night I sat up to watch till twelve o'clock, when mother made me go to bed."

" I 'll watch to-night," said Arthur, "and give 'em a lesson with a good load of beans from the old shotgun."

"It wouldn't pay," replied his father. "I concluded last night that all the melons in the world were n't worth a night's sleep. They 'll have to go, and next year I 'll know more than to plant any."

"You go and help Amy pick currants, and let me talk to the boy a little," said Mrs. Steele, coming up and taking Arthur off for a promenade up the broad path.

"How pretty Amy has grown," said he, glancing with a pleased smile at the girl as she looked up at her father. "I suppose the young men are making sheep's eyes at her already."

"It does n't do them any good if they are," said Mrs. Steele, decisively. "She 's only sixteen and a little girl yet, and has sense enough to know it."

"What had she been crying for when I arrived? I saw her eyes were as red as the currants."

"Oh, dear!" replied Mrs. Steele, with a sigh of vexation, "it was her troubles at the Seminary. You know we let her go as a day scholar this summer. Some of the girls slight and snub her, and she is very unhappy about it."

"Why, what on earth can anybody have against Amy?" demanded Arthur, in indignant surprise.

"I suppose it 's because some of the little hussies from the city have taken the notion that they won't associate with a mechanic's daughter, although Amy is very careful not to say it in so many words, for fear of hurting my feelings. But I suspect that 's about where the shoe pinches."

Arthur muttered something between an oath and a grunt, expressing the emphasis of the one and the disgust of the other.

" I tell Amy it is foolish to mind their airs, but I 'm really afraid it spoils the poor girl's happiness."

" Why don't you send her away to boarding-school, if it is so serious a matter as that? "

" We can't afford it," said his mother, whereto Arthur promptly replied : —

" I 'll pay her expenses. I 'm making a good deal more money than I know what to do with, and I 'd really like the chance of doing a little good."

His mother glanced at him with affectionate pride.

" You 're always wanting to pay somebody's expenses, or make somebody a present. It 's really unsafe, when you 're around, to indicate that one is n't perfectly contented. But you caught me up too quickly. I was going to say that we could n't spare her from home, anyhow. She 's the light of the house. Besides that, if it comes to objections, I 've my notions about boarding-schools, and I 'd trust no girl of mine at one that was n't within sight of her home. No, she 'll have to keep on here and bear it as she can, though it 's pretty hard, I know. The trouble to-night was, that Lina Maynard, who is one of the older girls, has invited nearly everybody at the Seminary except Amy to a birthday party to-morrow. Little minx, I could shake her. And the worst of it is, Amy thinks there's nobody like Lina Maynard."

After tea it was still light, and Arthur and Amy went out to walk. In spite of the ten years difference in their ages, he always enjoyed her company as well as anybody's in the world, because she was so refreshingly childlike and natural. Every chord of feeling answered so true and clear to the touch, that to talk with her was like playing on a musical instrument, only far more delightful. Arthur had looked forward to walks and talks with Amy as among the jolliest treats of his vacation. She tried her best now to seem light-hearted, and to entertain him with the local gossip, for which he always depended on her. But she couldn't simulate the vivacious and eager air that had been the chief charm of her talk. As he glanced down, he was grieved to see the sad set of the pretty child face at his side, and how still had grown the fountain of smiles in the hazel eyes that were wont to send their ripples outward in constant succession. It is to be feared that under his breath he applied some very ungentlemanly language to Lina Maynard and her clique, whose nonsenical ill-nature had hurt this little girl's feelings so sorely, and incidentally spoiled half the fun of his vacation.

"There, there, you needn't talk any more," he finally said, rather rudely, half vexed with her, as helpful people are wont to be with those they can do nothing to help.

She looked up in grieved surprise, but before he could speak again, they came face to face with a party of girls coming from the direction of the Seminary.

There were six or seven of them, perhaps, but Arthur only got the impression of one and a lot of others. The one was a rather tall girl of lithe figure and unusually fine carriage. Her olive complexion was lighted with great black eyes that rested on you with an air of imperturbable assurance, as penetrating as it was negligent. She was talking, and her companions were listening and laughing. As they came face to face with Arthur and Amy, he saw that they barely noticed her, while glancing at him rather curiously, with the boldness of girls in a crowd of their own sex. They evidently observed that he was a stranger to the village, and of quite a different style from that of the country bumpkins and rural exquisites they were accustomed to meeting. There was in the big black eyes, as they had met his a moment, a suggestion of interest that was strangely flattering, and left a trace of not unpleasant agitation.

"Who was that?" he asked, as they passed out of hearing.

He only thought of asking for one, although there were six, nor she apparently of answering differently.

"Lina Maynard. They are 'Sem.' girls."

It was a dulled voice she spoke in, quite unlike

her usual eager way of giving information. She, poor thing, was terribly afraid he would ask her why they did not seem acquainted with her, and it would have been a painful humiliation to have explained. Arthur was conscious that he no longer had exactly the same feeling of merely contemptuous annoyance toward Lina Maynard, on account of her treatment of Amy. He sympathized as much with his sister, of course, but somehow felt that to be recognized by Lina Maynard was not such a childish ambition as he had taken for granted.

It was dusk when they reached home and found Mr. and Mrs. Steele on the piazza, which served as an out-door parlor in summer, with a neighbor who had dropped in to see Arthur. So he got out his cigar-case and told stories of city life and interesting law cases to an intent audience till the nine o'clock bell rang, and the neighbor " guessed he 'd go home," and forthwith proved that his guess was right by going.

" 'Gad, I 'd forgotten all about the watermelons! Perhaps they 're at 'em already!'" cried Arthur, jumping up and running around the end of the piazza to the garden.

When he returned, it was to meet a combined volley of protestations against his foolish project of keeping watch all night, from his father, his mother, and Amy. But he declared it was no use talking; and where were the gun and the beans? So they adjourned from the piazza, a lamp was lit, the articles were hunted up, and the gun duly loaded with a good charge of powder and a pint of hard beans. It was about ten o'clock when Arthur, with a parting protest from his mother, went out into the garden, lugging his gun and a big easy-chair, while Amy followed, bringing one or two wraps, and a shocking old overcoat hunted up in the garret, for the chill hours after midnight.

The front of Mr. Steele's lot abutted on one of the pleasantest and most thickly housed streets of the village; but the lot was deep, and the rear end rested on a road bordered by few houses, and separated from the garden by a rail fence easy to climb over or through. The watermelon patch was located close to this fence, and thus in full view and temptingly accessible from the road.

Undoubtedly the human conscience, and especially the boyish article, recognizes a broad difference between the theft of growing crops — of apples on the trees, for instance, or corn on the stalk, or melons in the field — and that of other species of property. The surreptitious appropriation of the former class of chattels is known in common parlance as " hooking," while the graver term " stealing " describes the same process in other cases. The distinction may arise from a feeling that, so long as crops remain rooted to the ground, they are nature's, not man's, and that nature can't be regarded as forming business contracts with some individuals to the exclusion of others, or in fact as

acceding to any of our human distinctions of *meum*
and *tuum*, however useful we find them. Ethical
philosophers may refuse to concede the sanction
of the popular distinction here alluded to between
"hooking" and stealing; but, after all, ethics is
not a deductive but an empirical science, and what
are morals but a collection of usages, like orthogra-
phy and orthoepy? However that may be, it is the
duty of the writer in this instance merely to call
attention to the prevalent popular sentiment on the
subject, without any attempt to justify it, and to
state that Arthur Steele had been too recently a
boy not to sympathize with it. And accordingly
he laid his plans to capture the expected depreda-
tors to-night from practical considerations wholly,
and quite without any sense of moral reprobation
toward them.

Closely adjoining the edge of the melon-patch
was a patch of green corn, standing ten feet high,
and at the fullest perfection of foliage. This
Arthur selected for his ambush, its position being
such that he could cut off the retreat to the fence
of any person who had once got among the melons.
Hewing down a hill of corn in the second row from
the front, he made a comfortable place for his easy-
chair. Amy lingered for a while, enjoying the
excitement of the occasion, and they talked in
whispers ; but finally Arthur sent her in, and as
her dress glimmered away down the garden path,
he settled himself comfortably for his watch.

In the faint moonlight he could just descry the dark shapes of the melons on the ground in front of him. The crickets were having a high time in the stubble around, and the night air drew sweet autumnal exhalations from the ground; for autumn begins by night a long time before it does by day. The night wind rustled in the corn with a crisp articulateness he had never noticed in daytime, and he felt like an eavesdropper. Then for a while he heard the music of some roving serenaders, down in the village, and grew pensive with the vague reminiscences of golden youth, romance, and the sweet past that nightly music suggests, — vague because apparently they are not reminiscences of the individual but of the race, a part of the consciousness and ideal of humanity. At last the music was succeeded by the baying of a dog in some distant farmyard, and then, ere the ocean of silence had fairly smoothed its surface over that, a horse began to kick violently in a neighboring barn. Some time after, a man chopped some kindlings in a shed a couple of lots off. Gradually, however, the noises ceased like the oft-returning yet steadily falling ebb of the tide, and Arthur experienced how many degrees there are of silence, each more utter than the last, so that the final and absolute degree must be something to which the utmost quiet obtainable on earth is uproar. One by one the lights went out in the houses, till the only ones left were in the windows of the Seminary, visible over the tree-tops a quarter of a mile away.

"The girls keep late hours," thought Arthur. And from that he fell to thinking of Lina Maynard and the careless, almost insolent, grace of her manner, and that indifferent yet penetrating glance of hers. Where did she come from? Probably from California, or the far West; he had heard that the girls out there were of a bolder, more unconventional type than at the East. What a pity she did not fancy Amy!

What was that moving across the melon-patch? He reached for his gun. It was only a cat, though, after all. The slight noise in the corn-patch attracted the animal's attention, and it came across and poked its head into the opening where Arthur sat. As the creature saw him, its start of surprise would have shattered the nervous system of anything but a cat. It stood half thrown back on its haunches, its ears flattened, its eyes glaring in a petrifaction of amazement. Arthur sat motionless as marble, laughing inwardly. For full two minutes the two stared at each other without moving a muscle, and then, without relaxing its tense attitude, the cat by almost imperceptible degrees withdrew one paw and then another, and, thus backing out of the corn-patch, turned around when at a safe distance and slunk away.

A few minutes later a dog, that enthusiast in perfumes, jumped through the fence and trotted across

the melon-patch, his nose to the ground, making a
collection of evening smells.   Arthur expected
nothing but that he would scent his neighborhood,
find him out, and set up a barking.   But, chancing
to strike the cat's trail, off went the dog on a full
run with nose to the ground.

Such were the varying humors of the night.
After the episode of the dog, feeling a little chilly,
Arthur enveloped himself in the tattered old overcoat and must have dropped into a nap.   Suddenly
he awoke.   Within ten feet of him, just in the act
of stooping over a huge melon, was a woman's figure.   He saw the face clearly as she rose.   Immortal gods! it was — But I am anticipating.

The discipline at Westville Seminary had been
shockingly lax since the long illness of the principal had left the easy-going first assistant teacher at
the head of affairs.   The girls ran all over the rules,
— had private theatricals, suppers, and games of
all sorts in their rooms at all hours of day or
night.   In the course of the evening whose events in
another sphere of life have been narrated, several
girls called at Lina Maynard's room to notify
her of the "spread" at Nell Barber's, No. 49, at
eleven o'clock.   They found her sitting in a low
rocking-chair, with an open letter in her hand and
a very pensive, discontented expression of countenance.

"Does he press for an answer, Lina?   We're
just in time to advise you," cried Nell Barber.

" Don't say Yes unless his eyes are blue," drawled a brunette.

" Unless they 're black, you mean," sharply amended a bright blonde.

" Make him elope with you," suggested Nell. " It will be such fun to have a real rope-ladder elopement at the Seminary, and we 'll all sit up and see it."

" Oh, do, do, Lina ! " chorused the others.

But Lina, apparently too much chagrined at something to be in a mood for jests, sat with her eyebrows petulantly contracted, her feet thrust out, and the hand holding the letter hanging by her side, her whole attitude indicating despondence.

" Still pensive ! It can't be he 's faithless ! " exclaimed Nell.

" Faithless to those eyes ! I should say not," cried the blonde, whom Lina called her sweetheart, and who claimed to be " engaged " to her according to boarding-school fashion.

" Don't mind him, dear," she went on, throwing herself on the floor, clasping her hands about Lina's knee, and leaning her cheek on it. " You make me so jealous. Have n't you got me, and ain't I enough ? "

" Plenty enough, dear," said Lina, stroking her cheek. " This is only from my brother Charley."

" The one at Watertown 'Sem.' ? "

" Yes," said Lina ; " and oh, girls," she went on, with gloomy energy, " we don't have any good

times at all compared with those boys. They do
really wicked things, hook apples, and carry off
people's gates and signs, and screw up tutors'
doors in the night, and have fights with what he
calls 'townies,' — I don't know exactly what they
are, — and everything. I thought before that we
were doing some things too, but we 're not, compared with all that, and I shall be so ashamed
when I meet him at home not to have anything to
tell except little bits of things."

A depressing pause followed. Lina's disparag-
ing view of achievements in the way of defying
the proprieties, of which all the girls had been
very proud, cast a profound gloom over the circle.
The blonde seemed to voice the common sentiment
when she said, resting her chin on Lina's knee,
and gazing pensively at the wall : —

"Oh, dear! that comes of being girls. We
might as well be good and done with it. We
can't be bad so as to amount to anything."

"Good or bad, we must eat," said Nell Barber.
"I must go and get the spread ready. I forgot
all about it, Lina ; but we came in just to invite
you. Eleven sharp, remember. Three knocks, a
pause, and another, you know. Come, girls."

The brunette followed her, but Lina's little
sweetheart remained.

"What have they got?" demanded the former
listlessly.

"Oh, Nell has a jar of preserves from home, and

I smuggled up a plate of dried beef from tea, and cook let us have some crackers and plates. We tried hard to get a watermelon there was in the pantry, but cook said she did n't dare let us have it. It 's for dinner to-morrow."

Lina's eyes suddenly became introspective; then after a moment she rose slowly and stood in her tracks with an expression of deep thought, absent-mindedly took one step, then another, and after a pause a third, finally pulling up before the mirror, into which she stared vacantly for a moment, and then muttered defiantly as she turned away: —

" We 'll see, Master Charley."

" Lina Maynard, what 's the matter with you? " cried the blonde, who had watched the pantomime with open mouth and growing eyes.

Lina turned and looked at her thoughtfully a moment, and then said with decisiveness: —

" You just go to Nell's, my dear, and say I 'm coming pretty soon; and if you say anything else, I 'll — I 'll never marry you."

The girls were in the habit of doing as Lina wanted them to, and the blonde went, pouting with unappeased curiosity.

To gain exit from the Seminary was a simple matter in these lax days, and five minutes later Lina was walking rapidly along the highway, her lips firm set, but her eyes apprehensively recon-noitring the road ahead, with frequent glances to each side and behind. Once she got over the

stone wall at the roadside in a considerable panic
and crouched in the dewy grass while a belated
villager passed, but it was without further adven-
ture that she finally turned into the road leading
behind Mr. Steele's lot, and after a brief search
identified the garden where she remembered seeing
some particularly fine melons, when out walking
a day or two previous. There they lay, just the
other side the fence, faintly visible in the dim light.

She could not help congratulating herself, by
the way, on the excellent behavior of her nerves,
whose tense, fine-strung condition was a positive
luxury, and she then and there understood how
men might delight in desperate risks for the mere
sake of the exalted and supreme sense of perfect
self-possession that danger brings to some natures.
Not, indeed, that she stopped to indulge any psy-
chological speculations. The coast was clear; not
a footfall or hoof-stroke sounded from the road,
and without delay she began to look about for a
wide place between the rails where she might get
through. Just as she found it, she was startled
by an unmistakable human snore, which seemed
to come from a patch of high corn close to the
melons, and she was fairly puzzled until she observed, about ten rods distant in the same line, an
open attic window. That explained its origin, and
with a passing self-congratulation that she had
made up her mind not to marry a man that snored,
she began to crawl through the fence. When

halfway through the thought struck her, — was n't
it like any other stealing, after all ? This crawling
between rails seemed dreadfully so. Her attitude,
squeezed between two rails and half across the
lower one, was neither graceful nor comfortable,
and perhaps that fact shortened her scruples.

" It can't be really stealing, for I don't feel like
a thief," was the logic that settled it, and the next
moment she had the novel sensation of having both
feet surreptitiously and feloniously on another
person's land. She decidedly did n't relish it, but
she would go ahead now and think of it afterward.
She was pretty sure she never would do it again,
anyhow, experiencing that common sort of repent-
ance beforehand for the thing she was about to do,
the precise moral value of which it would be interesting to inquire. It ought to count for something, for, if it does n't hinder the act, at least it
spoils the fun of it. Here was a melon at her
feet ; should she take it ? That was a bigger one
further on, and her imperious conscientiousness
compelled her to go ten steps further into the
enemy's country to get it, for now that she was
committed to the undertaking, she was bound to
do the best she could.

To stoop, to break the vine, and to secure the
melon were an instant's work ; but as she bent,
the high corn before her waved violently and a big
farmer-looking man in a slouch hat and shocking
old coat sprang out and seized her by the arm,

with a grip not painful but sickeningly firm, exclaiming as he did so : —

" Wal, I swan ter gosh, if 't ain't a gal ! "

Lina dropped the melon, and, barely recalling
the peculiar circumstances in time to suppress a
scream, made a silent, desperate effort to break
away. But her captor's hold was not even shaken,
and he laughed at the impotence of her attempt.
In all her petted life she had never been held a
moment against her will, and it needed not the
added considerations that this man was a coarse,
unknown boor, the place retired, the time midnight, and herself in the position of a criminal, to
give her a feeling of abject terror so great as to
amount to positive nausea, as she realized her utter
powerlessness in his hands.

" So you 've been a-stealin' my melons, hey? "
he demanded gruffly.

The slight shake with which the question was
enforced deprived her of the last vestige of dignity
and self-assertion. She relapsed into the mental
condition of a juvenile culprit undergoing correc-
tion.   Now that she was caught, she no longer
thought of her offense as venial. The grasp of her
captor seemed to put an end to all possible hair-
splitting on that point, and prove that it was nothing more nor less than stealing, and a sense of
guilt left her without any moral support against
her fright.   She was only conscious of utter humiliation, and an abject desire to beg off on any terms.

" What do you go round stealin' folks's melons
for, young woman ? Don't yer folks bring yer up
better 'n that ? It 's a dodrotted shame to 'em, ef
they don't. What did ye want with the melons ?
Don't they give yer enough to eat ter home,
hey ? "

" We were going to have some supper, sir,"
she replied, in a scared, breathless tone, with a
little hope of propitiating him by being extremely
civil and explicit in her replies.

" Who was havin' supper to this time er
night ? " he snorted incredulously.

" We girls," was the faint reply.

" What gals ? "

Had she got to tell where she came from and be
identified ? She could n't, she would n't. But
again came that dreadful shake, and the words
faltered out : —

" Over at the Seminary, sir."

" Whew ! so ye 're one er them, are ye ? What 's
yer name ? "

Cold dew stood on the poor girl's forehead.
She was silent. He might kill her, but she
would n't disgrace her father's name.

" What 's yer name ? " he repeated, with another
shake.

She was still silent, though limp as a rag in his
grasp.

" Wal," said he sharply, after waiting a half minute to see if she would answer, " I guess ye 'll

be more confidin' like to the jedge when he inquiries
in the mornin'. A night in the lock-up makes
folks wonderful civil. Now I'll jest trouble ye to
come along to the police office," and he walked
her along by the arm toward the house.

As the horrible degradation to which she was
exposed flashed upon Lina, the last remnant of
her self-control gave way, and, hanging back with
all her might against his hand, she burst into
sobs.

"Oh, don't, don't! It will kill me. I'll tell
you my name. It's Lina Maynard. My father
is a rich merchant in New York, Broadway, No.
743. He will give you anything, if you let me go.
Anything you want. Oh, please don't! Oh,
don't! I couldn't! I couldn't!"

In this terror-stricken, wild-eyed girl, her face
streaming with tears, and every lineament con-
vulsed with abject dread, there was little enough
to remind Arthur Steele of the queenly maiden
who had favored him with a glance of negligent
curiosity that afternoon. He stopped marching
her along and said reflectively : —

"Lina Maynard, hey! Then you must be the
gal that's down on Amy Steele and wouldn't ask
her to the party to-morrow. Say, ain't yer the
one?"

Lina was too much bewildered by the sudden
change of tack to do more than stammer inarticu-
lately. I am afraid that in her terror she would

have been capable of denying it, if she had thought that would help her. Her captor reflected more deeply, scratched his head, and finally, assuming a diplomatic attitude by thrusting his hands in his pocket, remarked : —

"I s'pose ye 'd like it dummed well ef I was to let yer go and say nothin' more about it. I reelly don't s'pose I 'd orter do it ; but it riles me to see Amy comin' home cryin' every day, and I 'll tell ye what I 'll do. Ef you 'll ask her to yer fandango to-morrer, and be friends with her arterward so she 'll come home happy and cheerful like, I 'll let ye go, and if ye don't, I 'll put ye in jug overnight, sure 's taxes. Say Yes or No now, quick ! "

"Yes, yes ! " Lina cried, with frantic eagerness.

There was scarcely any possible ransom he could have asked that she would not have instantly given. She dared not credit her ears, and stood gazing at him in intense, appealing suspense, as if he might be about to revoke his offer. But instead of that, he turned down the huge collar of the old overcoat, took it off, threw it on the ground, and, turning up the slouch of his hat, stood before her a very good-looking and well-dressed young gentleman, whom she at once recognized and at length identified in her mind as the one walking with Amy that afternoon, which now seemed weeks ago. He bowed very low, and said earnestly enough, though smiling : —

"I humbly beg your pardon."

Lina stared at him with dumb amazement, and he went on : —

" I am Arthur Steele. I came home on a vacation to-day, and was sitting up to watch father's melon-patch for the pure fun of it, expecting to catch some small boys, and when I caught you, I couldn't resist the temptation of a little farce. As for Amy, that only occurred to me at the last; and if you think it unfair, you may have your promise back."

Lina had now measurably recovered her equanimity, and, ignoring his explanation, demanded, as she looked around : —

" How am I to get out of this dreadful place ? " mentally contemplating meanwhile the impossibility of clambering through that fence with a young gentleman looking on.

" I will let down the bars," he said, and they turned toward the fence.

" Let's see, this is your melon, is it not ? " he observed, stooping to pick up the booty Lina had dropped in her first panic. " You must keep that anyhow. You 've earned it."

Since the tables turned so unexpectedly in her favor, Lina had recovered her dignity in some degree, and had become very freezing toward this young man, by whom she began to feel she had been very badly treated. In this reaction of indignation she had really almost forgotten how she came in the garden at all. But this reference to

the melon quite upset her new equanimity, and as
Arthur grinned broadly she blushed and stood
there in awful confusion. Finally she blurted
out : —

"I did n't want your stupid melon. I only
wanted some fun. I can't explain, and I don't care
whether you understand it or not."

Tears of vexation glittered in her eyes. He
sobered instantly, and said, with an air of the
utmost deference : —

"Pardon me for laughing, and do me the justice to believe that I 'm in no sort of danger of misunderstanding you. I hooked too many melons
myself as a boy not to sympathize perfectly. But
you must really let me carry the melon home for
you. What would the girls say, if you returned
empty-handed ? "

"Well, I will take the melon," she said, half
defiantly ; "but I should prefer not to have your
company."

He did not reply till he had let down the bars,
and then said : —

"The streets are not safe at this hour, and you 've
had frights enough for one night."

She made no further objections, and with the
watermelon poised on his shoulder he walked by
her side, neither speaking a word, till they reached
the gate of the Seminary grounds. There she
stopped, and, turning, extended her hands for the
melon. As he gave it to her their eyes met a

moment, and their mutual appreciation of the
humor of the situation expressed itself in an
irrepressible smile that seemed instantly to make
them acquainted, and she responded almost kindly
to his low " Good-evening."

Amy came home jubilant next day. Lina Maynard had invited her to her party, and had been
ever so good to her, and there was nobody in the
world like Lina. Arthur listened and said nothing. All the next week it was the same story
of Lina's beauty, good-nature, cleverness, and per-
fections generally, and, above all, her goodness to
herself, Amy Steele. Lina was indeed fulfilling
her promise with generous over-measure. And after
once taking up with Amy, the sweet simplicity and
enthusiastic loyalty of the child to herself won her
heart completely. The other girls wondered, but
Lina Maynard's freaks always set the fashion, and
Amy, to her astonishment and boundless delight,
found herself the pet of the Seminary. The little
blonde, Lina's sweetheart, alone rebelled against
the new order of things and was furiously jealous,
for which she was promptly snubbed by Lina, and
Amy taken into her place. And meanwhile Lina
caught herself several times wondering whether
Arthur Steele was satisfied with the way she was
keeping her pledge.

It was Wednesday night, and Arthur was to return to New York Thursday morning. Although
he had walked the street every afternoon and had

met nearly all the other girls at the Seminary, he
had not seen Lina again. His mother, whom he
took about a good deal on pleasure drives, seriously
wondered if the eagerness of city life was really
spoiling his faculty for leisurely pleasures. He
always seemed to be looking out ahead for something, instead of quietly enjoying the passing sights
and scenery. He had consented to accompany
Amy to a little church sociable on the evening
before his departure. It was a species of entertainment which he detested, but he thought he
might possibly meet Lina there, as Amy had said
some of the Seminary girls would be present.

At once, on entering the vestry, he caught sight
of her at the other end of the room among a group
of girls. At the sound of the closing door she
glanced up with an involuntary gesture of expectancy, and their eyes met. She looked confused,
and instantly averted her face. There was plenty
of recognition in her expression, but she did not bow,
the real reason being that she was too much embarrassed to think of it. But during the week he had
so many times canvassed the chances of her recognizing him when they should meet that he had
become quite morbid about it, and manifested the
usual alacrity of persons in that state of mind in
jumping at conclusions they wish to avoid. He
had been a fool to think that she would recognize
him as an acquaintance. What had he done but
to insult her, and what associations save distress-

ing ones could she have with him? He would
exchange a few greetings with old friends, and
then quietly slink off home and go to packing up.
He was rather sorry for his mother ; she would
feel so badly to have him moody and cross on the
last evening at home.   Just then some one touched
his sleeve, and looking around he saw Amy.   She
put her flushed little face close to his ear and
whispered : —

"Lina said I might introduce you.   Isn't she
beautiful, though, to-night?   Of course you 'll fall
in love with her, but you must n't try to cut me
out."

Arthur was Amy's ideal of gentlemanly ease and
polish, and she had been very proud of having so
fine a city brother to introduce to the girls.   Imagine her astonishment and chagrin when she saw him
standing before Lina with an exaggeration of the
agitated, sheepish air the girls made such fun of in
their rural admirers !   But if that surprised her,
what was her amazement to see Lina looking
equally confused, and blushing to where her neck
curved beneath the lace, although the brave eyes
met his fairly !   A wise instinct told Amy that
here was something she did n't understand, and
she had better go away, and she did.

" The melon was very good, Mr. Steele," said
Lina demurely, with a glimmer of fun in her
black eyes.

" Miss Maynard, I don't know how I shall beg

pardon, or humble myself enough for my out-
rageous treatment of you," burst forth Arthur. "I
don't know what I should have done if I had n't
had an opportunity for apologizing pretty soon, and
now I scarcely dare look you in the face."

His chagrin and self-reproach were genuine
enough, but he might have left off that last, for he
had n't been looking anywhere else since he came
into the room.

"You did shake me rather hard," she said, with
a smiling contraction of the black eyebrows.

Good heavens! had he actually shaken this
divine creature, — this Cleopatra of a girl, whose
queenly brow gave her hair the look of a coronet!
He groaned in spirit, and looked so self-reproachful
and chagrined that she laughed.

"I don't know about forgiving you for that, but
I 'm so grateful you did n't take me to the lock-up
that I suppose I ought not to mind the shaking."

"But, Miss Maynard, you surely don't think
I was in earnest about that?" he exclaimed, in
strenuous deprecation.

"I don't know, I 'm sure," she said doubtfully.
"You looked as if you were capable of it."

He was going on to protest still farther when she
interrupted him, and said laughingly : —

"You take to apologizing so naturally that I 'd
nearly forgotten that it was not you but I who was
the real culprit. I must really make a few excuses
myself before I hear any more from you."

And then she told him all about her brother Charley's letter, and the spirit of emulation that had got her into trouble. It was easy enough to joke about certain aspects of the matter; but when she came to talk in plain language about her performances that night, she became so much embarrassed and stumbled so badly that Arthur felt very ill at ease.

" And when I think what *would* have happened if I'd fallen into anybody's hands but yours, you seem almost like a deliverer." At which Arthur had another access of humiliation to think how unchivalrously he had treated this princess in disguise. How he would like to catch somebody else abusing her that way! And then he told her all that he had thought and felt about her during the stealing scene, and she gave her side of the drama, to their intense mutual interést.

" Is n't it about time we were going home, Arthur?" said Amy's voice.

He glanced up. The room was nearly empty, and the party from the Seminary were waiting for Lina.

" Miss Maynard, may I call upon you in New York during vacation?"

" I should be happy to see you."

" *Au revoir*, then!"

" *Au revoir!*"

A POSITIVE ROMANCE

My friend Hammond is a bachelor, and lives in chambers in New York. Whenever we meet on my occasional visits to the city, he insists on my spending the night with him. On one of these occasions we had been at the opera during the evening, and had witnessed an ovation to a beautiful and famous singer. We had been stirred by the enthusiasm of the audience, and on our walk home fell to discussing a theme suggested by the scene; namely, the tendency of man to assume a worshipful attitude towards woman, and the reason for it. Was it merely a phase of the passional relation between the sexes, or had it some deeper and more mysterious significance?

When I mentioned the former idea, Hammond demanded why this tendency was not reciprocal between the sexes. As a matter of fact, while women showed endless devotion and fondness for men, their feeling was without the strain of adoration. Particular men's qualities of mind or heart might excite the enthusiastic admiration of women, but such admiration was for cause, and in no way confounded with the worshipful reverence which it was man's instinct to extend to woman as woman, with secondary reference to her qualities as a particular person. No fact in the relations of men and women, he declared, was more striking than this contrast in their mutual attitudes. It was the feminine, not the masculine, ideal which supplied the inspiration of art and the aroma of literature, which was found enshrined in the customs and common speech of mankind. To this I replied that man, being the dominant sex, had imposed his worship on the race as a conquering nation, its gods on the conquered. He, not woman, had been the creator of the art, the literature, and the language which were dedicated to her. Had woman been the dominant sex, the reverse might have happened, and man been obliged to stand upon a pedestal and be worshiped.

Hammond laughed, but declared that I was all wrong. Man's tendency to worship woman, while naturally blending with his passional attraction towards her, did not spring from the instinct of sex, but from the instinct of race, — a far deeper and generally unrecognized impulse. Even though woman should become some day the dominant sex, man need suffer no apprehension of being worshiped. His modesty would be respected.

Some time later, when we had cozily established ourselves before a sea-coal fire in Hammond's quarters, with divers creature comforts at hand for one of our usual symposiums, the subject came up again; and under conditions so favorable to discursiveness our talk took a wide range.

"By the way," said I, apropos of some remark he had made, "talking about the adoration of woman, did not that crack-brained Frenchman, Auguste Comte, propose something of the sort as a feature of his 'Religion of Humanity'?"

Hammond nodded.

"I wonder," I said, "whether that feature of his scheme was ever actually practiced by his followers. I should like to get a chance to ask a Positivist about that, if indeed there are any in America."

Hammond smoked in silence for some time, and finally said, quietly, "Possibly I might tell you something about it myself."

"Hello!" I exclaimed. "How long since you have been a Positivist?"

"About twenty-five years," was the matter-of-fact reply.

"A Positivist of twenty-five years' standing," I ejaculated, "and never told of it! Why have you hid your light under a bushel all this while?"

"I said that it was twenty-five years since I had been a Positivist," replied Hammond; "as long, in fact, as it is since I have been a sophomore. Both experiences belonged to the same year of my college course, and, perhaps you may infer, to the same stage of intellectual development. For about six months at that time I was as ardent a convert, I fancy, as the Religion of Humanity ever had."

"I thought you had told me all about yourself long ago," I said. "How is it that you have kept so mum about this experience ? I should fancy it must have been a decidedly odd one."

" It was a very odd one," replied Hammond, — " the strangest passage, on the whole, I think, in my life. I have never spoken of it, because it is one of those emotional experiences which no man likes to relate unless he is sure of being understood. To tell it to most men would be casting pearls before swine. I have always meant to tell you when a suitable opportunity came up."

" You know," he said, when I had signified my eagerness to hear, " that I graduated at Leroy College. It was a little one-horse institution, but blue as a whetstone in its orthodoxy ; and with my father, who was a clergyman of a very strait sect and staid views, that fact covered a multitude of shortcomings. I was nineteen when I entered, and consequently twenty when, at the beginning of sophomore year, I came under the charge of Professor Regnier. He was a Frenchman, but spoke English with perfect ease and precision and a very slight accent. At the time I knew him, he was probably sixty. His hair was quite gray, but his mustache and imperial were still dark. It was rumored among the students that he had left his native land for political reasons, having played for too high stakes at the national game of revolution. True or not, the report naturally heightened the interest which his personality had for us.

" He made it his business to know personally all

the students in his classes ; and as it is not easy
for a man of sixty, especially if he is also their
teacher, to become really acquainted with students
of twenty, the fact may be taken as evidence of his
unusual tact. He was, I think, the most fascinating man I ever saw. His insight into character
was like magic, his manners were charming, and
his Gallic vivacity made him seem like a boy.
Gradually, while still remaining to the rest of the
students a genial and friendly instructor, he sin-
gled out a smaller circle of particular intimates.
Of these I was one, and I believe the most trusted.

" Of course we boys were immensely flattered by
the partiality of such a man ; but equally of course
the pursuit of his own pleasure could scarcely have
been the motive which impelled him to seek our
companionship. It was, in fact, a motive as unselfish as that of the missionary who leaves the
comforts and refinements of civilization and exiles
himself among savages that he may win them to
his faith. He had been a personal friend and
disciple of Auguste Comte, then but lately dead,
and on coming to America had sought his present
employment, not merely as a means of livelihood,
but equally for the opportunity it offered for pro-
pagating the new gospel among young men. Do
you know much about what Positivism is ? "

I confessed that I knew next to nothing, —
scarcely more than that there was such a thing.

" I shall not bore you with an account of it,"

resumed Hammond, " further than to say that it is
a scheme for the perfection of the human race.   It
rejects as idle all theories of superhuman intelli-
gences, and declares the supreme object of the
individual love and devotion should be humanity.
The rational demonstration of the truth of this
system is sought in the course of history, which
is claimed to prove Positivism the finality of social
evolution.   You will find anything else you want
to know about it in the books.   I dare say you will
not be converted ; but if you were nineteen instead
of twice that, with Hippolyte Regnier to indoctri-
nate you, I fancy the result would be about what it
was in my case.

" His personal influence over us, and the intoxicating flattery implied in being seriously reasoned
with on themes so lofty by a man whom we so
greatly admired, would have gone far, no doubt, to
commend to us any form of opinions he might have
taught ; but there were not lacking other reasons
to account for his success in converting. us.   As for
Comte's dogmatic denial of superhuman existence,
and his fanciful schemes of new society, we were
too young and crude to realize how unphilosophic
was the former, how impossible and undesirable
was the latter.   While accepting them as facts of a
new creed, they meant little to us, nor did Regnier
much insist upon them.   What most he did insist
on was the ethical side of Positivism, — the idea of
the essential unity of the individual with the im-

mortal race of man, and his obvious duty to forget self in its service. What could be better adapted to affect generous and impassioned boys than an appeal like this? The magnificent audacity of it, the assumption of man's essential nobleness, the contemptuous refusal to make any terms with selfishness, captivated our imaginations. I know now, indeed, that this enthusiasm of humanity, this passion of self-abnegation, which I thought a new religion, was the heart of the old religions. In its new-fangled disguise the truth and virtue of the doctrine were still operative, and the emotional crisis through which I passed I found was as essentially religious as it was in form unorthodox.

"At the end of sophomore year there were a half-dozen very positive young Positivists in our class. The pride of intellect which we felt in our new enlightenment was intoxicating. To be able to look down from a serene height, with compassion frequently tempered by contempt, upon the rest of the world still groping in the mists of childish superstition, was prodigiously to the taste of youths of eighteen and twenty. How, to be sure, we did turn up our noses at the homely teachings in the college chapel on Sundays! Well do I remember attending my father's church when at home on vacation, and endeavoring to assume the mental attitude of a curious traveler in a Buddhist temple. Together with the intellectual vanity which it fostered, our new faith was commended to us by its flavor of the secret, the hazardous, and the forbidden. We were delightfully conscious of being concerned in a species of conspiracy, which if it came to light would convulse the college and the community, have us expelled, and cause no end of scandal to the public.

"But the more I took my new faith in earnest and tried to make of it the religion it claimed to be, I was troubled by a lack that seemed to be inherent. Humanity, the object of our devotion, was but an abstraction, a rhetorical expression for a mass of individuals. To these individuals I might indeed render affection, service, compassion, tenderness, self-sacrifice; but their number and pettiness forbade me the glow of adoration with which service was touched in religions which offered a personified object of adoration. When, finally, I confided these troubles to Regnier, I expected to be rebuked; but on the contrary, and to my great discomfiture, he embraced me effusively after the Gallic manner. He said that he had been waiting for the time when in the course of my development I should become conscious of the need I had confessed before explaining to me the provision made for it by Positivism.

"To start with, he put in, as a sort of special plea for Positivism, that it was not singular among religions in recognizing as the object of devotion an abstraction, the mode of the existence of which was a mystery. As a solace to their votaries and

an aid to their faith, nearly all religions recognized
sacred emblems ; not indeed to be confounded in
clear minds with the original object of devotion,
but worthy of reverence in its place, as its special
representative and reminder.   In precisely this
sense the sacred emblem of humanity was woman.

" Of course, Positivism claiming to be a creed
of demonstration, not of faith, Regnier did not ask
me to receive this proposition as his mere statement, but proceeded to establish its reasonableness
by logic.   I am going to give you what I remember of his argument, because I believe still, as I
did when I heard it, that it is the only philosophical explanation of the instinctive reverence of
man for woman which we have been talking about
to-night.   It was given to me, of course, as a doctrine peculiar to Positivism ; but I don't know of
any form of religious belief inconsistent with the
recognition of the sacred quality of womanhood on
the grounds given by Regnier.   Indeed, I am by
no means sure whether the doctrine as I received
it is orthodox Positivism at all.   I have reason to
think that Regnier was quite too original a character for a very good interpreter, and should be
interested to know how far his ideas were his own
and how far his master's.

" First he pointed out to me as matter of fact
that there was no more striking feature of the
modern and humane as compared with the ancient
and barbaric world than the constantly growing

tendency of the most civilized races to apotheosize womanhood. The virgin ideal had been set up by the larger part of Christendom as the object of divine honors. The age of chivalry had translated for all time the language of love into that of worship. Art had personified under the feminine form every noble and affecting ideal of the race, till now it was in the name of woman that man's better part adjured his baser in every sort of strife towards the divine. Is it alleged that it is man's passion for woman that has moved him thus in a sort to deify the sex? Passion is no teacher of reverence. Moreover, it is as the race outgrows the dominion of passion that it recognizes the worshipfulness of woman. The gross and sensual recognize in her no element of sacredness. It is the clear soul of the boy, the poet, and the seer which is most surely aware of it. Equally vain is it to seek the explanation in any general superiority of woman to man, either moral or mental. Her qualities are indeed in engaging contrast with his, but on the whole no such superiority has ever been maintained. How, then, were we to account for a phenomenon so great in its proportions that either it indicates a world-wide madness infecting the noblest nations while sparing the basest, or else must be the outcome of some profound monition of nature, which, in proportion as man's upward evolution progresses, he becomes capable of apprehending? Why this impassioned exaltation by him of his tender companion? What is the secret spring that makes her the ceaseless fountain of lofty inspiration she is to him? What is the hint of divinity in her gentle mien that brings him to his knees? Who is this goddess veiled in woman whom men instinctively reverence yet cannot name?

"The adoration of woman, which may almost be called the natural religion of the modern man, springs from his recognition, instinctive when not conscious, that she is in an express sense, as he is not, the type, the representative, and the symbol of the race from which he springs, of that immortal and mystical life in which the secret of his own is hid. She is this by virtue, not of her personal qualities, but of the mother-sex, which, overbearing in part her individuality, consecrates her to the interests of the race, and makes her the channel of those irresistible attractions by which humanity exists and men are made to serve it. As compared with woman's peculiar identification with the race, man's relation to it is an exterior one. By his constitution he is above all an individual, and that is the natural line of his development. The love of woman is the centripetal attraction which in due time brings him back from the individual tangent to blend him again with mankind. In returning to woman he returns to humanity. All that there is in man's sentiment for woman which is higher than passion and larger than personal tenderness

— all, that is to say, which makes his love for her the grand passion which in noble hearts it is — is the fact that under this form his passion for the race finds expression. Mysterious ties, subtending consciousness, bind him, though seemingly separate, to the mighty life of humanity, his greater self, and these are the chords which, when ' Love took up the harp of life,' . . . ' passed in music out of sight.' In woman humanity is enshrined and made concrete for the homage of man. This is the mighty indwelling which causes her to suggest something more august than herself, and invests her with an impersonal majesty commanding reverence.

" You may imagine with what power such a doctrine as this, set forth by an enthusiast like Regnier, appealed to the mind of an impassioned boy of twenty, as yet pure as a girl, but long vaguely stirred by the master passion of our nature. The other tenets of the Religion of Humanity had been impressed upon me by argument, but at the mere statement of this my heart responded, *O Dea Certe!*

" Subsequently, in response to my questioning, Regnier explained to me how the master had recommended his disciples to give practical effect to the cult of womanhood. I must remember that it was nothing new and nothing peculiar to Positivism for men to adore women to the point even of idolatry. Lovers constantly were doing it. But

in these cases the worshipers did not look beyond
the personality of the idol. Possibly, no doubt,
some dim apprehension of the true grounds of
woman's worshipfulness might mingle with the
lover's sentiment, but it was very far from being
the clear and distinct sense necessary to redeem
his homage from the charge of extravagance. On
the other hand, the spirit in which women received
the homage men rendered them was usually as
mistaken as that in which it was offered. Either,
on the one hand, from an impulse of personal modesty they deprecated it, or, on the other hand, they
accepted it as a gratification to their personal vanity. In either case, they equally misapprehended
their true and valid title to worship, which, while
personal qualities might enhance or partially ob-
scure it, was itself in root more than personal, and
consisted in the martyr and mother sex which so
peculiarly sacrificed and consecrated them to the
interests of humanity as to draw to them the homage and loyalty of all men who loved their race.
It had been the counsel of his master, Regnier
said, that, while his disciples should hold all women in exalted reverence, they should peculiarly
address this general sentiment to some particular
woman, who, being of the same faith, should be
able to accept it worthily and without self-exalta-
tion, in the spirit in which it was offered.

" Of course the reflection was obvious that in
the existing conditions of the Positivist propaganda

in America it would be impossible to find a woman
capable of understanding, much less of accepting,
such a relation, and, therefore, that to me the cult
which I had been taught must remain entirely
theoretical. Homage from men which did not
insure to the titillation of the vanity would seem to
women, as usually educated, equally incomprehen-
sible and unprofitable.

"It was in recognition of this situation that
Regnier ended by making a proposition which testified, more strongly than anything else could have
done, both to the enthusiasm and sincerity with
which he himself held the faith he preached, and
to his confidence in my own equal singleness of
heart. He had never before spoken of his personal
history or home life. Several times I had spent
the evening at his house, but on these occasions I
had seen only himself. Certain womanly belongings, however, which I had noticed, and the sound
of a piano once or twice, had suggested that the
house might not be without a feminine presence.
The professor now told me that long ago in France,
for a few short, blissful years, he had been the husband of the sweetest of women. She had left behind a daughter, the sole companion of his life and
the apple of his eye. She lived in complete seclu-
sion, rarely even leaving the house. He did not
desire her to make acquaintances in this country,
nor indeed was she able to speak a word of any
language but her own. There was no question of

my making her acquaintance in the ordinary sense,
or even of meeting her a second time, but if I desired to testify my new appreciation of the sacred
quality of womanhood, it was possible that she
might consent to receive my homage in the name
of her sex. He could not be sure what she would
say, but he would speak with her about it.

" The following day, a note from him requesting
that I should call at his house that evening intimated that he had succeeded in carrying his point.
When I called at the time set, he told me that he
had found it more difficult than he had anticipated
to gain his daughter's consent to see me. She had
been very reluctant to assume the attitude required
of her, and only her respect for his wishes and the
good of the cause, and the assurance he had given
her of the entire ingenuousness of my own motive,
had induced her finally to yield. After some talk
as to the significance of the interview before me,
which I was too much agitated to comprehend, he
bade me follow him.

" As may readily be supposed, my fancy, from
the moment Regnier had suggested this interview,
had been exceedingly busy with conjectures as to
the sort of scene it would prove, and especially as
to the personality of her who was to be the central figure. Except his intimation that the interview would be necessarily without interchange of
speech and presumably brief, scarcely more, probably, than a confrontation, he had told me nothing.

Of course, however, my fancies had not failed to take some form. I think I had a general expectation of finding myself in the presence of a beautiful woman, statuesquely shaped and posed. I imagine that I rather expected her to be enthroned or standing upon some sort of dais, and I am sure that I should not have been surprised had there been some artificial arrangement of lights as in a theatre to add effectiveness to the figure.

" I followed Regnier through several rooms without raising my eyes. Presently he paused and said, ' My daughter.'

" Thrilling with the premonition of a vision of imperious or melting loveliness which should compel my homage by its mere aspect, I raised my eyes to find myself facing a plain-featured, plainly dressed young woman, not ill-looking certainly, but destitute of a single trait striking enough to have won a second glance from me had I met her on the street.

" Her father need not have told me of her reluctance to assume the part his wishes had imposed upon her. For the fraction of an instant only, a pair of black eyes had met mine, and then she had bent her face as low as she could. The downcast head, the burning cheeks, the quick heaving of the breast, the pendent arms, with tensely interlacing fingers and palms turned downward, all told the story of a shy and sensitive girl submitting from a sense of duty to a painful ordeal.

"The sudden and complete wreck of all my preconceptions as to her appearance, as well as the accessories of the scene, left me for a few moments fairly dazed. Not only were my highly wrought expectations as to the present interview brought to humiliating discomfiture, but the influence of the disillusionment instantly retroacted with the effect of making the entire noble and romantic cult which had led up to this unlucky confrontation seem a mere farrago of extravagant and baseless sentiment. What on earth had Regnier been thinking of, to plan deliberately a situation calculated to turn a cherished sentiment into ridicule? If he had seriously thought his daughter capable of supporting the rôle he had assigned her, had there ever been a like case of parental fatuity?

"But even as I indignantly asked myself this question, I saw a great light, and recognized that the trouble was neither with Regnier's fatuity nor with his daughter's lack of charms, but with myself, and a most unworthy misconception into which I had fallen as to the whole object and purport of this interview. What had the beauty or the lack of beauty of this girl to do with the present occasion? I was not here to render homage to her for the beauty of her sex, but for its perpetual consecration and everlasting martyrdom to my race. The revulsion of feeling which followed the recognition of the grossness of the mistake I

had made had no doubt the effect of greatly inten-
sifying my emotions. I was overcome with contrition for the unworthiness with which I had
stood before this girl who had so trusted to my
magnanimity, appraising her like a sensualist when
I should have been on my knees before her. A
reaction of compunctious loyalty made my very
heartstrings ache. I saw now how well it had
been for a weak-minded fool like myself that she
had not chanced to be beautiful or even pretty, for
then I should have cheated myself of all that distinguished this solemn meeting from the merest
lover's antics. I won in that moment an impression of the tawdriness of mere beauty which I
have never gotten over. It seemed to me then,
and more or less has ever since, that the beauty of
women is a sort of veil which hides from superficial
eyes the true adorableness of womanhood.

"Unable longer to resist the magnetism of my
gaze, her eyes rose slowly to mine. At their first
meeting, her face became crimson ; but as she did
not avert her eyes, and continued to look into
mine, the flush paled swiftly from her face, and
with it all the other evidences of her embarrassment passed as quickly away, leaving her bearing
wholly changed. It was plain that through my
eyes, which in that moment must have been truly
windows of my soul, she had read my inmost
thoughts, and had perceived how altogether impertinent to their quality self-consciousness on her

part would be. As with a gaze growing ever
more serene and steadfast she continued to read
my thoughts, her face changed, and from the look
of a shy and timid maiden it gradually took on
that of a conscious goddess. Then, as still she
read on, there came another change. The soft
black eyes grew softer and yet softer, and then
slowly filled with tears till they were like brimming vases. She did not smile, but her brows
and lips assumed a look of benignant sweetness
indescribable.

" In that moment no supernatural aureole would
have added sacredness to that head, or myth of
heavenly origin have made that figure seem more
adorable. With right good-will I sank upon my
knees. She reached forth her hand to me and I
pressed my lips to it. I lifted up the hem of her
dress and kissed it. There was a rustle of garments. I looked up and she was gone.

" I suppose immediately after that I must have
left the house. I only know that the dawn found
me miles out of town, walking aimlessly about and
talking to myself."

Hammond poured himself a glass of wine, drunk
it slowly, and then fell into a profound reverie,
apparently forgetful of my presence.

" Is that all ? " I asked at last. " Did you not
see her again ? "

" No," he answered, " I never saw her again.
Probably, as her father had intimated, he did not

intend that I should. But circumstances also prevented. The very next day there was an explosion in college. There had been a Judas among my fellow-disciples, and the faculty had been informed of the Positivist propaganda going on under their noses. I was suspended for six months. When I returned to college, Regnier had disappeared. He had of course been promptly dismissed, and it was rumored that he had gone back to France. He had left no trace, and I never heard of him again or of his daughter. I don't even know the name of the woman I worshiped."

LOST

THE 25th of May, 1866, was no doubt to many a quite indifferent date, but to two persons it was the saddest day of their lives. Charles Randall that day left Bonn, Germany, to catch the steamer home to America, and Ida Werner was left with a mountain of grief on her gentle bosom, which must be melted away drop by drop, in tears, before she could breathe freely again.

A year before, Randall, hunting for apartments, his last term at the university just begun, had seen the announcement, "*Zimmer zu vermiethen*," in the hall below the flat where the Werners lived. Ida answered his ring, for her father was still at his government office, and her mother had gone out to the market to buy the supper. She would much rather her mother had been at home to show the gentleman the rooms; but, knowing that they could not afford to lose a chance to rent them, she plucked up courage, and, candle in hand, showed him through the suite. When he came next day with his baggage, he learned for the first time what manner of apartments he had engaged; for although he had protracted the investigation the previous evening to the furthest corner, and had

been most exacting as to explanations, he had
really rented the rooms entirely on account of a
certain light in which a set of Madonna features,
in auburn hair, had shown at the first opening of
the door.

A year had passed since this, and a week ago a
letter from home had stated that his father, indignant at his unexplained stay six months beyond
the end of his course, had sent him one last remit-
tance, barely sufficient for a steamer ticket, with
the intimation that if he did not return on a set
day, he must thenceforth attend to his own ex-
chequer. The 25th was the last day on which he
could leave Bonn to catch the requisite steamer.
Had it been in November, nature at least would
have sympathized ; it was cruel that their autumn
time of separation should fall in the spring, when
the sky is full of bounteous promise and the earth
of blissful trust.

Love is so improvident that a parting a year
away is no more feared than death, and a month's
end seems dim and distant. But a week, — a week
only, — that even to love is short, and the beginning of the end. The chilling mist that rose from
the gulf of separation so near before them over-
shadowed all the brief remnant of their path.
They were constantly together. But a silence had
come upon them. Never had words seemed idler,
they had so much to say. They could say nothing
that did not mock the weight on their hearts, and

seem trivial and impertinent because it was exclusive of more important matter. The utmost they could do was to lay their hearts open toward each other to receive every least impression of voice, and look, and manner, to be remembered afterward. At evening they went into the minster church, and, sitting in the shadows, listened to the sweet, shrill choir of boys whose music distilled the honey of sorrow; and as the deep bass organ chords gripped their hearts with the tones that underlie all weal and woe, they looked in each other's eyes, and did for a space feel so near that all the separation that could come after seemed but a trifling thing.

It was all arranged between them. He was to earn money, or get a position in business, and return in a year or two at most and bring her to America.

"Oh," she said once, "if I could but sleep till thou comest again to wake me, how blessed I should be; but, alas, I must wake all through the desolate time!"

Although for the most part she comforted him rather than he her, yet at times she gave way, and once suddenly turned to him and hid her face on his breast, and said, trembling with tearless sobs: —

"I know I shall never see thee more, Karl. Thou wilt forget me in thy great, far land and wilt love another. My heart tells me so."

And then she raised her head, and her streaming eyes blazed with anger.

"I will hover about thee, and if thou lovest
another, I will kill her as she sleeps by thy side."

And the woman must have loved him much who,
after seeing that look of hers, would have married
him. But a moment after she was listening with
abject ear to his promises.

The day came at last. He was to leave at three
o'clock. After the noontide meal, Ida's mother
sat with them and they talked a little about America, Frau Werner exerting herself to give a cheerful tone to the conversation, and Randall answering her questions absently and without taking his
eyes off Ida, who felt herself beginning to be
seized with a nervous trembling. At last Frau
Werner rose and silently left the room, looking
back at them as she closed the door with eyes full
of tears. Then, as if by a common impulse, they
rose and put their arms about each other's necks,
and their lips met in a long, shuddering kiss.
The breath came quicker and quicker ; sobs broke
the kisses ; tears poured down and made them salt
and bitter, as parting kisses should be in which
sweetness is mockery. Hitherto they had controlled their feelings, or rather she had controlled
him ; but it was no use any longer, for the time
had come, and they abandoned themselves to the
terrible voluptuousness of unrestrained grief, in
which there is a strange, meaningless suggestion of

power, as though it might possibly be a force that could affect or remove its own cause if but wild and strong enough.

"Herr Randall, the carriage waits and you will lose the train," said Frau Werner from the door, in a husky voice.

"I will not go, by God!" he swore, as he felt her clasp convulsively strengthen at the summons. The lesser must yield to the greater, and no loss or gain on earth was worth the grief upon her face. His father might disinherit him, America might sink, but she must smile again. And she did, — brave, true girl and lover. The devotion his resolute words proved was like a strong nervine to restore her self-control. She smiled as well as her trembling lips would let her, and said, as she loosed him from her arms: —

"No, thou must go, Karl. But thou wilt return, *nicht wahr?*"

I would not venture to say how many times he rushed to the door, and, glancing back at her as she stood there desolate, followed his glance once more to her side. Finally, Frau Werner led him as one dazed to the carriage, and the impatient driver drove off at full speed.

It is seven years later, and Randall is pacing the deck of an ocean steamer, outward bound from New York. It is the evening of the first day out. Here and there passengers are leaning over the

bulwarks, pensively regarding the sinking sun as
it sets for the first time between them and their
native land, or maybe taking in with awed faces
the wonder of the deep, which has haunted their
imaginations from childhood. Others are already
busily striking up acquaintances with fellow-pas-
sengers, and a bridal pair over yonder sit thrilling
with the sense of isolation from the world that
so emphasizes their mutual dependence and all-
importance to each other. And other groups are
talking business, and referring to money and mar-
kets in New York, London, and Frankfort as
glibly as if they were on land, much to the secret
shock of certain raw tourists, who marvel at the in-
sensitiveness of men who, thus speeding between
two worlds, and freshly in the presence of the
most august and awful form of nature, can keep
their minds so steadily fixed upon cash-books and
ledgers.

But Randall, as, with the habit of an old voy-
ager, he already falls to pacing the deck, is too
much engrossed with his own thoughts to pay
much heed to these things. Only, as he passes a
group of Germans, and the familiar accents of the
sweet, homely tongue fall on his ear, he pauses,
and lingers near.

The darkness gathers, the breeze freshens, the
waves come tumbling out of the east, and the motion of the ship increases as she rears upward to
meet them. The groups on deck are thinning out

fast, as the passengers go below to enjoy the fear-
some novelty of the first night at sea, and to compose themselves to sleep as it were in the hollow of
God's hand. But long into the night Randall's
cigar still marks his pacing up and down as he
ponders, with alternations of tender, hopeful glow
and sad foreboding, the chances of his quest. Will
he find her ?

It is necessary to go back a little. When Randall reached America on his return from Germany,
he immediately began to sow his wild oats, and
gave his whole mind to it. Answering Ida's letters got to be a bore, and he gradually ceased
doing it. Then came a few sad reproaches from
her, and their correspondence ceased. Meanwhile,
having had his youthful fling, he settled down as
a steady young man of business. One day he was
surprised to observe that he had of late insensibly
fallen into the habit of thinking a good deal in a
pensive sort of way about Ida and those German
days. The notion occurred to him that he would
hunt up her picture, which he had not thought of
in five years. With misty eyes and crowding
memories he pored over it, and a wave of regretful, yearning tenderness filled his breast.

Late one night, after long search, he found
among his papers a bundle of her old letters, already growing yellow. Being exceedingly rusty
in his German, he had to study them out word by
word. That night, till the sky grew gray in the

east, he sat there turning the pages of the diction-
ary with wet eyes and glowing face, and selecting
definitions by the test of the heart. He found
that some of these letters he had never before
taken the pains to read through. In the bitterness of his indignation, he cursed the fool who had
thrown away a love so loyal and priceless.

All this time he had been thinking of Ida as if
dead, so far off in another world did those days
seem. It was with extraordinary effect that the
idea finally flashed upon him that she was probably alive, and now in the prime of her beauty.
After a period of feverish and impassioned excitement, he wrote a letter full of wild regret and
beseeching, and an ineffable tenderness. Then he
waited. After a long time it came back from the
German dead-letter office. There was no person
of the name at the address. She had left Bonn,
then. Hastily setting his affairs in order, he
sailed for Germany on the next steamer.

The incidents of the voyage were a blank in his
mind. On reaching Bonn, he went straight from
the station to the old house in ——strasse. As
he turned into it from the scarcely less familiar
streets leading thither, and noted each accustomed
landmark, he seemed to have just returned to tea
from an afternoon lecture at the university. In
every feature of the street some memory lurked,
and, as he passed, threw out delaying tendrils,
clutching at his heart. Rudely he broke away,

hastening on to that house near the end of the street, in each of whose quaint windows fancy framed the longed-for face. She was not there, he knew, but for a while he stood on the other side of the street, unmindful of the stares and jostling of the passers-by, gazing at the house-front, and letting himself imagine from moment to moment that her figure might flit across some window, or issue from the door, basket in hand, for the evening market-ing, on which journey he had so often accompanied her. At length, crossing the street, he inquired for the Werner family. The present tenants had never heard the name. Perhaps the tenants from whom they had received the house might be better informed. Where were they? They had moved to Cologne. He next went to the Bonn police-office, and from the records kept there, in which pretty much everything about every citizen is set down, ascertained that several years previous Herr Werner had died of apoplexy, and that no one of the name was now resident in the city. Next day he went to Cologne, hunted up the former tenants of the house, and found that they remembered quite distinctly the Werner family, and the death of the father and only breadwinner. It had left the mother and daughter quite without resources, as Randall had known must probably have been the case. His informants had heard that they had gone to Düsseldorf.

His search had become a fever. After waiting

seven years, a delay of ten minutes was unendurable. The trains seemed to creep. And yet, on reaching Düsseldorf, he did not at once go about his search, but said to himself : —

" Let me not risk the killing of my last hope till I have warmed myself with it one more night, for to-morrow there may be no more warmth in it."

He went to a hotel, ordered a room and a bottle of wine, and sat over it all night, indulging the belief that he would find her the next day. He denied his imagination nothing, but conjured up before his mind's eye the lovely vision of her fairest hour, complete even to the turn of the neck, the ribbon in the hair, and the light in the blue eyes. So he would turn into the street. Yes, here was the number. Then he rings the bell. She comes to the door. She regards him a moment indifferently. Then amazed recognition, love, happiness, transfigure her face. " Ida !" " Karl !" and he clasps her sobbing to his bosom, from which she shall never be sundered again.

The result of his search next day was the discovery that mother and daughter had been at Düsseldorf until about four years previous, where the mother had died of consumption, and the daughter had removed, leaving no address. The lodgings occupied by them were of a wretched character, showing that their circumstances must have been very much reduced.

There was now no further clue to guide his

search. It was destined that the last he was to know of her should be that she was thrown on the tender mercies of the world, — her last friend gone, her last penny expended. She was buried out of his sight, not in the peaceful grave, with its tender associations, but buried alive in the living world ; hopelessly hid in the huge, writhing confusion of humanity. He lingered in the folly of despair about those sordid lodgings in Düsseldorf, as one might circle vainly about the spot in the ocean where some pearl of great price had fallen overboard.

After a while he roused again, and began putting advertisements for Ida into the principal newspapers of Germany, and making random visits to towns all about to consult directories and police records. A singular sort of misanthropy possessed him. He cursed the multitude of towns and villages that reduced the chances in his favor to so small a thing. He cursed the teeming throngs of men, women, and children, in whose mass she was lost, as a jewel in a mountain of rubbish. Had he possessed the power, he would in those days, without an instant's hesitation, have swept the bewildering, obstructing millions of Germany out of existence, as the miner washes away the earth to bring to light the grain of gold in his pan. He must have scanned a million women's faces in that weary search, and the bitterness of that million-fold disappointment left its trace in a feeling of aversion for the feminine countenance and figure that he was long in overcoming.

Knowing that only by some desperate chance he could hope to meet her in his random wanderings, it seemed to him that he was more likely to be successful by resigning as far as possible all volition, and leaving the guidance of the search to chance ; as if Fortune were best disposed toward those who most entirely abdicated intelligence and trusted themselves to her. He sacredly followed every impulse, never making up his mind an hour before at what station he should leave the cars, and turning to the right or left in his wanderings through the streets of cities, as much as possible without intellectual choice. Sometimes, waking suddenly in the middle of the night, he would rise, dress with eager haste, and sally out to wander through the dark streets, thinking he might be led of Providence to meet her. And, once out, nothing but utter exhaustion could drive him back ; for how could he tell but in the moment after he had gone, she might pass ? He had recourse to every superstition of sortilege, clairvoyance, presentiment, and dreams. And all the time his desperation was singularly akin to hope. He dared revile no seeming failure, not knowing but just that was the necessary link in the chain of accidents destined to bring him face to face with her. The darkest hour might usher in the sunburst. The possibility that this was at last the blessed chance lit up his eyes ten thousand times as they fell on some new face.

But at last he found himself back in Bonn, with the feverish infatuation of the gambler, which had succeeded hope in his mind, succeeded in turn by utter despair! His sole occupation now was revisiting the spots which he had frequented with her in that happy year. As one who has lost a princely fortune sits down at length to enumerate the little items of property that happen to be attached to his person, disregarded before but now his all, so Randall counted up like a miser the little store of memories that were thenceforth to be his all. Wonderfully, the smallest details of those days came back to him. The very seats they sat in at public places, the shops they entered together, their promenades and the pausing-places on them, revived in memory under a concentrated inward gaze like invisible paintings brought over heat.

One afternoon, after wandering about the city for some hours, he turned into a park to rest. As he approached his usual bench, sacred to him because Ida and he in the old days had often sat there, he was annoyed to see it already occupied by a pleasant-faced, matronly looking German woman, who was complacently listening to the chatter of a couple of small children. Randall threw himself upon the unoccupied end of the bench, rather hoping that his gloomy and preoccupied air might cause them to depart and leave him to his melancholy reverie. And, indeed, it was not long before the children stopped their play and gathered timidly about their mother, and soon after the bench tilted slightly as she relieved it of her substantial charms, saying in a cheery, pleasant voice : —

"Come, little ones, the father will be at home before us."

It was a secluded part of the garden, and the plentiful color left her cheeks as the odd gentleman at the other end of the bench turned with a great start at the sound of her voice, and transfixed her with a questioning look. But in a moment he said : —

"Pardon me, madame, a thousand times. The sound of your voice so reminded me of a friend I have lost that I looked up involuntarily."

The woman responded with good-natured assurances that he had not at all alarmed her. Meanwhile Randall had an opportunity to notice that, in spite of the thick-waisted and generally matronly figure, there were, now he came to look closely, several rather marked resemblances to Ida. The eyes were of the same blue tint, though about half as large, the cheeks being twice as full. In spite of the ugly style of dressing it, he saw also that the hair was like Ida's; and as for the nose, that feature which changes least, it might have been taken out of Ida's own face. As may be supposed, he was thoroughly disgusted to be reminded of that sweet girlish vision by this broadly moulded, com-

fortable-looking matron. His romantic mood was
scattered for that evening at least, and he knew
he should not get the prosaic suggestions of the
unfortunate resemblance out of his mind for a
week at least. It would torment him as a humor-
ous association spoils a sacred hymn.

He bowed with rather an ill grace, and was about
to retire, when a certain peculiar turn of the neck,
as the lady acknowledged his salute, caught his eye
and turned him to stone. Good God ! this woman
was Ida !

He stood there in a condition of mental paraly-
sis. The whole fabric of his thinking and feeling
for months of intense emotional experience had
instantly been annihilated, and he was left in the
midst of a great void in his consciousness out of
touching-reach of anything. There was no sharp
pang, but just a bewildered numbness. A few filaments only of the romantic feeling for Ida that
filled his mind a moment before still lingered, floating about it, unattached to anything, like vague
neuralgic feelings in an amputated stump, as if to
remind him of what had been there.

All this was as instantaneous as a galvanic shock
the moment he had recognized — let us not say
Ida, but this evidence that she was no more. It
occurred to him that the woman, who stood staring,
was in common politeness entitled to some explanation. He was in just that state of mind when,
the only serious interest having suddenly dropped

out of the life, the minor conventionalities loom up
as peculiarly important and obligatory.

"You were Fraülein Ida Werner, and lived at
No. —— ——strasse in 1866, *nicht wahr?*"

He spoke in a cold, dead tone, as if making a
necessary but distasteful explanation to a stranger.

"Yes, truly," replied the woman curiously;
"but my name is now Frau Stein," glancing at
the children, who had been staring open-mouthed
at the queer man.

"Do you remember Karl Randall?   I am he."

The most formal of old acquaintances could
hardly have recalled himself in a more indifferent
manner.

"*Herr Gott im Himmel!*" exclaimed the wo-
man, with the liveliest surprise and interest.
"Karl! Is it possible? Yes, now I recognize you.
Surely! surely!"

She clapped one hand to her bosom, and dropped
on the bench to recover herself.   Fleshy people,
overcome by agitation, are rather disagreeable objects.   Randall stood looking at her with a singular
expression of aversion on his listless face.   But,
after panting a few times, the woman recovered her
vivacity and began to ply him vigorously with exclamations and questions, beaming the while with
delighted interest.   He answered her like a schoolboy, too destitute of presence of mind to do otherwise than to yield passively to her impulse.   But
he made no inquiries whatever of her, and did not

distantly allude to the reason of his presence in Germany. As he stood there looking at her, the real facts about that matter struck him as so absurd and incredible that he could not believe them himself.

Pretty soon he observed that she was becoming a little conscious in her air, and giving a slightly sentimental turn to the conversation. It was not for some time that he saw her drift, so utterly without connection in his mind were Ida and this comfortable matron before him; and when he did, a smile at the exquisite absurdity of the thing barely twitched the corners of his mouth, and ended in a sad, puzzled stare that rather put the other out of countenance.

But the children had now for some time been whimpering for supper and home, and at length Frau Stein rose, and, with an urgent request that Randall should call on her and see her husband, bade him a cordial adieu. He stood there watching her out of sight, with an unconscious smile of the most refined and subtle cynicism. Then he sat down and stared vacantly at the close-cropped grass on the opposite side of the path. By what handle should he lay hold of his thoughts?

That woman could not retroact and touch the memory of Ida. That dear vision remained intact. He drew forth his locket, and opening it gazed passionately at the fair girlish face, now so hopelessly passed away. By that blessed picture he could hold her and defy the woman. Remembering that fat, jolly, comfortable matron, he should not at least ever again have to reproach himself with his cruel treatment of Ida. And yet why not? What had the woman to do with her? She had suffered as much as if the woman had not forgotten it all. His reckoning was with Ida, — was with her. Where should he find her? In what limbo could he imagine her? Ah, that was the wildering cruelty of it. She was not this woman, nor was she dead in any conceivable natural way so that her girlish spirit might have remained eternally fixed. She was nothing. She was nowhere. She existed only in this locket, and her only soul was in his heart, far more surely than in this woman who had forgotten her.

Death was a hopeful, cheerful state compared to that nameless nothingness that was her portion. For had she been dead, he could still have loved her soul; but now she had none. The soul that once she had, and, if she had then died, might have kept, had been forfeited by living on, and had passed to this woman, and would from her pass on further till finally fixed and vested in the decrepitude of age by death. So, then, it was death and not life that secured the soul, and his sweet Ida had none because she had not died in time. Ah! had not he heard somewhere that the soul is immortal and never dies? Where, then, was Ida's? She had disappeared utterly out of the universe. She had been transformed, destroyed, swallowed up in this woman, a living sepulchre, more cruel than the grave, for it devoured the soul as well as the body. Pah! this prating about immortality was absurd, convicted of meaninglessness before a tragedy like this; for what was an immortality worth that was given to her last decrepit phase of life, after all its beauty and strength and loveliness had passed soulless away? To be aught but a mockery, immortality must be as manifold as the manifold phases of life. Since life devours so many souls, why suppose death will spare the last one?

But he would contend with destiny. Painters should multiply the face in his locket. He would immortalize her in a poem. He would constantly keep the lamp trimmed and burning before her shrine in his heart. She should live in spite of the woman.

But he could now never make amends to her for the suffering his cruel, neglectful youth had caused her. He had scarcely realized before how much the longing to make good that wrong had influenced his quest of her. Tears of remorse for an unatonable crime gathered in his eyes. He might, indeed, enrich this woman, or educate her children, or pension her husband; but that would be no atonement to Ida.

And then, as if to intensify that remorse by showing still more clearly the impossibility of atonement, it flashed on him that he who loved Ida was not the one to atone for an offense of which he would be incapable, which had been committed by one who despised her love. Justice was a meaningless word, and amends were never possible, nor can men ever make atonement; for, ere the debt is paid, the atonement made, one who is not the sufferer stands to receive it; while, on the other hand, the one who atones is not the offender, but one who comes after him, loathing his offense and himself incapable of it. The dead must bury their dead. And, thus pondering from personal to general thoughts, the turmoil of his feelings gradually calmed, and a restful melancholy, vague and tender, filled the aching void in his heart.

WITH THE EYES SHUT

RAILROAD rides are naturally tiresome to persons who cannot read on the cars, and, being one of those unfortunates, I resigned myself, on taking my seat in the train, to several hours of tedium, alleviated only by such cat-naps as I might achieve. Partly on account of my infirmity, though more on account of a taste for rural quiet and retirement, my railroad journeys are few and far between. Strange as the statement may seem in days like these, it had actually been five years since I had been on an express train of a trunk line. Now, as every one knows, the improvements in the conveniences of the best equipped trains have in that period been very great, and for a considerable time I found myself amply entertained in taking note first of one ingenious device and then of another, and wondering what would come next. At the end of the first hour, however, I was pleased to find that I was growing comfortably drowsy, and proceeded to compose myself for a nap, which I hoped might last to my destination.

Presently I was touched on the shoulder, and a train boy asked me if I would not like something to read. I replied, rather petulantly, that I could not read on the cars, and only wanted to be let alone.

"Beg pardon, sir," the train boy replied, "but I 'll give you a book you can read with your eyes shut. Guess you have n't taken this line lately," he added, as I looked up offended at what seemed impertinence. "We 've been furnishing the new-fashioned phonographed books and magazines on this train for six months now, and passengers have got so they won't have anything else."

Probably this piece of information ought to have astonished me more than it did, but I had read enough about the wonders of the phonograph to be prepared in a vague sort of way for almost anything which might be related of it, and for the rest, after the air-brakes, the steam heat, the electric lights and annunciators, the vestibuled cars, and other delightful novelties I had just been admiring, almost anything seemed likely in the way of railway conveniences. Accordingly, when the boy proceeded to rattle off a list of the latest novels, I stopped him with the name of one which I had heard favorable mention of, and told him I would try that.

He was good enough to commend my choice. "That 's a good one," he said. "It 's all the rage. Half the train 's on it this trip. Where 'll you begin?"

"Where? Why, at the beginning. Where else?" I replied.

" All right.   Did n't know but you might have
partly read it.   Put you on at any chapter or
page, you know.   Put you on at first chapter with
next batch in five minutes, soon as the batch that 's
on now gets through."

He unlocked a little box at the side of my seat,
collected the price of three hours' reading at five
cents an hour, and went on down the aisle.   Presently I heard the tinkle of a bell from the box
which he had unlocked.   Following the example
of others around me, I took from it a sort of two-
pronged fork with the tines spread in the simili-
tude of a chicken's wishbone.   This contrivance,
which was attached to the side of the car by a
cord, I proceeded to apply to my ears, as I saw the
others doing.

For the next three hours I scarcely altered my
position, so completely was I enthralled by my
novel experience.   Few persons can fail to have
made the observation that if the tones of the
human voice did not have a charm for us in themselves apart from the ideas they convey, conversation to a great extent would soon be given up, so
little is the real intellectual interest of the topics
with which it is chiefly concerned.   When, then,
the sympathetic influence of the voice is lent to
the enhancement of matter of high intrinsic interest, it is not strange that the attention should be
enchained.   A good story is highly entertaining
even when we have to get at it by the roundabout

means of spelling out the signs that stand for the words, and imagining them uttered, and then imagining what they would mean if uttered. What, then, shall be said of the delight of sitting at one's ease, with closed eyes, listening to the same story poured into one's ears in the strong, sweet, musical tones of a perfect mistress of the art of story-telling, and of the expression and excitation by means of the voice of every emotion?

When, at the conclusion of the story, the train boy came to lock up the box, I could not refrain from expressing my satisfaction in strong terms. In reply he volunteered the information that next month the cars for day trips on that line would be further fitted up with phonographic guide-books of the country the train passed through, so connected by clock-work with the running gear of the cars that the guide-book would call attention to every object in the landscape, and furnish the pertinent information — statistical, topographical, biographical, historical, romantic, or legendary, as it might be — just at the time the train had reached the most favorable point of view. It was believed that this arrangement (for which, as it would work automatically and require little attendance, being used or not, according to pleasure, by the passenger, there would be no charge) would do much to attract travel to the road. His explanation was interrupted by the announcement in loud, clear, and deliberate tones, which no one could have had any excuse for misunderstanding, that the train was now approaching the city of my destination. As I looked around in amazement to discover what manner of brakeman this might be whom I had understood, the train boy said, with a grin, " That's our new phonographic annunciator."

Hamage had written me that he would be at the station, but something had evidently prevented him from keeping the appointment, and as it was late, I went at once to a hotel and to bed. I was tired and slept heavily ; once or twice I woke up, after dreaming there were people in my room talking to me, but quickly dropped off to sleep again. Finally I awoke, and did not so soon fall asleep. Presently I found myself sitting up in bed with half a dozen extraordinary sensations contending for right of way along my backbone. What had startled me was the voice of a young woman, who could not have been standing more than ten feet from my bed. If the tones of her voice were any guide, she was not only a young woman, but a very charming one.

" My dear sir," she had said, " you may possibly be interested in knowing that it now wants just a quarter of three."

For a few moments I thought — well, I will not undertake the impossible task of telling what extraordinary conjectures occurred to me by way of accounting for the presence of this young woman in my room before the true explanation of the matter occurred to me. For, of course, when my experience that afternoon on the train flashed through my mind, I guessed at once that the solution of the mystery was in all probability merely a phonographic device for announcing the hour. Nevertheless, so thrilling and lifelike in effect were the tones of the voice I had heard that I confess I had not the nerve to light the gas to investigate till I had indued my more essential garments. Of course I found no lady in the room, but only a clock. I had not particularly noticed it on going to bed, because it looked like any other clock, and so now it continued to behave until the hands pointed to three. Then, instead of leaving me to infer the time from the arbitrary symbolism of three strokes on a bell, the same voice which had before electrified me informed me, in tones which would have lent a charm to the driest of statistical details, what the hour was. I had never before been impressed with any particular interest attaching to the hour of three in the morning, but as I heard it announced in those low, rich, thrilling contralto tones, it appeared fairly to coruscate with previously latent suggestions of romance and poetry, which, if somewhat vague, were very pleasing. Turning out the gas that I might the more easily imagine the bewitching presence which the voice suggested, I went back to bed, and lay awake there until morning, enjoying the society of my bodiless companion and the delicious shock of her quarter-hourly remarks. To make the illusion more complete and the more unsuggestive of the mechanical explanation which I knew of course was the real one, the phrase in which the announcement of the hour was made was never twice the same.

Right was Solomon when he said that there was nothing new under the sun. Sardanapalus or Semiramis herself would not have been at all startled to hear a human voice proclaim the hour. The phonographic clock had but replaced the slave whose business, standing by the noiseless water-clock, it was to keep tale of the moments as they dropped, ages before they had been taught to tick.

In the morning, on descending, I went first to the clerk's office to inquire for letters, thinking Hamage, who knew I would go to that hotel if any, might have addressed me there. The clerk handed me a small oblong box. I suppose I stared at it in a rather helpless way, for presently he said : " I beg your pardon, but I see you are a stranger. If you will permit me, I will show you how to read your letter."

I gave him the box, from which he took a device of spindles and cylinders, and placed it deftly within another small box which stood on the desk. Attached to this was one of the two-pronged ear-trumpets I already knew the use of. As I placed it in position, the clerk touched a spring in the box, which set some sort of motor going, and at once the familiar tones of Dick Hamage's voice expressed his regret that an accident had prevented his meeting me the night before, and informed me that he would be at the hotel by the time I had breakfasted.

The letter ended, the obliging clerk removed the cylinders from the box on the desk, replaced them in that they had come in, and returned it to me.

" Is n't it rather tantalizing," said I, " to receive one of these letters when there is no little machine like this at hand to make it speak?"

" It does n't often happen," replied the clerk, " that anybody is caught without his indispensable, or at least where he cannot borrow one."

" His indispensable!" I exclaimed. " What may that be?"

In reply the clerk directed my attention to a little box, not wholly unlike a case for a binocular glass, which, now that he spoke of it, I saw was carried, slung at the side, by every person in sight.

" We call it the indispensable because it is indispensable, as, no doubt, you will soon find for yourself."

In the breakfast-room a number of ladies and gentlemen were engaged as they sat at table in reading, or rather in listening to, their morning's

correspondence. A greater or smaller pile of little
boxes lay beside their plates, and one after another
they took from each its cylinders, placed them in
their indispensables, and held the latter to their
ears. The expression of the face in reading is so
largely affected by the necessary fixity of the eyes
that intelligence is absorbed from the printed or
written page with scarcely a change of countenance, which when communicated by the voice
evokes a responsive play of features. I had never
been struck so forcibly by this obvious reflection
as I was in observing the expression of the faces
of these people as they listened to their correspond-
ents. Disappointment, pleased surprise, chagrin,
disgust, indignation, and amusement were alternately so legible on their faces that it was perfectly
easy for one to be sure in most cases what the
tenor at least of the letter was. It occurred to me
that while in the old time the pleasure of receiving letters had been so far balanced by this drudg-
ery of writing them as to keep correspondence
within some bounds, nothing less than freight
trains could suffice for the mail service in these
days, when to write was but to speak, and to listen
was to read.

After I had given my order, the waiter brought
a curious-looking oblong case, with an ear-trumpet
attached, and, placing it before me, went away. I
foresaw that I should have to ask a good many
questions before I got through, and, if I did not

mean to be a bore, I had best ask as few as necessary. I determined to find out what this trap was
without assistance. The words "Daily Morning
Herald" sufficiently indicated that it was a newspaper. I suspected that a certain big knob, if
pushed, would set it going. But, for all I knew,
it might start in the middle of the advertisements.
I looked closer. There were a number of printed
slips upon the face of the machine, arranged about
a circle like the numbers on a dial. They were
evidently the headings of news articles. In the
middle of the circle was a little pointer, like the
hand of a clock, moving on a pivot. I pushed this
pointer around to a certain caption, and then, with
the air of being perfectly familiar with the machine, I put the pronged trumpet to my ears and
pressed the big knob. Precisely! It worked like
a charm; so much like a charm, indeed, that I
should certainly have allowed my breakfast to cool
had I been obliged to choose between that and my
newspaper. The inventor of the apparatus had,
however, provided against so painful a dilemma by
a simple attachment to the trumpet, which held it
securely in position upon the shoulders behind the
head, while the hands were left free for knife and
fork. Having slyly noted the manner in which
my neighbors had effected the adjustments, I imi-
tated their example with a careless air, and presently, like them, was absorbing physical and mental aliment simultaneously.

While I was thus delightfully engaged, I was not less delightfully interrupted by Hamage, who, having arrived at the hotel, and learned that I was in the breakfast-room, came in and sat down beside me. After telling him how much I admired the new sort of newspapers, I offered one criticism, which was that there seemed to be no way by which one could skip dull paragraphs or uninteresting details.

"The invention would, indeed, be very far from a success," he said, "if there were no such provision, but there is."

He made me put on the trumpet again, and, having set the machine going, told me to press on a certain knob, at first gently, afterward as hard as I pleased. I did so, and found that the effect of the "skipper," as he called the knob, was to quicken the utterance of the phonograph in proportion to the pressure to at least tenfold the usual rate of speed, while at any moment, if a word of interest caught the ear, the ordinary rate of delivery was resumed, and by another adjustment the machine could be made to go back and repeat as much as desired.

When I told Hamage of my experience of the night before with the talking clock in my room, he laughed uproariously.

"I am very glad you mentioned this just now," he said, when he had quieted himself. "We have a couple of hours before the train goes out to my

place, and I 'll take you through Orton's establishment, where they make a specialty of these talking
clocks. I have a number of them in my house, and,
as I don't want to have you scared to death in the
night-watches, you had better get some notion of
what clocks nowadays are expected to do."

Orton's, where we found ourselves half an hour
later, proved to be a very extensive establishment,
the firm making a specialty of horological novelties,
and particularly of the new phonographic time-
pieces. The manager, who was a personal friend
of Hamage's, and proved very obliging, said that
the latter were fast driving the old-fashioned striking clocks out of use.

" And no wonder," he exclaimed ; " the old-fashioned striker was an unmitigated nuisance. Let
alone the brutality of announcing the hour to a refined household by four, eight, or ten rude bangs,
without introduction or apology, this method of
announcement was not even tolerably intelligible.
Unless you happened to be attentive at the moment
the din began, you could never be sure of your count
of strokes so as to be positive whether it was eight,
nine, ten, or eleven. As to the half and quarter
strokes, they were wholly useless unless you chanced
to know what was the last hour struck. And then,
too, I should like to ask you why, in the name of
common sense, it should take twelve times as long
to tell you it is twelve o'clock as it does to tell you
it is one."

The manager laughed as heartily as Hamage had done on learning of my scare of the night before.

" It was lucky for you," he said, " that the clock in your room happened to be a simple time announcer, otherwise you might easily have been startled half out of your wits." I became myself quite of the same opinion by the time he had shown us something of his assortment of clocks. The mere announcing of the hours and quarters of hours was the simplest of the functions of these wonderful and yet simple instruments. There were few of them which were not arranged to " improve the time," as the old-fashioned prayer-meeting phrase was. People's ideas differing widely as to what constitutes improvement of time, the clocks varied accordingly in the nature of the edification they provided. There were religious and sectarian clocks, moral clocks, philosophical clocks, free-thinking and infidel clocks, literary and poetical clocks, educational clocks, frivolous and bacchanalian clocks. In the religious clock department were to be found Catholic, Presbyterian, Methodist, Episcopal, and Baptist time-pieces, which, in connection with the announcement of the hour and quarter, repeated some tenet of the sect with a proof text. There were also Talmage clocks, and Spurgeon clocks, and Storrs clocks, and Brooks clocks, which respectively marked the flight of time by phrases taken from the sermons of these eminent divines, and repeated in precisely the voice and

accents of the original delivery. In startling prox-
imity to the religious department I was shown the
skeptical clocks. So near were they, indeed, that
when, as I stood there, the various time-pieces announced the hour of ten, the war of opinions that
followed was calculated to unsettle the firmest convictions. The observations of an Ingersoll which
stood near me were particularly startling. The
effect of an actual wrangle was the greater from
the fact that all these individual clocks were surmounted by effigies of the authors of the sentiments
they repeated.

I was glad to escape from this turmoil to the
calmer atmosphere of the philosophical and literary
clock department. For persons with a taste for
antique moralizing, the sayings of Plato, Epictetus,
and Marcus Aurelius had here, so to speak, been
set to time. Modern wisdom was represented by a
row of clocks surmounted by the heads of famous
maxim-makers, from Rochefoucauld to Josh Bil-
lings. As for the literary clocks, their number
and variety were endless. All the great authors
were represented. Of the Dickens clocks alone
there were half a dozen, with selections from his
greatest stories. When I suggested that, captivat-
ing as such clocks must be, one might in time grow
weary of hearing the same sentiments reiterated,
the manager pointed out that the phonographic
cylinders were removable, and could be replaced by
other sayings by the same author or on the same

theme at any time. If one tired of an author altogether, he could have the head unscrewed from the
top of the clock and that of some other celebrity
substituted, with a brand-new repertory.

"I can imagine," I said, "that these talking
clocks must be a great resource for invalids especially, and for those who cannot sleep at night.
But, on the other hand, how is it when people want
or need to sleep? Is not one of them quite too
interesting a companion at such a time?"

"Those who are used to it," replied the manager,
"are no more disturbed by the talking clock than
we used to be by the striking clock. However, to
avoid all possible inconvenience to invalids, this
little lever is provided, which at a touch will throw
the phonograph out of gear or back again. It is
customary when we put a talking or singing clock
into a bedroom to put in an electric connection, so
that by pressing a button at the head of the bed a
person, without raising the head from the pillow,
can start or stop the phonographic gear, as well
as ascertain the time, on the repeater principle as
applied to watches."

Hamage now said that we had only time to catch
the train, but our conductor insisted that we should
stop to see a novelty of phonographic invention,
which, although not exactly in their line, had been
sent them for exhibition by the inventor. It was a
device for meeting the criticism frequently made
upon the churches of a lack of attention and cor-

diality in welcoming strangers. It was to be placed
in the lobby of the church, and had an arm extending like a pump-handle. Any stranger on taking
this and moving it up and down would be welcomed
in the pastor's own voice, and continue to be welcomed as long as he kept up the motion. While
this welcome would be limited to general remarks
of regard and esteem, ample provision was made
for strangers who desired to be more particularly
inquired into. A number of small buttons on the
front of the contrivance bore respectively the words,
" Male," " Female," " Married," " Unmarried,"
" Widow," " Children," " No Children," etc., etc.
By pressing the one of these buttons corresponding to his or her condition, the stranger would be
addressed in terms probably quite as accurately
adapted to his or her condition and needs as would
be any inquiries a preoccupied clergyman would
be likely to make under similar circumstances. I
could readily see the necessity of some such substitute for the pastor, when I was informed that every
prominent clergyman was now in the habit of sup-
plying at least a dozen or two pulpits simultaneously, appearing by turns in one of them personally,
and by phonograph in the others.

The inventor of the contrivance for welcoming
strangers was, it appeared, applying the same idea
to machines for discharging many other of the
more perfunctory obligations of social intercourse.
One being made for the convenience of the Presi-

dent of the United States at public receptions was
provided with forty-two buttons for the different
States, and others for the principal cities of the
Union, so that a caller, by proper manipulation,
might, while shaking a handle, be addressed in
regard to his home interests with an exactness of
information as remarkable as that of the traveling
statesmen who rise from the gazetteer to astonish
the inhabitants of Wayback Crossing with the
precise figures of their town valuation and birth
rate, while the engine is taking in water.

We had by this time spent so much time that
on finally starting for the railroad station we had
to walk quite briskly. As we were hurrying along
the street, my attention was arrested by a musical
sound, distinct though not loud, proceeding apparently from the indispensable which Hamage, like
everybody else I had seen, wore at his side. Stopping abruptly, he stepped aside from the throng,
and, lifting the indispensable quickly to his ear,
touched something, and exclaiming, " Oh, yes, to
be sure ! " dropped the instrument to his side.

Then he said to me : " I am reminded that I
promised my wife to bring home some story-books
for the children when I was in town to-day. The
store is only a few steps down the street." As
we went along, he explained to me that nobody
any longer pretended to charge his mind with the
recollection of duties or engagements of any sort.
Everybody depended upon his indispensable to

remind him in time of all undertakings and responsibilities. This service it was able to render
by virtue of a simple enough adjustment of a
phonographic cylinder charged with the necessary
word or phrase to the clockwork in the indispensable, so that at any time fixed upon in setting the
arrangement an alarm would sound, and, the indispensable being raised to the ear, the phonograph
would deliver its message, which at any subsequent
time might be called up and repeated. To all
persons charged with weighty responsibilities de-
pending upon accuracy of memory for their correct
discharge, this feature of the indispensable rendered it, according to Hamage, and indeed quite
obviously, an indispensable truly. To the railroad engineer it served the purpose not only of
a time-piece, for the works of the indispensable
include a watch, but to its ever vigilant alarm he
could intrust his running orders, and, while his
mind was wholly concentrated upon present duties,
rest secure that he would be reminded at just the
proper time of trains which he must avoid and
switches he must make. To the indispensable of
the business man the reminder attachment was not
less necessary. Provided with that, his notes need
never go to protest through carelessness, nor, however absorbed, was he in danger of forgetting an
appointment.

Thanks to these portable memories it was, moreover, now possible for a wife to intrust to her

husband the most complex messages to the dress-maker. All she had to do was to whisper the communication into her husband's indispensable while he was at breakfast, and set the alarm at an hour when he would be in the city.

" And in like manner, I suppose," suggested I, " if she wishes him to return at a certain hour from the club or the lodge, she can depend on his indispensable to remind him of his domestic duties at the proper moment, and in terms and tones which will make the total repudiation of connubial allegiance the only alternative of obedience. It is a very clever invention, and I don't wonder that it is popular with the ladies; but does it not occur to you that the inventor, if a man, was slightly inconsiderate? The rule of the American wife has hitherto been a despotism which could be tem-pered by a bad memory. Apparently, it is to be no longer tempered at all."

Hamage laughed, but his mirth was evidently a little forced, and I inferred that the reflection I had suggested had called up certain reminis-cences not wholly exhilarating. Being fortunate, however, in the possession of a mercurial tempera-ment, he presently rallied, and continued his praises of the artificial memory provided by the indispen-sable. In spite of the criticism which I had made upon it, I confess I was not a little moved by his description of its advantages to absent-minded men, of whom I am chief. Think of the gain alike in serenity and force of intellect enjoyed by the man who sits down to work absolutely free from that accursed cloud on the mind of things he has got to remember to do, and can only avoid totally forgetting by wasting tenfold the time required finally to do them in making sure by frequent rehearsals that he has not forgotten them! The only way that one of these trivialities ever sticks to the mind is by wearing a sore spot in it which heals slowly. If a man does not forget it, it is for the same reason that he remembers a grain of sand in his eye. I am conscious that my own mind is full of cicatrices of remembered things, and long ere this it would have been peppered with them like a colander, had I not a good while ago, in self-defense, absolutely refused to be held accountable for forgetting anything not connected with my regular business.

While firmly believing my course in this matter to have been justifiable and necessary, I have not been insensible to the domestic odium which it has brought upon me, and could but welcome a device which promised to enable me to regain the esteem of my family while retaining the use of my mind for professional purposes.

As the most convenient conceivable receptacle of hasty memoranda of ideas and suggestions, the indispensable also most strongly commended itself to me as a man who lives by writing. How convenient when a flash of inspiration comes to one in the night-time, instead of taking cold and waking the family in order to save it for posterity, just to whisper it into the ear of an indispensable at one's bedside, and be able to know it in the morning for the rubbish such untimely conceptions usually are! How often, likewise, would such a machine save in all their first vividness suggestive fancies, anticipated details, and other notions worth preserving, which occur to one in the full flow of composition, but are irrelevant to what is at the moment in hand! I determined that I must have an indispensable.

The bookstore, when we arrived there, proved to be the most extraordinary sort of bookstore I had ever entered, there not being a book in it. Instead of books, the shelves and counters were occupied with rows of small boxes.

"Almost all books now, you see, are phonographed," said Hamage.

"The change seems to be a popular one," I said, "to judge by the crowd of book-buyers." For the counters were, indeed, thronged with customers as I had never seen those of a bookstore before.

"The people at those counters are not purchasers, but borrowers," Hamage replied; and then he explained that whereas the old-fashioned printed book, being handled by the reader, was damaged by use, and therefore had either to be purchased outright or borrowed at high rates of hire, the phonograph of a book being not handled, but merely revolved in a machine, was but little injured by use, and therefore phonographed books could be lent out for an infinitesimal price. Everybody had at home a phonograph box of standard size and adjustments, to which all phonographic cylinders were gauged. I suggested that the phonograph, at any rate, could scarcely have replaced picture-books. But here, it seemed, I was mistaken, for it appeared that illustrations were adapted to phonographed books by the simple plan of arranging them in a continuous panorama, which by a connecting gear was made to unroll behind the glass front of the phonograph case as the course of the narrative demanded.

"But, bless my soul!" I exclaïmed, "everybody surely is not content to borrow their books? They must want to have books of their own, to keep in their libraries."

"Of course," said Hamage. "What I said about borrowing books applies only to current literature of the ephemeral sort. Everybody wants books of permanent value in his library. Over yonder is the department of the establishment set apart for book-buyers."

The counter which he indicated being less crowded than those of the borrowing department, I expressed a desire to examine some of the phonographed books. As we were waiting for attendance, I observed that some of the customers seemed very particular about their purchases, and insisted upon testing several phonographs bearing the same title before making a selection. As the phonographs seemed exact counterparts in appearance, I did not understand this till Hamage explained that differences as to style and quality of elocution left quite as great a range of choice in phonographed books as varieties in type, paper, and binding did in printed ones. This I presently found to be the case when the clerk, under Hamage's direction, began waiting on me. In succession I tried half a dozen editions of Tennyson by as many different elocutionists, and by the time I had heard

" Where Claribel low lieth "

rendered by a soprano, a contralto, a bass, and a baritone, each with the full effect of its quality and the personal equation besides, I was quite ready to admit that selecting phonographed books for one's library was as much more difficult as it was incomparably more fascinating than suiting one's self with printed editions. Indeed, Hamage admitted that nowadays nobody with any taste for literature — if the word may for convenience be retained — thought of contenting himself with less than half a dozen renderings of the great poets and dramatists.

" By the way," he said to the clerk, "won't you just let my friend try the Booth-Barrett Company's 'Othello'? It is, you understand," he added to me, " the exact phonographic reproduction of the play as actually rendered by the company."

Upon his suggestion, the attendant had taken down a phonograph case and placed it on the counter. The front was an imitation of a theatre with the curtain down. As I. placed the transmitter to my ears, the clerk touched a spring and the curtain rolled up, displaying a perfect picture of the stage in the opening scene. Simultaneously the action of the play began, as if the pictured men upon the stage were talking. Here was no question of losing half that was said and guessing the rest. Not a word, not a syllable, not a whispered aside of the actors, was lost; and as the play proceeded the pictures changed, showing every important change of attitude on the part of the actors. Of course the figures, being pictures, did not move, but their presentation in so many successive attitudes presented the effect of movement, and made it quite possible to imagine that the voices in my ears were really theirs. I am exceedingly fond of the drama, but the amount of effort and physical inconvenience necessary to witness a play has rendered my indulgence in this pleasure infrequent. Others might not have agreed with me, but I confess that none of the ingenious applications of the phonograph which I had seen seemed to be so well worth while as this.

Hamage had left me to make his purchases, and found me on his return still sitting spellbound.

"Come, come," he said, laughing, "I have Shakespeare complete at home, and you shall sit up all night, if you choose, hearing plays. But come along now, I want to take you upstairs before we go."

He had several bundles. One, he told me, was a new novel for his wife, with some fairy stories for the children, — all, of course, phonographs. Besides, he had bought an indispensable for his little boy.

" There is no class," he said, " whose burdens the phonograph has done so much to lighten as parents. Mothers no longer have to make themselves hoarse telling the children stories on rainy days to keep them out of mischief. It is only necessary to plant the most roguish lad before a phonograph of some nursery classic, to be sure of his whereabouts and his behavior till the machine runs down, when another set of cylinders can be introduced, and the entertainment carried on. As for the babies, Patti sings mine to sleep at bedtime, and, if they wake up in the night, she is never too drowsy to do it over again. When the children grow too big to be longer tied to their mother's apron-strings, they still remain, thanks to the children's indispensable, though out of her sight, within sound of her voice. Whatever charges or instructions she desires them not to forget, whatever hours or duties she would have them be sure to remember, she depends on the indispensable to remind them of."

At this I cried out. " It is all very well for the

mothers," I said, "but the lot of the orphan must seem enviable to a boy compelled to wear about such an instrument of his own subjugation. If boys were what they were in my day, the rate at which their indispensables would get unaccountably lost or broken would be alarming."

Hamage laughed, and admitted that the one he was carrying home was the fourth he had bought for his boy within a month. He agreed with me that it was hard to see how a boy was to get his growth under quite so much government; but his wife, and indeed the ladies generally, insisted that the application of the phonograph to family government was the greatest invention of the age.

Then I asked a question which had repeatedly occurred to me that day, — What had become of the printers?

"Naturally," replied Hamage, "they have had a rather hard time of it. Some classes of books, however, are still printed, and probably will continue to be for some time, although reading, as well as writing, is getting to be an increasingly rare accomplishment."

"Do you mean that your schools do not teach reading and writing?" I exclaimed.

"Oh, yes, they are still taught; but as the pupils need them little after leaving school, — or even in school, for that matter, all their text-books being phonographic, — they usually keep the acquirements about as long as a college graduate does his

Greek. There is a strong movement already on foot to drop reading and writing entirely from the school course, but probably a compromise will be made for the present by substituting a shorthand or phonetic system, based upon the direct interpretation of the sound-waves themselves. This is, of course, the only logical method for the visual interpretation of sound. Students and men of research, however, will always need to understand how to read print, as much of the old literature will probably never repay phonographing."

" But," I said, " I notice that you still use printed phrases, as superscriptions, titles, and so forth."

" So we do," replied Hamage, " but phonographic substitutes could be easily devised in these cases, and no doubt will soon have to be supplied in deference to the growing number of those who cannot read."

" Did I understand you," I asked, " that the text-books in your schools even are phonographs ? "

" Certainly," replied Hamage; " our children are taught by phonographs, recite to phonographs, and are examined by phonographs."

" Bless my soul ! " I ejaculated.

" By all means," replied Hamage; " but there is really nothing to be astonished at. People learn and remember by impressions of sound instead of sight, that is all. The printer is, by the way, not the only artisan whose occupation phonography has destroyed. Since the disuse of print, opticians have mostly gone to the poor-house. The sense of sight was indeed terribly overburdened previous to the introduction of the phonograph, and, now that the sense of hearing is beginning to assume its proper share of work, it would be strange if an improvement in the condition of the people's eyes were not noticeable. Physiologists, moreover, promise us not only an improved vision, but a generally improved physique, especially in respect to bodily carriage, now that reading, writing, and study no longer involves, as formerly, the sedentary attitude with twisted spine and stooping shoulders. The phonograph has at last made it possible to expand the mind without cramping the body."

"It is a striking comment on the revolution wrought by the general introduction of the phonograph," I observed, "that whereas the misfortune of blindness used formerly to be the infirmity which most completely cut a man off from the world of books, which remained open to the deaf, the case is now precisely reversed."

"Yes," said Hamage, "it is certainly a curious reversal, but not so complete as you fancy. By the new improvements in the intensifier, it is expected to enable all, except the stone-deaf, to enjoy the phonograph, even when connected, as on railroad trains, with a common telephonic wire. The stone-deaf will of course be dependent upon printed books prepared for their benefit, as raised-letter books used to be for the blind."

As we entered the elevator to ascend to the upper floors of the establishment, Hamage explained that he wanted me to see, before I left, the process of phonographing books, which was the modern substitute for printing them. Of course, he said, the phonographs of dramatic works were taken at the theatres during the representations of plays, and those of public orations and sermons are either similarly obtained, or, if a revised version is desired, the orator re-delivers his address in the improved form to a phonograph; but the great mass of publications were phonographed by professional elocutionists employed by the large publishing houses, of which this was one. He was acquainted with one of these elocutionists, and was taking me to his room.

We were so fortunate as to find him disengaged. Something, he said, had broken about the machinery, and he was idle while it was being repaired. His work-room was an odd kind of place. It was shaped something like the interior of a rather short egg. His place was on a sort of pulpit in the middle of the small end, while at the opposite end, directly before him, and for some distance along the sides toward the middle, were arranged tiers of phonographs. These were his audience, but by no means all of it. By telephonic communication he was able to address simultaneously other congregations of phonographs in other chambers at any distance. He said that in one instance, where the demand for a popular book was very great, he had charged five thousand phonographs at once with it.

I suggested that the saving of printers, pressmen, bookbinders, and costly machinery, together with the comparative indestructibility of phonographed as compared with printed books, must make them very cheap.

"They would be," said Hamage, "if popular elocutionists, such as Playwell here, did not charge so like fun for their services. The public has taken it into its head that he is the only first-class elocutionist, and won't buy anybody else's work. Consequently the authors stipulate that he shall interpret their productions, and the publishers, between the public and the authors, are at his mercy."

Playwell laughed. "I must make my hay while the sun shines," he said. "Some other elocutionist will be the fashion next year, and then I shall only get hack-work to do. Besides, there is really a great deal more work in my business than people will believe. For example, after I get an author's copy" —

"Written?" I interjected.

"Sometimes it is written phonetically, but most authors dictate to a phonograph. Well, when I get it, I take it home and study it, perhaps a couple of days, perhaps a couple of weeks, sometimes, if it is really an important work, a month or two, in order to get into sympathy with the ideas, and decide on the proper style of rendering. All this is hard work, and has to be paid for."

At this point our conversation was broken off by Hamage, who declared that, if we were to catch the last train out of town before noon, we had no time to lose.

Of the trip out to Hamage's place I recall nothing. I was, in fact, aroused from a sound nap by the stopping of the train and the bustle of the departing passengers. Hamage had disappeared. As I groped about, gathering up my belongings, and vaguely wondering what had become of my companion, he rushed into the car, and, grasping my hand, gave me an enthusiastic welcome. I opened my mouth to demand what sort of a joke this belated greeting might be intended for, but, on second thought, I concluded not to raise the point. The fact is, when I came to observe that the time was not noon, but late in the evening, and that the train was the one I had left home on, and that I had not even changed my seat in the car since then, it occurred to me that Hamage might not understand allusions to the forenoon we had spent together. Later that same evening, however, the consternation of my host and hostess at my frequent and violent explosions of apparently causeless hilarity left me no choice but to make a clean breast of my preposterous experience. The moral they drew from it was the charming one that, if I would but oftener come to see them, a railroad trip would not so upset my wits.

AT PINNEY'S RANCH

JOHN LANSING first met Mary Hollister at the house of his friend Pinney, whose wife was her sister. She had soft gray eyes, a pretty color in her cheeks, rosy lips, and a charming figure. In the course of the evening somebody suggested mind-reading as a pastime, and Lansing, who had some powers, or supposed powers, in that direction, although he laughed at them himself, experimented in turn with the ladies. He failed with nearly every subject until it came Mary Hollister's turn. As she placed her soft palm in his, closed her eyes, and gave herself up to his influence, he knew that he should succeed with her, and so he did. She proved a remarkably sympathetic subject, and Lansing was himself surprised, and the spectators fairly thrilled, by the feats he was able to perform by her aid. After that evening he met her often, and there was more equally remarkable mind-reading; and then mind-reading was dropped for heart-reading, and the old, old story they read in each other's hearts had more fascination for them than the new science. Having once discovered that their hearts beat in unison, they took no more interest in the relation of their minds.

The action proper of this story begins four years after their marriage, with a very shocking event, — nothing less than the murder of Austin Flint, who was found dead one morning in the house in which he lived alone. Lansing had no hand in the deed, but he might almost as well have had ; for, while absolutely guiltless, he was caught in one of those nets of circumstance which no foresight can avoid, whereby innocent men are sometimes snared help-lessly, and delivered over to a horrid death. There had been a misunderstanding between him and the dead man, and only a couple of days before the murder, they had exchanged blows on the street. When Flint was found dead, in the lack of any other clue, people thought of Lansing. He real-ized that this was so, and remained silent as to a fact which otherwise he would have testified to at the inquest, but which he feared might now imperil him. He had been at Austin Flint's house the night of the murder, and might have committed it, so far as opportunity was concerned. In reality, the motive of his visit was anything but murderous. Deeply chagrined by the scandal of the fight, he had gone to Flint to apologize, and to make up their quarrel. But he knew very well that nobody would believe that this was his true object in seek-ing his enemy secretly by night, while the admis-sion of the visit would complete a circumstantial evidence against him stronger than had often hanged men. He believed that no one but the dead man knew of the call, and that it would never be found out. He had not told his wife of it at the time, and still less afterward, on account of the anxiety she would feel at his position.

Two weeks passed, and he was beginning to breathe freely in the assurance of safety, when, like a thunderbolt from a cloud that seems to have passed over, the catastrophe came. A friend met him on the street one day, and warned him to escape while he could. It appeared that he had been seen to enter Flint's house that night. His concealment of the fact had been accepted as corroborating evidence of his guilt, and the police, who had shadowed him from the first, might arrest him at any moment. The conviction that he was guilty, which the friend who told him this evidently had, was a terrible comment on the desperateness of his position. He walked home as in a dream. His wife had gone out to a neighbor's. His little boy came to him, and clambered on his knee. "Papa, what makes your face so wet?" he asked, for there were great drops on his forehead. Then his wife came in, her face white, her eyes full of horror. "Oh, John!" she exclaimed. "They say you were at Mr. Flint's that night, and they are going to arrest you. Oh, John, what does it mean? Why don't you speak? I shall go mad, if you do not speak. You were not there! Tell me that you were not there!" The ghastly face he raised to hers might well have seemed to confess everything.

At least she seemed to take it so, and in a fit of hysterical weeping sank to the floor, and buried her face in her hands upon a chair. The children, alarmed at the scene, began to cry. It was growing dark, and as he looked out of the window, Lansing saw an officer and a number of other persons approaching the house. They were coming to arrest him. Animal terror, the instinct of self-preservation, seized upon his faculties, stunned and demoralized as he was by the suddenness with which this calamity had come upon him. He opened the door and fled, with a score of men and boys yelling in pursuit. He ran wildly, blindly, making incredible leaps and bounds over obstacles. As men sometimes do in nightmares, he argued with himself, as he ran, whether this could possibly be a waking experience, and inclined to think that it could not. It must be a dream. It was too fantastically horrible to be anything else.

Presently he saw just before him the eddying, swirling current of the river, swollen by a freshet. Still half convinced that he was in a nightmare, and, if he could but shake it off, should awake in his warm bed, he plunged headlong in, and was at once swirled out of sight of his pursuers beneath the darkening sky. A blow from a floating object caused him to throw up his arms, and, clutching something solid, he clambered upon a shed carried away by the freshet from an up-river farm. All night he drifted with the swift current, and in the morning landed in safety thirty miles below the village from which he had fled for life.

So John Lansing, for no fault whatever except an error of judgment, if even it was that, was banished from home, and separated from his family almost as hopelessly as if he were dead. To return would be to meet an accusation of murder to which his flight had added overwhelming weight. To write to his wife might be to put the officers of the law, who doubtless watched her closely, upon his scent.

Under an assumed name he made his way to the far West, and, joining the rush to the silver mines of Colorado, was among the lucky ones. At the end of three years he was a rich man. What he had made the money for, he could not tell, except that the engrossment of the struggle had helped him to forget his wretchedness. Not that he ever did forget it. His wife and babies, from whose embraces he had been so suddenly torn, were always in his thoughts. Above all, he could not forget the look of horror in his wife's eyes in that last terrible scene. To see her again, and convince her, if not others, that he was innocent, was a need which so grew upon him that, at the end of three years, he determined to take his life in his hand and return home openly. This life of exile was not worth living.

One day, in the course of setting his affairs in order for his return, he was visiting a mining camp

remote from the settlements, when a voice addressed
him by his old name, and looking around he saw
Pinney. The latter's first words, as soon as his
astonishment and delight had found some expression, assured Lansing that he was no longer in
danger. The murderer of Austin Flint had been
discovered, convicted, and hanged two years previous. As for Lansing, it had been taken for granted
that he was drowned when he leaped into the river,
and there had been no further search for him. His
wife had been broken-hearted ever since, but she
and the children were otherwise well, according to
the last letters received by Pinney, who, with his
wife, had moved out to Colorado a year previous.

Of course Lansing's only idea now was to get
home as fast as steam could carry him; but they
were one hundred miles from the railroad, and the
only communication was by stage. It would get
up from the railroad the next day, and go back
the following morning. Pinney took Lansing out
to his ranch, some miles from the mining camp, to
pass the interval. The first thing he asked Mrs.
Pinney was if she had a photograph of his wife.
When she brought him one, he durst not look at it
before his hosts. Not till he had gone to his room
and locked the door did he trust himself to see
again the face of his beloved Mary.

That evening Mrs. Pinney told him how his wife
and children had fared in his absence. Her father
had helped them at first, but after his death Mary

had depended upon needlework for support, finding
it hard to make the two ends meet.

Lansing groaned at hearing this, but Mrs. Pinney comforted him. It was well worth while having
troubles, she said, if they could be made up to one,
as all Mary's would be to her when she saw her
husband.

The upcoming stage brought the mail, and next
day Pinney rode into camp to get his weekly newspaper, and engage a passage down the next morning
for Lansing. The day dragged terribly to the latter, who stayed at the ranch. He was quite unfit
for any social purpose, as Mrs. Pinney, to whom
a guest in that lonely place was a rare treat, found
to her sorrow, though indeed she could not blame
him for being poor company. He passed hours,
locked in his room, brooding over Mary's picture.
The rest of the day he spent wandering about
the place, smiling and talking to himself like an
imbecile, as he dreamed of the happiness so soon
to crown his trials. If he could have put himself
in communication with Mary by telegraph during
this period of waiting, it would have been easier
to get through, but the nearest telegraph station
was at the railroad. In the afternoon he saddled
a horse and rode about the country, thus disposing
of a couple of hours.

When he came back to the house, he saw that
Pinney had returned, for his horse was tethered to
a post of the front piazza. The doors and windows

of the living-room were open, and as he reached the front door, he heard Pinney and his wife talking in agitated tones.

"Oh, how could God let such an awful thing happen?" she was exclaiming, in a voice broken by hysterical sobbing. "I'm sure there was never anything half so horrible before. Just as John was coming home to her, and she worshiping him so, and he her! Oh, it will kill him! Who is going to tell him? Who can tell him?"

"He must not be told to-day," said Pinney's voice. "We must keep it from him at least for to-day."

Lansing entered the room. "Is she dead?" he asked quietly. He could not doubt, from what he had overheard, that she was.

"God help him! He'll have to know it now," exclaimed Pinney.

"Is she dead?" repeated Lansing.

"No, she isn't dead."

"Is she dying, then?"

"No, she is well."

"It's the children, then?"

"No," answered Pinney. "They are all right."

"Then, in God's name, what is it?" demanded Lansing, unable to conceive what serious evil could have happened to him, if nothing had befallen his wife and babies.

"We can't keep it from him now," said Pinney to his wife. "You'll have to give him her letter."

" Can't you tell me what it is ? Why do you keep me in suspense ? " asked Lansing, in a voice husky with a dread he knew not of what.

" I can't, man. Don't ask me ! " groaned Pinney. " It 's better that you should read it."

Mrs. Pinney's face expressed an agony of compassion as, still half clutching it, she held out a letter to Lansing. " John, oh, John," she sobbed; "remember, she 's not to blame ! She does n't know."

The letter was in his wife's handwriting, addressed to Mrs. Pinney, and read as follows : —

You will be surprised by what I am going to tell you. You, who know how I loved John, must have taken it for granted that I would never marry again. Not that it could matter to him. Too well I feel the gulf between the dead and living to fancy that his peace could be troubled by any of the weaknesses of mortal hearts. Indeed, he often used to tell me that, if he died, he wanted me to marry again, if ever I felt like doing so; but in those happy days I was always sure that I should be taken first. It was he who was to go first, though, and now it is for the sake of his children that I am going to do what I never thought I could. I am going to marry again. As they grow older and need more, I find it impossible for me to support them, though I do not mind how hard I work, and would wear my fingers to the

bone rather than take any other man's name after
being John's wife. But I cannot care for them
as they should be cared for. Johnny is now six,
and ought to go to school, but I cannot dress him
decently enough to send him. Mary has outgrown
all her clothes, and I cannot get her more. Her
feet are too tender to go bare, and I cannot buy
her shoes. I get less and less sewing since the
new dressmaker came to the village, and soon shall
have none. We live, oh so plainly! For myself
I should not care, but the children are growing
and need better food. They are John's children,
and for their sake I have brought myself to do
what I never could have done but for them. I
have promised to marry Mr. Whitcomb. I have
not deceived him as to why alone I marry him.
He has promised to care for the children as his
own, and to send Johnny to college, for I know
his father would have wanted him to go. It will
be a very quiet wedding, of course. Mr. Whitcomb has had some cards printed to send to a
few friends, and I inclose one to you. I cannot
say that I wish you could be present, for it will be
anything but a joyful day to me. But when I
meet John in heaven, he will hold me to account
for the children he left me, and this is the only
way by which I can provide for them. So long
as it is well with them, I ought not to care for myself.   Your sister,

                                MARY LANSING.

The card announced that the wedding would take place at the home of the bride, at six o'clock on the afternoon of the 27th of June.

It was June 27 that day, and it was nearly five o'clock. "The Lord help you!" ejaculated Pinney, as he saw, by the ashen hue which overspread Lansing's face, that the full realization of his situation had come home to him. "We meant to keep it from you till to-morrow. It might be a little easier not to know it till it was over than now, when it is going on, and you not able to lift a finger to stop it."

"Oh, John," cried Mrs. Pinney once more; "remember, she does n't know!" and, sobbing hysterically, she fled from the room, unable to endure the sight of Lansing's face.

He had fallen into a chair, and was motionless, save for the slow and labored breathing which shook his body. As he sat there in Pinney's ranch this pleasant afternoon, the wife whom he worshiped never so passionately as now, at their home one thousand miles away, was holding another man by the hand, and promising to be his wife.

It was five minutes to five by the clock on the wall before him. It therefore wanted but five minutes of six, the hour of the wedding, at home, the difference in time being just an hour. In the years of his exile, by way of enhancing the vividness of his dreams of home, he had calculated exactly the difference in time from various points in Colorado, so that he could say to himself, "Now Mary is putting the babies to bed;" "Now it is her own bedtime;" "Now she is waking up;" or "Now the church-bells are ringing, and she is walking to church." He was accustomed to carry these two standards of time always in his head, reading one by the other, and it was this habit, bred of doting fondness, which now would compel him to follow, as if he were a spectator, minute by minute, each step of the scene being enacted so far away.

People were prompt at weddings. No doubt already the few guests were arriving, stared at by the neighbors from their windows. The complacent bridegroom was by this time on his way to the home of the bride, or perhaps knocking at the door. Lansing knew him well, an elderly, well-to-do furniture-maker, who had been used to express a fatherly admiration for Mary. The bride was upstairs in her chamber, putting the finishing touches to her toilet; or, at this very moment, it might be, was descending the stairs to take the bridegoom's arm and go in to be married.

Lansing gasped. The mountain wind was blowing through the room, but he was suffocating.

Pinney's voice, seeming to come from very far away, was in his ears. "Rouse yourself, for God's sake! Don't give it all up that way. I believe there's a chance yet. Remember the mind-reading you used to do with her. You could put almost anything into her mind by just willing it there. That's what I mean. Will her to stop what she is doing now. Perhaps you may save her yet. There's a chance you may do it. I don't say there's more than a chance, but there's that. There's a bare chance. That's better than giving up. I've heard of such things being done. I've read of them. Try it, for God's sake! Don't give up."

At any previous moment of his life the suggestion that he could, by mere will power, move the mind of a person a thousand miles away, so as to reverse a deliberate decision, would have appeared to Lansing as wholly preposterous as no doubt it does to any who read these lines. But a man, however logical he may be on land, will grasp at a straw when drowning, as if it were a log. Pinney had no need to use arguments or adjurations to induce Lansing to adopt his suggestion. The man before him was in no mood to balance probabilities against improbabilities. It was enough that the project offered a chance of success, albeit infinitesimal; for on the other hand there was nothing but an intolerable despair, and a fate that truly seemed more than flesh and blood could bear.

Lansing had sprung to his feet while Pinney was speaking. "I'm going to try it, and may God Almighty help me!" he cried, in a terrible voice.

"Amen!" echoed Pinney.

Lansing sank into his chair again, and sat leaning slightly forward, in a rigid attitude. The
expression of his eyes at once became fixed. His
features grew tense, and the muscles of his face
stood out. As if to steady the mental strain by
a physical one, he had taken from the table a
horseshoe which had lain there, and held it in a
convulsive grip.

Pinney had made this extraordinary suggestion
in the hope of diverting Lansing's mind for a
moment from his terrible situation, and with not
so much faith even as he feigned that it would be
of any practical avail. But now, as he looked
upon the ghastly face before him, and realized the
tremendous concentration of purpose, the agony
of will, which it expressed, he was impressed that
it would not be marvelous if some marvel should
be the issue. Certainly, if the will really had any
such power as Lansing was trying to exert, as so
many theorists maintained, there could never arise
circumstances better calculated than these to call
forth a supreme assertion of the faculty. He
went out of the room on tiptoe, and left his friend
alone to fight this strange and terrible battle with
the powers of the air for the honor of his wife and
his own.

There was little enough need of any preliminary
effort on Lansing's part to fix his thoughts upon
Mary. It was only requisite that to the intensity
of the mental vision, with which he had before

imagined her, should be added the activity of the
will, turning the former mood of despair into one
of resistance. He knew in what room of their
house the wedding party must now be gathered,
and was able to represent to himself the scene
there as vividly as if he had been present. He
saw the relatives assembled; he saw Mr. Davenport, the minister, and, facing him, the bridal
couple, in the only spot where they could well
stand, before the fireplace. But from all the others, from the guests, from the minister, from the
bridegroom, he turned his thoughts, to fix them
on the bride alone. He saw her as if through
the small end of an immensely long telescope, distinctly, but at an immeasurable distance. On this
face his mental gaze was riveted, as by conclusive
efforts his will strove to reach and move hers
against the thing that she was doing. Although
his former experiments in mental phenomena had
in a measure familiarized him with the mode of
addressing his powers to such an undertaking as
this, yet the present effort was on a scale so much
vaster that his will for a time seemed appalled,
and refused to go out from him, as a bird put
forth from a ship at sea returns again and again
before daring to essay the distant flight to land.
He felt that he was gaining nothing. He was as
one who beats the air. It was all he could do to
struggle against the influences that tended to deflect
and dissipate his thoughts. Again and again a

conviction of the uselessness of the attempt, of the madness of imagining that a mere man could send a wish, like a voice, across a continent, laid its paralyzing touch upon his will, and nothing but a sense of the black horror which failure meant enabled him to throw it off. If he but once admitted the idea of failing, all was lost. He must believe that he could do this thing, or he surely could not. To question it was to surrender his wife ; to despair was to abandon her to her fate. So, as a wrestler strains against a mighty antagonist, his will strained and tugged in supreme stress against the impalpable obstruction of space, and, fighting despair with despair, doggedly held to its purpose, and sought to keep his faculties unremittingly streaming to one end. Finally, as this tremendous effort, which made minutes seem hours, went on, there came a sense of efficiency, the feeling of achieving something. From this consciousness was first born a faith, no longer desperate, but rational, that he might succeed, and with faith came an instantaneous tenfold multiplication of force. The overflow of energy lost the tendency to dissipation and became steady. The will appeared to be getting the mental faculties more perfectly in hand, if the expression may be used, not only concentrating but fairly fusing them together by the intensity with which it drove them to their object. It was time. Already, perhaps, Mary was about to utter the vows that would give her to another. Lansing's lips moved. As if he were standing at her side, he murmured with strained and labored utterance ejaculations of appeal and adjuration.

Then came the climax of the stupendous struggle. He became aware of a sensation so amazing that I know not if it can be described at all, — a sensation comparable to that which comes up the mile-long sounding-line, telling that it touches bottom. Fainter far, as much finer as is mind than matter, yet not less unmistakable, was the thrill which told the man, agonizing on that lonely mountain of Colorado, that the will which he had sent forth to touch the mind of another, a thousand miles away, had found its resting-place, and the chain between them was complete. No longer projected at random into the void, but as if it sent along an established medium of communication, his will now seemed to work upon hers, not uncertainly and with difficulty, but as if in immediate contact. Simultaneously, also, its mood changed. No more appealing, agonizing, desperate, it became insistent, imperious, dominating. For only a few moments it remained at this pitch, and then, the mental tension suddenly relaxing, he aroused to a perception of his surroundings, of which toward the last he had become oblivious. He was drenched with perspiration and completely exhausted. The iron horseshoe which he had held in his hands was drawn halfway out.

Thirty-six hours later, Lansing, accompanied by Pinney, climbed down from the stage at the railroad station. During the interval Lansing had neither eaten nor slept. If at moments in that time he was able to indulge the hope that his tremendous experiment had been successful, for the main part the overwhelming presumption of common sense and common experience against such a notion made it seem childish folly to entertain it.

At the station was to be sent the dispatch, the reply to which would determine Mary's fate and his own. Pinney signed it, so that, if the worst were true, Lansing's existence might still remain a secret; for of going back to her in that case, to make her a sharer of his shame, there was no thought on his part. The dispatch was addressed to Mr. Davenport, Mary's minister, and merely asked if the wedding had taken place.

They had to wait two hours for the answer. When it came, Lansing was without on the platform, and Pinney was in the office. The operator mercifully shortened his suspense by reading the purport of the message from the tape: "The dispatch in answer to yours says that the wedding did not take place."

Pinney sprang out upon the platform. At sight of Lansing's look of ghastly questioning, the tears blinded him, and he could not speak, but the wild exultation of his face and gestures was speech enough.

The second day following, Lansing clasped his wife to his breast, and this is the story she told him, interrupted with weepings and shudderings and ecstatic embraces of reassurance. The reasons which had determined her, in disregard of the dictates of her own heart, to marry again, have been sufficiently intimated in her letter to Mrs. Pinney. For the rest, Mr. Whitcomb was a highly respectable man, whom she esteemed and believed to be good and worthy. When the hour set for the marriage arrived, and she took her place by his side before the minister and the guests, her heart indeed was like lead, but her mind calm and resolved. The preliminary prayer was long, and it was natural, as it went on, that her thoughts should go back to the day when she had thus stood by another's side. She had ado to crowd back the scalding tears, as she contrasted her present mood of resignation with the mingling of virginal timidity and the abandon of love in her heart that other day. Suddenly, seeming to rise out of this painful contrast of the past and the present, a feeling of abhorrence for the act to which she was committed possessed her mind. She had all along shrunk from it, as any sensitive woman might from a marriage without love, but there had been nothing in that shrinking to compare in intensity with this uncontrollable aversion which now seized upon her to the idea of holding a wife's relation to the man by her side. It had all

at once come over her that she could not do it.
Nevertheless she was a sensible and rational woman as well as a sweet and lovely one. Whatever might be the origin of this sudden repugnance, she knew it had none in reason. She was
fulfilling a promise which she had maturely considered, and neither in justice to herself nor the
man to whom she had given it could she let a
purely hysterical attack like this prevent its con-
summation. She called reason and common sense
to her aid, and resolutely struggled to banish the
distressing fancies that assailed her. The moisture
stood out upon her forehead with the severity of
the conflict, which momentarily increased. At
last the minister ended his prayer, of which she
had not heard a word. The bridal pair were bid-
den to take each other by the hand. As the bridegroom's fingers closed around hers, she could not
avoid a shudder as at a loathsome contact. It
was only by a supreme effort of self-control that
she restrained from snatching her hand away with
a scream. She did not hear what the minister
went on to say. Every faculty was concentrated
on the struggle, which had now become one of
desperation, to repress an outbreak of the storm
that was raging within. For, despite the shuddering protest of every instinct and the wild repulsion with which every nerve tingled, she was determined to go through the ceremony. But though
the will in its citadel still held out, she knew that

it could not be for long. Each wave of emotion that it withstood was higher, stronger, than the last. She felt that it was going, going. She prayed that the minister might be quick, while yet she retained a little self-command, and give her an opportunity to utter some binding vow which should make good her solemn engagement, and avert the scandal of the outbreak on the verge of which she was trembling. "Do you," said the minister to Mr. Whitcomb, "take this woman whom you hold by the hand to be your wife, to honor, protect, and love while you live?" "I do," replied the bridegroom promptly. "Do you," said the minister, looking at Mary, "take the man whom you hold by the hand to be your husband, to love and honor while you live?" Mary tried to say "Yes," but at the effort there surged up against it an opposition that was almost tangible in its overpowering force. No longer merely operating upon her sensibilities, the inexplicable influence that was conquering her now seized on her physical functions, and laid its interdict upon her tongue. Three times she strove to throw off the incubus, to speak, but in vain. Great drops were on her forehead; she was deadly pale, and her eyes were wild and staring; her features twitched as in a spasm, while she stood there struggling with the invisible power that sealed her lips. There was a sudden movement among the spectators; they were whispering together. They saw that something was wrong. " Do you thus promise? " repeated the minister, after a pause. " Nod, if you can't speak," murmured the bridegroom. His words were the hiss of a serpent in her ears. Her will resisted no longer; her soul was wholly possessed by unreasoning terror of the man and horror of the marriage. " No! no! no!" she screamed in piercing tones, and snatching her hand from the bridegroom, she threw herself upon the breast of the astonished minister, sobbing wildly as she clung to him, " Save me, save me! Take me away! I can't marry him, — I can't! Oh, I can't! "

The wedding broke up in confusion, and that is the way, if you choose to think so, that John Lansing, one thousand miles away, saved his wife from marrying another man.

" If you choose to think so," I say, for it is perfectly competent to argue that the influence to which Mary Lansing yielded was merely an hysterical attack, not wholly strange at such a moment in the case of a woman devoted to her first husband, and reluctantly consenting to second nuptials. On this theory, Lansing's simultaneous agony at Pinney's ranch in Colorado was merely a coincidence; interesting, perhaps, but unnecessary to account for his wife's behavior. That John and Mary Lansing should reject with indignation this simple method of accounting for their great deliverance is not at all surprising in view of the common proclivity of people to be impressed with the extraordinary side of circumstances which affect themselves; nor is there any reason why their opinion of the true explanation of the facts should be given more weight than another's. The writer, who has merely endeavored to put this story into narrative form, has formed no opinion on it which is satisfactory to himself, and therefore abstains from any effort to influence the reader's judgment.

TO WHOM THIS MAY COME

It is now about a year since I took passage at Calcutta in the ship Adelaide for New York. We had baffling weather till New Amsterdam Island was sighted, where we took a new point of departure. Three days later, a terrible gale struck us. Four days we flew before it, whither, no one knew, for neither sun, moon, nor stars were at any time visible, and we could take no observation. Toward midnight of the fourth day, the glare of lightning revealed the Adelaide in a hopeless position, close in upon a low-lying shore, and driving straight toward it. All around and astern far out to sea was such a maze of rocks and shoals that it was a miracle we had come so far. Presently the ship struck, and almost instantly went to pieces, so great was the violence of the sea. I gave myself up for lost, and was indeed already past the worst of drowning, when I was recalled to consciousness by being thrown with a tremendous shock upon the beach. I had just strength enough to drag myself above the reach of the waves, and then I fell down and knew no more.

When I awoke, the storm was over. The sun, already halfway up the sky, had dried my clothing, and renewed the vigor of my bruised and aching limbs. On sea or shore I saw no vestige of my ship or my companions, of whom I appeared the sole survivor. I was not, however, alone. A group of persons, apparently the inhabitants of the country, stood near, observing me with looks of friendliness which at once freed me from apprehension as to my treatment at their hands. They were a white and handsome people, evidently of a high order of civilization, though I recognized in them the traits of no race with which I was familiar.

Seeing that it was evidently their idea of etiquette to leave it to strangers to open conversation, I addressed them in English, but failed to elicit any response beyond deprecating smiles. I then accosted them successively in the French, German, Italian, Spanish, Dutch, and Portuguese tongues, but with no better results. I began to be very much puzzled as to what could possibly be the nationality of a white and evidently civilized race to which no one of the tongues of the great seafaring nations was intelligible. The oddest thing of all was the unbroken silence with which they contemplated my efforts to open communication with them. It was as if they were agreed not to give me a clue to their language by even a whisper; for while they regarded one another with looks of smiling intelligence, they did not once open their lips. But if this behavior suggested that they were amusing themselves at my expense, that presumption was negatived by the unmistakable friendliness and sympathy which their whole bearing expressed.

A most extraordinary conjecture occurred to me. Could it be that these strange people were dumb? Such a freak of nature as an entire race thus afflicted had never indeed been heard of, but who could say what wonders the unexplored vasts of the great Southern Ocean might thus far have hid from human ken? Now, among the scraps of useless information which lumbered my mind was an acquaintance with the deaf-and-dumb alphabet, and forthwith I began to spell out with my fingers some of the phrases I had already uttered to so little effect. My resort to the sign language overcame the last remnant of gravity in the already profusely smiling group. The small boys now rolled on the ground in convulsions of mirth, while the grave and reverend seniors, who had hitherto kept them in check, were fain momentarily to avert their faces, and I could see their bodies shaking with laughter. The greatest clown in the world never received a more flattering tribute to his powers to amuse than had been called forth by mine to make myself understood. Naturally, however, I was not flattered, but on the contrary entirely discomfited. Angry I could not well be, for the deprecating manner in which all, excepting of course the boys, yielded to their perception of the ridiculous, and the distress they showed at their failure in self-control, made me seem the aggressor. It was as if they were very sorry for me, and ready to put themselves wholly at my service, if I would only refrain from reducing them to a state of disability by being so exquisitely absurd. Certainly this evidently amiable race had a very embarrassing way of receiving strangers.

Just at this moment, when my bewilderment was fast verging on exasperation, relief came. The circle opened, and a little elderly man, who had evidently come in haste, confronted me, and, bowing very politely, addressed me in English. His voice was the most pitiable abortion of a voice I had ever heard. While having all the defects in articulation of a child's who is just beginning to talk, it was not even a child's in strength of tone, being in fact a mere alternation of squeaks and whispers inaudible a rod away. With some difficulty I was, however, able to follow him pretty nearly.

" As the official interpreter," he said, " I extend you a cordial welcome to these islands. I was sent for as soon as you were discovered, but being at some distance, I was unable to arrive until this moment. I regret this, as my presence would have saved you embarrassment. My countrymen desire me to intercede with you to pardon the wholly involuntary and uncontrollable mirth pro-

voked by your attempts to communicate with them.
You see, they understood you perfectly well, but
could not answer you."

"Merciful heavens!" I exclaimed, horrified to
find my surmise correct; "can it be that they are
all thus afflicted? Is it possible that you are the
only man among them who has the power of
speech?"

Again it appeared that, quite unintentionally,
I had said something excruciatingly funny; for
at my speech there arose a sound of gentle laughter from the group, now augmented to quite an
assemblage, which drowned the plashing of the
waves on the beach at our feet. Even the interpreter smiled.

"Do they think it so amusing to be dumb?" I
asked.

"They find it very amusing," replied the interpreter, "that their inability to speak should be
regarded by any one as an affliction; for it is by
the voluntary disuse of the organs of articulation
that they have lost the power of speech, and, as
a consequence, the ability even to understand
speech."

"But," said I, somewhat puzzled by this statement, "did n't you just tell me that they understood me, though they could not reply, and are
they not laughing now at what I just said?"

"It is you they understood, not your words,"
answered the interpreter. "Our speech now is

gibberish to them, as unintelligible in itself as the growling of animals; but they know what we are saying, because they know our thoughts. You must know that these are the islands of the mind-readers."

Such were the circumstances of my introduction to this extraordinary people. The official interpreter being charged by virtue of his office with the first entertainment of shipwrecked members of the talking nations, I became his guest, and passed a number of days under his roof before going out to any considerable extent among the people. My first impression had been the somewhat oppressive one that the power to read the thoughts of others could be possessed only by beings of a superior order to man. It was the first effort of the interpreter to disabuse me of this notion. It appeared from his account that the experience of the mind-readers was a case simply of a slight acceleration, from special causes, of the course of universal human evolution, which in time was destined to lead to the disuse of speech and the substitution of direct mental vision on the part of all races. This rapid evolution of these islanders was accounted for by their peculiar origin and circumstances.

Some three centuries before Christ, one of the Parthian kings of Persia, of the dynasty of the Arsacidæ, undertook a persecution of the sooth-sayers and magicians in his realms. These people were credited with supernatural powers by popular prejudice, but in fact were merely persons of special gifts in the way of hypnotizing, mind-reading, thought transference, and such arts, which they exercised for their own gain.

Too much in awe of the soothsayers to do them outright violence, the king resolved to banish them, and to this end put them, with their families, on ships and sent them to Ceylon. When, however, the fleet was in the neighborhood of that island, a great storm scattered it, and one of the ships, after being driven for many days before the tempest, was wrecked upon one of an archipelago of uninhabited islands far to the south, where the survivors settled. Naturally, the posterity of the parents possessed of such peculiar gifts had developed extraordinary psychical powers.

Having set before them the end of evolving a new and advanced order of humanity, they had aided the development of these powers by a rigid system of stirpiculture. The result was that, after a few centuries, mind-reading became so general that language fell into disuse as a means of communicating ideas. For many generations the power of speech still remained voluntary, but gradually the vocal organs had become atrophied, and for several hundred years the power of articulation had been wholly lost. Infants for a few months after birth did, indeed, still emit inarticulate cries, but at an age when in less advanced races these cries began to be articulate, the children of the mind-readers developed the power of direct vision, and ceased to attempt to use the voice.

The fact that the existence of the mind-readers had never been found out by the rest of the world was explained by two considerations. In the first place, the group of islands was small, and occupied a corner of the Indian Ocean quite out of the ordinary track of ships. In the second place, the approach to the islands was rendered so desperately perilous by terrible currents, and the maze of outlying rocks and shoals, that it was next to impossible for any ship to touch their shores save as a wreck. No ship at least had ever done so in the two thousand years since the mind-readers' own arrival, and the Adelaide had made the one hundred and twenty-third such wreck.

Apart from motives of humanity, the mind-readers made strenuous efforts to rescue shipwrecked persons, for from them alone, through the interpreters, could they obtain information of the outside world. Little enough this proved when, as often happened, the sole survivor of the shipwreck was some ignorant sailor, who had no news to communicate beyond the latest varieties of forecastle blasphemy. My hosts gratefully assured me that, as a person of some little education, they considered me a veritable godsend. No less a task was mine than to relate to them the history of the world for the past two centuries, and often did I wish, for their sakes, that I had made a more exact study of it.

It is solely for the purpose of communicating with shipwrecked strangers of the talking nations that the office of the interpreters exists. When, as from time to time happens, a child is born with some powers of articulation, he is set apart, and trained to talk in the interpreters' college. Of course the partial atrophy of the vocal organs, from which even the best interpreters suffer, renders many of the sounds of language impossible for them. None, for instance, can pronounce *v*, *f*, or *s ;* and as to the sound represented by *th*, it is five generations since the last interpreter lived who could utter it. But for the occasional intermarriage of shipwrecked strangers with the islanders, it is probable that the supply of interpreters would have long ere this quite failed.

I imagine that the very unpleasant sensations which followed the realization that I was among people who, while inscrutable to me, knew my every thought, were very much what any one would have experienced in the same case. They were very comparable to the panic which accidental nudity causes a person among races whose custom it is to conceal the figure with drapery. I wanted to run away and hide myself. If I analyzed my feeling, it did not seem to arise so much from the consciousness of any particularly heinous secrets, as from the knowledge of a swarm of fatuous, ill-natured, and unseemly thoughts and half thoughts concerning those around me, and concerning myself, which it was insufferable that any person should peruse in however benevolent a spirit. But while my chagrin and distress on this account were at first intense, they were also very short-lived, for almost immediately I discovered that the very knowledge that my mind was overlooked by others operated to check thoughts that might be painful to them, and that, too, without more effort of the will than a kindly person exerts to check the utterance of disagreeable remarks. As a very few lessons in the elements of courtesy cures a decent person of inconsiderate speaking, so a brief experience among the mind-readers went far in my case to check inconsiderate thinking. It must not be supposed, however, that courtesy among the mind-readers prevents them from thinking pointedly and freely concerning one another upon serious occasions, any more than the finest courtesy among the talking races restrains them from speaking to one another with entire plainness when it it desirable to do so. Indeed, among the mind-readers, politeness never can extend to the point of insincerity, as among talking nations, seeing that it is always one another's real and inmost thought that they read. I may fitly mention here, though it was not till later that I fully understood why it must necessarily be so, that one need feel far less chagrin at the complete revelation of his weaknesses to a mind-reader than at the slightest betrayal of them to one of another race. For the very reason that the mind-reader reads all your thoughts, particular thoughts are judged with reference to the general tenor of thought. Your characteristic and habitual frame of mind is what he takes account of. No one need fear being misjudged by a mind-reader on account of sentiments or emotions which are not representative of the real character or general attitude. Justice may, indeed, be said to be a necessary consequence of mind-reading.

As regards the interpreter himself, the instinct of courtesy was not long needed to check wanton or offensive thoughts. In all my life before, I had been very slow to form friendships, but before I had been three days in the company of this stranger of a strange race, I had become enthusiastically devoted to him. It was impossible not to be. The peculiar joy of friendship is the sense of being understood by our friend as we are not by others, and yet of being loved in spite of the understanding. Now here was one whose every word testified to a knowledge of my secret thoughts and motives which the oldest and nearest of my former friends had never, and could never, have approximated. Had such a knowledge bred in him contempt of me, I should neither have blamed him nor been at all surprised. Judge, then, whether the cordial friendliness which he showed was likely to leave me indifferent.

Imagine my incredulity when he informed me that our friendship was not based upon more than ordinary mutual suitability of temperaments. The faculty of mind-reading, he explained, brought minds so close together, and so heightened sympathy, that the lowest order of friendship between mind-readers implied a mutual delight such as only rare friends enjoyed among other races. He assured me that later on, when I came to know others of his race, I should find, by the far greater intensity of sympathy and affection I should conceive for some of them, how true this saying was.

It may be inquired how, on beginning to mingle with the mind-readers in general, I managed to communicate with them, seeing that, while they could read my thoughts, they could not, like the interpreter, respond to them by speech. I must here explain that, while these people have no use for a spoken language, a written language is needful for purposes of record. They consequently all know how to write. Do they, then, write Persian? Luckily for me, no. It appears that, for a long period after mind-reading was fully developed, not only was spoken language disused, but also written, no records whatever having been kept during this period. The delight of the people in the newly found power of direct mind-to-mind vision, whereby pictures of the total mental state were communicated, instead of the imperfect descriptions of single thoughts which words at best could give, induced an invincible distaste for the laborious impotence of language.

When, however, the first intellectual intoxication had, after several generations, somewhat sobered down, it was recognized that records of the past were desirable, and that the despised medium of words was needful to preserve it. Persian had meanwhile been wholly forgotten. In order to avoid the prodigious task of inventing a complete new language, the institution of the interpreters was now set up, with the idea of acquiring through them a knowledge of some of the languages of the outside world from the mariners wrecked on the islands.

Owing to the fact that most of the castaway ships were English, a better knowledge of that tongue was acquired than of any other, and it was adopted as the written language of the people. As a rule, my acquaintances wrote slowly and laboriously, and yet the fact that they knew exactly what was in my mind rendered their responses so apt that, in my conversations with the slowest speller of them all, the interchange of thought was as rapid and incomparably more accurate and satisfactory than the fastest talkers attain to.

It was but a very short time after I had begun to extend my acquaintance among the mind-readers before I discovered how truly the interpreter had told me that I should find others to whom, on account of greater natural congeniality, I should become more strongly attached than I had been to him. This was in no wise, however, because I loved him less, but them more. I would fain write particularly of some of these beloved friends, comrades of my heart, from whom I first learned the undreamed-of possibilities of human friendship, and how ravishing the satisfactions of sympathy may be. Who, among those who may read this, has not known that sense of a gulf fixed between soul and soul which mocks love! Who has not felt that loneliness which oppresses the heart that loves it best! Think no longer that this gulf is eternally fixed, or is any necessity of human nature. It has no existence for the race of our fellow-men which I describe, and by that fact we may be assured that eventually it will be bridged also for us. Like the touch of shoulder to shoulder, like the clasping of hands, is the contact of their minds and their sensation of sympathy.

I say that I would fain speak more particularly of some of my friends, but waning strength forbids, and moreover, now that I think of it, another consideration would render any comparison of their characters rather confusing than instructive to a reader. This is the fact that, in common with the rest of the mind-readers, they had no names. Every one had, indeed, an arbitrary sign for his designation in records, but it has no sound value. A

register of these names is kept, so they can at any
time be ascertained, but it is very common to meet
persons who have forgotten titles which are used
solely for biographical and official purposes.   For
social intercourse names are of course superfluous,
for these people accost one another merely by a
mental act of attention, and refer to third persons
by transferring their mental pictures, — something
as dumb persons might by means of photographs.
Something so, I say, for in the pictures of one
another's personalities which the mind-readers conceive, the physical aspect, as might be expected
with people who directly contemplate each other's
minds and hearts, is a subordinate element.

I have already told how my first qualms of morbid self-consciousness at knowing that my mind
was an open book to all around me disappeared as
I learned that the very completeness of the disclos-
ure of my thoughts and motives was a guarantee
that I would be judged with a fairness and a sympathy such as even self-judgment cannot pretend
to, affected as that is by so many subtle reactions.
The assurance of being so judged by every one
might well seem an inestimable privilege to one
accustomed to a world in which not even the tenderest love is any pledge of comprehension, and yet
I soon discovered that open-mindedness had a still
greater profit than this.   How shall I describe the
delightful exhilaration of moral health and clean-
ness, the breezy oxygenated mental condition, which

resulted from the consciousness that I had absolutely nothing concealed! Truly I may say that I
enjoyed myself. I think surely that no one needs
to have had my marvelous experience to sympathize with this portion of it. Are we not all ready
to agree that this having a curtained chamber where
we may go to grovel, out of the sight of our fellows,
troubled only by a vague apprehension that God
may look over the top, is the most demoralizing
incident in the human condition? It is the existence within the soul of this secure refuge of lies
which has always been the despair of the saint and
the exultation of the knave. It is the foul cellar
which taints the whole house above, be it never
so fine.

What stronger testimony could there be to the
instinctive consciousness that concealment is de-
bauching, and openness our only cure, than the
world-old conviction of the virtue of confession for
the soul, and that the uttermost exposing of one's
worst and foulest is the first step toward moral
health? The wickedest man, if he could but somehow attain to writhe himself inside out as to his
soul, so that its full sickness could be seen, would
feel ready for a new life. Nevertheless, owing to
the utter impotence of the words to convey mental
conditions in their totality, or to give other than
mere distortions of them, confession is, we must
needs admit, but a mockery of that longing for
self-revelation to which it testifies. But think

what health and soundness there must be for souls
among a people who see in every face a conscience
which, unlike their own, they cannot sophisticate,
who confess one another with a glance, and shrive
with a smile! Ah, friends, let me now predict,
though ages may elapse before the slow event shall
justify me, that in no way will the mutual vision
of minds, when at last it shall be perfected, so enhance the blessedness of mankind as by rending
the veil of self, and leaving no spot of darkness in
the mind for lies to hide in. Then shall the soul
no longer be a coal smoking among ashes, but a
star in a crystal sphere.

From what I have said of the delights which
friendship among the mind-readers derives from
the perfection of the mental rapport, it may be
imagined how intoxicating must be the experience
when one of the friends is a woman, and the subtle
attractions and correspondences of sex touch with
passion the intellectual sympathy. With my first
venturing into society I had begun, to their extreme
amusement, to fall in love with the women right
and left. In the perfect frankness which is the
condition of all intercourse among this people,
these adorable women told me that what I felt was
only friendship, which was a very good thing, but
wholly different from love, as I should well know
if I were beloved. It was difficult to believe that
the melting emotions which I had experienced in
their company were the result merely of the friendly

and kindly attitude of their minds toward mine; but when I found that I was affected in the same way by every gracious woman I met, I had to make up my mind that they must be right about it, and that I should have to adapt myself to a world in which, friendship being a passion, love must needs be nothing less than rapture.

The homely proverb, "Every Jack has his Gill," may, I suppose, be taken to mean that for all men there are certain women expressly suited by mental and moral as well as by physical constitution. It is a thought painful, rather than cheering, that this may be the truth, so altogether do the chances preponderate against the ability of these elect ones to recognize each other even if they meet, seeing that speech is so inadequate and so misleading a medium of self-revelation. But among the mind-readers, the search for one's ideal mate is a quest reasonably sure of being crowned with success, and no one dreams of wedding unless it be; for so to do, they consider, would be to throw away the choicest blessing of life, and not alone to wrong themselves and their unfound mates, but likewise those whom they themselves and those undiscovered mates might wed. Therefore, passionate pilgrims, they go from isle to isle till they find each other, and, as the population of the islands is but small, the pilgrimage is not often long.

When I met her first we were in company, and I was struck by the sudden stir and the looks of touched and smiling interest with which all around turned and regarded us, the women with moistened eyes. They had read her thought when she saw me, but this I did not know, neither what was the custom in these matters, till afterward. But I knew, from the moment she first fixed her eyes on me, and I felt her mind brooding upon mine, how truly I had been told by those other women that the feeling with which they had inspired me was not love.

With people who become acquainted at a glance, and old friends in an hour, wooing is naturally not a long process. Indeed, it may be said that between lovers among mind-readers there is no wooing, but merely recognition. The day after we met, she became mine.

Perhaps I cannot better illustrate how subordinate the merely physical element is in the impression which mind-readers form of their friends than by mentioning an incident that occurred some months after our union. This was my discovery, wholly by accident, that my love, in whose society I had almost constantly been, had not the least idea what was the color of my eyes, or whether my hair and complexion were light or dark. Of course, as soon as I asked her the question, she read the answer in my mind, but she admitted that she had previously had no distinct impression on those points. On the other hand, if in the blackest midnight I should come to her, she would not need to ask who the comer was. It is by the mind, not the eye, that these people know one another. It is really only in their relations to soulless and inanimate things that they need eyes at all.

It must not be supposed that their disregard of one another's bodily aspect grows out of any ascetic sentiment. It is merely a necessary consequence of their power of directly apprehending mind, that whenever mind is closely associated with matter the latter is comparatively neglected on account of the greater interest of the former, suffering as lesser things always do when placed in immediate contrast with greater. Art is with them confined to the inanimate, the human form having, for the reason mentioned, ceased to inspire the artist. It will be naturally and quite correctly inferred that among such a race physical beauty is not the important factor in human fortune and felicity that it elsewhere is. The absolute openness of their minds and hearts to one another makes their happiness far more dependent on the moral and mental qualities of their companions than upon their physical. A genial temperament, a wide-grasping, godlike intellect, a poet soul, are incomparably more fascinating to them than the most dazzling combination conceivable of mere bodily graces.

A woman of mind and heart has no more need of beauty to win love in these islands than a beauty elsewhere of mind or heart. I should mention here, perhaps, that this race, which makes so little account of physical beauty, is itself a singularly handsome one. This is owing doubtless in part to the absolute compatibility of temperaments in all the marriages, and partly also to the reaction upon the body of a state of ideal mental and moral health and placidity.

Not being myself a mind-reader, the fact that my love was rarely beautiful in form and face had doubtless no little part in attracting my devotion. This, of course, she knew, as she knew all my thoughts, and, knowing my limitations, tolerated and forgave the element of sensuousness in my passion. But if it must have seemed to her so little worthy in comparison with the high spiritual communion which her race know as love, to me it became, by virtue of her almost superhuman relation to me, an ecstasy more ravishing surely than any lover of my race tasted before. The ache at the heart of the intensest love is the impotence of words to make it perfectly understood to its object. But my passion was without this pang, for my heart was absolutely open to her I loved. Lovers may imagine, but I cannot describe, the ecstatic thrill of communion into which this consciousness transformed every tender emotion. As I considered what mutual love must be where both parties are mind-readers, I realized the high communion which my sweet companion had sacrificed for me.

She might indeed comprehend her lover and his love for her, but the higher satisfaction of knowing that she was comprehended by him and her love understood, she had foregone. For that I should ever attain the power of mind-reading was out of the question, the faculty never having been developed in a single lifetime.

Why my inability should move my dear companion to such depths of pity I was not able fully to understand until I learned that mind-reading is chiefly held desirable, not for the knowledge of others which it gives its possessors, but for the self-knowledge which is its reflex effect. Of all they see in the minds of others, that which concerns them most is the reflection of themselves, the photographs of their own characters. The most obvious consequence of the self-knowledge thus forced upon them is to render them alike incapable of self-conceit or self-depreciation. Every one must needs always think of himself as he is, being no more able to do otherwise than is a man in a hall of mirrors to cherish delusions as to his personal appearance.

But self-knowledge means to the mind-readers much more than this, — nothing less, indeed, than a shifting of the sense of identity. When a man sees himself in a mirror, he is compelled to distinguish between the bodily self he sees and his real self, which is within and unseen. When in turn the mind-reader comes to see the mental and moral self reflected in other minds as in mirrors, the same thing happens. He is compelled to distinguish between this mental and moral self which has been made objective to him, and can be contemplated by him as impartially as if it were another's, from the inner ego which still remains subjective, unseen, and indefinable. In this inner ego the mind-readers recognize the essential identity and being, the noumenal self, the core of the soul, and the true hiding of its eternal life, to which the mind as well as the body is but the garment of a day.

The effect of such a philosophy as this — which, indeed, with the mind-readers is rather an instinctive consciousness than a philosophy — must obviously be to impart a sense of wonderful superiority to the vicissitudes of this earthly state, and a singular serenity in the midst of the haps and mishaps which threaten or befall the personality. They did indeed appear to me, as I never dreamed men could attain to be, lords of themselves.

It was because I might not hope to attain this enfranchisement from the false ego of the apparent self, without which life seemed to her race scarcely worth living, that my love so pitied me.

But I must hasten on, leaving a thousand things unsaid, to relate the lamentable catastrophe to which it is owing that, instead of being still a resident of those blessed islands, in the full enjoyment of that intimate and ravishing companionship which by contrast would forever dim the pleasures of all other human society, I recall the bright picture as a memory under other skies.

Among a people who are compelled by the very constitution of their minds to put themselves in the places of others, the sympathy which is the inevitable consequence of perfect comprehension renders envy, hatred, and uncharitableness impossible. But of course there are people less genially constituted than others, and these are necessarily the objects of a certain distaste on the part of associates. Now, owing to the unhindered impact of minds upon one another, the anguish of persons so regarded, despite the tenderest consideration of those about them, is so great that they beg the grace of exile, that, being out of the way, people may think less frequently upon them. There are numerous small islets, scarcely more than rocks, lying to the north of the archipelago, and on these the unfortunates are permitted to live. Only one lives on each islet, as they cannot endure each other even as well as the more happily constituted can endure them. From time to time supplies of food are taken to them, and of course, any time they wish to take the risk, they are permitted to return to society.

Now, as I have said, the fact which, even more than their out-of-the-way location, makes the islands of the mind-readers unapproachable, is the violence with which the great antarctic current, owing

probably to some configuration of the ocean bed,
together with the innumerable rocks and shoals,
flows through and about the archipelago.

Ships making the islands from the southward
are caught by this current and drawn among the
rocks, to their almost certain destruction; while,
owing to the violence with which the current sets
to the north, it is not possible to approach at all
from that direction, or at least it has never been
accomplished. Indeed, so powerful are the currents
that even the boats which cross the narrow straits
between the main islands and the islets of the
unfortunate, to carry the latter their supplies, are
ferried over by cables, not trusting to oar or sail.

The brother of my love had charge of one of
the boats engaged in this transportation, and, being
desirous of visiting the islets, I accepted an invitation to accompany him on one of his trips. I
know nothing of how the accident happened, but
in the fiercest part of the current of one of the
straits we parted from the cable and were swept
out to sea. There was no question of stemming
the boiling current, our utmost endeavors barely
sufficing to avoid being dashed to pieces on the
rocks. From the first, there was no hope of our
winning back to the land, and so swiftly did we
drift that by noon — the accident having befallen
in the morning — the islands, which are low-lying,
had sunk beneath the southwestern horizon.

Among these mind-readers, distance is not an insuperable obstacle to the transfer of thought. My companion was in communication with our friends, and from time to time conveyed to me messages of anguish from my dear love; for, being well aware of the nature of the currents and the unapproachableness of the islands, those we had left behind, as well as we ourselves, knew well we should see each other's faces no more. For five days we continued to drift to the northwest, in no danger of starvation, owing to our lading of provisions, but constrained to unintermitting watch and ward by the roughness of the weather. On the fifth day my companion died from exposure and exhaustion. He died very quietly, — indeed, with great appearance of relief. The life of the mind-readers while yet they are in the body is so largely spiritual that the idea of an existence wholly so, which seems vague and chill to us, suggests to them a state only slightly more refined than they already know on earth.

After that I suppose I must have fallen into an unconscious state, from which I roused to find myself on an American ship bound for New York, surrounded by people whose only means of communicating with one another is to keep up while together a constant clatter of hissing, guttural, and explosive noises, eked out by all manner of facial contortions and bodily gestures. I frequently find myself staring open-mouthed at those who address me, too much struck by their grotesque appearance to bethink myself of replying.

I find that I shall not live out the voyage, and I do not care to. From my experience of the people on the ship, I can judge how I should fare on land amid the stunning Babel of a nation of talkers. And my friends, — God bless them! how lonely I should feel in their very presence! Nay, what satisfaction or consolation, what but bitter mockery, could I ever more find in such human sympathy and companionship as suffice others and once sufficed me, — I who have seen and known what I have seen and known! Ah, yes, doubtless it is far better I should die; but the knowledge of the things that I have seen I feel should not perish with me. For hope's sake, men should not miss the glimpse of the higher, sun-bathed reaches of the upward path they plod. So thinking, I have written out some account of my wonderful experience, though briefer far, by reason of my weakness, than fits the greatness of the matter. The captain seems an honest, well-meaning man, and to him I shall confide the narrative, charging him, on touching shore, to see it safely in the hands of some one who will bring it to the world's ear.

NOTE. — The extent of my own connection with the foregoing document is sufficiently indicated by the author himself in the final paragraph. — E. B.